Godiva

NERYS JONES

Godiva

MACMILLAN

First published 2008 by Macmillan
an imprint of Pan Macmillan Ltd
Pan Macmillan, 20 New Wharf Road, London N1 9RR
Basingstoke and Oxford
Associated companies throughout the world
www.panmacmillan.com

ISBN 978-0-230-53068-3

A CIP catalogue record for this book is available from
the British Library.

Map designed by Raymond Turvey

Typeset by SetSystems Ltd, Saffron Walden, Essex
Printed and bound in Great Britain by
Mackays of Chatham plc, Chatham, Kent

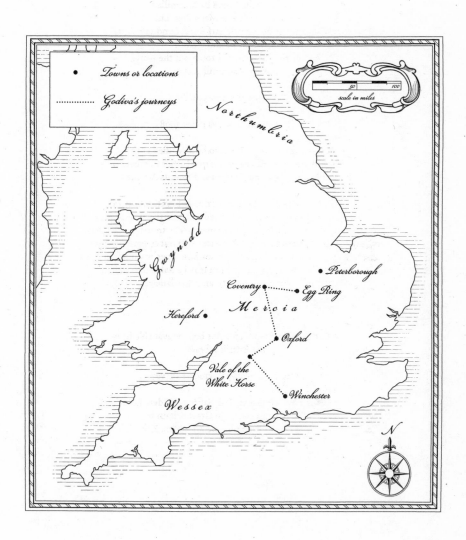

Glossary

Burgh: a walled, defended town.

Churl (Ango-Saxon *ceorl*): a member of the lowest class of the free population.

Fyrd: the army recruited from the regions.

Godweb: best-quality fabric, whether of linen, wool or silk.

Heregeld (sometimes known as *geld*): literally, the 'army tax', imposed by Danish kings in England.

Housecarl (house-churl): a member of the armed entourage of a lord who lived under his own roof and travelled with him.

Reeve: the steward of an estate.

Scopman: a storyteller and entertainer, often in the service of a lord.

Thegn: a land-owner who also held political office at a regional level.

Wergeld: blood-money, a fine paid as compensation to the relatives of a victim of homicide.

Pronunciation

Godiva's name was pronounced 'Good-eva' and written as *Godgifu* in early English. *Godgifu* meant 'the good gift'. The name of her husband, Leofric, was pronounced 'Lovric' and appears as such in this novel. *Leofric* meant 'beloved leader'.

One

A marsh mist had drifted in overnight and settled on the Sherbourne, clinging to the frayed riverbanks and tingeing the early morning air with a dank, sulphurous mustiness. Above the banks, low ridges of drier earth lay listless in the weak light of the breaking dawn, like drunks still debilitated by the excesses of the previous night. As a weak shaft of sunlight broke through the mist, the dawn chorus, excitedly feasting on sluggish worms, fell suddenly silent, as if resolving this day would repay no further effort. Only the horse-flies and wasps continued to rise through the brightening daylight in venomous, buzzing joy from the rubbish on the unpaved streets that led across town and up to the market place. There, at the summit of a low hill, two old churches and a new stone-built Benedictine priory jostled each other for holy precedence. In their midst stood the brightly painted town cross, whose tall outline and clear-cut shadow symbolized the harmony of the market as money changed hands below. Men, women and children swatted their foreheads, cursed and braced themselves for a morning of irritation and effort. The more forbearing raised their eyes, gazed at the churches and signed the cross in hope of an answer to a forgotten prayer. Then they too steeled themselves for the labours that lay ahead. A day that seemed like any other in that sullen summer of 1045 was getting under way in the new town of Coventry.

Less than half a mile to the south, the lane that ran from the town took a sharp turn and led directly into the yard of the manor of Cheylesmore. A stranger arriving here might have taken this to be another country, far from Coventry, for there was nothing languid about the scene now taking place in the manor. In the centre of the yard a small, wizened woman in a long hemp apron stood on a mounting block beside the stable and issued a stream of commands to whoever came her way. Boys were sent off with long poles to fish the shallow rivers that threaded through the bogs that lay south of the manor; slaves were ordered to sweep the dung from the yard and fill the potholes and cart ruts with fresh clay and gravel; men from the hall were told to appraise the supplies for the coming night's feast and report any shortages; and the women who cooked and served food were informed of the menu and the order in which their day's work would unfold.

Her instructions delivered, the old woman, Gwen – not really old, but work-worn and snappy, and therefore nicknamed 'the corgi' – trudged off towards the far end of the yard and the large wattle-and-daub hut where the sick and injured of the manor were sent to recuperate. With everyone now at work, she felt once more the emptiness that prevailed during the absence of the rulers of the household. It recalled the desolation of other houses she had known – set alight, overgrown and finally abandoned. She shuddered, then squeezed her eyes shut and sent up a sudden, informal prayer: *please, Mary, bring Godiva home in good time this evening; protect Earl Lovric from all enemies and may the wounded be few tonight; please, Mary, bring my darling Alfgar home with his father, and let Milly marry and go away soon. Amen. Oh, and keep an eye on Harry, far away with Earl Siward. And may the rain stop and the cows get well. God help us and give us a good feast tonight* and keep famine away this year. Mother Mary, pray for us sinners down here on this Earth. Amen again.

By evening, their work done, the servants reassembled in the yard of the manor house. Men and women who rarely had time to worry about their appearance now fidgeted with belts and hoods, straightened their wrinkly hose and twisted skirts and tidied away loose wisps of hair. At last, having satisfied Gwen's unsparing scrutiny, they straightened up and settled down to stare intently at the lane that led out through the manor's entrance towards the town, the abbey and the low, rolling woodlands of Mercia.

A prolonged moment of silence occupied the crowded yard until, hesitantly at first, a murmur started amongst those nearest the entrance, and then a loud cheer went up. Someone had spotted the small pennant that fluttered on the tip of the spear that the earl's outrider carried above his head. Moments later the outrider came trotting into the yard and the crowd erupted in cries of welcome, so rowdy that his brightly caparisoned horse reared up and bared his teeth as if about to enter battle. The outrider let his stallion continue rearing, performing 'the dance of the drums' on his hind legs and impressing on the people of the manor the glory and strangeness of the world of warfare. Soon the herald arrived, displaying a banner emblazoned with the black eagle of the Earls of Mercia, hanging from a trumpet which the herald raised to his lips and blew repeatedly, making a harsh sound like the screech of a battlefield crow protecting its carrion. Brown war-dogs surged into the yard, baying, frothing and yelping, straining at the leashes and tugging their handlers. Next came the battle stallions, clattering over the stones at the yard's entrance, snorting and whinnying as they recognized the scents of home.

Tension mounted as the servants awaited the entrance of the

housecarls – Earl Lovric's nucleus of fully armed men who stayed at his side when his other soldiers became farmers again and decamped to their own villages. They could hear them approaching, their voices thundering a marching song that boasted of their courage in combat and the glory of their lord. As the singing grew louder the hall-master, Odo, picked up the refrain and everyone else joined in. The housecarls tramped into the manor yard with their blood-stained spears and battered shields at their sides, grim-faced men who kept up a stony front while their eyes searched the crowd for the one particular face that meant home. Some in the crowd searched too, wondering who would come limping in last, or arrive on a stretcher, and who would not be coming home at all this time. But most eyes followed the swinging stride of the housecarls' captain, who flourished a tall pike on which was fixed the old trophy skull of a Viking, contemptuously crowned with his own battered helmet. As they came to a full stop before the line of servants, the herald produced his drum and began the tattoo that announced the ritual of home-coming.

'Out,' shouted the captain, pointing at the Viking skull. The housecarls pointed their spears at the skull and shouted in unison, 'Out! Out! Out!'

The servants then took up the shout, and the war-dogs, thrilled at the sound of so many throats in full cry like a pack of hounds, howled along with them. Some of the smaller children took fright and were hurried away, while older boys thought longingly of dropping their spades and taking up arms, and girls wondered whether they would ever see anything more distant than the parish church.

Once things had settled down again, Odo and his hall-men rushed to clear the yard of dogs and horses, and the assembly of servants and soldiers regrouped to greet the last arrival in the yard. As always, the Earl of Mercia waited until there was silence before making his entrance. He rode in alone at a walking pace on the biggest stallion of all, his mailed gloves still on his hands, his shield and sword at his side, his ceremonial cape with its feathery black eagle about his shoulders, and his helmet pulled down over his face. All could now see what he looked like when he was away from the manor and carrying out his duties as a commander. He rode once round the circle of servants with his helmet closed, and then once more with his visor up, and then brought his horse to a halt. Slowly he unbuckled his helmet, rubbed his chin and dismounted.

He stared round at the yard of the manor, and felt his heart suddenly quicken. Godiva would appear at any moment now – radiant, serene, the lady of the manor in her best *godweb* mantle, offering mead from the old horn first to him and then to his second in command. This was the high point of the homecoming, all the more intense for its unvarying ceremony: something he could dream about when he was away because he could count on it being always the same, and she too always the same.

Still, as he waited, he could not help but take stock of the details of his surroundings, as though he was still on campaign and alert to hidden dangers. The yard was neater than he remembered, and more prosperous. A weak part of the palisade had been patched with new, pale timber and the entrance to the courtyard was paved with smooth river stones that kept the mud down more effectively than the broken old bricks that had been there before. He remembered those bricks from the time he lamed a horse on them and he was glad they were gone. Then he noticed the windows and gritted his teeth. So, she had done it after all – put in glass despite his objections that windowpanes were too expensive and hard to repair. What else had she done that he wouldn't like? He started to sweep the courtyard with his glittering blue eyes that could still, after five decades, count the number of horsemen in a column half a mile away. Then, tearing into his concentration, there came a shriek.

'Papa!'

'Milly!'

He spun round as a daintily dressed girl gathered up her skirts and raced across the yard to throw herself into his arms. The earl embraced his stepdaughter, then pushed her to arm's length and looked at her appraisingly.

'Little Mill, you're blooming! You were just a big child when I left and now, suddenly, you're all grown-up.'

'Thank you, papa.'

'That means you must have your wedding feast with no delay. It's long overdue. But I promise on my oath we'll do it before summer ends.'

'Ends?'

'Yes. That'll give your mother and Gwen enough time to prepare. It's not so far off – so you can stop frowning, my girl. Come, Milly, won't you forgive me for having made you wait? I came home as soon as I could.'

'Papa, I'd forgive you anything,' said Milly with a forced smile, vowing silently to have her feast sooner than September, no matter what her stepfather said now.

'Well then, forgive me this. I'm going to have to talk with you later. A good long talk about your wedding and the lands we will give you. But first I need to talk alone with your mother. At once.'

He scanned the crowd in the yard, looking for Godiva's face.

'Where is she?' he said, his throat suddenly tightening. 'She's supposed to be here when the men come home.'

'I can't say, father,' Milly said uncertainly. It worried her when her parents quarrelled, as they seemed to do more often since leaving Hereford and coming to Coventry. 'There's cattle sickness all about. Perhaps she had to go and look.' But Lovric's scowl only deepened and Milly clammed up.

Just then fresh noises came from the entrance to the yard and everyone turned to look that way. Godiva's outrider, blowing a horn, came trotting in, followed immediately by her liveried herald. Lovric swore into his beard at this ostentation and turned away from his waiting soldiers in embarrassment.

But then Godiva appeared, riding high on a tall palomino mare, horse and rider a swirl of chestnut, cream and pale gold, and his anger faded like an enemy that had briefly raised his flag, but passed on to another destination. She saw him and gave her broad smile, the smile that raised her cheeks like the curtains on a new morning and brought light into eyes so soft and grey that he always wanted to pull her close, no matter how much she maddened him. Dressed in men's riding leggings and a long, divided tunic, she stayed up on her horse and shouted instructions to the stable hands. With arms folded, Lovric stared at her, noting how flushed she was and guessing that she had sped home from some mission. Anxiously his men watched him assess his beautiful wife. The manor was their haven; no one wanted the earl to be angry at home. Stillness settled on the yard again as Godiva finished her tasks and rode up to Lovric. Smiling, she dismounted.

'Welcome home, Lord Lovric,' she said formally, bowing and pulling off her leather riding cap. Her bright-yellow hair tumbled out and swept the straw-covered ground before he had a chance to raise her face to receive his kiss.

'Eva, my love,' he murmured, so softly that only Godiva heard, and then he wrapped her in his arms.

A sigh of relief escaped from the crowd. The horn was found and filled with mead. Godiva took it and raised it to Lovric's lips. He passed it to his second in command, and then it was refilled and put into the hands of every hero who had shed the blood of an enemy during the months away from home, the months during which the flowers had blossomed in the manor's gardens, the honey gathered and the nectar fermented. The sweet mead was time-distilled, a homage to home.

In the bedchamber of the manor house Lovric shut the oaken door firmly behind him and turned to face Godiva. His anger, though much diminished, hadn't entirely gone, and Godiva, after eighteen years of marriage, was quite prepared to deal with it.

'I know you wanted me in the yard for your arrival,' she said quickly. 'I'm always there for you. But this time was different. It was a matter of law and order. That's why I took the herald and the flag. People are nervous, what with the food supply dwindling and the cows sickening, and now there's been an unexpected death. I had to show them I cared.'

'Perhaps,' Lovric answered, ignoring her explanation. 'But it looked disrespectful, not being in the yard for the homecoming.' He knew he was being unfair. An unexplained death had to be investigated at once, and that would take the best part of a day. He was finding fault only because his disappointment, though short-lived, had taken his breath away. 'Well, what did you manage to find out?'

'The dead man came from another lordship. Elfthryth and her daughter believe it was a suicide.'

'How could they tell? You put too much trust in these so-called wise women.'

Godiva ignored the jibe. 'Elfthryth said that he made sure he would die when he jumped off the tree. Killers are not so careful. They wouldn't care if they hanged a man twice or more.'

'Anything else?'

'Drovers stopped at the pool in Stivichall a few days ago. This man could have been with them, got into a fight perhaps or got too drunk and been left behind. Perhaps no one wanted him any more, and he decided to end it.'

'Perhaps.'

'I came back as quickly as I could.'

'I'm sure you did.' Suddenly, as it always did, the last of his anger vanished abruptly. He took her hand and kissed it. 'I'm sorry, Eva. You did the right thing. I shouldn't have been so annoyed.'

'You're tired.'

'And so are you.'

She nodded and sighed. Though she was no stranger to death, the sight of the hanged man's body had shaken her. He was prematurely aged, thin and toothless, and the illusion of a smile on his twisted, blackened mouth suggested he was grateful for any release from his wretched life. She had stood over him as the wise women finished their work, and then told her chaplain to lead everyone in prayer for the forgiveness of his soul. The servants were told to take the corpse to Coventry for burial and tell the monks of St Mary's to say a mass for him at her expense. After that she talked with the men of the tithing and decided they should go ahead with a search for possible killers, in case the death was not a suicide. Finally, on her way home, she made a detour to see a family of lepers whose health had recently deteriorated. The woman of the family had come to the gate that barred the world from their infected home and in her arms there was a new, malnourished baby. Godiva gave her a coin and promised she would send more soon. Then, halfway to Cheyles-more, while crossing a shallow ford, the outrider had spotted the carcass of a cow lying in a stream that fed a drinking pool. It was a very recent death, for the flies had only just started work on the hide. The owner had to be found and brought to dispose of the animal's remains, and messengers sent to the hamlet whose drinking water was now polluted. It took a while to find the owner, for no one would admit to possessing a cow that had sickened to death and put other animals at risk. Hours later than she intended, Godiva had turned her horse's head towards Coventry and ridden home at dangerous speed for her reunion with Lovric.

She sat heavily on the edge of the bed. Lovric poured her a glass of red wine, sat beside her and held her hand in a silence that grew ever more companionable. He felt comfortable with her at last. He thanked God.

'We've been apart so long, Eva,' he said at last. 'Let's lie down and continue our talking later.'

She closed her eyes and turned her face to take the kiss with which he always sought to repair whatever small injuries they had inflicted on each other since last they lay together. Then, softening, she put her arms around his neck, reclined and let him find his way slowly through the layers of her riding clothes.

About an hour later she woke up to find him sitting near the window with an empty glass of wine in his hand.

'Now, my love,' he said, 'there is something important I must discuss with you.'

'Not now, Lovric – the feast is starting soon.'

'I'm not attending. My men have seen enough of me. They won't mind my absence as long as they get well fed.'

'But my people will mind. They've worked so hard...'

'Eva, I can't feast and make plans with you at the same time.'

She felt once more the weight of duty, a weight that seemed to have sat on her for as long as she could remember, crushing even minor pleasures. Inevitably, the manor and its routines took second place to the needs of the earldom and the kingdom. Lovric's responsibilities kept them all enmeshed in chains of responsibility that ran upwards from the merest slave to the lonely pinnacle of the king himself. She knew that, she was resigned to it – and yet these days it irked her, as though her efforts in Coventry meant little in the scheme of things, and little to Lovric.

She sent for Gwen to apologize for their absence from the feast and asked for more wine. Then she lit extra candles, locked the chamber door and settled down to listen. As Lovric started talking, with too much detail at first about troop movements and fords, supply lines and defended points, and then with growing urgency about deaths and rapes, betrayals and burning towns, she shut her eyes to concentrate. And gradually, behind her closed lids, a picture formed.

It was Hereford once more. The mountains to the west rose black against the night, winds howled and rain slashed the faces of fugitives. Words were screamed out in English and Welsh, and then in French. Gruffydd ap Llywelyn was coming to take back the lands of his ancestors. Alfgar – Lovric's beloved son Alfgar – sought out the Welsh prince. They could make terms, he said. The Welshman laughed at the thought and waved him away. No, said Alfgar – either they would come to terms, or the Normans would come in and vanquish them all. There would be castles everywhere, bristling with garrisons at the ready, just as there were already in the Vexin, the borderland of Normandy, which Ralph of Mantes had brought to heel. Now Ralph is starting to get a grip on the Welsh borders. Soon he will get reinforcements from Normandy and come after them all, Welsh and English, with equal venom. And then they could all forget forever what justice and freedom had been like.

Gruffydd stopped laughing, embraced Alfgar like a brother and took him far up the winding valley of the Wye to a secret fortress that Alfgar had never heard of and whose name no one would tell. There they had talked for days and nights with no fear of King Edward's spies, all of them talking in Welsh, for

Alfgar knew the language from his childhood days with Gwen in Hereford. We are Britons, they agreed, enemies but Britons. Ralph of Mantes is a foreigner, and though he speaks French he is as bad as any Dane or Norwegian or any other Viking. Men like him are finding footholds all over England and, piecemeal and unopposed, with the backing of the despicable King Edward they will carve up these islands between them, just as other Northmen did before, with fire, axe and longboat.

'But you see, Eva, Ralph of Mantes is the king's sworn man.'

Godiva opened her eyes to find Lovric pacing the room and clenching his fists.

'And so Alfgar is being accused of treason.'

She felt the breath leave her body as if from a blow. Alfgar was her stepson, and the eldest and most turbulent of the children – her favourite – the one who made her laugh most, the one who went riding with her whenever he could and who taught her to use a sword. Where Milly aroused her sense of obligation, and the memory of Harry stirred up tenderness, the thought of Alfgar filled her with joy.

'There must be a mistake,' she said at last.

'No. Edward has decided to make an example of him. Plotting against Ralph is now held to be treason against the king. I've got this,' Lovric said, holding up a scrolled letter. 'I've been summoned to Winchester to defend Alfgar.'

'But where is he now?' she asked, her words muffled by the great fear that had taken her by the throat.

'In hiding. But he is reckless and likes to pick fights. He might break cover and then anything could happen.'

'Then you must go to Winchester at once, Lovric, before matters get worse for him.'

'Yes,' he said. Then his voice trailed off uncertainly.

'What else is wrong?'

'You must come too, Godiva. You must come with me.'

'What? I can't. I am desperately needed here, and I could do nothing to help in Winchester. Just go and come back as quickly as possible, Lovric.'

'But I need you with me. You're coming. I've decided.'

Godiva stepped away from him and put her hands angrily on her hips.

'Don't talk to me like that, Lovric. You know I have responsibilities in Coventry. And you know that Edward does not like me. It would irritate him to see me at Winchester.'

'No.'

He turned away to pace the room, but she pursued him, insisting that he listen to her. 'I have too much on my hands to be able to leave. Milly's wedding is overdue. And there's the priory. Prior Edwin is wilful and lazy. As for Coventry, I may have to feed the townspeople from my own barns. The wheat harvest is probably going to fail and the dull weather is holding back the fruit and vegetables, too. And now, making everything ten times worse, there's cattle plague, cutting into people's milk supply. God knows where it will all end. I've noticed some of the townspeople already looking pinched and pallid. If this goes on much longer they'll fall ill...'

'They will not, Godiva. Not so quickly. We won't be away much more than a month. People can stand a little bit of hardship until then.'

'Lovric, that's callous.'

'No, it's realistic. They have greater reserves than they let on. Every year folk say they are going to die of famine before the end of summer, and they hardly ever do. You worry too much.'

'But so do they. They need me here, if only to reassure them.'

'But I need you more.'

He had never entreated her so stubbornly before and she wondered what was worrying him. Perhaps it was his advancing age. He should be handing over the affairs of the earldom to

Alfgar soon, if only Alfgar were ready for such responsibilities. But no, it couldn't be that: Lovric was still fit and strong and looked every inch the Earl of Mercia.

'My dear,' she began softly, 'You're hiding something from me. If you want me to come to Winchester, tell me what it is.'

'What?'

'What you're hiding.'

'I'm not...'

'For God's sake, Lovric! Tell me what the matter is. Otherwise I won't even think of coming with you.'

His instinct when confronted by anyone – whether king, common soldier or his own wife – was to conceal, to bluff or lie, or even to bully. This instinct was all the stronger when he wanted to protect someone he loved. Forced into revelations, he grew clumsy.

'You must tell me,' she said softly, knowing how he was struggling with himself.

'I wanted to wait. I didn't want you wringing your hands and weeping all the way to Winchester.'

In the silence that followed, Godiva gazed at her husband's bowed head. His hair, though shot with grey and silver, was still thick and strong, and his neck retained the suppleness of a much younger man, so that his head drooped like the stem of a wilting flower whenever he was worried. How strange, she thought, that such a subtle stamp of uniqueness should pass from father to son, and that a whole family of soldiers should exhibit this hint of vulnerability. His father had this neck droop, so did Alfgar, and even Harry bowed his neck like this when he was only eight. Suddenly her heart lurched and she seized his hand.

Lovric said nothing. He is remembering, Godiva thought, how I cried and wrung my hands when Harry went north to Siward. I lamented for days, as though my little boy was being led to his death and not to a loving upbringing with good foster-parents, an arrangement that was not just normal, but deeply honourable. Yet to me it was a tragedy.

Now she tried to remain composed. 'This is about Harry, isn't it? You must tell me, my love.'

'I'm sorry,' he whispered back. Then, seeing the horror on her face, he rushed on. 'No. Don't misunderstand. The boy is well...'

'Then what is the matter?'

'Harry is well, but I have bad news about him: the king has ordered Siward to bring Harry to Winchester.' He paused, gripped the hilt of his sword and blurted out the rest of it. 'Harry is to be held hostage for Alfgar's good conduct.'

'What?' she whispered furiously, keeping her voice down in case there were servants nearby. 'Our son a hostage? Hostages are what kings take from defeated enemies, not from allies. And hostages are those they kill or blind and castrate when they are displeased in any way. Nobody can guarantee peace on the Welsh border – not the king, not you, not anyone. What will Edward do if there is a Welsh raid? Blame Alfgar and hang Harry? Oh dear God, what will you do, Lovric?'

He took a deep breath and seemed to calm down. 'Edward won't harm Harry just because of a border raid. This is a gesture, to show others – his Norman friends in Hereford – that he can bring the English earls and their sons to heel, and frighten their wives as well.'

Godiva leaped up from her seat and slammed her hand on the wall beside him. 'Damn this king!' she hissed. 'Damn this Norman whore's bastard son!'

'Hush! Take heart,' he said, putting his arms around her. 'Edward bluffs all the time. He won't know what to do next and then he will tire of the situation. It's happened before, even with his mother.' He paused and wiped away her tears. 'Remember when he imprisoned old Queen Emma?'

'Yes.'

'She cursed the whole nation of the English in French. Everyone thought we'd seen the last of her, but just a year later she was back at court, as arrogant as ever and scolding everyone. It will be the same with Harry – just a short spell as a hostage and then Siward and I will have the boy out of court and back with us, safe and sound. You'll see.'

'Better by far never to put him in harm's way.'

'Yes, but I have no choice in this matter.'

'And, obviously, neither do I.'

'Then you'll come to Winchester with me?'

'Yes. I'll come.'

'Are you sure?'

'What else could I do? I want to see Harry before he is handed over to the king. I want to hold him and kiss him again. I want to show him I have not forgotten him after these nine long years apart.'

She stopped to control herself and wipe away the tears that had gathered. When she resumed she sounded like the practical woman she was – the woman who, on her own, had planned and financed the building of a splendid abbey, who had supervised builders and interviewed traders before licensing them to settle in her town. She spoke in a voice that she recognized as her own, but it was not the one in which she had said goodbye to Harry. She had changed so much, and he must have changed even more. She was unsure what she feared most: his forthcoming imprisonment or her own encounter with a son who had grown up without her.

'Lovric, we must ensure he gets well treated – not put in prison, or kept in chains. And I must find someone to take care of his food and bedding and clothing. Perhaps I could plead for him with Queen Edith – she has no children, but she is a woman and she might have more compassion than the king...'

She talked on, running through all the things she might be

able to do to help her youngest child. Lovric saw that her spirits were rising and did not interrupt. He himself was so full of foreboding about the king's intentions that the less he said now, the better. Gradually she talked herself into a mood of confidence. She had faced many difficulties before, on her own and with Lovric. They would prevail again, she was sure. Lovric would make Alfgar's peace with the king, and then there would be no reason for Harry to remain a hostage. As for Coventry, the weather might well improve, and as Lovric said, her fears were probably exaggerated. The abbey was an urgent matter, but Prior Edwin could be dealt with quickly, in one decisive conversation. Her problems were far smaller than they had seemed only an hour ago. She put her arms round Lovric and kissed him tenderly as though forgiving him for some misdeed, some guilt that had yet to be discovered. Awkwardly he briefly returned her kiss.

Godiva usually awoke at the second crowing of the rooster that ruled the dung heap on the north side of the palisade. But this morning, just when she needed her full share of sleep for the busy day ahead, her eyes sprang open before the first sliver of pink cut through the clouded sky. Beside her Lovric was snoring and, though they were only soft snores, they were too loud for a woman used to sleeping on her own. She thought of taking a candle and going to the room downstairs where Gwen and Milly slept together on low pallets beside the hearth. She could slip in beside them and get another hour or two of rest. Then the reason for her abrupt awakening came to her. It was Edwin, her unsatisfactory prior. She had to talk to him before leaving Coventry, and to catch him in his quarters she had to confront him at dawn.

Edwin, a man distinguished only by his passion for angling, had been elected prior of St Mary's because he was Lovric's second cousin, and Lovric had insisted that Godiva appoint a relative to head her new priory. Otherwise, he argued, the priory lands would drift out of their control. In their circle of kin only Edwin was available, and this became the chief argument for his suitability. As a result, Godiva found herself putting up with a brazen unscrupulousness she had never had to deal with before. When eyebrows were raised, for instance, at Edwin's frequent absences from St Mary's, he would point out that he merely followed in the footsteps of the great apostle, Peter the Fisherman, whose altar stood in the priory. The people of the town, used to the riddling of churchmen, nodded in agreement, smiled to his face and laughed with scorn behind his back. Godiva, meanwhile, busy with other matters and anxious to avoid having to replace him, left Edwin undisturbed.

First light was dawning as the low side-door of St Mary's resounded to the loud banging of the iron door-knocker. Behind the door the chanting of dawn prayers continued undisturbed. Minutes passed and Godiva's attendant began to hit the door angrily until she whispered that the monks were not answering for their own reasons. In the silence that followed a light appeared, flickering in a small casement window above the door. Then shuffling footsteps could be heard, low voices conferring and finally the grating of a key turning in the lock.

'My lady!' a reedy voice gasped from the crack that now appeared beside the door.

'Let me in, and go and get Prior Edwin.'

More time went by and Godiva was growing enraged, when Edwin came hurrying around a corner in the company of a freckled blond boy, known to everyone in Coventry as Cherub. The prior was flustered and the boy looked unhappy.

'My beloved daughter in Christ...' Edwin began.

'Take me somewhere private. I must talk to you,' she said, looking past him.

Edwin, noticing the asperity of her tone, signed the cross and led the way towards the refectory, near which there was a small room set aside for private meetings and emergencies.

'Whatever is troubling your soul, beloved in Christ?' he began again, as disarmingly as possible.

'My soul is in good health, but not my priory. There are several matters that I committed to your attention weeks ago, and they remain unattended. I must leave today on an unexpected journey to Winchester with the earl. I do not need the additional worry of wondering when you, Edwin, will stop procrastinating and carry out my instructions.'

'Ah, you must mean the matter of the arm of St Augustine. You see, beloved lady, this is a delicate business. I have tried...'

'You have not! It is our most important relic – once in the treasury of Queen Emma herself – and you let it remain in obscurity in St Michael's, and no mention of moving it to my priory. This is a disgrace!'

'But I really did try. The secular clergy are not reform-minded, you see. They view the holy arm as their own personal property.'

'Well, Father Godric will inform them this morning, before we leave, that this relic is to be moved at once to St Mary's. And that you will perform this act with all due ceremony, prayers and reverence. And speed.'

'Very well, very well. I shall pray for the Virgin's assistance in ending this dispute amicably.'

'There is no dispute,' Godiva shouted. 'And if I find a feud going on when I return home, I'll know that you caused it. I'm warning you, Edwin, any more meddling and you will go back to that little prebendary you held outside Hereford.'

Edwin hung his head and said nothing, but Godiva caught a brief flash of menace when he glanced at her for a moment.

She got up, moved towards the door in a great volume of cloth and glared back at him. 'When I come back from Winchester you will tell me what you have done. Do you understand?'

The prior made no reply. The resentful look on his face had hardened. Suddenly, unwilling to leave him in such a bad mood, she softened. 'I am not as displeased as perhaps I sound. Together we shall do better in future,' she said, and kissed him lightly on the cheek.

This was the Christian kiss of forgiveness, but it filled Edwin with disgust. With an effort he summoned his look of pained love for humanity, the look that he often used with women to conceal the revulsion he felt for the softness of their lips and the sweet manners that he knew to be a gift from Satan to his first daughter. Still, his hand trembled a little, for Godiva was not only a beautiful woman, but one with great power over him, and though he knew he owed her gratitude, he hated the humiliation he felt in her presence. How wonderful it would be to take her down a peg or two, but without bringing himself down as well. Then the realism that had served him so well over the years reasserted itself. Nothing but God or Satan could bring Godiva down: she was rich in her own right, healthy, beloved of her powerful husband and all those who surrounded her, a celebrated beauty and with no secret blemishes. He signed the cross and kissed her hand.

Godiva closed the door behind her with relief and rebuked herself for not having dealt with Edwin sooner. She looked back at her luminous priory and acknowledged that, despite his absurdity, there was something about Edwin that had inclined her to avoid him. That would have to change if they were to develop St Mary's as a centre of pilgrimage. When she got back from Winchester, she would make an effort to draw closer to him. It might be a good idea, for example, to start confessing to him sometimes, instead of relying so much on her uneducated chaplain, Father Godric. Edwin was undoubtedly sly and self-indulgent, but with encouragement and appreciation he would probably change. Most people, she had found, preferred to let their better qualities shine. She thought for a moment about all the masons and woodworkers she had supervised until recently, and how some had been arrogant, others crude and yet others confused at taking orders from a woman. Yet in the end they had all become cooperative. Optimistic and resolved, she crossed herself, thanked Mary for her priory and headed back to Cheylesmore manor to face the day and the journey that lay ahead. Had she looked back she might have felt differently. Prior Edwin was glaring after her, and squeezing Cherub's neck until the pain brought tears to his eyes. But Godiva was facing the road ahead, thinking of all she had to do next, and did not turn round again.

Two

*G*odiva entered Cheylesmore to find the yard stirring. Inside the manor house she greeted Gwen and went up to her bedchamber, where she found Lovric standing, already dressed, and gazing through the glass window into the yard below.

'Went to see Prior Edwin, did you? I saw you coming up the lane.'

'Yes, I think I'll have an obedient prior from now on.'

'Good. I like your new windows. You were right about putting in glass after all. You can see everything that's going on down in the yard. Gwen's had the slaves out at dawn to sweep up after last night and get the yard ready for our departure. We're lucky she's still fit for work. But are you training someone to replace her?'

Godiva went to the window. 'There is one new man. That one over there, talking with Odo and Arne.' She pointed at a young man in a green huntsman's tunic, wearing a feather in his cap. 'He came here as a gift from the king. His name is Bret – Beorhtric of Nottingham.'

Lovric raised his eyebrows and examined the man.

'Edward sent him to us early this spring to develop our stag hunting. You complained to him that there were too many boars in our forests and too few stags.'

'I don't remember saying that.'

'Well, it's true anyway. You were probably drunk when you said it. They say Edward is always cold sober and never forgets a thing.'

'Never forgets his Psalms and such. Bring the man up and let me meet him.'

Godiva opened the window and leaned out into the yard. The man in green appeared to start when she called his name, then he bowed respectfully.

'That's odd,' Lovric said as he peered over her shoulder. 'This fellow does not quite have the build of a huntsman. More like the shape and movement of a swordsman. He's been in someone's army.'

He beckoned to the man and, in less than a minute, he was up the stairs and knocking on the door of the chamber. In one glance Lovric detected all the marks of the huntsman on him — the calluses on his fingers, the narrowing of the right eye, the slight stoop forward from the waist and a supple, feline walk. Then Lovric glanced down.

'What's wrong there?' he said, pointing at Bret's foot. 'You look like some men I've seen who've been in the iron boot for a while. Been in trouble, have you?'

Bret looked offended. 'My foot would be far worse if it had been in the boot, sir. It would be crushed. It is only my ankle that is wrong. Look,' he pulled off his loose suede boot.

Godiva looked away, embarrassed that Lovric was putting her huntsman through an uncalled-for test of his innocence. Lovric ignored her and scrutinized the man's lower leg carefully, concluding that Bret might yet have been tortured with the iron boot, but perhaps only briefly until he talked his way out of it.

'Well? What happened to you, if not the boot?'

'I was caught in a stirrup during a fall two years ago and got dragged by my ankle. I won't use the damn things any more.

That was the reason I left military service. John, the chief huntsman, will tell you, sir. I always ride foot-free now.'

Lovric put aside his moment of doubt. He looked Bret over once more and thought what a fine specimen he was – tall and broad-shouldered, well spoken and handsome, with an open, tanned face and dark-green eyes that seemed to flicker in the light of the candles. The two talked for a few minutes more about the forests, the weather and the increase in the signs of poaching, and then they shook hands and Bret, bowing reticently to Godiva, made to leave. She smiled apologetically at him, and seeing the sympathy in her eyes he smiled back at her, so warmly that she felt she had not really noticed him before. As he walked away she stared after him for a moment, wondering why she had seen so little of him since his arrival at Cheylesmore. But then the demands of the day reclaimed her, and her attention moved on to the complications of last-minute packing for a journey that would see them ride through forests, sleep at humble thegns' halls and dine in the presence of a king and queen.

By noon the riding party was almost ready to leave. Gwen stood next to Godiva in the yard, taking last-minute instructions and trying not to show her annoyance at the unexpected disruption of her routines. Milly stood to one side, arms folded, not talking to her parents, but making her presence and her anger palpable. Odo, as steward of the hall, strode around, arguing with his assistant, Arne, both of them trying to count heads and make sure that no one assigned to hall duties had managed to slip into the riding party. Young girls from the dairy came rushing in, franti-cally seeking out their lovers and pressing small plaited straw crosses into their hands. Agatha, seventeen years old and the only rider amongst the women of the manor, sat up on her horse, pretty and flushed with excitement and longing to go. Then she spotted her mother, who seemed to be smiling and waving farewell. Agatha waved back, only to realize that Bertha was not waving, but shaking her hard little fist in warning.

'Bugger off,' Agatha murmured, too quietly for her mother to understand, but loud enough for Godiva to overhear.

'None of that, or you stay home and help Bertha repair clothes all summer,' Godiva scolded.

Agatha bit her lip, as she had done since she was three whenever she felt ashamed. All of a sudden, Godiva saw her again as a child, Harry's playmate in the manor gardens of Hereford. He had called her his sister and told everyone he would marry her when he grew up. Her eyes burned. But this was no time for tears: the departure had begun. Godiva took her place alongside Lovric and urged her horse on.

A short while after leaving the manor the riding party reached a lane that wound east through the Forest of Arden towards a junction with an old Roman road. From here they would continue unimpeded and straight south to Oxford. A great hush fell on the riders as they entered the undisturbed world of Arden, where even quiet words seemed harsh and alien. All round them were oaks that had been young when Guinevere and Launcelot lingered beneath their branches. They towered now like tall kings, garlanded in glittering raindrops, and from beneath their canopy shy creatures offered their eyes and ears briefly to the light, and then took fright and dived into holes or plunged deeper into the beckoning green shadows behind them. Godiva was so silent that Lovric wondered if she was brooding about what lay ahead of them in Winchester. In fact, she had plunged into reverie about the sprites whose mischief had entertained her childhood years in Sherwood Forest and those of her children in the Forest of Haye. Puck would be lurking nearby, cloaked in leaves and hiding in a cluster of toadstools, or sliding down a dusty sunbeam through the trees to the earth below. And the Fairy Queen must be here too, swinging on the catkins and coating herself in golden dust, raising the petals of her gossamer skirts to tease the elves and the butterflies. In this paradise she and her children were forever young and safe and joyful.

Lovric grew silent beside her, enjoying a reprieve from his constant military vigilance. The whole riding party gradually fell into a similar consoling trance, and it was not until late afternoon when they were deep in the forest that sounds of human activity brought them all down to earth. Shouting and the sound of axe blows against timber, and then the dismal creak and sigh of a crashing tree, announced the presence of woodsmen ahead of them. There would be charcoal-burners nearby, and Lovric halted the riding party, told them to water the horses and announced that he would go ahead alone to procure some charcoal water for his burning stomach. Godiva, saying she wanted some charcoal and flaxseed poultice for the medicine chest, followed him.

The forest, though it was legally within Lovric's domain, was in fact beyond anyone's control. The king talked about imposing his authority over all the greenwood, but the forests of England were too big and his servants too few, and they remained as they had always been – a world apart from the human web of fields, pastures and gardens. Nevertheless, Lovric felt safe, for his riding party was surrounded by a penumbra of scouts, and no one had reported trouble from the route ahead. It was, then, with a shock that he brought his horse to a sharp halt as soon as he entered the glade in which the charcoal-burners had made camp. He tried to get Godiva to go back, but it was too late. She drew alongside him and took in the scene before them.

The camp was a big, commercial one, with several smouldering fires on the go at the same time, slowly hardening wood into the charred substance that would heat the furnaces where metal ores were smelted to make, above all else, weapons. There was money to be made from charcoal, and foreigners had moved in recently with licences to operate and with the cheapest labour they could get their hands on. This inevitably consisted of men and women who had been enslaved as punishment for serious crimes, and of these the very cheapest, and the least likely to run away successfully, were those whose punishment included mutilation. It was these who now faced Lovric and Godiva: a filthy, ragged woman with holes like two accusing eyes where her nose had been, and three men who seemed intact until they shouted at the intruders to go away, waving their arms and making indecipherable noises with their tongueless mouths. In the background were other coal-blackened workers, and walking between them were several overseers with whips. Lovric took the reins of Godiva's horse and jerked its head away. They retreated from the glade and returned to the riding party without a word.

Lovric knew that the scene in the camp had reminded her of the perils facing Alfgar and Harry. It was true that as men of high birth they would not be subject to flogging or mutilation, but there were other cruelties that could be inflicted upon them in captivity. She would know that. To distract her attention he began to run through the pleasures that lay ahead as they crossed lands that belonged to his thegns, Wulfwin and Waga. They were men she knew well and liked – men whose halls would be open to them, whose wives would offer mead and ale, whose daughters would sing, and whose *scopman* would tell an exciting or funny tale. Then there would be bed, and because he was the overlord, Lovric would have a quiet place of his own to lie with Godiva. So different was this, he told her, from his long tours of duty in the troublespots of the land, where no welcome awaited and no wife was there at night, and where the only shelter was a leather tent, hauled with great effort up hill and down dale in the pursuit of elusive, evanescent peace.

She smiled at his efforts to cheer her, a deliberately composed smile, intended to show him that she had calmed down and put the brutal scene in the forest behind her. But Lovric was not deceived, nor did he know what else to say to her. He turned towards her again and looked at her riding clothes – the close-fitting leather tunic and the tight cap that was unflattering, but which, because she had worn them both for years, he found enchanting.

'My lady,' he began, and then found he couldn't say what was on his mind. She knew he loved her, but he told her that so often, in the same plain old words, it seemed pointless to keep saying it. Then, to her surprise, he cleared his throat and started to sing. Lovric had a strong, tuneful baritone that Godiva had not heard for months. She joined in the song too, and then the trumpeter, at the head of the column, picked up his penny whistle with his free hand and accompanied them. Behind them someone pulled out a small flat drum, and down the line of horsemen several found their knick-knack bones or spoons, and soon everyone was making music. The horses pricked up their ears and though their pace remained unchanged, it grew livelier as manes were tossed and tails swished. Then, suddenly, from far down the line, rising like a blackbird's song, came the tenor voice of an unknown soldier. Lovric held up his hand and passed the message back: bring that man up here to sing with me.

It was the new huntsman, Beorhtric of Nottingham. Only now did Godiva realize that he had been tacked on to the end of the line. He came trotting forward and pulled up alongside the head of the column, where he bowed his head in greeting to Lovric.

'Do you know the ballad of the Mill at Stoneleigh?' asked Lovric. Bret nodded. 'Then let us sing it together. I shall be the man and you shall be the girl, since you can do the high notes.'

Godiva glanced across at Bret curiously and he nodded back diffidently. She thought how dull he was, despite his good looks and his ability to sing, and how he probably had no conversation other than forests and hunting. But then, as his husky voice soared effortlessly up the scale, from a distance no further than the cream-throated song thrush that sat on the small apple tree beside her open window at night, a violent thrill passed through her heart, making her blush deeply and turn away. Lovric saw none of this, but Bret did, and afterwards, when Lovric sent him back to his place at the rear of the column, he vowed he would stay there and call no more attention to himself on this journey, for the likes and dislikes of powerful people are fickle, and he was not a man who could afford a fall from grace.

Two days later the little group from Mercia prayed silently for protection from all foreigners as the church towers of busy, clerical, long-robed Oxford came into view. They were now leaving their homeland and crossing into King Alfred's old kingdom of Wessex, where the frontier line had been drawn against the Danish invaders, drawn and held by means of *burghs* like this walled town. Today this was still Wessex territory, and that night they would lodge with one of Earl Godwin's thegns, a man named Wiglaf, undistinguished, but rich and loyal to the overlord of Wessex.

As her horse ambled carefully through the congested streets, Godiva thought how big Oxford seemed and how full of monks and priests, and of nuns and laundresses, kitchen maids and the other women of vague occupation who always seemed present in abundance wherever there were many monks gathered together. But there were few children, she noticed. To her mind this gave Oxford an air of purpose and order such as one never found in ordinary towns like Coventry, where small voices and hands wrought constant havoc. Everywhere she looked she saw churches, many small and old and built in a familiar squat Anglo-Saxon style, but some much grander and hinting of links with Normandy and beyond. They crossed over an arched stone bridge that amazed Godiva with its solidity and graceful lines – for

Coventry was still getting by with pontoons and flat bridges – and then, entering another quarter of the city, encountered yet more and even greater churches. There would be relics here in abundance, she thought, and wondered whether she could visit a shrine. Immediately, though, thoughts of Alfgar and Harry put paid to that idea: speed was the essence of this journey.

It didn't take long to reach Wiglaf's home, an old-fashioned manor house with a detached feasting hall standing to the rear. As soon as they dismounted, Wiglaf's house-steward appeared to show them through the yard to the manor-house door, where a moment later the lord of the manor appeared, arrayed despite the early hour in rich, heavy clothes designed to impress his guests. Lovric, a soldier to his marrow, glanced disapprovingly at Wiglaf's silver embroidery, but then pulled himself together and played the diplomat. Wiglaf bowed to Godiva, uttered a rudimentary greeting and then with no explanation took Lovric by the arm and led him away. Godiva stared after them for a moment, thinking how Wiglaf's shiny threads showed up his oafish manners. Then she shrugged and turned to enter his home.

As she stepped into the manor house the scents of seasoned oak, beer and fresh bread greeted her, and in the background, teasing the appetite, the smell of slowly roasting meat. Despite the master, the house was delightful – dark and polished, well swept and padded out with thick cushions and colourful hangings, a sanctuary of comfort for aching bones in the cold of winter and cool shade on dusty, fly-ridden summer days. And as for luxury, this house had carpets – small, it was true, but carpets nonetheless. Godiva, who had rarely seen anything but straw and hides on floors, stepped tentatively on to the first, a dark-red oblong whose intricate pattern glowed with a sheen that one never saw on wool, no matter what was done to it. She leaped back, realising that she was stepping on foreign silk, and just then she heard a delicate step behind her. Godiva readied herself for a cold welcome from a jealous hostess, and turned around. But Wiglaf's wife was also beautiful, and much younger than Godiva. What money buys, she thought, remembering the bandy legs and shapeless face of the lord of the manor.

Adelheid, who wanted to be called Adel, exuded kindness and consideration. She took Godiva's hand and did not let it go until they had toured every room. Agatha was told how to look after her mistress in this unfamiliar house, and Father Godric was sent to a priest's room so that he could pray for everyone and stay out of the way. Adel sent the servants off to the kitchen and brought Godiva to a small dining room used only by the family when they wanted to be alone together. They talked, as women always did on occasions such as this, about their children and their ancestors, about the price of wool, meat and horses, and about their latest purchases of lands and livestock. Only after they had learned a lot about each other and started to feel a warmth that reached beyond courtesy, did Adel raise the matter of husbands.

'I have been lucky,' she confided. 'I married as my father ordered me, and I didn't love Wiglaf until after our first child was born. But when I saw the child in his arms, and how he swore so fiercely to protect him and me from all danger – then I fell in love with him.'

Godiva was no longer used to the way young women confided in each other about men, but felt she had to respond. 'I was lucky too,' she said. 'I fell in love with Lovric at first sight, and he turned out to be as good as he looks.'

'And is he strong?'

'What do you mean?'

'I mean,' Adel said hesitantly, 'in times of trouble, does he grow angry with you? Or deceive you?'

'No,' Godiva replied firmly, unwilling to go into details with Adel about Lovric's occasional bouts of bad temper.

'That is what I worry about,' Adel continued, lowering her

voice in case a servant might hear. 'I fear my husband will grow cold again if bad times come back to England. I could go without food, or firewood, or servants, but I could not go back again to being without love.'

Godiva took Adel's hand, the way she would have liked to do with her daughter, if only Milly did not always repel her gestures of concern. 'There won't be bad times. You shouldn't worry. Too many powerful lords want peace.'

'I know. But I also know that Wiglaf is worried, and he won't tell me why. The hall is full of strange men who have come down from the north – but I only know that because my maid heard Danish and northern accents. All of a sudden Wiglaf won't talk to me, and if I ask him anything he gets angry.'

There was a pause in the conversation as neither knew what to say next. Godiva's words of reassurance now seemed hollow, and Adel thought she had given too much away. Now she changed the subject.

'There will be a great feast tonight in the hall. You must come! You will, won't you, dear Godiva?'

Dismayed, Godiva explained that all her good feasting clothes had been sent on ahead to Winchester.

'But you can borrow anything you want from me,' Adel persisted. 'A *godweb* cowl, for instance, to brighten up a plain dress. And your maid can put extra braids around your ears where they will show under your headdress. Oh, you will look beautiful tonight, and rich and glorious!'

'We shall see,' Godiva said, suddenly irritated by Adel's nervous, vapid conversation. 'I may need to rest tonight, Adel. The journey was long and there is much more ahead. I'm not quite the rider I was. I'll send Agatha to let you know later.'

Adel nodded, smiled and then, as Godiva left, she seemed to dab one eye to blot un unspilled tear.

*

In the event, there was no question of Godiva keeping up appearances that night. As she sat with Agatha in the guest chamber before a large mirror, Lovric came in, breathless and bringing news. The sight of him, appearing like a ghost in the mirror, alarmed Agatha, who left without being told.

Godiva rose to greet him. 'Lovric, whatever...?'

'Sit. Eva, I have news. Earl Siward is here in Oxford.'

'Something is wrong, isn't it?'

'Something is changing. We are not going directly to Winchester as I planned. Earl Godwin has asked for a secret meeting with me. We are to go south from here into the heart of Wessex, to meet Godwin in secret.'

'But, Lovric, we can't afford this delay. The boys...'

'This must take precedence. This meeting will affect my standing in England. It will either strengthen or weaken my hand in dealing with Edward.'

'What do you mean?'

'Siward came all the way from Northumbria to Oxford to arrange this meeting. No one else knows about it. Father Godric and Agatha will come with us, of course, but they must not be told where we are going. If Edward knew he would suspect that Siward, Godwin and I are conspiring to overthrow him.'

For a moment Godiva said nothing as she tried to digest this latest twist in the kingdom's fortunes. Upheavals were taking place in the king's circle, so much was clear. Lovric was losing favour, judging by the recent threats to his sons. Yet his old rival, Godwin, also seemed to be breaking ranks and falling out with the king, just when his position was growing ever stronger. It made no sense to her, but Lovric was not going to enlighten her. For safety's sake, he would tell her only what he absolutely had to.

'Where do we meet Godwin?'

'Near Uffington, in the Berkshire Downs, where King Alfred's old castle stands.'

'In the Vale of the White Horse?'

'Yes.'

'Then,' she said decidedly, 'we had better pay our respects to the Goddess while we're there. I will invoke her help for the boys. After all, she gave me Harry.'

Lovric, who had little patience with overcredulity, surprised Godiva by making no objection. 'We need better luck,' he said, 'than we've been getting from the prayers of those monks of yours at St Mary's.'

Godiva ignored the barb and continued. 'You should walk along the White Horse's back with me too. That makes the magic stronger.'

Lovric nodded, though with a shadow of embarrassment beginning to darken his face. Religion of any sort, he thought, was best left to women and perfumed men in skirts.

'Now,' he said, slapping his knees to announce a complete change of mood. 'I have something else to tell you, something that will cheer you up.'

'Is it news of the boys?'

'Not quite what you want to hear, but enough to make you very happy.'

'Is it Harry? Oh, my God, did Siward bring Harry here with him?'

'Yes.'

'Mother of God! I thought he'd already sailed to Southampton for Winchester. When can I see him?'

'Now,' Lovric said. 'As soon as you are ready.'

It was growing dark. Agatha lit several candles and arranged Godiva's hair and veil so that her son would not be dismayed at how much older she looked than on the day he saw her last, nearly nine years ago. Agatha then left the room and Godiva paced the floor, her heart racing. Despite the avalanche of plans under which she had buried her fears, she remained angry and anxious at the fate that had befallen her son while he was far away from her. She crossed herself and called on Mary, recalling again the time when he left home to be fostered at the court of Siward in Northumbria, and the terrible grief that had gripped her then. Harry was her first-born son, one who had taken a long time to conceive, and the only living child of her union with Lovric. As they parted she had kissed his cheek and he had squared his shoulders like the warrior he would have to become, and she had remembered then, as if it were just yesterday, the neck of her son when he was an infant, tucked into his chest like a chick in its shell, so frail and delicate it was impossible to think a man would grow from this. She had wept for so long that Lovric promised on oath that he would have Harry back home with her before he was eighteen. That would have been this Christmas. It might still be, God willing.

The door creaked open and someone gave a small soft knock. How like him, she thought. He still enters first and knocks afterwards. Then, unable to hold back, she ran to the door and pulled him into the room and into her arms. Lovric had let him come alone and she would have him all to herself for a while.

'My son, my son,' she repeated, and it was to be a long time before she could hear him say, 'Mother, I'm all right. Don't cry, mother.'

And it was much, much longer – not until after he had told her where he'd travelled, which thegns he knew, how good his skills with arms were, the greatest adventure he'd had (which was when he saw the Pictish warrior princess, Gruoch, the wife of Macbeth, in armour and off to battle) and how kind his foster-mother was (at which Godiva choked as relief and resentment collided) – only when they were finished with all this recounting of years spent apart, only then could Godiva bring herself to talk about their bitter circumstances.

'But you are not coming back home with me, my darling. You are to go to Winchester and remain there.'

'As Edward's hostage? Yes, I know that, mother.'

He spoke these words with that cool indifference that young men of his rank were taught to produce under the worst of circumstances. But he said it with a northern – indeed a Danish – accent, and this sounded so rustic and uncouth to her ears that she gave a little laugh.

'What's wrong with that, mother?' he asked, more earnestly now. 'Siward says I won't be held for more than three months. Less than that, if father gets Alfgar off the hook again. Siward has even made a bet with me. If I'm still with Edward in six months' time, then I'm to get Siward's youngest daughter to wife.'

'Wife? I forbid it! You're far too young.'

'I'm not! But I won't win the bet,' he said cheerfully. 'And anyway, I don't want a wife. I will be home with you by Christmas, you'll see.'

There was a loud knock on the door and Lovric entered.

'Harry will dine in the hall tonight,' Lovric announced, beaming proudly. 'I will have the pleasure of showing off this fine young man of mine to my thegns, who have not seen him since he was a child.'

'Good, I'm sure,' Godiva said coldly.

'And won't you come to the feast, too? Other noblewomen will be there.'

'I don't know them, and I am not fit for company tonight,' she said, and then, before she could bite her tongue, she rushed on, 'and nobody but a fool would expect his wife to smile and dine and be merry at a feast when her son is to be made a hostage.'

Harry looked in alarm at his father, who signalled for the boy to leave.

'I must go to this feast,' Lovric said when he was out of

earshot, 'in order to show Edward's spies that I do not feel afraid, and therefore that I firmly believe in Alfgar's innocence. I thought you'd understand that.'

'I do,' she answered. 'Lovric – I'm sorry I called you a fool before Harry.'

She's losing her nerve, he thought. Seeing Harry had undone her composure. It was like this sometimes on the battlefield – a soldier, full of resolve, would suddenly see the face of a long-lost friend, and would fall into a tailspin as all that had ever been lost took its place alongside all that might soon be lost, in one dark embrace of despair.

'Eva,' he said, softening. 'You don't have to play the part that I must. You can grieve for Harry. You have the right. Even if the king is only playing a game with us, and even if Harry will be home soon, it is still hard to see your boy being made a hostage.'

'Yes,' she said, taking his hand. 'But I too must try to keep up appearances. This feast is important for Wiglaf and Adel.'

'Wiglaf is not important, just rich. Dine well in your room now with Agatha, and go to sleep early. You'll need to be rested for this journey through Wessex that starts tomorrow.'

A little later Agatha returned and set down a silver inlaid tray on the table. She looked down at Godiva, who had fallen asleep, half-dressed for the feast, and lamented silently for her troubled mistress. Then, as instructed by her mother, she found Godiva's rosary of precious stones, wrapped it round her hand and started to recite the English paternoster quietly. But she had only arrived at 'thy kingdom come' when Godiva sat up briskly and started praying too. When they reached the end of the prayer, Godiva repeated loudly, 'Let thy kingdom come upon our Earth, and not that bastard Edward's. Amen.'

Agatha gasped in astonishment and then, before she could shut her mouth as her mother had warned her to, she blurted out her own thoughts on Edward. 'True word, my lady! He be a right bastard. All Saxon folk know that. You ain't got nothing to fear from long, tall Neddy. Ain't nothing in his trousers, they say. Forty years old, married, and still a virgin! And boasting of it, too! It ain't right, and he ain't no man. So how can he win against a real man like the earl? Ain't going to happen. Our Harry be home by Christmas or Candlemas, you'll see. Mark my words.'

'Perhaps you are right, child,' said Godiva, happy to give the conversation over to someone so young and blithe that in comparison ladyship seemed a dismal, useless thing. What common Saxon mother would let her son be taken hostage? Not one. They would fall on their knives first. But she, Godiva, second to no woman in the land but Queen Edith and old Queen Emma, could not do that. She had to fall in with her husband's plans and keep a straight face when she met the creature they called king. But not tonight.

'Tell me again, Agatha,' she laughed, pouring the maid a full glass of rich red wine, 'tell me what folk say about long, tall Neddy. And Queen Edith.'

Agatha took a huge gulp of the unfamiliar beverage, downing it as she would a mug of beer at home, and continued with the delicious destruction of the king's dignity. 'They call him Unwed Ned and her Needy Eady. Why, you can guess. What with all that chastity, virginity and other things folk don't understand the why of…'

'But it's said he's so holy that one touch of his hand heals the sick,' Godiva mocked.

'One sickness heals another, they reckon. That hand of his been up to no good, all on its own.'

The evening wore on tipsily, until it was not only dark, but silent outside. Agatha snuffed out most of the candles and went off to her own sleeping space outside the chamber door. Grand folk, she thought as she buried herself in a rough black blanket, them ain't no better than we be. Laugh just like us, and tears as wet. Some day, though, we'll be rid of them all, mark my words. Common folk can see what's coming. Normans be coming, that's what. Well, good riddance to all these rich earls and thegns we got now. Though not to my own good, kind lady here, not to mistress Good-Eva, may Mary and Freya bless her and keep her, and me and my mother too, amen.

Three

Several hours later Godiva woke up to a headache and an empty bed. Lovric must have slept in Wiglaf's hall last night with Siward, Harry and the northern thegns, huddling together round the great fire to strengthen the vows of friendship that bound together these men who met infrequently and not always in accord.

Despite the early hour, sounds of human activity could be heard outside. From a nearby monastery there drifted the first prayers of Lauds, defying sleep, darkness and the rhythms of the earth. And then, from much nearer at hand and growing louder, there came the muffled sound of horses being walked slowly over straw-strewn cobbles and men talking quietly to each other.

She got up, shivering in the night air, and went to the window. Below, in the yard, soldiers were assembling rapidly by torchlight. They were pouring in from the hall, from the house-carls' quarters and from the stables. Some were beginning to mount their horses. Anxiously she scanned the flame-lit faces in the crowd, searching for Lovric. Instead her eyes alighted on a man of similar build and age and wearing a red cloak just like Lovric's, but with no black eagle on it. It had a bold design in white, black and gold across the back, showing a bear rampant

above two war axes that lay across each other, and both axes
Viking. This was none other than the Dane, Siward, Earl of
Northumbria and arch-enemy of the deadly Scot, Macbeth;
Siward, the third partner in the fractious, unpredictable triumvi-
rate of earls that now held England together; Siward, kind foster-
father of her beloved Harry.

Godiva had never met the Earl of the North. Now she longed
to run down and thank him, and beg him to urge Edward to
abandon his demands for a hostage. But even as the thought
entered her mind it petered out. For there, riding up to Siward
on a gleaming, sloe-black stallion, was Harry. He was dressed all
in black as though to match his horse, and his fair hair fell down
his back in the Norse fashion. A young page, a boy of about
Harry's age and dressed like him, took hold of the reins of his
horse. The page turned and spoke to Harry, who looked down
and smiled at him with such warmth that she knew at once he
was a foster-brother, one of Siward's sons. It gladdened her that
Harry had grown up with love in Siward's court, and yet that open
smile of his frightened her. He looked like a boy at the start of a
wonderful adventure and not one whose life, liberty and dignity
were at risk. She longed to talk with him again, this time to warn
him realistically of the dangers he faced. She opened the casement a crack and thought of shouting down to him. He was
beautiful as only the young are at that exact moment when
childhood, its work done, finally departs, and her heart ached
with love. But she stood transfixed, with the cold of the floor
rising into her feet and confusion paralysing her will.

'Eva!'

She spun around. 'Lovric?'

'They are going now. Going to Winchester.'

'Already?' She turned back to the window.

'Yes. Don't embarrass Harry.'

'I wasn't going to.'

'Liar,' he said, but he said it fondly and pulled her back under the bedclothes and started rubbing her cold feet.

'You'll see him again in Winchester,' he went on. 'Don't worry. I'm sending my thegns and my housecarls ahead of us with Siward. They'll ride into the city together under my banner, after Siward and the northern thegns. Edward will see them – or his spies will – and will see that all the country stands behind Harry and his safety.'

'Lovric?'

She put her hands up to him, cradling his face, and looked into his eyes. Shadowed under his brows by the candlelight, they gave only a hint of his mood, but enough for her to know he was calm and resolved.

'I trust you.'

'You're trying to, I know that.'

They smiled at each other for the first time since early yesterday, and Lovric, knowing he had an hour at least before he should go down to the yard and give everyone orders, decided to see what they might make of this interval alone together.

A little later they made their way down to the family dining room where Godiva and Adel had talked yesterday. Despite her worries, Lovric had cheered her up with his undiminished appetite for love, a love that seemed able to resist whatever misery the previous day had brought or the next one might hold. A servant brought in a wooden bowl of oatmeal porridge. In the background she could smell frying bacon, black pudding and baking bread. It was what they usually ate at Cheylesmore in the mornings, and no doubt the same breakfast was being prepared in every prosperous kitchen in all parts of Britain at this very time of day. She almost felt at home in Adel's house, and looked round, hoping to see the lady of the manor come in. Lovric, who had eaten before dawn in the hall, went off to see how the preparations for departure were going in the yard. As he stepped out he almost knocked over Adel, and for the first time Godiva realized how slight and fragile she was.

'Is your food good?' Adel asked anxiously. 'If not, I can get you something else. Griddle cakes. Buttermilk. Or an omelette? And more meat and cheese of course.'

She fluttered on, waving her hands around distractedly. The excitable young woman of yesterday had vanished: in her place was a bewildered girl whose headdress lay wrapped untidily across most of her face.

'My food is good,' Godiva murmured, 'but what has happened to you?'

'Nothing. I cannot say,' Adel muttered, looking round to see where the servants were.

Godiva got to her feet and took Adel by her thin shoulders. She pulled back the side of her headdress and inspected the bruise.

'Why?'

Adel hung her head and said nothing.

'My first husband would hit me too,' Godiva said, putting her arm round her. 'He was my daughter Milly's father and I thought I would never escape him.'

Adel remained silent.

'What happened last night?'

Adel swallowed several times and then started to whisper. 'When you did not appear at the feast, Wiglaf was angry. He wants to impress his lord, Earl Godwin, so it was important to manage Lovric's visit well. I told him I thought something had happened between you and Lovric, but he would have none of that. No, I was a bad hostess and somehow I put you off coming. When the feast was over he came to our chamber. He was drunk and we quarrelled. Then he hit me. I have not seen him since.'

'Oh, my dear!' Godiva said, taking Adel by the arm. 'But you know, there was fear in the air last night. Lovric and I argued too, and he slept in the hall. Still, men cannot hit women, however much they might argue.'

Adel looked down again and didn't answer.

'You could divorce if he won't control himself,' Godiva said. 'Threaten him. You have your rights, and your own property. Say you'll take back your dowry.'

'I know about my rights,' Adel answered, wiping her eyes. 'But my father would not take my side. Well, you can see how rich Wiglaf is, and Father has taken loans from him. Big loans.' She sighed heavily. 'And there are other reasons, too.' Godiva glanced down at Adel's small round belly and guessed what these might be. Adel smiled effacingly and backed away into her kitchen. Godiva stared after her and thanked Mary that mortality and luck had relieved her of a man very much like Wiglaf. Lovric, no matter what his faults, was a man she would love forever.

Shortly afterwards the small riding party that was due to go south to meet Earl Godwin assembled by the door of the manor house. Lovric now appeared, not on his own massive war stallion, but on a smaller mare belonging to Wiglaf. He had also taken off his cloak with its identifying black eagle and was wearing ordinary thegn's clothing. He was almost unrecognizable. Godiva too was in her ordinary riding jacket, which Agatha had pulled out of the travelling luggage. She smiled at Agatha, who smiled back with the studied dignity of one struggling with a hangover, she was relieved to see her mistress both sober and good-tempered, for she had got up this morning worrying that she would be blamed for last night's drinking, especially if the earl found out about it.

Father Godric was in the saddle too, fingering his rosary repentantly. Godiva looked him over carefully. The priest was unusually indifferent to wine, but his delight in the company of bawds was well known. He had gone to his little priest-room early last night and had not been seen for hours. But the look of contrition on his face suggested that he had gained little pleasure compared to the amount of sin he had committed. Good, thought Godiva, who pitied his wife. May his none-too-private parts suffer whore's itch all day.

Once they were in proper order for departure, a group of lightly armed horsemen, led by an unusually taciturn captain, surrounded them. Indeed, it was soon apparent that all the members of the Wessex guard were as surly and uncommunicative as their captain, as though the old wars between their country and the men of Mercia were far from forgotten. It was, then, a wary and silent riding party that left Wiglaf's hall, heading south-west towards the Vale of the White Horse and a meeting with the Lord of the South, Godwin of Wessex.

Two days later the Berkshire Downs rose out of the woodlands like the velvet breasts of the living earth. A marked change of mood now settled on all the riders: a softening of temper, more patience with the tiring horses and a greater interest in each other. For the first time Godwin's captain of the guard spoke to his charges in friendly tones, telling them to slow down.

'She's coming into view soon,' he said. 'Dismount and follow me and you'll see her properly. It's not a sight to miss, sir, lady.'

Godiva, who had seen the White Horse at Uffington long ago, and seen other White Horses too, carved on the hills in several parts of Mercia, had yet to see the fabled image at the necessary distance. Expectantly she followed the captain and Lovric up a narrow path that led from the lane to a stile and on round a bramble-strewn bend. Then, suddenly, there it was – its clear white-chalk outline spread out over the hill and facing them directly across a fold in the land, the forelegs prancing, the long tail flowing behind, and the head, mysteriously beaked, pointing the way forward. And right in the middle of the horse's face, staring up at the sky, was that large, round and magical eye, the eye that everyone came to see. Complete silence took hold of the group, except that Father Godric was mumbling a prayer as quietly as he could, asking God's forgiveness for coming to this pagan place.

'It's a good time for walking her back, sir,' said the captain, taking in the signs of the weather and noting the dryness of the soil beneath their feet. 'But my instructions are to take you straight to the house, sir.'

Agatha noticed how the man had mentioned no names on this whole journey, and she signed the cross on her bosom. As far as she was concerned, they were alone in Wessex, a foreign country to a Mercian girl, and they were alone with armed strangers. God only knew what Lord Lovric was up to. Godric saw her bite her lip and he said another prayer, this one a bland benediction for travellers that he could say out loud without offending the presiding pagan spirits. And then the group stumbled back down the path to their horses and were on their way to the meeting place.

A few minutes later the captain pointed ahead as their destination came into view. It was an unlikely house for an earl and his lady to visit, no more than two rooms built of wattle and daub, with one thatched roof over both of them. Scattered around were some other structures – a couple of small huts, an open-air pen for the temporary quartering of horses and what appeared to be several graves. The whole scene had an air of abandonment about it. But there was one mark of distinction, the only sign that, despite the coming and going of tribes and legions, old gods and new priests, here was still a place of great importance. This was the network of tracks and paths that sat like a cobweb on the hillside and converged here. It was where people came first, before they walked the Horse.

An elderly, long-bearded man came out to greet them and

show Lovric and Godiva into the house. Inside it was dark, despite the strength of the late-afternoon sun, and the man called for candles. A woman of similar age, her toothless face sunken and shadowed, appeared from the other room carrying small oil lamps. Godiva started in surprise at the sight of these, for the lamps were made of solid gold and set around with rubies that lit up with fire like the flames rising from the scented wicks. The poverty of this place was only partial; it was meant to mislead.

'Great lord,' the old man began. 'Greetings. Earl Godwin is here already. Are you prepared, sir? If so, send the maid and the priest outside.'

After Godric and Agatha had gone, the door to the other little room opened again, and in strode Godwin of Wessex, the man most of England thought should be king. He stood there before them, not quite as tall as Lovric, and nowhere near as handsome, thought Godiva, noting his beaky nose and low brow, but strong as an ox, heavy as a plough, and full of the force that everyone saw as royal, though there was scarcely a drop of king's blood in his veins. He put out his hand at once, and Lovric shook it. Then, with surprising grace, he took Godiva's hand, kissed it lightly and motioned them to be seated.

All round the room ran benches built into the walls. They were strewn with cushions whose worn tapestry covers told of many other secret meetings held here over the years.

'Welcome to the oldest shrine in the land of Wessex,' said Godwin, in such a pronounced south-Saxon accent that Godiva had to struggle to pick out his words. 'I make no apology that it is a pagan centre, and that the old man and woman in there are priests of the Horse's cult. My bishops know about this place, but turn a blind eye to its existence. This means that I can come here with no clerical spies to hinder me in my business.'

'And what is our business?' Lovric asked.

Godwin passed Godiva a glass of wine and another to Lovric.

'It is the business of our children, sir,' Godwin answered in a level voice. 'And the business of our king, and thus our country. And of your son, Alfgar, and my son, Sveign; my daughter Edith, and now your Harry, and soon after that, any one of our other children. They are all young; the boys are looking for lands, looking to lead armies, to have noblewomen to wife and to start raising children. They are all prepared to defy the king, and to obey their fathers only when it suits them.' He paused and looked at Lovric and Godiva intently.

'I know that,' Lovric said.

'But what you perhaps do not know,' said Godwin, a touch of sympathy entering his voice, 'is news that came down to me from Hereford while you were still on your way to Oxford. Alfgar has been captured...'

'Holy Mary,' Godiva whispered. 'Is he hurt?'

'I'm sorry, lady, I know nothing more. But it is certain that he will soon be in the hands of the king, like your Harry.'

'I thank you,' Lovric said, motionless but for the clenching and unclenching of his fists. 'This changes the situation I will face in Winchester. It will be harder now to bargain with Edward.'

Godwin nodded and then paused again, as though gathering his energies before resuming.

'This is not all,' he said at last, 'I have bad news of my own, but not the sort that can be talked about where men drink in thegns' halls or where laws are bound at meetings of the Witan. It concerns Edith.' He paused and looked at Godiva's averted face. 'Godiva?'

'Yes?' she turned to face him, and Godwin, seeing her clearly and at close quarters for the first time, was taken aback. He had glimpsed her at a distance over the years, veiled like the other ladies of Edward's court, and riding or walking beside Lovric on great royal occasions, and thus he knew of her beauty chiefly by report, for everyone said that the Earl of Mercia had the best woman in England and loved her beyond all reason. By now, he thought, age seemed to have confirmed this legendary beauty, suggesting there was permanence and an inexplicable depth to her grace.

'Tell me,' he said, as carefully as he could, 'would you say, as a married woman, that you could have taken Edward to be your husband? Or would you have wished your daughter to be his wife?'

'No.'

'Godiva...' Lovric began.

'I must speak the truth, Lovric. I wouldn't wish that man on any woman. When he came to Coventry, to the dedication of my priory, he said nothing to me for two whole days, but he kept his eyes on me the whole time, and they were wet and cold. It was a look I can't describe well – contempt, some revulsion, but also a kind of amusement. It's hard to pin down what it meant. I took it that he was sneering at me, but then I saw that he looked at everyone that way, though not at Lovric and one or two men he fears. With them he stared at the ground and looked pious.' She took a deep breath and thought for a moment. 'Earl Godwin,' she continued soberly, 'women say Edward is unmanly. My maid tells me the common women laugh and make up stories about him all through the land.'

'Thank you,' said Godwin. 'You say what my own wife says. Every night Gytha weeps and says that we have wronged Edith, that she was plucked as a young girl from the convent at Wilton and delivered to the bed of a man unfit for any woman – but a certain kind of whore.'

Lovric shot Godwin an unguarded look of concern. He knows, thought Godwin, looking back at him. It shows in Lovric's eyes, in the absence of shock or curiosity. He knows about Edward's strange ways, and he has said nothing to his wife or anyone else in order to protect Edward's position. And perhaps to muffle the cries of his own conscience, as he takes his wife to meet the king. Takes her as I sent Edith, knowingly putting her at risk. Godwin scrutinized Lovric: there were no signs of guilt in his eyes, none of the evasiveness, the self-pity, the confusion that marks the faces of guilty men. But nothing had happened yet. Edward had not touched Godiva. Yet he was sure to try, of that Godwin was sure. He turned his gaze towards her. She was composed again, and she was lively, not like a woman enduring suppressed fear or resentment. He felt sure she knew nothing about the king's orders. No, she was going to Winchester like a good mother, anxious to do what she could for her captured sons and, like a good wife, trustingly cooperating with her husband's request that she accompany him.

Lovric in turn examined Godwin. The man looked like someone who had struggled to come to a difficult decision, and was still struggling, trying to find the right words to phrase what he had to say next. He would make his announcement soon, declaring the reason for this meeting.

'Where does this leave us?' Lovric asked.

'Edith, my daughter,' Godwin began, and stopped in dismay at what he had to relate. Then he started again, but from a different angle. 'Lovric, for many years I have opposed you and Siward. I cannot pretend that this was for any reason other than that I wanted to be king myself, or at least to be the grandfather of the next king and control the man who now sits on the throne. I have failed in both my aims.'

'Both?'

'Yes. I cannot be king. None of us can. Not one of us is strong enough alone to topple him. Nor will I be grandfather to Edith's children with Edward. There will be no such children, ever. I want to make a pact with you, as I have already done with Siward, to support this monarchy until Edward meets his natural end. Division will only weaken us, and the kingdom of England will pass to the Normans or to the Danes. We must work towards a smooth succession after Edward's death.'

Lovric stared at Godwin. For all his farmer's forthrightness and good cheer, the man was full of guile. If henceforth he had to trust him, he would need to know more about the reasons for his willingness to cooperate fully with Siward and himself. He would have to probe.

'My good lord,' he began in his smoothest diplomatic manner. 'It is not clear to me why Edith should not bear an heir to Edward. She is young, and the marriage is not yet three years old. One knows of many marriages that remained unfruitful for years, and yet eventually yielded several children.'

Godwin said nothing and seemed unwilling to take the conversation further.

Godiva put her hand on his, startling him with a gentle touch of sympathy. 'It is hard to be a parent of grown children and watch them suffer life's hardships.'

Her words seemed to dissolve whatever pride or sorrow had been stopping the Earl of Wessex from getting to the heart of the matter. 'As you must know,' he said, still holding her hand and letting his speech stream out in a torrent, 'for the whole country knows this – Edith's marriage is not consummated. I thought this would be a passing matter. But now Edith tells her mother that Edward will never consummate the marriage. Never. Not that he can't, but that he refuses to. The bastard will not bed my daughter.'

Lovric frowned down at his hands. 'I too had hoped the king's marriage would eventually be consummated, and I too have started to think otherwise.'

'But surely,' Godiva intervened, 'if Edward once took religious vows of celibacy, as some say, he is released from them, by the very act of marriage.'

'He never took vows.' Godwin spat into the corner of the

room. 'He would not bind himself to anything in this world. He wears the black Benedictine robe merely because he likes it. It is an affectation. He's worn it ever since he arrived in Normandy, after his father died and his mother sent him away.'

'Others say he is spiting his mother,' Godiva continued. 'Queen Emma will be angry to have no royal grandchildren. Perhaps he will change...'

'Perhaps.'

'It must have driven him mad when she married King Canute, and then produced heirs that we all preferred to Edward. To be betrayed, disinherited, by your own mother! But if he could forgive her, he might change and decide to have children.'

Godwin seemed not to be listening, but brooding on something.

'What does your wife think?' Godiva went on, trying to draw him back into the discussion.

'Oh, Gytha believes that is true,' he said wearily. 'She says that Edward's story is like the tale the Danish *scopmen* tell about a prince of Denmark whose mother did something similar. A certain Hamlet. It left him so twisted in his mind that he could never decide anything or love any woman...'

'And yet,' Lovric interrupted, 'I know that Edward can be decisive sometimes, and astute too.'

'Intelligent, or learned?' Godiva asked.

'Both. He reads every day, and plays games that I haven't even heard of. I used to play chess with him when I visited court, but no longer. It is embarrassing how quickly he checkmates me. As to his celibacy, I think it is a reasoned decision. I think it may be his way of avoiding assassination. As long as he remains married, we will keep hoping for heirs from him. Then, if we got one...'

'No,' Godwin said, leaning forward onto his hands and looking up from under his haggard brows. He seemed to have come to a decision. 'Forgive me now, Godiva, for my coarse words. Lovric, I have to say this. The problem with our king is not about politics. It is about fucking. It is about men and women, birth and families. He hates it all.'

He stood up suddenly and started circling the small room.

'Go on, sir,' Lovric said. 'No one will ever learn from us what you have to say.'

Godwin continued to pace the room, clasping and unclasping his hands. Like racing clouds, conflicting emotions showed on his face, one chasing the other, nothing lasting. Rage predominated, but disgust followed quickly, then pity and sorrow as he thought, perhaps, of his daughter. Afterwards came pride, making its case for silence, then fear and confusion as the need for comradeship and understanding from an equal came to the fore. In the end, with a gasp that almost resulted in tears, it was the last that prevailed. Godwin had to tell another man what was on his mind.

'Very well,' he said quietly. 'Let it be known. Edith says that about three months after her marriage, the old queen mother came to see her, and brought with her two fine Norman whores, dressed as nuns. You see, Emma hoped the problem – the non-consummation of the marriage – was due to Edith's inexperience. But when Edith told the whores what Edward had been doing, they shook their heads and went and told Emma she should not hope for grandchildren from this marriage. Men don't change after thirty, they both agreed, not in this respect, and so there was nothing they could do. Now Edith was young, pretty enough and not half as innocent as everyone assumed. Gytha had made sure of that...'

Lovric's eyes met Godiva's. They had both heard the rumours that Gytha was growing rich by finding the prettiest girls amongst the captives brought to the Wessex ports and selling them on at a huge profit, after a bit of polishing up, to the Danish emporia controlled by her kin. Of course Gytha would know what to tell Edith about bed-work with a man. But Godwin, unaware of the revulsion that had overtaken his guests, ploughed on.

'...So our Edith was quite ready, for her part, to conceive heirs to the throne. But Edward was not. No, that man had other practices he much preferred to lying with a young woman, and Edith didn't know what they meant. But the whores did, and apparently so did old Emma, for she went into one of her rages against Edward in which all that could be heard were the words "*scopman*", in the sense of story-maker and joker, and "watchman," and then "*scopophiliac*" – one who enjoys his own eyes more than his male parts – a word some learned man must have taught her, long ago, when she may once have tried to understand her son. I still don't understand what this means myself. All I know is that Edith says he makes her dress up like a baby...'

'Swaddling bands?' Godiva asked.

'Yes. Bunting. Then he calls her "baby" and "daughter" and she must cry and suck her thumb and call him "daddy". And...' Godwin put his head in his hands and continued in a whisper, '...there are worse things he does also, but I won't say what they are. She consents to all this because the Norman whores told her that it was possible, if she lay very still and closed her eyes, that the king would quickly do the deed and she might conceive. But now,' said Godwin, shaking his head in bitter disbelief, 'after going through so much unnatural torment, Edith says that Edward refuses to beget an heir. She does what the whores suggested and it is almost successful. But then Edward, our king, spills his royal seed. On purpose. And he tells her it is his pleasure to continue to do so, and she, as queen, must submit to his pleasure.'

Godiva looked up at Lovric and saw the embarrassment on his face.

'Good lord,' said Lovric, 'you did not have to tell me so much.'

This is shameful to your daughter, and to your noble house. And to you, my friend.'

But Godwin refused to be cheered by this promise of friendship from his oldest rival, and seemed to want to unburden himself further.

'He will devise some torture for you, too,' he said, looking at Godiva, 'something inventive and entertaining, something that will make you want to rise in rebellion. His pleasure, you see, is in putting you in his own position – of having to suffer people he can't endure, such as his mother, and us, the earls. He enjoys making you want to rebel, because he knows you won't do it – it is not in your interest – and so you must sit there at his command, itching and unable to scratch. That's what he wants to watch. That is why his mother calls him the jester, the *scopman*, and the watchman. He teases, like a cruel child tormenting the servants' children, and this can drive grown men to fury because he is the king and none of us are children. No one knows how to respond, or even what game he is playing.'

'Very well,' said Lovric cautiously, 'I will take heed, Godwin. I will be alert for provocation and try not to respond. There is no doubt that we must keep the country at peace until there is a better English heir in sight. Or else we will be ruled by foreign lords again.'

Godwin stood up now and shook Lovric's hand. Suddenly he looked younger, like a man who had put down a heavy burden.

'Come,' he said, 'we have talked enough. The light is still good. We have time to walk the White Horse's back together.'

'You too?' Godiva asked, surprised.

'I go there twice a year. I go on my own and place my coin at the centre of the eye. The old woman picks it up later. She keeps the donations of pilgrims in a chest,' he nodded at the other room, 'and whenever an impoverished woman is in labour she sends money for the midwife, or a wet nurse if the mother dies.'

'Many years ago I went there to try to conceive,' Godiva said. 'And afterwards I got Harry. I went back once after that to give thanks, as one must. This time, I will make a greater offering for his life, and his brother's.'

'I go there,' Godwin said, 'to look across at Alfred's Castle and tell myself that I must not give up his work. Strange, isn't it, that I, the grandson of a farmer, should be carrying on the great king's fight, while the man with full royal blood sits idly on his throne, playing despicable games? Matters have not gone as we expected. When Edith married Edward, I thought of hanging up my sword and going to live in peace in a monastery. I don't think of that any more. There is more danger now to Wessex, and all the regions and islands of Britain, as each year passes and Edward remains childless on the throne and his Norman friends circle like vultures, waiting for the death of Alfred's kingdom.'

It was a strange little procession that left the priests' house a few minutes later: two famous earls in ordinary clothing, a beautiful lady carrying a heavy bag of money, a pretty maid with her eyes agog and a priest who was frantically thumbing his rosary. As they neared the point of departure on the hillside where pilgrims stepped into the trench and the deep carved line of the horse's back began, Godiva raised her eyes and beheld, spread all around them, the hearth fires of dozens of Wessex farms, lighting up for the night, warming the mothers and fathers, children and servants who were coming together after their day's work, all thanking God for the peace that let them do so, and some thanking the Goddess for the new life that lay quietly suckling in a corner of the room. Oh, dear mother Mary, she prayed, let us have peace, no matter what this king of ours may do.

'I was thinking,' Lovric said, breaking the silence as they walked back later to the priests' house. 'Perhaps, if you would arrange an escort for her, Godwin, my wife should go back now to Coventry.'

'No,' Godiva exclaimed, 'I intend to see Alfgar and Harry. Nothing could change my mind.'

'It might be better, though...'

'No.' Godwin cut into their growing argument. 'Edith says that Edward is looking forward to meeting Godiva again, at court this time, as you plead for Alfgar's life. If you cheat him of his desires he'll take some revenge. He has both your boys in his hands, remember.'

He rubbed the sweat from his brow and Godiva, looking at him carefully, could see that he really was a man on the cusp of age, a man who would have been well placed in the walled herb garden of some luxurious monastery, not travelling the roads of the kingdom trying to keep at bay its slowly approaching doom. He took her hand and kissed it, and then in a whisper told her to be strong and wise in dealing with whatever the future held for her. They watched him go alone, down a bridle path that went due south towards his nearest manor house. In the distance they could see torches, moving towards him in a neat column. His bodyguard would meet him soon, probably at the ford over the small river in the valley below, and then the guard assigned to protect Lovric and Godiva would come and lead them on to wherever they would spend the night. It would have been the same had Godwin come to Lovric's Mercia – the same distrust, the same protection, the same formality. You could almost think this is a safe country in which we live, thought Godiva. Safe and so dignified. How hard, then, to understand why it should be quaking beneath our feet, not from the tramp of foreign armies, but as though the solid British rock and turf on which we stand is composed of quicksand, caverns and reeking, treacherous bogs, pitted with holes and inhabited by hidden enemies. She crossed herself again: it was time to ride once more.

Four

As the moon emerged from between thinning clouds, the Wessex captain led the horses down a gravel path towards the banks of a fast-flowing, powerful stream and the entrance to the upper decks of a wooden mill house. The horses, along with Agatha and Father Godric, were taken off at once to separate quarters in the nearby hamlet that housed the carpenters, masons and other attendants of the mill, while Godiva and Lovric were brought into the miller's house to rest for the night. The miller and his wife greeted them correctly, made no attempt at small talk and showed them at once to a large open room that contained a bed, a table laden with food and wine and everything a guest could want for the night.

'Wessex hospitality!' the miller said, allowing himself one pleasantry and pointing at the sacks of flour that lined the walls of the room. 'Earl Godwin likes to send me his special guests.'

Lovric could see why. The sound of the rushing water and the clattering of the turning wheel drowned out all other noise. The bags of flour would further hinder any eavesdroppers with their ears to the walls. Lovric and Godiva ate alone and in silence for a while, as each reviewed the events of the day.

'That was a strange meeting,' Godiva said at last, putting down her tankard of beer. 'Godwin could have won your friendship without shaming himself like that. I can't see what he gained from it.'

But I can, Lovric thought, continuing to gnaw at his ham bone. He saw into me at that meeting. He knows that Edward ordered me to bring Godiva to Winchester. That she herself now wants to come is irrelevant: I would have persuaded her anyway. Godwin has guessed that I've told her nothing about the king's orders. He and I are sharing a similar humiliation. Edward is playing with us endlessly, and we can't stop him, short of hurling his chess board in his face and starting a war that we can't afford. It is right that Godwin and I strengthen our alliance; we have this shame in common. And yet, I do not trust him. He has left his daughter to the king's mercies, and today he exposed her to my scorn, and Godiva's, too. Something is happening in the House of Godwin. Some secret crumbling.

'And why was he so sure the king expects me in Winchester?' Godiva went on, ignoring his silence. 'Is Edward guessing that I'll appear, or did you make him a promise, Lovric?'

'No,' he lied, longing to tell her the truth, but afraid she might start to despise him. It was better that she did not know. 'Let us talk about Edith,' he said, putting the bone down and wiping his hands. 'Some may pity her, but she is still the queen, and no matter what her father and brothers may think, there is every chance she will want to remain queen. She will continue to please and indulge Edward. She will see you as a rival, because of your beauty and because you have children. And he will see you as challenging him, because of your priory. Only the king may shine with holiness in this land, Godiva.'

'I had the same thought about Edith,' she replied. 'If she can't have children, she must be worrying about her future.'

'Indeed she is. It is said she is growing closer to two of her brothers – her many hungry brothers. She will be trying to get them lands...'

'Mine!' Godiva gasped.

'No, Eva. There are easier targets for Edith's schemes.'

'I'm not so sure, Lovric. You are away so much, and we have very few men-at-arms at Cheylesmore. We are not so far from the northern Wessex border, and if something were to happen, if some of the sons of Godwin came over...'

'They wouldn't dare,' he said, taking her hand again.

But Godiva, deep in thought, didn't respond.

'My love,' he said anxiously, 'when we are in Winchester, don't mingle too much. The less you have to do with Edward or Edith, the better.'

Godiva made no reply. Then she seemed to nod agreement. Lovric felt his heart sink. In Winchester she would have to dissemble and calculate. That was not the Godiva he knew and loved. Oh God, he swore into his beard and clenched his fist round the hilt of his sword. How sweet it would be at this very moment to plunge cold steel into the royal viscera and relieve England of Edward, that obstruction lodged high up in its bowels, bringing misery and holding back the life of the whole country.

Lovric took his hand off the hilt, gave Godiva an unconvincing pat of reassurance on her arm, and asked for her help in unbuckling his belt and getting him ready for bed. Five minutes later the earl, who never lost a minute's sleep even in howling storms on the night before battle, was dead to the world, while beside him lay his wife, listening to the tumbling water and worrying about her captive sons and, for the first time since marrying Lovric, worrying profoundly about her own future, too.

From the Vale of the White Horse the route to Winchester lay south and east through countryside that was less wet and forested than southern Mercia, and that seemed altogether older as a site of human habitation. The ride became pleasanter now that the prospect before them was downland, open fields and meadows, rather than woodland, coppice and tall marsh grass. Lovric made such an effort to keep up the spirits of his small party – Godiva, Agatha and Father Godric – that even the taciturn Wessex captain of the guard joined in the banter and started telling southern jokes, the sort of village jokes that didn't travel well and which none of the Mercians had heard before. Lovric roared with laughter as though he had nothing more challenging ahead of him than a pleasant ride along a well-maintained road in good weather.

Godiva, unable to produce more than the occasional tepid smile, wondered about his state of mind. He must be terribly anxious to display such exaggerated good cheer. This was what he did, he told her, when he had to lead his men into battle on the following dawn. But whatever awaited them in Winchester, it was probably nothing Lovric had fought before.

They came to a stop at a rendezvous point beside a ford on the River Kennet. Here the Wessex guard handed over the duty of escorting the Earl of Mercia to a small detachment of Lovric's own men, drawn from amongst those who had come down with him from Coventry. The captain of the Mercians greeted Lovric and Godiva, bowed coldly to his Wessex counterpart and then led his party straight on until they were out of view of Godwin's men. But at the first sheltered spot on the path that ran above the river they slowed down, and the captain approached Lovric to deliver his news.

'My lord,' he began, 'the rest of your men are with Earl Siward in Winchester, awaiting your arrival. Sir, I was sent back here to meet you after we were stopped by an envoy of the king.'

Lovric tried to conceal his dismay. 'So, the king knows about my meeting with Earl Godwin?'

'It appears so, sir.'

Lovric, distracted, let his gaze wander over his soldiers as he tried to weigh the implications of the latest news. Suddenly his eyes alighted on Bret, sitting in the middle of the other soldiers on a stallion that belonged to one of Lovric's oldest followers.

'What is Bret doing here, on Cenric's horse?' he demanded.

'Bret rides stirrupless, sir,' said the captain, 'and Siward thought it would not look right, to parade to Winchester gate with him in the midst of your guard and his feet hanging down like two dirty socks, sir.'

'And Cenric?'

'He and Bret exchanged horses. Cenric's stallion prefers to have the stirrups off.'

Lovric nodded amiably at Bret.

'Earl Siward instructs me to tell Earl Lovric, sir,' the captain of the guard went on. 'The king commands that the Earl of Mercia and the lady go at once, on arrival in the city, to Winchester prison, sir.'

Lovric, knowing the captain was watching him for any twitch of fear, remained motionless.

'The king,' the captain continued, 'has said that you are to be permitted an interview there, sir, in the prison. With Lord Alfgar.'

Godiva had been sitting silently all this while, preoccupied and confused by the sudden fast beating of her heart at the sight of Bret so near by. As though bitten by a snake, she swivelled in her saddle.

'Prison! Why isn't Alfgar in the king's quarters? What does this mean, Lovric?'

It usually meant only one thing: that the prisoner would be tortured to extract information, and then either blinded and castrated or hanged like a thief. Edward rarely used his prisons for anything else. Anyone he meant to spare was exiled at once. Lovric knew this and so did his men, and now he saw them all staring at him, sullen, anxious and looking for leadership.

'It means I must talk with the king as soon as possible.' Then he leaned over to Godiva and in a whisper told her to get ready for fast riding, adding, 'If Alfgar has been harmed, I will raise the *fyrd* all over Mercia and go to war against the king.'

Their arrival in Winchester a few hours later lacked all the usual pageantry that accompanied a nobleman's entry with his retinue into a walled royal town. They reached the approaches of the city under cover of darkness, and were stopped at a good distance before the city wall by a heavily armed officer who brusquely ordered Lovric's guard to hand over their weapons and go to the housecarls' quarters near the south wall. King's men now surrounded Lovric, Godiva, Agatha and Father Godric, and marched them off on foot as though they were under arrest. Godiva noticed that Agatha was trembling and had started to cry.

'Not one tear!' she snapped at the girl. 'You represent me. Make Father Godric pray with you quietly.'

Shuddering with fear, Godric began to stutter out the paternoster, so quietly that it did nothing to calm Agatha's apprehension. Only Godiva's stern glances did that.

Their way led through a warren of old, poorly lit streets, full of people quietly concluding their day's labours. Some of these looked up curiously at the king's men leading a lord and lady on these unceremonious paths, and one or two nudged each other knowingly, for rumours had swept the city since Alfgar was brought in, dishonourably heaped with chains and sitting in an ox-cart. But soon the little group passed out of the civilian settlement and entered through the west gate of the city wall and into the planned grid of streets laid down in the time of King Alfred for his administration, his soldiers and his priests. And there before them rose the towers of the cathedral – holy, regal and transcendent. We should have been allowed to come here first to pray, Godiva thought bitterly. A king who calls himself 'the Confessor' should have thought of that and made arrangements for us. Instead they passed round the side of the cathedral, alongside the precinct wall, and marched on towards the king's fort down a lane that ran alongside it, coming to a halt in front of a squat oak door, its planks reinforced with rivets of iron. It was a mean and menacing hole in the wall, and nothing could have made it plainer that this was the entrance of a passage to prison.

The captain of the escort shouted out a password. Then, it seemed for several minutes, nothing happened. Godiva glared at Agatha, who had forced herself into a state of unnatural calm, and Agatha looked back meekly, understanding that her ladyship was controlling her own fear by bossing around her maid. The poor thing, thought Agatha. How terrible to find yourself at this door to who knows what kind of horror, and your own son within. She crossed herself and began to say the beautiful prayer she had recently learned by rote and half-understood, 'Ave Maria, gratia plena ... benedicta tu in mulieribus...'

Godiva, hearing her, immediately remembered Mary at the foot of the cross.

'Dear God,' she murmured, 'I am like any other woman who must see her child suffer. Help me now.'

Then, while her thoughts were on Calvary, the door swung slowly open. A turnkey stood there, dressed in black and reeking of stale beer.

'The Lord Lovric,' he said, with all the contempt that servants can squeeze into inoffensive words, 'may enter his majesty's prison.'

Lovric took Godiva's hand and stepped forward. But the turnkey raised his arm and blocked their way.

'We both go in,' Lovric growled. 'She is the mother, for Christ's sake.'

'Orders,' said the man, staring insolently at Godiva.

'Go and check your orders again,' said Lovric. The man stared back at him until Lovric found his purse and pulled out a silver coin. 'My good man,' he said, his voice splintering like ice as he extended his hand.

The turnkey took the coin, tested it on a back tooth and then retreated into the tunnel that led into the heart of the prison. In a moment he was back, the door was thrown wide open and Lovric and Godiva passed under the thick lintel, into a place that stank of old fear, of dirt and of recent death.

'Alfgar?'

There was no answer from the corner of the dark room. One torch flickered high above, giving just enough light for them to see that there was a pile of blankets and straw at the opposite side of the room.

'Alfgar, my son?'

Lovric went up to the pile and started to pull back a blanket. Then Godiva came near. In her hand she held a blue glass bottle. She cracked the seal open and inhaled the fragrance of mead, honey and the Mercian herbs and foreign bitters that the wise woman of Coventry had blended for her. From out of the pile there emerged a blackened hand, and then a face, shoulders and neck, and very soon the bottle found its way to Alfgar's mouth, which sucked on its tonic contents until Godiva pulled it away, fearing an overdose.

Alfgar threw off the straw and blankets, sending a cloud of fleas leaping for cover, and leaned back on his hands to get a good look at his parents. They were haggard, he thought, and showing their age. His own appearance he knew to be appalling. There was blood caked in his matted black hair, an untended gash running down his right cheek and needing urgent cleaning and dressing, and he stank of his own urine. But now he was grinning.

'I'm not in as bad a way as I look,' he said, smiling at Godiva and then at his father. 'When they brought me here I buried myself in this heap of blankets and slept. The food they give you is so bad there's no point sitting up for it. I put it in the corner by the torch and it kept the rats away from me.'

'Well, what is your story?' Lovric asked. 'It had better be good.'

'It's not much of a story, actually,' Alfgar replied, 'but it is different from the one that is being put about.'

Lovric produced a skin bag full of wine from under his cloak, and then two cold pork chops and a hunk of bread. He passed them to Alfgar and told him to eat quickly so that he would have the strength to talk sense.

'It started innocently enough in a tavern in Hereford,' Alfgar began. 'I'd gone there – it's a decent, clean place, with good ale and nice girls – with this Welshman called Dafydd, who'd just sold me a horse, a lovely chestnut three-year-old . . .'

'For God's sake,' Lovric roared, 'get to the bloody point, man.'

'Well, father, this is the point. We were having a pleasant, relaxing time, eating and drinking, and just getting into the mood with a nice little tart called Mari and a big Saxon girl, and the whole town was quiet because it was midweek and there had been no disturbances for a while, when in bursts Ralph of Mantes' man, Robert de la Vexin, with half a dozen armed ruffians. Everyone dived for cover, but Dafydd and I put our hands up, nice and peaceful, and let them take us off. We thought there was some mistake and it would get sorted out with Ralph straight away. Instead of that, they put the Saxon girl in the stocks, sent Mari back without a penny over the Welsh border, and punched us up before dumping us overnight in Ralph's pit. The next day I was on a horse and riding here to Winchester at top speed. Then, when I got to the city wall, they put me in a cart, trailed me through the town and people threw dung at me. I still don't know what this is all about, but the officer in charge of this jail tells me I'm charged with murder and with refusing to answer to law.'

'I'm prepared to believe you,' said Lovric guardedly. 'But tell me why it happened. What's been going on in Hereford? And where are your men now?'

'They're over the Welsh border.'

'With Gruffydd ap Llywelyn?'

'Yes.'

Lovric groaned and shook his head despairingly.

'But they only fled to him after I was taken away,' said Alfgar. 'Until then Hereford was enjoying peace. The Welsh were able to come to market and sell their livestock, and the English were able to charge them entry tolls and sell them ale and whores. Everyone was happy. Now it'll be back to the Welsh raiding and the English clamouring to take the *fyrd* over the ford to knock their heads in. This is bad for everyone.'

'Except Ralph of Mantes. It will seem that only he can keep the peace on this part of the Welsh border. Edward can continue to favour his Normans and we won't be able to complain about it.'

'Quite so, father.'

'What do you want me to do, son?'

'You, father? Nothing. I want to go to trial.'

'You'd have to undergo an ordeal, you know. You can't swear a stronger oath than a king's man like Ralph.'

'Then I'll do it,' Alfgar said, as though plunging his hand into boiling water was nothing to worry about.

'No! You will not!' Godiva cut in. 'I've seen more ordeals than either of you, and I can tell you, you may prove your innocence, but your hand will never be good again. Your grip will be weak. You won't wield a sword or axe, and even if they let you use your left hand for the ordeal, it means you won't be able to manage a shield properly or hold a bow. Your fighting days would end, Alfgar. Let your father intervene with the king…'

'Spoken like a caring mother,' said a thin, sibilant voice from the door. All three turned in surprise to look at the speaker, a monk it seemed, judging by his black robe and his sandals. He stood there motionless, his colourless eyes glassy in the light of the torch. A silent priest behind him held a jewelled cross above his head. Then, as the visitor raised his hand to sign the cross, his ring came into view, a massive jewel that could belong to only one man in England.

'Your majesty,' said Lovric, rising dutifully.

'Greetings, my lord,' Godiva said, rising to her feet, bowing and crossing herself.

Alfgar said nothing.

'You are not to disturb your soul, good lady,' said Edward, ignoring the two men before him. 'You see, mindful of our Lord Jesus' command that we forgive one another, and having given thought to the matter at hand, and realizing that the father knows full well how to restrain the son, I have decided to release Alfgar. There will be no charges.'

'That's because the charges were lies,' Alfgar shouted.

'Your majesty,' Lovric began. 'If blood-money can be proven to be due, it should be paid.'

'I will pay it myself if need be,' Edward replied vaguely. 'You need have no concern, good earl. And you, my lady, my dear Godiva, you especially should have no fear. Your soul is as dear to your king as it is to our Lord Jesus. Do you not know that? I have been praying for you – for your great suffering, your dreadful agony as a mother.'

He smiled at Godiva, who felt a shiver cross her shoulders and pulled her cloak tightly round her chin.

'It is not so simple,' Lovric persisted. 'Alfgar must clear his name.'

Suddenly Edward burst into life like a coiled snake, hissing across the room.

'Is not the life of your son enough for you? Will you play games with me, Lovric of Mercia? Alfgar's name cannot be cleared. Who knows what happens on the borders of Mercia when Englishmen intrigue with foreigners...?'

'Foreigners? No, Britons!' Alfgar shouted. 'The Welsh are my fellow Britons. It is your Norman friends who are the foreigners, and who knows what happens when you give them a free hand? You don't know, king. I'd swear that on oath.'

'Take your life, you wretch,' Edward said, suddenly tired of the confrontation. 'Take your life and thank God for his mercy and for your king's.'

And with that he gathered his robe to his long, slight frame, sighed plaintively and shook out one of his wrists as though he had spent too much time writing in the scriptorium. After he left, the aroma of incense lingered disturbingly in the room.

'He smells like a whore,' Alfgar spat.

'Alfgar! He smells of church,' said Godiva crossly.

'And you smell like a latrine,' said his father. 'First you must be cleaned up and properly dressed, and then we'll dine as well as we can tonight at the king's guest quarters. However little sense we can make of Edward, at least you are here with us now, Alfgar – apparently a free man.'

'All well and good,' Alfgar said. 'But you still have to find out what Edward plans to do with Harry.'

'Harry? What do you know about that?'

'They brought him here on the same day as me. I even spoke with him.'

'He was here, in this foul prison?' Godiva shuddered. 'I told you,' she said to Lovric, 'I told you there was no guarantee that Harry would be treated well.'

'Don't worry, mother,' Alfgar said gently. 'He was in good spirits, and he wasn't shackled. He was only here for an hour and then they took him off.'

'Look at it this way, Eva,' Lovric said. 'Edward seems to have done his worst with Alfgar. He's probably getting bored already with trying to play games with the Mercians. And with Alfgar released, there is no excuse for keeping Harry hostage. We could all be gone from here by the end of the week. You could be back in Coventry soon, Eva.'

Lovric began to tell Alfgar about Godiva's successes with the priory and the town, about the new glass windows in the manor house, and how she had started improving the game reserves in the forests. But Alfgar wasn't listening. He knew that Edward had many other charges he could bring against him, and that one day he would strike again. The arrest in Hereford was just a shot across his bows. Edward would wait. There was no gain to be made from arresting an earl's son and having to deal with his father, too. No, he would wait till Alfgar succeeded his father as Earl of Mercia, and then he would pounce. There would be an ambush somewhere, or a trap, and Hereford and the marches of Mercia would be delivered to Edward's Normans. And so he, Alfgar, had better go on plotting to put another king on the throne of England before his father died. There was plenty for him to be thinking about, without wasting time listening to stories about his mother's shops and monks in a town that he hardly knew.

But if he thought his father had not noticed his wandering attention, Alfgar underestimated the Earl of Mercia, a man who had risen to the height of power, and had stayed there, by missing very little, and never letting on what he had not missed. So later, after a meal of suckling pig, served with sausage, baked apples, bread and cheese, Alfgar was surprised when his father turned to him and gave him his orders.

'You are to go to Peterborough, my boy,' he announced.

Alfgar put down the long strip of pork rind on which he had been gnawing, wiped the fat from his chin and stared coldly at his father. 'Whatever for?'

'We have interests there, as you know. We need to start pressing our rights to rents. I'm not bringing in as much money as I need.'

'And my men?' Alfgar replied.

'I'm going to send for them in the morning, and send some money to them, too.'

'Father, they will not follow me to the Fens. There's nothing there but monks and eels.'

'If they love you as their lord, they'll follow you anywhere,' said Lovric unsympathetically. 'Besides, the Fens are the haunt of Vikings, even in times of peace. You never know when you'll find their boats banked beside some creek in tall reeds, and then you'll have a hell of a fight on your hands. Learn to tackle the bastards in their favourite hide-holes and when you are Earl of Mercia in my place you'll be able to do more than just trade horses with the Welsh.'

'Damn it, father,' Alfgar exploded, 'I was doing far more than that.'

'Quite so, son. You were plotting to overthrow your king. I know it. He knows it. And he's just biding his time as far as you are concerned. Meanwhile, there's nowhere better for you now than Peterborough.'

'No, Lovric, don't send him so far away,' said Godiva. 'Why Peterborough?'

Lovric looked at her, and then back at Alfgar's disconcerted face, and started to laugh.

'Why? Because Peterborough has no whorehouses, no Welshmen, and it is on the other side of the country from Hereford. It is not a prison, but it will be an exile. And my God! How much does my son and chief heir deserve it. Exile, yes! With fat eels and thin monks!' He laughed again, sounding cheerful for the first time in days.

Alfgar took Godiva's hand and gave it a kiss. 'Don't worry,

mother,' he said, far more equably than she expected. 'Father is right. Hereford was getting uncomfortable. The Welsh were bringing some Irish in on our plans, and I could not control things. It was too much, and it was giving Gruffydd's cousins in Gwynedd too much power. No, going to Peterborough is not such a bad idea at all.'

Godiva looked at him sceptically. 'What else do you fancy about the Fens?'

'Eel pie. Does a man's back good, I'm told. I'll get a warm welcome when I return to the bawdy houses of Hereford. And some thegns' halls as well.'

She slapped the unwounded side of his head. 'You'll get a wife and settle down,' she retorted and leaned her head against his shoulder. 'And you can give me grandchildren, and let me make clothes for them and sing them to sleep.'

'Yes, mother. Whatever will make you happy. I promise.'

And with these empty words from the wild son she loved so much, Godiva closed her eyes. They would soon all be safe again, and even if Alfgar had to go to Peterborough for a while, he could probably return to Coventry soon – perhaps at Christmas, when Harry would surely be home, too. All the family together, safe at home for a while. She could think of nothing better except permanent peace, and that was as unattainable as heaven on Earth. She dozed off by the fire long before the dinner was over, and father and son kept on talking, all disagreement between them put aside for the time being.

Very late at night, as the candles started to burn down low and flicker, Agatha came into the room, trailing blankets she had pulled off the bed in the sleeping chamber. She tucked up Lovric and Godiva, who were entwined together, and made sure their feet were warm. Then, as she was still bent over, she felt a hand rise up within her skirt and knowingly stroke the soft skin behind her knee. For a moment, enthralled, she hesitated. Then her mother came to mind, steaming with fury, and Agatha span round and stamped on the erring hand.

'Off with you to Peterborough, you lout,' she hissed. 'And good riddance. Wait till I tell your mother.'

Alfgar groaned and turned over. 'Well then, girl, tuck me up at least,' he grumbled.

None too gently Agatha wrapped him in two blankets and left. Alfgar, curled up like a cat, listened to his father's breath deepen and his mother's soft sighs start to fade. These sounds made him think of his family and how it never changed, no matter how many years passed. It was something he could count on, and that was more than many could say. He thought of his men, most of whom were alone in the world. He thought of the Mercian marches, how beautiful they were, and how one day he would have a home there and perhaps a castle of the sort the Normans were starting to build – a place where you could keep a family safe while you went off to do battle. He thought too how much he owed his father. It was because of him that this awful day that had started in filth and well-hidden fear had ended in comfort at a hearth with his mother and father, food and drink. His thoughts strayed on to the possibility of a girl's delightful thighs, parting in welcome tomorrow or the day after, if only he was more subtle with her, and she did not complain to Godiva.

Suddenly he sat bolt upright. Godiva! Why was his mother in Winchester? No one had explained that to him. She had no business being here, for this was no pleasure trip or saint's pilgrimage that Lovric was undertaking. Pleading with the king was men's business. He looked at his father's sleeping back. The old fox was hiding something; keeping secrets from him again. And he expected to be trusted? Fury took hold of Alfgar and he struggled to get out of his blankets. Moments later he tiptoed out of the room and went into Agatha's little cupboard of a sleeping space. He shook her awake and closed his hand over her mouth.

'I am going,' he said. 'When my parents rise, tell them I've gone – I'm on my way to Peterborough.'

Agatha bit his hand and wrenched his fingers away. 'No, I won't,' she growled. 'That'd get me into trouble. Get the porter to tell them. Get off me now. Leave me be.'

In answer Alfgar took her head in both his hands, kissed her hungrily and let her fall back into her bed. Then, in a swirl of dust, he was gone.

Agatha lay where she was, her heart pounding, longing for him to come back, do more and show her what it was like to be unvirtuous, wilful and on fire with life. But then, as ever, came the crushing memory of her mother's cautions, ringing in her ears and telling her, over and over again: you are only a lady's maid, Agatha, and very lucky to be that. So no high-jinks for you, my girl, just duties and minding your manners. Remember that. If some lad comes interfering with you, slap his face and curse him. Courting and all that – it's for the lords and ladies. Ladies like Godiva, thought Agatha, and for a moment she felt bitterly jealous of her beloved mistress, she who had buried one husband and gained a better one, who was admired by handsome young Bret, and was even, it seemed, sought after by the king. Oh, fortunate lady, so rich and fair, so loved and loving, what a joy her life must be! Agatha shed a few tears of self-pity and invoked her guardian angel: '*Angele dei, qui custos es mei*,' repeating the prayer several times over, until her eyes grew heavy and she sank into the remnants of her night's sleep.

Five

Late in the morning, much later than she started work at home in Cheylesmore manor, Agatha pushed open the window beside the door to Godiva's chamber and rubbed her eyes in sleepy disbelief. After weeks of rain and overcast skies in Coventry, the sight of busy, sunlit Winchester dazzled and disturbed her. She started to fret at once. What on earth would her lady wear today, on her first public appearance in this royal *burgh*? Lovric had said last night that they should stroll around with him next day and take in the strange sights of the town, for it would occupy their minds until they were able to see the king and plead for Harry. Godiva had agreed, though without much enthusiasm, Agatha noticed. Now, with this summery weather, she would feel even less inclined to walk around with Lovric and grow all dusty, hot and bothered. All her good, proper dresses were long-sleeved. At home she wore them only briefly on warm days, but here in Winchester and this inconvenient royal hostelry she would be stuck in them all day long and by afternoon she would smell like a cat. Goddamit, Agatha murmured to herself. If ever her mother heard of that, she would box her ears.

The memory of Bertha scolding and slapping everyone during spring-cleaning sharpened her wits. She must have included something suitable for a day like today. Agatha brightened up and set off to find out where these light clothes might have gone.

Two hours later Godiva stood at the threshold of the hostelry, waiting for Lovric and wondering what to do with the rest of the morning. Thanks to Agatha's enterprise, she was now arrayed in a sleeveless, narrow, pale-green tunic made of lightest linen lawn, her hair dressed in two golden coils that covered both ears like a pair of iridescent shells, and a necklace of small pearls falling between her breasts. Around her forehead sat a thin silver filet from which hung the flimsiest of white silk veils that fluttered away in the soft breeze, covering nothing at all of her neck and shoulders. A passing monk paused in amazement as the word 'naked' formed in his mind, and crossed himself to expunge the image of those two creamy, slender limbs that hung from near the woman's breasts all the way down to that secret grove where Eve had wrought the destruction of mankind. He crossed himself again and hurried away, unnoticed by Godiva, who was frowning with displeasure at the strong, dazzling sunlight.

The maid was once more a very worried girl. Godiva was in a bad temper this morning and had refused to accept a little silk stole from Agatha, saying that she wouldn't wear it and was sure to lose it. She seemed oblivious to the impropriety of revealing her bare arms so boldly, though she covered them up all the time on Sundays in St Mary's, Coventry. Was she showing off? It was a possibility, thought Agatha, for she had Lovric with her and she always made a show of herself for him. Then again, she probably didn't realize exactly how she looked. There were no large mirrors here, and it was a long time since Godiva had seen herself in this thin dress. Agatha wanted to say something to her, but couldn't find the words. How do you tell your mistress that she looks like the Fairy Queen? Or the Virgin herself? It was impossible. No, it was up to the earl to have a word with her, and if he didn't then it was no one else's business.

But Lovric, who could not understood why monks these days wanted to hide the beauty of women so thoroughly, seemed delighted with Godiva's appearance when he arrived back at the hostelry after some early business.

'My love,' he said, and stroked her bare arm, rather too sensuously in such a public place, thought Agatha, looking away and wondering why the earl's well-known discretion seemed a bit tattered this morning. 'Come and stroll in the sunshine with me,' he continued. 'Let's put our troubles aside for a while.'

Godiva just stared at him. She still had not got over her annoyance at Alfgar's abrupt dawn departure with no farewells.

'Do come, Eva,' Lovric persisted.

'All I want is an audience for you with the king, and for me with the queen,' she replied. 'And then I want to go home.'

'It will be soon. Today or tomorrow. Try to worry less, Eva. Come out and enjoy yourself...'

Godiva examined him critically. He seemed a bit flustered, as though his early morning business, whatever it was, had not gone too well. His determination to have some fun seemed forced. But that was his way when he was under pressure. Sulkily she nodded assent to the proposed walk through Winchester, and took his hand.

Well, that's that, Agatha sighed. At least with Lovric accompanying them everywhere like a big old mountain, no one would dare insult Godiva's bare arms.

They set off in a tight little knot – Lovric and Godiva arm in arm, and Father Godric and Agatha following behind – huddling together because it was strange to be amongst strangers without a big band of their own armed men protecting them. Lovric still had his insignia and his sword, and people made way for him, knowing him to be a high-ranking lord. Yet even he seemed diminished, like all the other important men in this royal *burgh*, whose followers had to sleep apart from their leaders and go about unarmed.

In order to feel more like his usual self, Lovric issued a constant flow of orders to look at this, look at that, go here and go there. Thus, without having thought about it, they found themselves quickly in the busiest part of a street that bisected what seemed to be the commercial quarter of the city. Here there was scarcely a monk in sight, but there were lords and ladies, common people, traders with stalls, cooks selling snacks, and entertainers of all sorts, dancing, tumbling, miming and making music. Everywhere they went there was raucous noise and tumult, laughter, shoving and shouting. Lovric forged ahead, making a safe path for the others, and not looking in the least where he was going. Soon they had reached a place where the crowd thickened and stood in one place, staring ahead. Rising above the general din that filled the square there could now be heard a persistent drumming and along with it, in time with it, an unearthly grunting. As they approached, people respectfully made way and then closed behind them, and soon they were caught at the front of a crowd that was watching, so people said, the very first dancing bear to come to Britain.

It was a terrible sight. The bear, following its instincts, kept trying to raise its head to smell whatever scents came to it on the air, but a ring sat in a hole in its nose, a sore and bleeding hole at which its keeper kept tugging, making the creature bow down unnaturally and submit to his commands. The bear shuffled pitifully, moving its huge legs in time to the beat of a drum being played by an expressionless little girl who sat on the ground nearby. Nothing less like dancing could possibly be imagined, nor was there anything funny in the spectacle, and yet people around them were jigging about and laughing. Someone poked Agatha in the arm and told her the bear had just arrived from the Magyar court, where the king's kinsman was a prince. It is a Russian bear, said the man, and in Russia there are bears prowling round all the villages. They capture them and make them dance, to teach the peasants to laugh at them instead of fearing them.

'Come,' said Lovric. 'This is Edward's idea of pleasure. It is what he'd like to do to his earls, I'm sure.'

Gladly all four pushed back towards the rim of stalls that lined the street. For a few minutes they examined the various goods that were on display, and Godiva noticed with disappointment that everything on offer in Winchester was far superior to the goods that arrived at her market in Coventry. The glassware had fewer bubbles and the colours were more varied and intense. The leather was softer and the patterns stamped onto the skins were elaborate and multicoloured. She bought a pair of ordinary shoes quickly, for she knew Lovric would not stand around for long while she hesitated, and then she regretted it, because she could have bought just such a pair for less in her own market. Next she went over to a stall where pieces of carved walrus ivory were on display. Here she chose a small comb for Agatha, as a gift for all her good service and because the girl owned nothing of any value. There were several large and intricately carved combs at the stall that she admired and thought of buying for herself, but hesitated at the price, even when the trader tried to goad her by telling how Queen Edith had bought several of them only yesterday, including some old ones that everyone thought were 'Roman'. But Godiva refused to be impressed and drifted off towards a jeweller's stall where several prosperous men and women were examining a display of decorative pins for fastening clothes. Here she chose a delicate silver brooch for holding together light wraps and shawls like the one Agatha had brought along for the walk. She put it on and Agatha was relieved to see that now Godiva's upper arms, at least, had disappeared modestly beneath an embroidered white silk stole.

Irritated by the constant reminders of how petty and poor her own town seemed compared with the glories of Winchester, Godiva was now as ready as Lovric to leave the market and do something else. As they edged through the last knot of people in the market-place throng, an avenue opened up before them. Down this road in the distance they could see and smell round, shining rumps and tossing manes. It was the horse fair, and from beyond it came the sound of men shouting and animals shrieking.

'Let's go there,' Godiva said. 'We need new blood-lines amongst the breeding mares at Cheylesmore. And we could bet on the cockfight or the dogs.'

Lovric was all for this, and had just started looking in his coin bag to see how much money he had on him, when someone tugged at his sleeve.

'My lord,' said a lanky youth in tattered hose. 'Ivar Haraldson would have a word.'

Over by a stand selling hot bread stood a very tall man. He turned, and Lovric saw that he was looking once again at the face of his Icelandic friend, Ivar quick-tongue, his companion on many nights beside camp fires on the wilder borders of the Danelaw.

'Still on the run?' Lovric laughed as he and Ivar embraced.

'No. I've made my peace with Ragnar, paid him all the blood-money he was due, and even shook the bastard's hand.'

Ivar smiled, showing his broken soldier-of-fortune teeth, but his slanting blue eyes glinted dangerously. Suddenly he turned towards Godiva, bowed briefly and looked quizzically at Lovric.

'Your woman?' he asked. 'The one you pined for so much? I can see why.'

He kissed her hand with a tenderness that was so at odds

with his general roughness that Godiva blushed and felt a lurch in her heart, followed by instant shame. This was the second such blush recently and she hoped that it meant no more than that she was coming to that age when women often felt flushed for no particular reason.

Lovric, with his back turned, saw nothing amiss. 'Yes, my woman Godiva,' he replied, turning and putting his arm round her shoulder and pulling her close. 'Yes, this is who I pined for. But you, man, were pining too – for a girl called Inga and a farm at Hella. Why aren't you back there with your sheep and goats, in the place you said was paradise?'

Ivar laughed. 'I was lying. There was no Inga, just an Irish slave called Brigid who will never be mine. As for Hella, I'm not rich enough to buy land there. To tell the truth, I've become so good at lying I've decided to stay in England where liars can always find a good lord. The pay I get for my stories here is better than what I can make from sheep in Iceland or even Greenland.'

'Are you a *scopman* now?'

'A *skald*, as we say at home.'

'Then,' said Lovric, 'you are also a bearer of news?'

Ivar shot his old friend a sharp look, for the true meaning of his question was, 'Do you still spy?'

'You could say that,' said Ivar, stepping back a few paces so that Godiva couldn't hear him. 'I need a new lord,' he whispered. 'Quickly. And I need to get out of this part of Britain. Can you commend me to Alfgar?'

'So, the word is out, is it, about Alfgar's movements?'

'Can you help me?' Ivar repeated.

'Does that mean I'm aiding a fugitive again?'

'Not this time, friend. I have some gambling debts, but not with the sort of men who are within the law.'

'You've kept your old vices,' said Lovric, 'and I suppose you've kept your old virtues, too.'

He took off a ring he often wore on his middle finger and passed it unobtrusively to Ivar.

'Show this to my captain, down in the housecarls' quarters, and get a horse from him. Go to Bristol and lie low. Alfgar will get there soon. Show him the ring, and give him this.' He passed a purse to Ivar and another for the Icelander to keep himself.

'But, Lovric, I'd heard Alfgar was off to Peterborough.'

'He is, but not for long. I've sent a messenger after him; from Peterborough he is to go to Bristol, then west to the Welsh coast, and beyond. You'll go with him.'

'Those are deep waters, old friend,' said Ivar, frowning.

'Don't worry, I'm not in rebellion, not yet. I'm just making my plans, in case . . .'

'Does she know what you're up to?' Ivar glanced at Godiva.

'No. No one does. I'm giving out misleading instructions to my men, until the last moment.'

Ivar nodded, looking again at Lovric's beautiful wife. 'Be careful with her. She still trusts you.'

'Yes, but she doesn't pry. Godiva is sensible . . .'

'Even so, she could start to feel deceived. And once a woman grows distrustful . . . take care, old friend.'

'I know my own wife,' Lovric snapped, 'and she knows me. She knows I can't tell her everything – for her safety as well as mine.'

Lovric noticed one or two well-dressed Norman youths near-by, watching them with interest.

'Walk with us now towards the horse market,' he said, taking Ivar's arm and steering him back to his little group. 'My lady wants to buy a mare, and then she wants to bet on the cockfights and the dogs.'

Ivar bowed again to Godiva, and then, being a common man himself, to Agatha and Father Godric. 'No,' he demurred, address-ing Godiva. 'Today is not a good day for going to the old serfs' town, where the gaming rings are. They put up a new gallows there last week and they hanged a thief last night. The body is still up, and men are drinking beer and looking for the mandrake root in the soil that has hanged-man's-seed in it. It's an unseemly place for womenfolk now. They'll cut him down at nightfall, so you could go tomorrow, lady, to buy your mare.'

Ivar excused himself and disappeared as quickly as he had come to their attention.

Godiva and Lovric, each preoccupied, turned silently back towards the centre of town, in the direction of the grand cathedral. It was time for a midday meal and they walked towards the hostelry, followed by Agatha and Godric, all of them keeping an eye open for somewhere more aromatic and less austere than the king's guest quarters, somewhere in which to find undiluted ale, good food and perhaps some fine company as well. Around them dozens of people with accents from all over England, as well as Normans, Danes, some Irish and a few Welsh, were going in and out of inns that seemed to occupy every other frontage on the long street.

They were on the verge of entering a promising establishment that Lovric remembered from his last visit to Winchester, when a beautiful woman, not unlike Godiva in stature and complexion, stepped out of the door, paused before them and seemed about to greet Lovric. On seeing Godiva, however, she turned away.

'Wait,' Lovric called after her. 'Estrith!'

The woman hesitated, but then came back to the door of the inn. 'The ale in here is watered down,' she murmured. 'Let me show you somewhere better.'

She led them round the corner and into an establishment run by servants of Earl Godwin, where Estrith said they would be well fed and well received. She smiled cautiously at Godiva, and then asked Lovric to step outside again to have a word with her. A few moments later he returned without her, and Godiva, annoyed and puzzled that there had been no introductions, raised her eyebrows.

'That woman – Estrith Gudmanson – is a member of the household of one the king's most valued counsellors, Robert de Champart, Bishop of Jumièges.'

'Is that why she is so beautiful and so well dressed,' Godiva sniped.

Lovric ignored her and went on. 'I learned something important from her. She is taking care of the affairs of a noblewoman from Kent who has annulled her marriage, on the bishop's advice, because she and her husband are cousins. There are no children in this case and the woman's dowry lands are now hers to do with as she wishes. The husband is angry and accusing Bishop Robert of ruining his marriage in order to get his hands on the wife's estates.'

'Is it true?'

'Estrith thinks so. The estates are extensive and they are already occupied by the bishop's soldiers.'

'Why did Estrith tell you this?'

'Because there is talk around the bishop's table that other rich noblewomen are coming to the same decision as the Kentish woman. Estrith said that if you and I are related, we should start to think up some story to deny it.'

'Well, I wouldn't give you up so easily, Lovric,' Godiva scoffed. 'And anyway we are no more than second cousins. This is nonsense. That woman was just trying to get your attention.'

'I don't think so. I've heard mention before now that the bishops are showing a lot of interest in the prohibited degrees of marriage.'

'Well, let them. If they ask, tell them that though we have a great-grandfather in common, everyone knows his wife was a king's mistress, and so it is more likely that one of us has royal blood than that we are related to each other.'

'Very clever,' Lovric laughed, but not as heartily as Godiva would have liked. She would have preferred it too had that pretty, knowledgeable woman not crossed their paths.

'Let's go somewhere else,' she said, getting up abruptly.

Estrith's connection with the tavern had clearly made it distasteful to Godiva, and Lovric agreed without a word. He took her hand and pushed his way through the crowd into the street, heading for the nearest respectable inn. With hunger mounting, they hurried to cross the threshold and were about to plunge into the dark, comforting interior, when a uniformed herald sprang up before Lovric and barred his way.

'Earl Lovric of Mercia,' he intoned. 'The king summons you at once to the cathedral. You are required to witness the signing of the charters this afternoon.'

'This is my dinner time,' Lovric fumed. 'Why was I not informed before now? What would you have done if you had found me down at the cockfight and spattered with blood? Is this how you manage the business of the realm?'

The messenger stood mute and expressionless, waiting for the nobleman's tirade to subside. They were all like this when they were summoned; they all implied that they would be better rulers than the king; they all ranted at the powerless messenger; then they all bowed low before the throne.

'Eva,' Lovric sighed, 'I'm sorry I must leave you. Go back now to the hostelry, and dine there, rest and wait for me.'

On another day she might have argued. But the heat was oppressive, her appetite poor and the morning had left her feeling that she had seen enough of Winchester. They kissed and parted, and Godiva, with Agatha and Father Godric now on either side of her, started back towards the hostelry.

Their way took them down the chief market street to where a narrow lane, crammed with people, flowed into the main cathedral road. The scene was one of bustle and business, but nothing that seemed unusual for this time of the week and day. Then, without warning, just as they arrived at the junction of the streets, a huge uproar broke out, and the three found themselves standing directly in the path of a hue and cry. A shopkeeper, flushed with rage, was giving chase to a pilferer and shouting 'stop, thief' and 'cut-purse' at the top of his voice, egged on by a band of citizens out to share his vengeance.

What happened next was unavoidable. Godric stumbled and notwithstanding his priestly garb got trampled, while a burly woman aflame with indignation pushed Agatha aside impatiently, leaving her pinned against a wall by the heaving crowd, unable to move in any direction. Meanwhile Godiva, caught off guard, found herself standing directly in the path of the fleeing man, whose legs were darting off to left and right at the same time, his clothes flying, and his arms, already bleeding from the shop-keeper's attempt to arrest him, lashing out at anyone who came near him.

Suddenly he saw her and stopped, like a condemned man who has just seen the astonishing face of his saviour. He lunged towards her and someone hit him on his back with a staff, thinking he was attacking the lady. The blow sent him sprawling at her feet and clutching at the hem of her dress, smearing it at once with mud and blood. He reached up for her hand and covered it with kisses, and in doing so dragged her white silk stole and the new brooch down to the ground where they fell under his thrashing legs.

'Mercy,' he shouted hoarsely. 'I am innocent. I repent. Save me, lady. Forgiveness! Sanctuary!'

Before she could tell him she had no power in this town to protect him, the mob was upon him. The merchant whose money he had taken seized him by the hair and pulled him backwards, his scalp so tight that Godiva thought it would tear away from his face.

'Mercy, lady,' the thief screamed.

'Wait,' she shouted at the crowd, in whose hands knives were already gleaming. For a moment they froze, yielding instinctively to the authority of a high-ranking person. Godiva put her hand on the man's shoulder and addressed the shopkeeper. 'Find a priest or a law-speaker. Give him justice as a man, not a dog's death on a street corner.'

Then the spell broke and the crowd's wrath flared up again. 'Take him to the gallows,' someone shouted. 'There's lawmen there, and a priest too, ready for the likes of him.'

'The gallows!' they all roared, and rushed on like a river just renewed by heavy rain, bearing the thief with them to his death and leaving Godiva alone in the street, her dress filthy and her servants cowering by a door.

'Good lady, forgive me!' Agatha cried as she ran over and put her own plain hemp wrap round Godiva's shoulders. 'The crowd came between us. Let us go to your chamber at once.'

With Agatha beside her and Father Godric walking ahead, Godiva began to make her way back to the hostelry as quickly as she could, keeping her head down to avoid the curious glances of passers-by and hoping desperately that she would meet no one who might recognize her in her present dishevelled state. But as it happened, the story of the lady and the thief had spread like wildfire through the streets, and those townsfolk who did stare at her did so with admiration rather than derision. At last, realizing that no one was ridiculing her, Godiva cautiously raised her eyes and looked round. The first person she saw was a woman whose small child called out, 'Good lady, good lady.'

'Well, it seems I have not ruined my name, after all,' she said to Agatha.

'No. If a thief thinks you can give sanctuary, other folk will think you are holy. Well, a bit holy, mistress.'

Godric turned round and added vaguely, 'Praise be!'

All three were calming down rapidly now. Indeed, the whole episode seemed about to be buried by food and an afternoon of rest, when round the corner came sailing a large band of stout and severe ladies, their sweating bodies swathed in woollen drapes that left not one inch of flesh exposed other than their unadorned hands and red faces. Accompanying and encircling them were armed guards and softly chanting priests, all of whom seemed to be following the unvoiced orders of a young woman whose blonde brows and lashes, sitting on a face as fluffy as a dandelion, gave the appearance of one of the albino rats that sometimes ran out of the barns in Cheylesmore manor. Was this Godwin's daughter, Godiva wondered? If so, she had grown thinner and prematurely lined since Godiva had glimpsed her at her wedding, and her nose seemed sharper and brows more prominent, as though with time and political pressure she was growing into her father's selfsame face. It had to be her: one so young and so imperious could only be Queen Edith. And it was she who now brought the assembly of ladies to a halt immediately before Godiva.

'Madam?' said Edith, looking Godiva up and down as though she were an old whore who had been brought to the reeve to pay her fines.

'Yes, Edith of Wessex,' Godiva replied clumsily, unsure how to address this woman who, in the eyes of most of England, was no queen because she was still a virgin and therefore no true wife to the king. Only the slightest quiver on one cheek showed that Edith resented Godiva's discourtesy.

'I believe,' she went on icily, 'that you were accosted by a common criminal. This has never happened to a noble in Winchester. One wonders why it should happen to you.' Again she looked reprovingly at Godiva's dirty dress and her bare forearms protruding from beneath Agatha's hemp stole. 'And I believe that the thief asked you for sanctuary,' she went on, dragging out her syllables to make everyone await the completion of her pronouncements. 'That was impious. Only the king and I may grant sanctuary in this city. I trust you did nothing to encourage anyone to believe that you have the holy powers of sanctuary, either here or in Coventry, or anywhere else, my lady Godiva?'

'No. I did nothing. Of course not,' Godiva replied at once. It was the wrong answer. Edith raised her pale brows as though expecting a better explanation. 'It happened so suddenly,' Godiva said, unable to make up a suitably self-effacing tale to flatter Edith. 'It was just very strange . . .'

'*Strange?*' the queen's voice was even lower and slower now. 'In the minds of simple folk what is "strange" is often taken to be miraculous. You had better be careful, madam, lest you give offence while you are with us in royal Winchester.'

And with that Edith averted her gaze and moved on, followed by her circle of attending ladies, their eyes down and faint smirks tucked into the corners of their mouths.

Godiva remained where she stood, her face beginning to flame, unable to move or decide what to do next. Around her some of the people who had gathered to watch the scene remained to stare and point at her. Two teenage boys called out 'Oo, the naughty lady got a spanking! Ha ha ha', and laughed until a man chased them away. Some little girls started to mimic the queen giving Godiva a dressing down, one wagging her finger and the other crying and rubbing her eyes. They left to go home with their new game, which Godiva realized would be registered at once in the compendium of local children's lore. A passing whore muttered, 'Never mind, lady. Mistress Edith do open her mouth more than her legs.' A wave of laughter rippled through the small crowd. Godiva felt their sympathy deepen her shame.

Suddenly Father Godric caught hold of her arm and pulled her with him.

'Walk behind me, lady,' he said and began to lead her quickly towards the hostelry.

Agatha took up position behind her, to show more deference to her humiliated mistress. Godiva walked in a cloud of misery between them, concentrating so hard on blocking out her surroundings that she barely heard the faint voice behind her chanting childishly, over and over again in a whisper, 'Needy Eedy, needy Eedy.'

The words couldn't wipe out the shame of the afternoon, but they helped Godiva as she struggled back to the privacy of her own chamber. Edith, she remembered, might be queen, but she was also Edward's victim. While her own shame was transient, Edith's was an enduring torment, day and night. She braced her shoulders, raised her head and walked on.

Agatha noticed and silently thanked, not Mary the consoler this time, but God the Father, the Lord God Almighty, the great judge and the avenger of wrongs, He who stands above kings and queens and gives hope to small people such as herself, the One she had never appealed to in person before, keeping Him in reserve for serious peril. Only when they arrived at the safety of the hostelry did Agatha realize what she had done – praying to Him was like ringing the bell in the town square of her mind and shouting, 'Danger! enemies! flee!' But there was nowhere to flee to, and no one to protect her but a woman who was not entirely safe herself. She felt her knees buckle as if they belonged to someone else. They seemed to be getting ready to do a lot more praying to the Lord God Almighty before Agatha would see Coventry again.

Six

It was late afternoon when Lovric returned to the hostelry. Agatha could tell from the heavy trudge of his ascending footsteps that he was tired and probably irascible. The door flew open and in he came, grunting and glaring, his clenched fist squeezing a scroll of parchment and his hose askew around his knees.

Agatha had been preparing for this moment. Now she rose and, instead of bowing and effacing herself as she usually did in Lovric's presence, she stood there before him, her feet planted before Godiva's door and her hands tightly clasped together. The only customary sign of deference she gave was a deep curtsy, but as soon as she straightened up she gazed at him with a look that was bold and even possibly defiant.

'Well, my girl?'

Despite her resolve, Agatha quailed. He reminded her of her father, drunk and demanding to confront her mother over some quarrel, and she, Agatha, a mere slip of a thing, standing before him to slow down the progress of his godlike rage and take the first blow herself.

'My lord,' she began uncertainly. 'Mistress is unwell.'

'Sick? Was the food bad at midday? We should have lodged at

the cathedral guest quarters, after all. You can count on monks to dine well.'

'No lord, the food was not bad here,' Agatha hesitated, and then she grasped the nettle. 'No, she was assaulted, sir.'

The expected blow did not fall. Lovric was not drunk and his command of his own violence was instinctive. Instead he gave her such a look of contempt that her heart froze over. She had failed in her first duty as a servant, which was to protect her mistress against everything. His silent condemnation made it hard for Agatha to find the words with which to relate what had happened. But when she spoke Lovric listened carefully, and only at the end, when Agatha described the encounter with Edith, did he utter one quiet curse.

'Go now and rest,' he told her, and then he entered the chamber where Godiva was still asleep.

Agatha did not go at once, but placed her ear firmly against the door and listened. From inside the room there came no sound at all. The master must be standing there, just looking down at Godiva, she thought. Mother Mary! Let him see how pale she is and have the sense to let her go home.

Inside the shuttered, candle-lit room, Lovric was indeed reflecting on the wisdom of being in Winchester, at Edward's command, with Godiva. He was ruminating too on the loyalty of the little maid. From the look on her face she had expected at least a slap, but she had risked it to deflect the greater anger that some husbands showed wives who had been dishonoured, albeit by accident and through no fault of their own.

He was deeply uneasy. Despite the gentle setting of this town – the way it rose unobtrusively out of the open chalk landscape, the way the long, low cathedral did not soar and dominate its surroundings, but nestled between gardens and water meadows beside the temperate River Itchen – there was something subtly awry in the spirit of the place. The insult to his wife intensified the anxiety he had felt all day since Alfgar's unexpected release. Glad as he was about that, it immediately raised questions about the king's motives in taking Harry hostage. Lovric had grave misgivings on that score, too grave to share with Godiva. Then there were all the other little jarring incidents that had taken place – unimportant in themselves, and yet cumulatively unsettling: the failure this morning of one of his spies to arrive at an early appointment; meeting Ivar quick-tongue, and him on the run again; encountering Estrith, a clerical courtesan bearing news of cold winds of change; Godiva feeling put out on finding her market to be so much poorer than Winchester's; and that gaunt monk, devouring the sight of her bare arms – something that she had not noticed, but he had.

How often it was that she did not see what was going on around her, he thought. Take Prior Edwin: she had let him continue in his ways unchecked for far too long. And take this visit to Winchester: why was she not on her guard, every second, for something to go wrong? Why did she plead for that thief, for instance, when it only drew more attention to her? She knew now that Edward was a strangely cruel man and she had long complained that he had taken an irrational disliking to her. Why was she not supremely cautious, as he was? He doubted that Edith had come upon Godiva just by chance, so soon after the thief fell at her feet. No: her informers had told her at once and she had sought out Godiva to rebuke and shame her. It was even possible that the whole incident of the thief had been staged. He found himself suddenly angry and sweating. He could not be everywhere, and he could not be at her side all the time. She was an adult woman and responsible for herself. That's all there was to it.

And yet, and yet. It was he who had brought Edwin to the abbey of St Mary's and ignored Godiva's misgivings, as he always did when he thought he knew best. And it was he who had brought her here, knowing full well the nature of Edward's mind and Edward's pleasures. He should have insisted on her going back. That is what husbands were supposed to do, he believed – make decisions about difficult things and force family members to comply. He could have done it, even if it was not his usual way with his wife, and even if it angered Edward. He did try, he remembered, but only feebly, and then he had relented and let her have her way about coming to see Alfgar and Harry. God almighty! What guilt he would feel if she suffered for this gamble he was taking to humour the king and stave off further attacks on his own authority. Such sudden attacks they had been. A mere year ago he would not have been able to imagine this rapid decline in his position – Normans at large in Hereford and he, the Earl of Mercia, having to flee; Godwin's kin nibbling away at the Mercian frontiers; two sons taken into captivity; and the Welsh up in arms again. All this, despite his great service to the king. Why did Edward want to damage him? What had he done to provoke his rage? Lovric, despite all the spies he employed, could see no reason for Edward's growing antagonism. It was so obvious that Godwin and his children were his real enemies amongst the English. The king was firing in the wrong direction.

But the king was no archer, Lovric mused. He got up and began to pace the room noisily. Edward's game was chess, a game at which he, Lovric, was a novice in comparison. All he could do now was watch out for the king's next move. In contrast, he reflected, his marriage was no chess game. God be thanked, his wife was his partner, not his opponent, and certainly not a pawn in any game. He had to treat her accordingly – stop deceiving her, as Ivar had been quick to point out; talk to her frankly instead. Then she could choose thoughtfully what to do the next time they were apart from each other. It was only fair.

He stumbled over a small stool that stood in the shadows and cursed it. Godiva stirred and put her arm across the embroidered coverlet. Lovric picked up her hand and kissed the underside of her forearm, and kept kissing it until her eyes opened.

'Hush! I know,' he said. 'There was no help for it. It was just an accident.'

'Edith...'

'Ignore that. She is less important than she thinks she is. The important thing is whether you should stay on with me, here in Winchester.'

'I hate this place.' She sat up and clasped his hands in hers. 'But, Lovric, the king still has Harry. I need to comfort the boy and make good arrangements for him. His food, his bedding, his candles ... I haven't even started on these matters yet. No, I must stay.'

'You have the right to make this choice, Eva. But if you stay, promise me you won't go anywhere without me again. Do you promise?'

'Of course.'

'Eva, listen,' he said abruptly. 'Do you remember that you asked me whether I'd promised the king to bring you here? I avoided your question. The truth is, Edward commanded me to bring you, on pain of Alfgar's life. I'm sorry, I deceived you.'

He looked so wretched, his shoulders so bowed with worries, that she sat up and put an arm round his neck and kissed him.

'Whyever would Edward tell you to bring me here?'

'Who knows? To see you suffer as you did in the prison, or to make Edith jealous. It could be any reason at all, depending on what fancy occupies his mind now. I'm not even sure if he remembers his command.'

'Listen, Lovric. I'm not angry about this. You've always kept some things from me – for my own good, you say – and this wasn't much of a deception. It changed nothing. I would have come with you anyway, once I knew Harry was being brought here as a captive.'

Lovric looked down at his hands.

'We are apart so long, so often,' she continued. 'Gaps open up between us, and then there are misunderstandings. But we are happy when we can be together and nothing comes between us.'

We are happy because she is forbearing, he thought, and remembering how only moments ago he had despised her kindness as weakness and gullibility, he felt ashamed again. This would not do. He got up and paced round the room. He had to regain command of himself. And so did she.

'Eva, if you were on a battlefield with me, I would tell you to get back up on your horse, brandish your sword and find your enemy. You need to confront Edith and face her down. Show her you don't give a damn about this afternoon.'

'How?'

'Come with me tonight to the feast at the king's castle. Edward will be satisfied if he sees you there – it'll show him I am still obedient. And Edith will be furious.'

'That's not exactly brandishing a sword, is it? It would be a gesture and no more. And empty gestures are childish and trivial. I'd rather confront Edward and accuse him of lying about Alfgar to favour his Normans. I'd like to do that at the feast tonight.'

Her voice had suddenly grown cold and Lovric didn't like it. She was right: he wanted her to make a gesture only, but no real attack on their enemies. He wanted her to remain soft, warm and waiting for him, not armed and fighting. And yet he knew she was good with the bow and the sword – Alfgar boasted how well he had taught her, and Odo joked that he'd follow her into combat any day. And no one could handle a horse better than she. He was keeping her in her place, or trying to, for his sake as well as hers. And he was failing, for even at home alone in Coventry, she was building up a town and an abbey, making money and gaining influence. And he? He was making play-war, feinting with gestures to parry Edward's gestures. He felt weak and disgraceful.

She was looking away from him towards the fire. He stared at her searchingly, finding again in her face that disturbing vision that sometimes emerged from her beauty, of a more chiselled profile, a sterner brow, an older heroine – but not at all what he wanted in his bed and at his board. She turned towards him and for a moment a spasm of fear flew up his spine.

'I've been meaning to say this for some time, Lovric, but I hesitated because you don't like me to interfere with your affairs. From everything you've said over the last two years – since we lost Hereford – it seems to me you should declare war on Edward. You and the other two earls. This cold, uncertain peace is nothing but a torment for everyone. What do you have to lose?'

It was the opening he knew he should take. Tell her plainly that this was his plan, and that it was already in motion. But he couldn't. They would have to talk for days on end about all the details, the dangers and unforeseeable factors. And what would he gain from that? Nothing but endless worry that she might let slip some crucial piece of knowledge; or worse, that she would come under suspicion before she could reach safety, and be captured and tortured. It didn't bear thinking about.

'No, Eva. There must not be civil war in England. Not ever, if possible.'

'Better that than a Norman conquest.'

'It won't come to that. Anyway, we'll talk about this again, I promise,' he said, half-believing himself. 'But as for now, we should take a small meal before we begin to dress for the night. It will be late before we eat again, and I doubt that our entertainment will take our minds off our hunger. Edward says we will be treated to choral music sung by monks, and readings from the Psalms throughout the evening. Don't expect to laugh much.

But look your best: make Edith of Wessex red-hot with envy. You will feel better, believe me.'

'There's only one thing that will do that.'

'Harry. Yes, I know.'

The king's castle, being built of heavy timber and surrounded by a deep ditch, was far less grand and modern in appearance than the cathedral, and certainly less beautiful. And yet in the fading twilight of the summer evening, as it blazed with militant welcome and scores of torches illumined the lawn before the great gate, it possessed a grim beauty of its own. Here the king's relatives, thegns, bishops and foreign guests, and the few great ladies who attended such occasions, assembled before going in formal procession through the entrance. Despite Edward's great love for the monastic life, the castle conveyed a clear impression of its overwhelming importance in matters of state. This was the place where the leading generals and their lieutenants would come together peaceably to talk over food and drink with the king and his advisers. It was the soldiers' world, the world of those who fought all the time, just as the cathedral was the domain of those who prayed ceaselessly. Its location in the southwest of the town, just within the walls, enhanced its military atmosphere, for in this quarter of the town the disarmed retainers of the lords and bishops were lodged, and here they strolled around in the evenings, taunting and eyeing each other menacingly.

Late in the evening Godiva and Lovric approached the castle through a gauntlet of young soldiers. Lovric looked around, hoping to see the faces of his own men of Mercia, and for a moment thought he glimpsed Bret amongst a group of armed king's men. But then he was gone and Lovric doubted that it was Bret after all. Once more, he resented the feeling of powerlessness that he had on the streets of Winchester and wanted to hurry into the castle and go straight to the great hall where the feast would take place. But protocol forbade such haste. Lovric and Godiva had to stand around and cool their heels like everyone else and wait for the heralds to sort them out in order of rank. Once the long line of worthies had been chivvied into place, the guests could proceed to enter the castle, but this procession too went at a slow and stately pace, for everyone had to pass before the careful gaze of the door-wardens, whose duty was the detection of impersonators and gatecrashers.

As they lingered near the front of the emerging line of guests, Lovric saw many faces that he knew, and a few that he had hoped never to see again.

'That group of men, all talking to each other and with their backs to everyone else, who are they?' Godiva asked.

'King's thegns, all of them,' he whispered. 'They were present at the cathedral today when the charters were confirmed, all signing, though I'm sure half of them can't write a word other than their own name. The big one with the long red hair is Ordgar. He was Ealdorman of Devon under King Canute, and now he's on his way up in Edward's favour. His brother is over there, also with long hair. They are good men. But that one,' he said, indicating with a tip of his head a burly, short man who was talking with Ordgar, 'that one is Orc. Greedy, and none too clever about it. He won't last much longer in the inner circle. The others are – let's see – Karl, Osgot Clapa and Thored, all Danes, but all men committed to Edward's rule. The rest are Saxons: there's Odda of Deerhurst, a kinsman of Edward, and Ordwulf, Beorhtric and the three Alfs. That's Aelfweard, Aelfgar and Aelfstan, all Wessex men of course, and all sensitive about any favours bestowed on Normans.'

'Are there any Normans here tonight?'

'Not many. Edward is trying to reassure the House of Godwin that it will not be supplanted soon by men of Normandy. But over there, amongst those clerics, that man in the beautiful robes is Robert de Champart, Bishop of Jumièges. He came over from Normandy with Edward, who trusts him completely.'

'Robert de Champart – that woman Estrith's patron?'

'And lover. Yes.'

The line of guests had now acquired proper form and it seemed they might soon start the entrance procession into the castle, when a commotion broke out amongst the heralds and orderlies standing at the far end of the line.

'Let me go forward! Forward, I say!' A strong female voice, heavily enriched with Danish vowels, rang out above the hum of the crowd. 'I am invited, and even if I am not, I have every right to be here. My children's grandmother was Edith, daughter of King Ethelred. She was a sister of King Edward . . .'

'Half-sister,' someone shouted.

Someone else said, 'Let her be. She's the only laugh we'll get tonight.'

'And my mother was sister to King Canute,' the woman roared. 'And my father was King of the Wends and ruled the North Sea . . .'

'Pirate-king,' yelled the first heckler.

'In any case, I was invited by the king,' she shouted again. 'Go and find out, you idle dogs!'

The senior door-warden disappeared inside the castle and came back out quickly.

'Humble apologies, great lady. Your place is at the head of the table, just before Earl Lovric of Mercia, and his lady, Godiva.' He paused. 'And your children are also kindly invited to the feast.'

At this Gunnhildr came storming up the line to take her place before Lovric. She was a big, dull blonde, much burdened with Baltic jewellery, and seemed to have faded greatly with the years, so grey was her visage. But now she was incandescent with unquenched rage. She stopped in front of Godiva, her eyes blazing.

'And who are you?' she demanded. 'Yes, yes, I know who your husband is. But who are *you*? Why are you here? Who are your father and brothers, and what lands do they hold? Where are your own lands?'

'Coventry. And many other parts of Warwickshire and the midlands of England,' Godiva replied calmly, slight amusement showing at her mouth. 'My brother is Thorkell, Sheriff of Leicester...'

'Is that all? Well, *we*,' said Gunnhildr, pointing at her two terrified little boys, 'all have royal blood. And that is why I come before your husband in the line tonight.' That said, she raised her imposing chin and looked past them to survey the other guests in the line, all of whom dropped their gaze as her eyes locked with theirs.

Lovric groaned inwardly; this woman was to be his chief dinner companion tonight. He could already feel his stomach acid flowing towards the patch where it hurt like fire. But there was no help for it. The line was moving forward, with Gunnhildr leading the way.

All went smoothly at first. The king's guests lined up soberly beside the vast, long, dining table and the narrow cushioned benches that ran alongside it. Once they were in their places the royal trumpeters announced the king's entrance, and all eyes turned to take in the sight of King Edward, processing slowly towards his ceremonial seat on a dais at the far end of the hall. Smiling and nodding benignly, he rustled forward slowly in his silks, giving all his guests an opportunity to examine every extraordinary inch of his robes. He was wearing tonight an ankle-length gown of dark blue, over which there sat a shorter tunic of undyed silk, richly patterned with roundels encircling pairs of panthers and griffins, all arranged in rows with pairs of hawks and doves between them. The tunic was closed by a row of gold toggles the size of acorns, and drawn in at the waist with a broad brocaded belt whose fringed ends, embroidered with fleurs-de-lis, fell to below his knees. He wore the tunic over a dazzling white silk shirt, whose hemlines at his neck and again at his wrists were finished with gold embroidery. And even though the banquet tonight was not of great state importance, he wore on his head a light replica of his coronation crown and carried in his hand a full-size copy of his sceptre. So splendid, and so very tall was Edward, that few noticed his queen walking beside him, draped in pale swathes of bland silk and drawing no attention away from the radiance of his majesty, whose ceremonial clothes she had herself embroidered.

As the envious guests remained standing, servants hurried to fill the tankards with beer and the goblets with wine, performing the role of the lady of the hall, a role that Queen Edith would not lower herself to play at this stage in the feast. Then a hush descended on the crowd as the king's chief steward stepped into the centre of the room and raised the old hunting horn to sound the call that would commence the feast. It was an eerie, thrilling sound, one that reminded everyone how often kings and thegns had met and feasted in this place before, and how many steps had led to those who were present being here tonight, to be honoured and affirmed, while some rival skulked at home or lay in a poor grave.

The trumpet fell silent and loud chatter started up as everyone sat down and greeted those next to them. Large wooden platters were placed before the guests, each one resting on a big flat square of bread, where the night's spills of gravy, grease, wine and beer would collect and soak into the bread, so that when it arrived next morning in the mouths of the poor, the crumbs from the king's table would taste of the feast on which the rich had dined.

Immediately afterwards the serving dishes and bowls appeared, some so large they were borne by three servants, one at each handle and a third fishing out whatever choice pieces a guest demanded. Godiva, because of Gunnhildr's loud voice, was unable to converse with Lovric, or with the man on her right, because he was drunk already and in danger of vomiting soon. She concentrated therefore on the long meal that lay ahead of her. She started with a pastry pie stuffed with larks' tongues, and then progressed quickly to slices of beef served with white bread, carrots and cabbage, mustard and horseradish. She gave the pork chops and chicken breasts that followed less attention, but all around her men were eating with undiminished appetite as dish followed dish, and whether delicate and luxurious like the oyster paste and the preserved quail's eggs, or coarse and common like the pigs' trotters and ox tails, everything was consumed with equal gusto. The only thing amiss, though no one seemed to care, was that the king wasn't eating at all. As for the queen, she merely picked fastidiously at her food and stared with unconcealed disgust at the earthliness of all around her. Edward too stared at those before him, but with a look of distant amusement and curiosity, as though the real feast for him was the sight of those he saw sitting before him and what might happen to them in the course of the evening.

At last, as the chewing slowed down and people began to talk more, Edward rose to his feet. The steward called for attention and then the king cleared his throat, smiled and turned to Gunnhildr.

'Dear lady,' he said, 'kindly step forward.'

'Me?' asked Gunnhildr disbelievingly.

'Yes. Beloved Gunnhildr. You. Come now, don't be shy. Step forward.'

The room grew silent quickly as people murmured, pointing out to each other how the corpulent Gunnhildr was struggling to swing her legs over the bench and get out of her place at the table. Lovric got up to help her and saw that Gunnhildr's brashness had vanished.

'And the children,' said Edward. 'Let them stand before me too, that we may see them clearly.'

Gunnhildr froze, but then she found her voice and called the two little boys, who came forward happily, mistaking this attention as a sign of kindness to come.

'I hear you dance well, Gunnhildr, and sing too.'

She shook her head in mute protest, but Edward clapped his hands and a flautist appeared, accompanied by a drummer. They started playing a fast dance that was almost a jig and Edward clapped along with them.

'Now dance, all three of you,' he said.

None of them knew any steps to such music, and Gunnhildr had to improvise and tell the boys what to do. In minutes they were stumbling and tripping her, while she pretended to smile and enjoy herself as she broke into a sweat and turned red.

'Enough!' the king announced. 'You disappoint me, Gunnhildr. You dance like a Russian bear. Try now to sing.'

Again the flautist started up, playing a well-known melody. Gunnhildr knew the words, but she had a voice that was quavering and off-key. By now the boys had seen people laughing at their mother and realized that they were being held up to ridicule. They snivelled copiously and Gunnhildr, still trying to sing, found herself having to wipe their noses with her own long sleeves. As the spectacle became agonizing, Godiva nudged Lovric questioningly.

'Leave her,' he whispered. 'It will stop soon.'

It did, but the torment only got worse for Gunnhildr. Edward clapped his hands again and the flautist stopped playing. From the far end of the hall a soldier blasted a single long note on a trumpet and all eyes turned in that direction, where stood a man, dishevelled and dirty, his hands bound. A gasp rose to the ceiling of the hall. The trumpeter hit the man on the side of his head and slowly, unable to walk properly, the captive stumbled forward towards Gunnhildr.

'What have you done to him?' Gunnhildr screamed.

'I had him questioned,' Edward answered blandly. 'Now tell my friends who this man is.'

'He is my cousin,' Gunnhildr said loudly, her fear chased away by outrage. 'You have dishonoured my family, king. This is not how free men are treated.'

'But this is how I treat traitors, free or not,' Edward replied. 'You conspired against me, Gunnhildr. Your kinsmen in Denmark were on their way here to try to take my throne.'

'That is not true,' she shouted back.

'There are men in this room who have heard your cousin's confession,' he answered. 'He leaves England tonight.' He nodded to the guards, who dragged the Dane away. 'But as for you, Gunnhildr, I may show mercy. You and your sons will forfeit your English lands of course, but you can stay here at court with me and my queen, as long as you can make some contribution. You could entertain us. It seems you have an unsuspected talent for making people laugh.'

Loud guffaws erupted in several parts of the room where Edward's most assiduous supporters sat. Others, out of pure inebriation, picked up the mirth, and soon the whole hall was laughing, pointing fingers at Gunnhildr, and some were laughing so hard they were taking to the pissing pots that sat under the table for late-night convenience. Gunnhildr turned round and stared at all of them in turn. For a moment she gained a dignity that no one had seen in her that evening. Then she started to walk down the length of the hall, her sons clinging to her gown, through wave after wave of increasingly obscene laughter.

So great was the noise that only those close to Edward heard him instruct his sergeant-at-arms, 'To Bruges with them at once, under guard, and with no servants at all, not even a maid. Let that woman do her own cooking and cleaning until she reaches Flanders. Make sure of that.'

Godiva turned to Lovric. 'I was sorry for her,' she said.

'I don't think she was guilty,' he whispered. 'He had no proof against her. That confession under torture meant nothing. Edward should have sent her away for a year and looked into her affairs. She was condemned through ridicule. That was not right.'

He shook his head and glanced round him. For all the noise in the hall there were others who were looking soberly round them too. Lovric caught the eye of one, a thegn of Siward's, and knew they were in agreement. In his treatment of Gunnhildr and her children, Edward had been dishonourable.

Dessert was now served, sweetmeats of many sorts, fruit and syrups, and nuts chopped in honey and eaten with little boat-shaped cakes made of crisp pastry. Godiva, however, had no appetite any more. Yet no one could leave the hall before the king, and so she sat there, making rather stilted conversation with Lovric.

Eventually Edward got up and declared that he would share a cup with each of his guests and then retire. He now progressed slowly round the table, starting from the far end of the hall, accompanied by three young monks who sang psalms and hymns in soft and doleful tones. Edith poured wine for the first time that night, and Edward, offering his cup to each guest, took a sip from the guest's own goblet and pronounced a blessing. Several minutes later the king and queen reached Lovric's place at the table. Edward smiled with pleasure at Godiva for so long that Lovric began to stir restlessly.

'My good earl, great lord of Mercia,' Edward intoned, 'how glad I am that you have kept your promise and brought your glorious lady to my city of Winchester. My lovely Godiva, welcome to my home.'

Edward now carefully exchanged cups with Lovric, whose strength was going into quelling the tremor in his sword arm. Then it was Godiva's turn. She steeled herself to smile politely at Edith, but the queen ignored her. Edward raised his goblet slightly so that Edith might add more wine. What happened next Godiva could not tell, for though she was staring into Edith's face and was sure the queen was concentrating and that her grasp was firm and steady, nevertheless, with a slight exclamation of surprise, Edith tipped out a large amount of red wine, spilling it so suddenly that the table was instantly awash in crimson and the middle of Godiva's dress was soaked in it.

Servants immediately appeared and began to undo the damage as well as they could, mopping around with linens and pitchers of water.

'It doesn't matter,' Godiva forced herself to say. 'My gown is dark; the stain will be faint and wear out.'

Edith, however, was on the attack at once. 'It was you!' she declared. 'You leaned forward and you jerked my arm. I saw you.'

Lovric, expecting Edward to side with Edith, braced himself for a difficult moment. But it was Edith who received an unpleasant surprise.

'Naughty girl!' Edward said, looking down from his great height.

'But...' she began.

'Naughty,' said Edward again, wagging his finger and looking at her with sadness, as though she were a promising pupil who had let down her devoted teacher. 'We will talk about this later, and how you shall make amends to me for spoiling my pretty dinner table. Off with you now. Go on! Bedtime!'

Taut with rage, Edith composed herself and walked out of the room with all possible speed, leaving Edward to give Godiva his complete attention.

'I shall properly compensate you for my wife's clumsiness,' he insisted, and then, within full view of Lovric, he lightly ran the back of his index finger along the wet patch on her dress, which sat clinging to her belly. Edward saw Lovric's knuckles whiten on the hilt of his sword and smiled with satisfaction. The evening had gone brilliantly. Now he would retire and take to his bed, though perhaps not before playing one more little game with Edith, something ordinary and simple tonight, like a light dessert after the rich meal he had just enjoyed so much.

He turned to go, and was surprised to hear Lovric address him. 'King,' he said, 'my wife and I must know soon about our son, Harry. Alfgar is now free. There can be no further need for a hostage. Harry…'

'Ah yes, freedom!' Edward sighed. 'That treasured word. That fool's gold. My good earl, freedom is a matter between God and man, not between men alone. Or women,' he added, smiling at Godiva. 'I will tell you about Harry in God's good time, cherished lady. And now, good earl, dear lady, goodnight. Goodnight to you all, my friends.'

And then he was gone, leaving Lovric and Godiva staring at each other and, over at the far side of the room, Siward's thegn, taking in the scene and guessing what had transpired. No release for young Harry. Fury amongst the earls. This is bad, and surely it is not going to get better. What mischief will the jester of England think of next? As Siward's thegn watched he saw Godiva turn towards him, caught the gleam of gold in her hair and around her long neck, and noticed how many other men were looking at her too, openly covetous no matter how powerful the man who stood at her side. It was obvious where Edward's interest would turn next. He left quickly to alert his lord with a coded message in Welsh addressed to Siward's master of ogham cryptograms: *llygaid y neidr ar nyth yr eryr. Siward gofalwch*; the snake's eyes are on the eagle's nest. Siward, beware.

Seven

'I can get most of the stain out,' Agatha insisted anxiously, fingering the wine-sodden gown. 'But the smell will linger unless I really scrub it, and then the dye would come off and leave you with a faded patch in the middle.'

Godiva said nothing.

'My mother would pull my hair if I did that,' Agatha chattered on, trying to ignore the silence that enveloped her mistress this morning. 'How could the queen be such a butterfingers? She don't want no practice in pouring wine, I'll warrant...'

'Just leave it,' Godiva said curtly. 'I won't need that dress again in Winchester.'

Agatha was too nervous to desist. 'But the smell will soak in and grow old and sour. Mould could grow in it. Mother always said...'

'Stop it, Agatha,' Godiva snapped. 'Leave me alone. I don't care about the dress.'

Agatha stared incredulously at Godiva, who was gazing out of the window. It was inconceivable that she would suddenly become indifferent to her black *godweb* feasting dress, the pride of her wardrobe and a gown of heirloom quality. The maid peered carefully from the corner of her eye at the side of her mistress's face. She lacked her usual glow this morning and her mouth had that downward, bitter droop at the corners that one saw so often in women of her age. Recent events had taken more of a toll on her than Agatha would have expected. She turned to hang the dress up to air near the window, breathing heavily as she struggled to hoist the heavy gown onto its hanger and lift it above her head.

'You seem tired today,' Godiva said.

Agatha, who felt perfectly well, looked at her in surprise. Her words were meant to be kind, she supposed, but her tone of voice continued to suggest annoyance.

'You've had a lot to do on this journey, child,' Godiva went on. 'Rest this afternoon. Borrow my bed and sleep there. The earl will not be back until early evening and I intend to go to the cathedral alone.'

Agatha gasped. 'But master says I must go with you everywhere.'

'And I say otherwise. Do as you are told, dear, and get some rest this afternoon.'

Agatha felt a surge of resentment. God only knew what trouble Godiva would land herself in, and this time Lovric would come down heavily on her maid, no matter what Godiva said now. Then, as Agatha pulled the curtain back from the bed, she noticed again how soft and inviting it was, compared to her own scratchy bundle of blankets. It would be very pleasant to have some time off and take a nap in this silky nest. Mistress could look after herself today, and good luck to her.

That afternoon Godiva stepped out onto the streets of Winchester on her own, and felt a sudden lifting of her spirits. The prospect of being free of Lovric's constant commands, Agatha's fussy ministrations and Godric's empty pieties, filled her with peace. On her own she seemed to have her wits about her again and felt confident that she would do better at avoiding mishaps than when others were at hand, distracting her with demands for cooperation, approval and the constant recognition of their presence. On her own, moreover, she felt detached from Lovric's political importance, and less of a magnet for whatever troubles his power might attract. For the first time in her life she really understood why so many wealthy women of her age, once they were widowed and released from the promises of marriage, dispensed with family life and put themselves in convents. Silence and contemplation. Peace, prayer and gardening.

From just around the corner a single bell, grave and finite, tolled the hour. *Tempus fugit*. But mortals do not fly or escape. Here on Earth they must labour forward, one foot ahead of the next, head down and hand on the plough. Daily life and the business of living it. No convent would open its doors to her for a long time to come – indeed never, unless she abandoned her plans for Coventry and the priory. Her only present hope of tranquillity lay in a couple of hours of solitude in a small obscure chapel, uninteresting to pilgrims and hidden in the depths of the glorious cathedral. Such a place must surely exist and the sooner she found it, the better. She pulled the light hood of her cloak round her face and started walking briskly down the street, dodging the lively traffic of royal servants, pilgrims, monks and vendors, and feeling with every step she took that her normal strength might soon return.

As she turned onto the main street, the wall of the cathedral precinct came into view, running alongside the street and forming a protective boundary round the sacred enclosure. Several carved archways offered entry into the precinct and Godiva went in through the most ornate of them, thinking it would lead directly towards the cathedral's west front and the entrance. Her assumption was shared by many others and soon she found herself being swept along by a thick stream of pilgrims, all reverential and awed, and all aiming at one place – the royal feretory of St Swithun, the gold and silver case provided by King Edgar to hold the saint's earthly remains. These now lay, following several removals and divisions amongst sister churches, in the apse behind the high altar, immediately beneath the throne of King Edward.

Cheek by jowl with young and old folk of all sorts, Godiva was soon struck by something that they had in common: few were healthy, and those that were fit were struggling with the care of invalids. There were crutches everywhere, tripping the sure-footed, and stained bandages were more abundant than good cloaks. Sighs, tears, lamentations and prayers for deliverance filled the air with a murmur too gentle for pain, but too persistent for comfort. Soon this mass of people would reach the feretory and here they would place the afflicted parts of their bodies as close to the holy bones as possible, inserting ulcerated feet and scabrous hands deep into the shrine, and pressing blind eyes and deaf ears against the golden cage. Desperate for this last chance to be healed, they pressed forward ever more insistently as they neared the massive west front of the cathedral and the main door into the nave.

Suddenly Godiva felt repelled by this tide of distress and its ineluctable drive towards its destination. She had not come to be healed, but to enjoy sacred beauty and divine peace. Pushing and struggling, excusing herself to old men who were trying to keep their place in the throng and to women fighting to hold on to fragile children, she worked her way sideways to break free of them and get on to the grass verge. Once there, she walked back a few paces until she stood alone, and then she stopped and raised her eyes. The reward for her effort – the vista of the precinct – now unfolded before her. To the left stood two churches and to the right what she guessed must be the royal palace. Directly before her rose the cathedral, now called the Old

Minster, and beyond that to its north stood the New Minster, whose enormous bell tower looked down over the entire enclosure. Behind both minsters she could see a part of the Nunnaminster, which was famous in Wessex and Mercia as a convent for princesses and queens, and to the south side of that stood the strong fortress of the bishop's castle.

Confused by the architectural riches of the precinct, Godiva focused her gaze on the Old Minster and its dazzling white stone frontage and towers. Unexpectedly, tears welled up in her eyes and sat there like offerings of gratitude for such astonishing beauty. In this cathedral, mute stone had been made to sing and dusty rock had been smoothed and shaped into a human paradise. How could the hands of mere men do this unless guided by the one divine hand that vivifies all things? Like many others before her who had stopped at the approach to the cathedral, Godiva was transfixed with joy. Minutes passed as she stood alone, her eyes following the lines of the cathedral eastwards towards the union of man and God at the High Altar, and upwards from that point towards the mystery of the heavens, whose stars and firmament, the doors of infinity, indicate that there, truly, lies the everlasting and only destiny of the human soul. Spontaneously she began to murmur the paternoster, and one or two people, seeing the beautiful woman wrapped in the love of God, crossed themselves as they passed near her.

Suddenly she stopped praying. Someone was coughing loudly behind her.

'Lady,' Father Godric began. 'Better to go inside to pray. I'll come with you.'

'No. I wish to be alone,' Godiva muttered in annoyance.

'Then I'll accompany you,' the chaplain said stubbornly. 'On your own you'll look like a holy one, a blessed pilgrim.'

Godiva raised her eyebrows, not understanding his meaning.

'You mustn't look too saintly in Queen Edith's city, lady.'

Godiva frowned, thinking how even Godric had more sense than she could muster in Winchester.

'Very well,' she agreed, and took his arm in the way she usually did as she walked round Coventry on those Sundays when Lovric was away from home.

Godric, for all his apparent lack of intellect, was an observant man. As they walked towards the cathedral's entrance he noticed two monks suddenly stop, confer and then turn off towards a small lane that seemed to lead to one side of the cathedral. One was memorably tall and the other short, and Godric was sure he had seen them watching Godiva at prayer, and talking to each other about her. That, in fact, was why he had approached her and persuaded her to go inside, for otherwise he would now be on his way to the other side of Winchester, to knock on the door of a woman of the town whose delightful acquaintance he was most anxious to renew. He stared at the monks until they disappeared from view through a side door into the cathedral, and thus engrossed he was taken aback and affronted when he realized that Godiva had stopped to acknowledge someone else. He turned to face the intruder and the other man turned towards him. It was Bret. He smiled at Godric, nodded his head politely, and then addressed Godiva as though her chaplain had vanished from the face of the Earth.

'My lady, good day,' said Bret, doffing his hat gracefully.

He had stepped forward from a group of young soldiers to greet Godiva. They now stared at her boldly, each one registering the emergence of a pale-pink blush that spread up her neck, delicately at first, and then proceeded to paint her cheeks a vivid, incriminating scarlet. Not since he sang his duet in the forest with Lovric had Godric resented Bret so much. This time he wanted to kill the man.

'Good sir!' Godiva replied, too taken aback to make appropriate conversation.

'May I offer you my protection to the door of the cathedral?' Bret responded with complete composure, ignoring Godiva's embarrassment.

'Not necessary!' Godric interrupted.

'Yes, of course,' Godiva replied, and at that Bret took Godric's place at Godiva's right side, leaving the chaplain to walk before them, swinging his staff angrily and repeating *maledictus est* to himself in a low growl.

Bret did not take Godiva's arm as her priest was permitted to. He merely walked so close to her side that his arm brushed against hers. The group of soldiers who had been with him now found their voices again and could be heard talking loudly, joking and occasionally laughing. Godric turned to glare at them, and for the first time noticed that they all wore over their chain-mail armour a white tunic emblazoned with the motif of a red cross. Devotees of St George, the patron saint of professional, mercenary soldiers, he knew, and wondered what they might be doing so far south as Winchester. He scowled at them and from their sudden silence knew they had been commenting on Godiva and her huntsman.

'How do you find Winchester?' Godiva asked Bret, keeping her eyes away from his.

'Well, lady,' Bret answered. 'I have made my donation at the shrine of St Swithun and heard the sound of a great organ for the first time. It is just as men describe it – a sound that seems to have come from the days of the creation of the world. But still, all your men of Coventry look forward to going home. There's nothing like a summer's day in the forest.'

'Yes. I look forward to that, too,' she replied as naturally as she could. 'I must come to the hunting lodge by the West Orchard and inspect our bridle paths. It's a long time since I did that. Who is there now?'

'John, the chief forester. My lodge is deeper in the forest.'

'I see,' she said, unable to think what else to say about the forest and thereby put off parting from Bret.

Sensing he was about to be dismissed, he dropped to one knee in the new Norman fashion and took hold of her hand and kissed it. To everyone watching it looked like a normal gesture of politeness – formal, stylised and elegant when performed by a man as lithe as Bret. But to Godiva it was no such thing. It was the first time she had felt his lips. It was a disastrous kiss, a catastrophe of skin and nerves, blood and heart. She might as well have been standing naked at the cathedral steps for all that she could prevent the world from seeing what she was feeling. Her heart was throbbing in her throat and not a single syllable of sense came out of her mouth.

Godric sprang to her rescue. 'Off with you now, good sir,' he said gruffly. 'Mistress needs to be at her prayers. And then she must hurry back to your master, Earl Lovric.'

Bret gave Godric a courteous little nod of acknowledgement, relieved that the chaplain had not been more openly rude, and walked off. As he went, Godiva's eyes followed him, unable to prevent herself from imagining his body beneath his clothing to be supple, smooth and strong, and longing so much to feel his kiss again that even his slight list seemed to be part of the essence of what made him magical. Suddenly, as she still watched, Bret stopped, accosted by an old monk. They talked only briefly, as though the monk were a pilgrim asking for directions, and then Bret disappeared, leaving Godiva feeling that the life had drained out of her.

'Well, lady, unless you wish me to pray with you, I will leave you now,' Godric said, in frosty tones such as Godiva had never heard from the placid priest before. Godiva ignored him. She had done nothing wrong and he could think what he liked, sinful fellow that he was.

'Good priest,' she replied tartly. 'I will pray alone, for both of

us.' Then she disappeared into the shadows of the vestibule at the mouth of the cathedral.

But her hopes for peace and solitude were dashed when she entered the nave. First it was the low buzz of prayer and conversation that she noticed, and the scudding and dragging of many feet and robes in motion, but then, as her eyes grew accustomed to the dim light, she saw them: the masses of sick pilgrims who had come in from the precinct, and with them, keeping them in order, the cathedral canons, deacons, vergers and others who worked here, and the many monks whose home was in the cloisters and the Benedictine city attached to the cathedral. These people, filling the nave and in constant motion, made it look more like a place of business than a retreat for tired souls seeking solace. This was what it meant to have a successful saint's cult in a big cathedral – indeed, this is how she would like Coventry to become one day, though inevitably on a smaller scale. Peace and prayer, she realized, would not be found here, in the central part of the cathedral, but off in some remote recess at the side.

Godiva therefore left the nave and started walking under the low pointed arches of one of the aisles. But even this was congested and she found herself moving forward in what seemed like a procession, though where it was going was hard to tell. Chapels opened up all along the aisle, offering the opportunity to make devotions to a favourite saint, but every one of them seemed as full as the aisle itself. Here and there she glimpsed plaques set into the stone slabs of the floor, and nearby the solemn carved sarcophagus of some royal or episcopal person – members of the ruling line of the West Saxon royal house, she knew, and also, because they had accepted Christ, Canute and other recent Danish kings.

Suddenly she found she was alongside the Lady Chapel, the main chapel for the veneration of the Virgin. This was not behind the high altar as it usually was, and so, surprised and pleased, she pushed her way in amongst the crowd that was jostling to buy tapers and to kneel briefly on the hard floor and pray. As she worked her way towards the altar, a small side-entrance came into view. Through this she could see another chapel, which seemed from its tapestry depicting the crucifixion to be for the veneration of Mary, Mother of Sorrows. This, she knew, was where she wanted to be, praying to the *mater dolorosa* on behalf of her beloved young son. But a locked and gilded gate barred the entrance and Godiva had to content herself with standing beside it and murmuring *Ave Maria* as others elbowed past, determined to place a lighted incense stick before the altar of Mary in Glory.

Her eyes were shut and so she did not see who opened the gilded gate. All she knew was that a voice whispered that if she wanted to come in, she should enter quickly so that the gate could be shut behind her at once. The speaker, in black robes, presented only his back to her view and then he was gone. As Godiva stepped forward into the chapel she found she had entered a treasury of jewel-encrusted silver altar plate, silk-woven tapestries, thick gold candlesticks and intricately carved wood. Some incense she had never encountered before – a compound of frankincense and rose, she thought – suffused the air and added to the atmosphere of heavenly richness. Entranced, she stared straight at the main altar for a few minutes, and only after saying another prayer did she become aware that yet another chapel lay behind the altar of Mary of Sorrows. And from there came the sound of music. Someone, it seemed, was playing very softly on a small organ, a miniature of the huge instrument that had recently been installed beside the cathedral's high altar. The faintness of the melody seemed like a plea for privacy, a demand for solitude at prayer and contemplation, and answered to her needs perfectly. Despite the mysteriousness of the labyrinth of chapels, and the gate that was now locked behind her, she stepped

forward without hesitation, drawn hypnotically on by the music
into the peace that it seemed to promise.

Inside it was almost completely dark. The music was coming
from behind another door, which was shut, and through small
cracks in it came faint glimmers of light. Godiva looked around
and found it impossible to tell what kind of chapel this might be.
It could have been devotional, with an altar to one of the lesser-
known aspects of the Virgin or her mother; or it could have been
a chantry, where mass was offered for the soul of a rich donor;
but it seemed so small and secluded that it might even be a
confessional. She groped around and found what seemed to be
a pew, a very small one that would hold only three or four people.
Then she sat down, closed her eyes and let the music carry her
away.

It seemed that this heavenly interlude lasted for a long time,
though perhaps it was no more than five minutes. Then, rather as
one smells rain even before the sky clouds over, she became
aware of a presence somewhere in the dark behind her. The
realization stole upon her for no apparent reason, for whoever
might be there was utterly still and silent. And yet, once aware of
the presence, she could no longer hear the music, or retain any
sense of the peace that had so gently embraced her since she had
entered this secluded chamber. It had gone completely, as though
she had never felt it, and in its place came an engulfing fear that
began to suck the air from the room. She turned abruptly and
surprised herself by calling out loudly, 'Who is there?' The only
answer was a deep sigh from the darkest corner of the room.

The door to the organ room opened and Godiva spun round
in the pew. The organ was surrounded by dozens of candles and
the room was filled with a light softer than daylight but almost
as strong. Against this backdrop a short monk appeared in black
silhouette, his arms stretched before him and holding aloft a big,
ornate crucifix that Godiva knew she had seen before. The monk,

she realized, was the man who was with the king in prison, when Alfgar had been there. According to Alfgar, he was known as Father Francis, the king's secret confessor. Others called him the Saxon traitor-priest.

'Godiva.'

The voice seemed to come from behind the monk, who was still standing motionless at the threshold to the little room, still holding the crucifix aloft. Godiva stared so hard at the organ room, trying to discover who had called to her, that she barely noticed, low on the floor at the monk's feet, something that appeared to be little more than a bundle of black cloth. Then this obscure figure spoke to her.

'Come here, my child. Come and pray with me.'

A long white hand reached up to her, its jewelled fingers glistening in the candle light.

'Come down on the floor and pray with me in the dust of which we are all made, and to which we so quickly return.'

'Your majesty!' she whispered, unable to move.

'Not majesty, except on Earth, but your brother in Christ eternal. Come, Godiva.'

As she approached hesitantly, he signalled with his hand for her to fall to her knees beside him. Edward then began to say the Lord's Prayer. Godiva accompanied him, but her thoughts were not on prayer at all, though that is what she had longed for and in just such a place as this. But not like this; not in fear. Not one godly thought occupied her mind: all she could think of was whether she could find her way back through the maze of chapels and side-chapels and get out quickly into the daylight and the streets of the town.

But this was not to be, for no sooner had Edward reached the end of the prayer in Latin than he began it again in English. '*Faeder ure, ddu dde eart on heofonum,*' he prayed as slowly as possible, drawing out each word as though to emphasize the

purity of his Saxon enunciation, notwithstanding his many Norman manners and habits. While this was going on, the deacon
who had played the organ came into the room and started to
drape the monk, Father Francis, in a long white chasuble, over
which he placed the richest stole that Godiva had ever seen
round a priest's neck. Then he hurried around at the altar, placing
on it with great care the chalice for the wine and the pyx for the
consecrated bread.

With a shock, Godiva realized they were going to celebrate a
mass. She groaned inwardly. She had only wanted to sit and pray,
'Veni, Sancte Spiritus' and then contemplate a holy image. That was
what she did in Coventry and it was what she liked most. But
now she was faced with the immensely long mass, only fragments
of which she could translate into English and even less of which
she understood theologically. Worse still, it was obviously going
to be a low mass, lacking music, and there would be nothing to
listen to but the voices of the monk and his server, droning on
unintelligibly for well over an hour. But she was trapped, and
would have to make a good show of gratitude for what everyone
would say was an extraordinary honour – a private mass with the
king.

As the service began Father Francis and the server, who were
busy declaring the celebrants' desire to approach the altar of God,
had their backs turned to Edward and Godiva. The king took this
opportunity to settle with her in the small pew, placing a kneeling
cushion before her, and encouraging her with smiles and nods to
be seated. Not wishing to offend, she took the cushion and then
her seat beside the king. Edward gave a long sigh and Godiva
turned to try to smile politely at him, only to find that the king's
often snide countenance was quite transformed. A kindly warmth
had descended on him, seeming to lift his brows, pulling all the
muscles into place and imparting to his face an appearance of
composure, blended curiously with extreme youth. To Godiva he

looked like a boy who has suddenly been made happy after some episode of bitter misery. For just a second she felt like reassuring him about whatever had saddened him. But then, perplexed, she thought better of it. She looked back at the monk and the server and, noticing they had now begun the general confession of sins, decided she would concentrate on the mass and try to ignore Edward. But that soon proved impossible, for at every mention of sins and sinners, of *delicta* and *pecatores*, Edward gave one of his sighs – sighs of contentment, it seemed, or satisfaction – and then, rather shockingly, thought Godiva, when they came to the *kyrie*, Edward joined in himself, beseeching the Father and the Son for mercy in tones that suggested relish rather than remorse.

After this, though, he fell silent, for the following sections of the mass, the Gloria and the Nicene Creed, were about praise and dogma, and made little mention of sin at all. She glanced sideways at him and thought that he seemed as bored as she was. More surprisingly, he did not react strongly to what came afterwards – the offering of the wine and the bread, with all the sacred words that went with that. This was the one part of the mass that Godiva fully appreciated, for this was the 'sacrifice' that would give her eternal and purified life after death. How or why, she was unsure, but it was enough to believe in this promise, the most amazing gift that anyone could offer.

Her spirits continued to rise as the service moved towards the Marian prayers that brought low mass to its unsung end. First came *Ave Maria*, followed at once by the even lovelier *Salve Regina*, to Godiva's mind the perfect prayer: '*mother of mercy, our life, our sweetness and our hope! To thee we cry, poor banished children of Eve, to thee do we send up our sighs, mourning and weeping in this valley of tears.*' Though she had prayed to Freya and the Great Goddess to conceive, it was to the Virgin with this prayer that she had turned when one of her children failed to survive his birth. She knew too that this would be the prayer she would say at her husband's death-bed and on her own. But Edward was not much moved by this, the climax of the end of the mass. It was over now and he got to his feet as Father Francis and the server cleared away the mass vessels and departed. Godiva tidied her cloak and wondered what she should say in parting. Edward, however, seemed in no hurry to let her go. He looked down at her with utmost tenderness, kissed the side of her cheek and took her hand.

'Dear, beloved lady,' he said softly and earnestly. 'How long I have waited for the opportunity to share the sacrifice of the mass with you, and to feel the sin lift for a moment from your beautiful shoulders. To have you with me, here in Winchester at last, is more than I had hoped for. I asked your husband two years ago to bring you here, but he refused. You may have noticed that I was not happy at the time of the investiture of your priory. You did notice, didn't you?'

Godiva, surprised at this explanation, nodded mutely.

'You see, the occasion was spoiled for me. Your achievement in bringing a Benedictine priory to a dark and wooded corner of my realm – I was moved, I was impressed, I wanted to embrace you. But I knew too that you needed to be shriven, as we all do – purified of your sin at a place where the Holy Spirit is at its strongest. You needed to receive the blessed sacrament here at Winchester in the aura of St Swithun. And your man,' he spat out the word contemptuously, 'forbade it. Yet, now, he has yielded. The Lord works wonders.'

'He ... we ... yielded because we were worried about our children, sire,' Godiva said, more bluntly than she intended. 'You had them in your possession. We came here to try to get them out of prison. We remain here, as you know, still waiting to learn about Harry.'

'Have no fears about Harry,' Edward replied. 'He is well. It is the prison of the sick soul you must worry about, Godiva.' As

Edward spoke, his finger caressed the back of her neck like a loose feather falling to Earth.

Godiva shuddered. 'My soul, and the souls of my family – we are not especially sick, sire,' she said. 'We pray, give alms to the poor, make confession. When we sin, we acknowledge it and repent.'

'You are wrong, beloved,' Edward said passionately. 'Sin is inherent. It is a stain that is never washed away. It is the animal that rises within us, strong and hearty, night and day, wanting to kill, eat, despoil, defile and, above all else, propagate its own kind. The mass only averts God's anger and God's loathing of us. Christ's death on the cross was terrible because God's revulsion at us is so immense. So do not make the mistake of thinking that when you have taken communion, you are truly cleansed. You remain in your animal filth, though you have won God's pardon for a short while after the mass, because you have participated in the sacrifice of His son by eating of His purifying body and drinking His cleansing blood.'

'I see,' said Godiva, suddenly dejected. 'It appears, then, that I have been mistaken, sire. For years, I found praying and contemplation and the giving of alms to be good and purifying.'

'I know,' said Edward pityingly. 'Some accused you of worldly ambition when you built your new priory, but I always said it was spiritual, not worldly, pride that was your fault. You think you are good. You think you understand God's ways. But you do not. You have a long road ahead of you, Godiva, before God will be able to bear to look at you in your vile nakedness.'

Godiva, though never afflicted by a weak stomach, felt a tide of acid rise suddenly in her throat. She put her chin down into her neck, breathed deeply and studied her feet in their small black shoes. Memories of rapture while contemplating the Virgin's boundless kindness came back to her. She had been so sure, all her life, that this was the heart of her religion, and that it was pure, strong and real. Had she been deluded, then? Was the God whose immaculate conception filled Mary's womb with everlasting joy not really a loving God at all, but a furious deity who had to be appeased with token blood and flesh, a scornful hater of the poor, pain-racked creatures called men that He himself had made, those imperfect angels whom He exposed to temptation and then let fall to Earth and death and damnation? She did not understand this at all. But she felt sure of one thing: the king was determined that sooner or later, one way or another, he would bring her to understand God in the way that he did, and in no other way. To his mind, this would be an act of love on his part. And she herself had seen a hidden part of his soul, a warm and remote recess where it was possible that love did really dwell in hiding.

She raised her head and glanced at him. The tenderness in his eyes was unmistakable. It was radiant, even saintly. What was she to think? That Edward was the cruel joker described by Godwin in such an agony of shame that there could be no doubting his sincerity? Or that Edward was in fact holy, self-sacrificing and totally misunderstood by the earls? Many others thought so. And yet, in the mere second that their eyes met and a question came to her lips, some swift change came about and his customary mocking expression was back in place. Her blood ran cold and she stepped away in case he tried to touch her once more with that insinuating, pointed finger of his.

'It is getting late, sire,' she said hesitantly, afraid of affronting him. 'My lord Lovric will be expecting me...'

Just then the cathedral bells interrupted, the eight chimes pealing all together to announce the arrival of one of the most important of the canonical hours: the eighteenth hour of the summer evening and the holy office of Vespers.

'You cannot leave now,' Edward said. 'Let us go and stand together in the nave and watch the cathedral choir, with the monks and the priests, perform the solemn rites of the ending of the light of day.'

Obviously, she had to stay. She heard the huge cathedral organ start up and braced herself to enter the nave with Edward. There, side by side, they would await Vespers and the coming of the dark.

Eight

A throne had been built for Edward behind the back of the high altar, a throne from which he could be seen by everyone in the cathedral, even during the most sacred moment of the mass when the priest said the secret prayer. But Edward did not ascend his throne. Instead he remained beside Godiva in the shadows under the arches of an aisle, about halfway down the nave.

Winchester cathedral had drained of people, for the vergers and deacons had swept out the pilgrims and the sickly devotees of St Swithun's bones, and only a few hardy faithful were left who were prepared to stand through the twelve psalms and the various prayers and short allusions that made up Vespers. Perhaps, Godiva reflected, Edward had not ascended his throne because there was little dignity in presiding over so small an audience in such a vast, empty space. Thank God for the organ, she thought. It filled the cavernous church with a great volume of sound, reverberating on the lower registers like storms in the black of the night of the first day, then rising like choirs of cherubim to the realms of the tiny twittering birds, created late on the evening when God turned his hand to flight and feathers. She stood there, entranced by the music and wishing she could own an organ and learn to play it, and waiting for what would happen next. At her side stood Edward, still as a stone, and also waiting.

Suddenly the music stopped and in the startling silence that followed a bell rang out, shrill and commanding. Then the organ let out a great boom and the processional music began. It was rude to turn and stare at the clergy at this point. Godiva looked straight ahead as they passed alongside her, lurching with importance as they always did, whether in royal cathedrals or in her own modest priory. She could only see the sides of their heads and bodies, but it was enough to take her breath away, for they were so numerous and resplendent. First came the bishop himself, Alfwold of Sherborne, newly consecrated as bishop and thin as a saint due to his famous frugality, but adorned in the richest of robes. After him came his archdeacon and the rest of the canons, all solemn, ageing monks. There then followed, after a meaningful interval, the minor orders – the door-keepers, lectors, sexton, exorcists and acolytes. Next came the choir, led by their master. Its members ranged in size from tall, fully grown men down to the small boys whose delicate, pure voices were so prized in churches everywhere. Straggling after these came a sizeable group of male catechumens, seeking baptism for the first time. Godiva thought they looked Danish, so broad of face and thick of leg were they all. And finally, at the tail end, there came shuffling a small number of penitents who had confessed to such deadly sins that before they could be readmitted to communion they needed to pray, fast and endure whatever else the bishop specified, and then get baptised all over again. Godiva stared curiously after them, but from where she was standing she couldn't tell anything about them, not even their ages, for they had recently been shaved in the style of the Roman tonsure and now looked like middle-aged men who were naturally balding at the crown. All four wore ash-white woolly robes of coarse, untreated wool, and all walked unshod on the cold tiled floor. One also dragged behind him a blood-stained piece of rope.

The whole procession came to a halt before the altar, and each section distributed itself to its proper place as the choir began to sing the Psalms of Vespers and the clergy prepared for the Office. Then the tall, sun-whitened, beeswax tapers and thick yellow candles were lit, casting light into corners of darkness and throwing shadows across hitherto plain surfaces. The cathedral, transformed for the passage of the night hours, had taken on an aura of new and even denser mystery.

Eventually, after what seemed like hours to Godiva, the service of Vespers drew to an end and Edward came out of the trance that had gripped him throughout. He bent down to whisper to Godiva, 'The day that God gave us has ended and has been blessed. The walls have gone up against the demons of the night. Are you not glad, beloved sister?'

'Yes,' she replied uncertainly. The lighting of the candles had reminded her of hearth and family. She wanted to get back to the hostelry and talk to Agatha again about the stain on the dress, and she wanted to dine with Lovric and listen to his tales of charters and land-grants, envy, greed and plotting.

'Then remember the gladness of this moment,' Edward said obscurely.

The music for the exit procession gathered momentum and the whole assembly of those who had performed the Office of Vespers now began to move slowly away from the altar, down the nave and towards the western doors of the cathedral. Godiva, able to see their faces for the first time, stared with unabashed interest at them all in turn, until, their heads hanging down and displaying their shining pates, there came the four penitents, shuffling their numbed bare feet and scratching wherever the raw wool robes chafed. They looked poverty-stricken, footsore and cringing, the beauty of their hair destroyed and all pride gone.

At the moment when they came alongside Edward, the king put out his hand and touched the shoulder of one. He gave a nervous start and, on seeing the king, signed the cross and dropped to his knees. Godiva looked on, feeling sorry for him and wondering what offence he had committed.

'Rise, poor sinner,' said Edward. Then, giving Godiva one of his smiles of melting sympathy, he took her hand and placed it in the hand of the penitent.

'My son, I give you the power to bless this woman,' Edward said.

For the first time the penitent looked at the woman who stood beside the king, and then he snatched back his hand in horror.

'Holy Mary, she is my earthly mother!' he gasped. 'Godiva, why are you here?'

'Harry?' Choking, she turned on the king. 'What have you done to him?' she shouted.

'Hush! Good lady, stay quiet. We are in God's house,' Edward protested.

'Look at him!' she carried on in a frantic whisper. 'You have degraded him. He cannot hold his head up and look me in the eye. I'm going to need answers about this. You were supposed to return him to us once you freed Alfgar.'

Edward nodded sympathetically. 'But he is free to return to you, are you not, Harry?'

'Yes, I am free to go,' Harry answered. 'But I have chosen to stay here. I will take holy orders, mother.'

'No, you won't,' Godiva hissed.

Harry looked at the king, hoping for guidance.

'You should talk alone to each other,' he said. 'Harry, your mother needs to understand your decision. And you will need her blessing, though you do not need her legal consent.' He turned towards a deacon who was hovering nearby. 'Lead this lady and this boy to the vestry and see that they are left alone.' Then he turned back to Godiva. 'It is well that you found out here and now what Harry has decided. The sooner he is able to begin his vocation, the better. And the sooner you know the truth, the better for the health of your soul and the peace of your mind – about which I care deeply, beloved sister.'

A hundred questions flooded Godiva's mind, but she stood there speechless until, after a moment of silence, Edward left.

A little later Godiva and Harry sat facing each other in a comfortable, candle-lit room within the vestry. The doors were shut and the organ music could scarcely be heard. They were alone, it seemed.

'Harry,' she began tenderly. 'Tell me what this means. Why are you doing penance?'

'So that I can be baptised again. At Easter.' His voice was tight with the difficulty of talking.

'But that is more than half a year from now!' she protested gently. 'What could you have done to earn such a long period of penitence?' She looked at him searchingly. 'You have done something bad, I assume. But if you can tell the monks of Winchester, you can tell your own mother.'

He lifted his head and gazed at her with such despair in his reddening eyes that she wanted to throw her arms round him like a cloak against a cold wind. But he had been away from her too long for such an embrace.

'You must tell me, son. Someone will tell your father soon, and then I'll find out anyway.'

This time Harry gave a wan smile and for a moment something like derision seemed present in his eyes.

Godiva struggled to retain her composure. 'Well,' she said, 'if you cannot tell me yet what your fault is, at least tell me what penance the bishop imposed on you. I saw another of the penitents dragging a rope. It had blood on it.'

'Yes. He committed rape on a child. He was flogged this afternoon, even though he is of noble birth.'

'And you?' she whispered.

'My only penance is prayer and fasting. No more than the daily routine of the monks.'

'Your sins can't be very serious then,' she said, trying to sound hopeful. Harry didn't reply. Godiva repeated her words. Still he said nothing, but hung his head very low. Suddenly she realized his shoulders were shaking and tears were falling on to his hands. The distance between them fell away at once and Godiva sank to the floor before him, lifted his hands and kissed them, and then took his face and kissed his wet cheeks.

'My darling,' she whispered, 'what in God's name have they done to you?'

'Edmund's gone,' he said at last, his face twisted with grief.

She waited for the gusts of sorrow to die down before asking more questions.

'Who is Edmund?' she began. Then, before he answered, she realized who he was. 'Your page. That's who he is, am I right?'

Harry looked at her curiously.

'I saw you together from an upstairs window,' she said. 'You were on horseback and he held the reins in the yard outside Wiglaf's hall in Oxford. He is a beautiful boy, like you.'

He started to cry again. 'They've sent him away forever. I may never see him again or hold his hand. He has to do penance for a year in Northumbria. And because he is not noble, they've already flogged him, in the prison in Winchester.'

'Not noble? But the boy I saw was one of your foster-brothers, one of Siward's sons. Wasn't he?'

'No. He is a churl, a poor farmer's son.'

'But what is his crime? Why a flogging for this boy?'

'For Christ's sake, mother, can't you guess? Look at me. Why am I so sad? Because I lost a friend? Just a friend?'

Slowly, like a mist stealing across a field and changing the appearance of everything, making sheep look big as ponies and trees vanish, it dawned on Godiva what Harry meant. Instinctively she pulled her hand away, and then immediately tried to put it back, but he refused her touch.

'Harry, tell me in plain words,' she said.

'I love Edmund. I love him as other men love women. That's all there is to say.'

The silence that sat between them was immense, a vast icefield over which nothing living moved and no horizon came in to view. Godiva did not know what to say. Harry got to his feet.

'I think you should go now, mother,' he said.

'Harry,' she whispered, 'I love you. You are my son. Nothing will change that.'

'I know, mother,' he replied gently, but with a new dryness in his voice. 'But your love will only help you, not me. I have to face my life as it is. There is nothing you can do for me.'

He started towards the vestry door, but Godiva, in panic, threw herself at him and seized his arm.

'Stay longer,' she pleaded. 'Let us talk more. We could talk about your vocation as a monk, if that's what you want. Or we could talk about Edmund. One day I would like to meet him. Anyone who loves you will be loved by me...'

He looked at her with what seemed like contempt. 'Mother, you don't know what you're talking about. My life won't be as you expected, coming to visit you at the family hearth, bringing family and friends with me...'

'Why not? It could be, I'm sure,' she trailed off in desperation, her longing outrunning her command of words. 'I'll talk to your father. I'll explain. He's sure to understand such things...'

But Harry stood by the door now, opening it. 'Father...' he began, and then he too ran out of words. And once again a faint look of derision and pity crossed his face.

Godiva left the cathedral without anyone seeming to notice. The king had disappeared and so had the most important priests and deacons. She supposed they were all busy now in the monkish city that sprang from one side of the cathedral, the labyrinth of Benedictine buildings that housed, fed and employed the multitude of monks amongst whom her son was now a citizen of the lowest rank – but yet a citizen. It was a whole world, able to swallow any man or boy, erasing his past and defining his future.

The long summer's day was dwindling into twilight as she made her way towards the hostelry. She wondered how she would tell Lovric and how he would react. Would he be disgusted, fearful and angry, or sad and compassionate? She had no idea, for love between men was not something they had ever discussed.

Deep in thought she turned a corner, and then came to an abrupt stop. Further down the street, his back turned to her, stood her husband, talking to a well-dressed woman and her maid. Godiva, not wishing to start explaining anything to Lovric until they were alone and in private, was about to go back and find another way to the hostelry, when the woman called out, 'Farewell, Lovric' and started to walk towards Godiva. Lovric turned round. Inevitably he saw his wife, and both women saw each other. It was Estrith, the tall, pretty woman, the one who had spoken to him beside the inn so recently, the one who took the Bishop of Jumièges to her bed. She smiled at Godiva, wished her good evening, and vanished.

'What are you doing out on your own at this hour, Godiva?' Lovric asked.

'I should think you are the one with a question to answer,' she whispered.

'That woman, you've met her already,' he replied without hesitation. 'If you must know, her husband once served with me in Gloucester. I've known her for years.'

'And is she a widow now? A bishop's whore, with some free time to pass with old friends?'

'Eva, you've no right,' Lovric sighed. 'Estrith is not my mistress, and she is not a whore. She was giving me news, that was all. You are the only woman I love. You know that. I know you do.'

But he said it irritably, and his words made no impression on her. She was on the point of saying that nothing would surprise her any more, but that would only lead on to the subject they had to discuss with great care, as soon as possible.

'Very well,' she said. 'We will say no more about Estrith – or any other such woman.'

He ignored the barb, and ignored too the utter coldness of her manner. Clearly she had been out on some business, and that was what he needed to hear about, not angry reprimands about an old love affair that had died out many years ago and which he would never, ever reveal to his wife.

In the hostelry Agatha had swept and tidied up the chamber used by Godiva and Lovric, lit candles and put fresh wood on the fire. A pitcher of wine and another of beer stood on a table near a low bench, where there were also tankards, wine glasses and a large dish of meat pasties. Though it was late, they would have a pleasant evening tonight, she thought, and get over all the fretting of the past few days. But as soon as she heard their voices on the stairs she knew it would not be like that, and she banished herself with the merest curtsy.

'Well?' Lovric asked Godiva.

'I went to pray, in the cathedral.'

'Alone? Godiva, you promised me you would not go out alone.'

'Father Godric accompanied me to the west wall. Then, inside, I was alone. People do pray alone, you know.'

'Then why are you so late?'

'The king delayed me.'

Lovric groaned. 'That is why I told you to stay in the hostelry. And you agreed. I told you, you can go out with me whenever you want to.'

'A church is different.'

'Obviously it is not. There was Edward, waiting for you, just as I feared.'

'No, he stumbled upon me...'

'Don't be ridiculous, Godiva. The cathedral is his headquarters. Every priest and servant is a spy, or a guard with a weapon under his robes.'

'Then why didn't you say so? It was the last thing I would expect in a holy place.'

Lovric felt again his frustration with Godiva, and then with himself. He wanted total compliance from her – and for very good reasons – and she was not capable of giving it. For better or worse, she was her own woman, and getting more so with every month she spent working on her plans in Coventry.

'You'd better tell me what else you have to say about this meeting,' he said testily.

'I met Harry in the cathedral.'

'Oh God, no.'

'Yes. I met him in the cathedral, at Vespers. Lovric, he was wearing ashen wool, penitential robes.'

Lovric slumped forward, put his head in his hands and signalled to her to tell him everything.

'And so,' she concluded several painful minutes later, 'the reason for all this – for the penance, for Harry's wish to take vows as a monk – is love between men. I don't understand. I thought it was something that takes place between little boys, and sometimes carries on when a man is too ugly or timid to get a woman's love. I thought it was a joke – not something that can ruin a strong young man's life. Harry will be lost to us. He will take vows and live in a monastery somewhere and never have children.'

Lovric finally sat up and looked her in the face. 'Eva, it did not have to be like this for Harry. If Edward had not interfered, if he had not demanded that Harry be brought to Winchester and turned over to the bishop, then the boy could have remained as he was in Siward's household. He could have had the life of a warrior, with honour, lands, respect, even a family one day, and he could have kept Edmund at his side...'

'Edmund?' she cut across him. 'How did you know his lover's name? I didn't mention it. I know I didn't.'

Lovric paused, looked away and then went on reluctantly. 'Siward told me three years ago that Harry seemed to fall in love with certain men. With my consent he arranged for him to meet a suitable companion. The two boys are now devoted. They have grown together as young soldiers. They conduct themselves decently and neither intrudes on other men's lives. No one despises them. This could have gone on until the relationship came to a natural end.'

'And I need never have known. Is that what you are saying, Lovric?' Godiva almost spat at him.

'I thought it better.'

'I am his mother! You had no right to deceive me.'

'But you might have taken it badly. Many parents do. There was no point in disturbing your peace of mind.'

'You don't trust me. You do not even know me any more,' she shouted. 'How could you even imagine that I would love him less? You say "many parents do", but I am not just any parent. I am your wife, and you know me. Then obviously you judge me to be weak and unreliable.'

'Mothers and sons...' he began, and then he stopped. 'I'm sorry,' he said miserably. 'You know me, Eva. You know I have grown used to keeping a great many things to myself. When I am in dangerous parts of the country I make decisions on my own. I have to. I am a commander. It is simply my habit now. But you are right that I should have talked with you about Harry. I'm sorry. Will you forgive me?'

Yes, she thought, but what about that woman, Estrith? She hadn't been trusted with the whole truth about her, she was sure of that. And then there was the matter of this visit to see the king: Lovric had not told her, at least not until they were already on their way to Winchester, that Edward had demanded her presence. Now he was apologizing for past acts of subterfuge while no doubt continuing to deceive.

'Will you forgive me?' he repeated.

'Will you stop keeping secrets from me?'

'I'll try,' he said, but even he knew his promise sounded hollow.

He got up and paced the floor. Godiva expected that when next he spoke he would sound decisive and look relieved. His mind would be racing ahead towards doing something, instead of dwelling on what lay between them – this sudden chasm of disillusionment in which small flowers of hatred were already seeding and waiting for a chance to bloom.

Godiva's mind was moving quickly too, but backwards, towards the memory of Adel, the little wife of Oxford, with her rich clothes, bruised cheek and ruined love. She shuddered, and then she pulled herself together. She would not harbour these resentments against Lovric. She would force herself, through sheer willpower, to hold on to her faith in him, the faith that had sustained her for years during his long, dreary absences.

'Lovric,' she said. 'I will forgive you. It is being here in Winchester that causes friction between us. Let us go home now. The king has had me in his presence, as he wished, and made me witness both my sons' humiliation. And I too have been humiliated in this horrible town. He must have had his fill of tormenting me by now.'

He threw his arms around her and kissed her thankfully. 'Yes,' he agreed, 'this place is unlucky for us. I am forced to ignore Edward's provocations, but it grows harder with each incident. Before anything else can happen you should go home at full speed.'

'Me? I should go home? Alone? I meant that we would go back together. That is what I meant, and I thought you did too.'

'There are a few more charters that we must debate.'

'No, Lovric! Come home with me. It's been a shock to learn about Harry. And I'm worried about what I'll have to face in Coventry. I would like your help when I get home, and I'd like to be comforted for once. You're never there with me when there's trouble...'

'But, Eva, be reasonable.'

'When I asked you to be reasonable, were you? No. You insisted I come here with you, and no good has come of it.'

'You wanted to come. You said you wanted to see Harry.'

'Yes, but you'd have talked me out of coming here unless you wanted it, too. I know you, Lovric. That is what you'd have done.'

'But I did want you here to comfort me.'

'Even that isn't quite true. You said it was for your comfort, but really it was to appease the king. But would Edward have made more mischief if I had refused to come to Winchester? I don't think so. I'm irrelevant to this great game of chess he is playing with you, the earls.'

'Alfgar was released, though...'

'But not because of anything I did. I never made a plea for

him. I need never have come here at all. But no! You had to
insist and have it all your way. Well, I came with you to comfort
you, as you asked. Now you can come home and comfort me.
Fair's fair, Lovric.'

He sighed deeply again and started to put his arm round her,
but backed off when he saw the fury on her face. She was right,
he knew. But he knew other things too, things that he had never
confided to Godiva. Things about war – civil war – and its great
imminence. He looked at her again and saw that her anger was
turning cold. Soon it would be hatred. It was worth the risk of
telling her a bit of the truth, he thought, if it would drive that
dreadful expression from her face.

'Listen, Eva,' he started. 'My love,' he tried again. 'I acknowledge that you are right. But my situation is more complicated
than it seems, and that is why I cannot come home with you
tomorrow.'

She crossed her arms and looked at him with utter scepticism.

'Alfgar,' he said very quietly, 'Alfgar did not go to Peterborough. I sent men to intercept him and tell him to go back west,
to Bristol, and then bring his soldiers down from the Welsh
border. I already opened secret negotiations myself with some of
the Welsh princes and their Irish allies six months ago. That's
what I was doing while I was away from you. I sailed from Bristol
to the Isle of Anglesey, off the north Wales coast, and we all met
there. I don't want to make war against the king, but if Edward
goes too far with his Norman friends, we'll attack him from the
west, Siward will come down from the north and Godwin will
destroy his navy and southern fortresses. We'll divide England
into three zones, abolish the monarchy and rule the country
through a council of earls and thegns. But we must be careful not
to jump too soon, before our plans are properly developed, or
we'll be destroyed. In the interim I must undermine Edward's
confidence, but without making him distrust me personally. I

need to spend several more days close to his side, building his faith in me, but also making him fear for his crown. Later, when one or two unexpected, major attacks have taken place – on Chester and Ludlow probably – Edward will be terrified. Then he'll eat out of our hands.'

'And you'll get Harry home first, before war begins?'

'Of course.'

Overwhelmed by the gravity of what she had just heard, Godiva could think of nothing more to say for the moment. She filled large glasses of red wine for each of them, and called in Agatha to play the lute and sing a soothing song while they ate the pasties and drank ever more wine, and when they finished that they turned to the beer. Agatha was not well trained, but she could hold a tune on the strings and she knew many ballads, including duets and three-part pieces. Soon all three were singing loudly. Then Father Godric asked permission to join in and the chamber quickly became a scene of rowdy good cheer such as would have seemed impossible a mere hour ago.

And yet, as the candles died down and she closed her eyes, sleep would not come to Godiva. War – how could she even think of welcoming that? She had seen enough village skirmishes at the border to know about burning farmhouses, little girls raped and mangled corpses polluting wells and streams. War was only worth it when peace was failing and military success seemed certain. But what had sounded so convincing when put in Lovric's commanding language seemed now, as she lay alone with her thoughts in the darkness, to be hopelessly difficult. Too many important men would have to put aside their competing interests and work together. Would Godwin do that? She almost laughed. He had said he wanted to cooperate with Siward and Lovric – but that was not the same as waging war with them against Edward. He hadn't said a word about that; no, he said they should work together to keep the king on the throne. This new plan of the earls – was it a plan? Or just one possibility? And who was in on it? Was Alfgar? No – he had seen nothing wrong with being sent to Peterborough, other than a shortage of whorehouses. Lovric had been vague, mentioning nothing more specific than possible attacks on Ludlow and Chester. But those were details she could have invented herself. He had talked in grand, general terms, quite unlike the detailed description he had given her of conditions on the Welsh border at the time of Alfgar's arrest. Yes, she concluded, he had been vague and possibly misleading. Perhaps, after all, he wanted to stay in Winchester for other reasons. Estrith, for instance.

Godiva tossed restlessly as Lovric's snores deepened, and when she finally fell asleep it was in a mood of cold, weary resignation, not the optimistic faith in their future that had flickered briefly when, just a short while ago, she had believed in what he was saying. She woke once in the night, sat up and remembered what she had just dreamed. It was her own voice, loudly telling her what she was determined to deny: I do not love him any more.

At dawn a rider set out from Winchester, carrying a pennant on which the House of Lovric's black eagle fluttered in the air. His mission was to tell all those who were to accommodate the Earl of Mercia's wife when they should expect her arrival and what kind of hospitality they owed her. Simple – that was the message. Godiva was going home with all possible speed and wanted no late-night feasting – nothing but sustenance, a bed, a stable and departure every day at dawn, until she was thankfully back in her own domain.

The riding party assembled at the north-west gate of the city as the cathedral bell tolled the eighth hour of the day. Lovric supervised the departure, making sure that the small group of men who would be Godiva's bodyguard were properly equipped and that their horses were up to a long, fast ride. There were eight men in all, enough for a journey through country that was free of bandits, and someone had decided to put Bret on the biggest stallion, riding alongside Godiva near the front of the group.

'You can handle this horse, can you, without stirrups?' Lovric asked Bret. 'He's a big one, and fast.'

'I trust so, sir,' Bret replied. 'The captain put me here alongside your lady.'

'Well, he knows more about these horses than I do,' Lovric observed. 'Good. You're doing well, man. Take care on this journey.'

'Without fail,' Bret replied.

The group had drawn up near the arch of the gate when a breathless messenger arrived. 'A gift for the lady,' he said to one of the servants. Then he saw Godiva and ran to her. 'This,' he said, 'is a parting gift from Queen Edith.' He thrust the small object, wrapped in blue silk and tied with gold braid, into Godiva's hand and then, without waiting for a reply, he left.

The little package opened easily, revealing inside what appeared to be nothing more than a strip of carved bone, lying on its side. Holding it up, Godiva could see it was a comb, yellowed with age and so worn that it had lost two or three of its teeth. It was made of rare, finely carved elephant ivory, and yet its design seemed familiar. On one end small flowers clustered, and on the other end, where one would hold the comb to use it, a knob protruded that seemed to show the figure of a woman astride a horse, with one leg hanging down the end of the comb. The woman was naked and had long, loose hair. A bird, so minute and worn it was hardly visible, perched on her shoulder with its beak open to sing.

'Agatha, what do you think of this?' Godiva asked.

'Old, mistress. Like them combs we saw in the market. The trader said Queen Edith bought some Roman ones.' She paused and examined the comb. 'But this ain't Roman, I'll warrant. This lady riding on a horse with a bird singing on her shoulder, that would be Rhiannon. Gwen told me all about her. The Welsh tell stories of her, but the priests don't like her. The horse, you see, mistress; Rhiannon was a horse spirit, or goddess maybe. I don't really know...' Agatha stopped, embarrassed at revealing how much she knew of pagan lore. She passed the comb back to Godiva, who looked at it again, even more suspiciously now.

'I'll throw it away,' she said, 'in some remote spot.'

'Oh no!' Agatha gasped. 'That would be pure unlucky, mistress. You'll have to keep her now you've got her. Just like you can't visit the White Horse only once.'

'Oh, Holy Mary!' Godiva whispered to herself as realization dawned on her. Edith knows, and the king must know too, that she had gone to the White Horse. Worse, they had performed the pagan ritual of walking the line of the Horse's back. In the eyes of the king, she and Lovric must be sinners no less than their younger son.

'Hide this thing,' she said to Agatha. 'We'll do something with it when we get home. But now, let us get out of Winchester as quickly as we can.'

As Lovric wished everyone a safe journey, Bret rode round the entire party, making sure they were all in properly matched pairs, and then he returned to Godiva's side and put her horse's reins in her hand. Even from some distance the warmth of the smile she gave him was obvious. To her husband, in contrast, she gave what even a priest could tell was a cool kiss of farewell.

The monk who stood watching in the shadows, his hood concealing his face, saw Lovric step back and take stock of the situation: his beautiful wife on her way home with an admirable young man at her side. The earl looked ill at ease and waved the riding party on abruptly. The monk smiled and disappeared into the crowd. Soon he was deep inside the royal palace, murmuring in the ear of the man who was expecting him.

'Has she gone?' Edward asked.

'Yes,' Father Francis answered. 'All is well, your majesty.'

'Yes,' Edward smiled. 'I believe all is very well.'

He went back to the game of chess that he was playing with the queen.

'You are playing a long game, child,' he said quietly as he observed her face. Her pallid cheek rested in her hand, motionless and thoughtful, a replica of the two ivory queens on the board.

'The better to amuse you, great lord,' she replied, keeping her eyes fixed on his bishop. 'And there will be more to amuse you soon, of that I am sure.'

'Oh yes,' said Edward. 'How good it is that we begin to truly understand each other, my dear little girl.'

'That is what daughters are for,' said Edith. 'To please their fathers. And you are the best daddy in the land, dear Edward.'

She took her hand away from her cheek and briefly widened her pale-blue eyes in mock-innocence. Edward examined her for several moments, rubbed his hand across his mouth thoughtfully, and then leaned forward to move his ivory bishop on the beautifully carved chess board that he had just received from a young admirer in Normandy, a certain William – a bastard unfortunately, but talented and promising. A boy to be encouraged, thought Edward, as he watched Edith stoop forward and stare intently like a heron at a fish in shallow water, taking stock of her position and appraising the exact moment and precise angle from which to strike next.

'Your move,' he said.

'Not yet. Let us dine now and continue later. There is no need to hurry this game, is there, Edward my dear? You are the king and I am your queen. It follows that we have all the time in the world to amuse ourselves.'

Nine

On the winding back roads where the horses often slowed to a trot there were many opportunities for Bret to converse with Godiva. Judging by appearances, though, it was she who led the talking, turning often towards him, gesturing and sometimes smiling. Agatha and Father Godric, deafened by the sound of the horses' hooves, observed the backs of their heads and kept watch for any untoward gesture. But nothing significant took place, and what had at first appeared to be too intimate an association between their mistress and the huntsman quickly became uninteresting. Soon the maid and the priest found themselves gossiping about people in Coventry and the state of affairs that would meet them when they got home. The thought of the difficulties that might lie ahead dampened their conversation as both wondered silently why they had been in such a rush to go back home and pick up the threads of troubled village life.

Sitting straight-backed on her horse, with her riding cap closing severely around her face, Godiva looked forbidding. Bret behaved as though he felt shy in her presence, talking only to answer some question of hers and looking at the way ahead, avoiding her eye. Occasionally he laughed loudly at something she said that was only slightly funny. By the end of the first day of riding side by side, Godiva felt sorry for him, as though he were a child and could do with more confidence.

'Bret,' she said, as they neared the farmhouse where they would spend the night, 'do you like being with us in Coventry?'

He mumbled assent.

'I ask because young men always seem to leave home to make their way in the world. It must be lonely and difficult.'

Again he refused to be drawn.

'Was it hard for you?'

'No. My father was a thegn's man. The thegn took me into his service as a housecarl. Later he sent me to join the housecarls at the king's estate in Cleley, in the Forest of Salcey. That's where I learned forestry and hunting.'

'But didn't you miss your family? Or have any difficulties?'

Bret slowed his horse slightly and took his time about answering. When next he spoke he seemed reluctant and embarrassed.

'Since you ask – yes, I did have some trouble, lady. At Cleley there was a man who harassed me. Excuse me for saying this, but this man wanted to lie with me.' He glanced at Godiva to see how she was taking this shift in the conversation. She had pursed her lips and was staring ahead. 'Because I refused him, he told an officer that I was trying to lie with him. He told the king, who summoned me.'

'I'm told the king hates love between men. Weren't you afraid?'

'No. He had the matter investigated and I was exonerated. But I had to leave Cleley because my enemy had many old friends. They were angry because he was sent away.'

'I'm surprised he wasn't punished more severely,' she said, her interest sharpening.

'The king is merciful, lady. He is a man with a deep understanding of the human heart. He wants to save souls, not crush people with punishment. If you knew him better you would admire him as much as I do.'

'But I know for a fact that he hates love between men.'

'He wishes to discourage it because it leads to suffering. He himself is celibate because he prefers that way of life, though it is not the choice of most men.'

'But people do not think he is choosing celibacy for good reasons. Many say that he does not like women and prefers strange practices performed in secret.'

'That notion is nothing but malice, put about by his enemies – Godwin and his family especially. He talked with me for a long time, and I never gained the sense that there was anything strange about him. He was sympathetic and he knows what ordinary men are like.'

'But surely celibacy is a strange preference, is it not?'

'The king is good, but not naive. He has made the right choice for himself, but he knows that men vary – some prefer whores, others amuse themselves alone, many want to keep a stable of mistresses. Yet others like their own sex. And some men – the majority I'd say, men like me – prefer to make love to a beautiful, well-grown woman.'

He looked across at her and noticed that she was blushing once more. He was afraid he might have been too obvious in his allusion to her, and waited to see whether she might distance herself. But if he was flirting, Godiva did not seem to realize it. Nothing in her manner changed, and the blush stayed on her cheeks, soft pink like bramble blossom.

'But as I said,' he continued, 'the king thinks man-love should be renounced, where that is possible. Young boys and youths can change their affections if encouraged at the right time.'

'Do you really think so?'

Her need for hope was transparent. Bret was almost sorry for

her, though not sorry enough to change the drift of their conversation.

'You can believe that, lady. Your Harry is in good hands. He will come back to you as the man you want him to be.'

'What?' Godiva took the reins of his horse and pulled him close. 'In God's name,' she whispered, 'how do you know about Harry?'

'His friend, Edmund, was at Cleley before being sent north to Siward's court. There were men from Cleley in Winchester – you saw me talking with them near the cathedral. One of them saw Edmund being taken to prison for a flogging. He bribed the guard to let them talk for a moment, and that is how we learned the story of Harry and Edmund. I must say, lady, Ed is a good lad and not deserving of a flogging, but the bishop must have thought Harry would feel such guilt at Edmund's pain that he would lose all desire for him. Harsh medicine, but for good results.'

'So everyone knows about Harry?'

She looked so sad that if he had been alone with her, he would have taken her into his arms at once. But that chance, he was becoming sure, would come again soon.

The farmhouse where they were to be quartered that night suddenly came into view in a shallow valley. In the fading light its vellum windowscreens flickered with the promise of comfort in a warm, candle-lit room beside a big fire at an open hearth. Godiva and Agatha would sleep there with the woman of the house, while Father Godric, Bret and the other horsemen would bed down in the barns. As Bret helped her dismount – with such propriety that even Agatha could find no fault with him tonight – Godiva thought how good it would be tomorrow, to ride beside him and talk with him again.

*

But next day she found that the captain of the guard had put a different horseman on her right. No explanation was offered and Godiva rode in complete silence until they reached a ford, where they dismounted to have some bread and cheese. She ate her rations quickly and then sent Agatha to tell the captain that Bret was to ride beside her again. She could see the man look puzzled and then gesticulate, but Agatha held her ground and argued with him. Finally he shrugged and Agatha returned.

'Disobedient,' she spat. 'Won't do as they're told. All them horsemen think they be lords themselves. They should have my mother in charge of them. What he said, mistress, was that Bret asked him last night if he could ride at the back. Seems he has some bet on with one of the men down the line and wants to keep an eye on who is winning. So he had to go, mistress. You know how these men cheat on each other, and Bret don't have no money and can't afford to lose a penny.'

'How do you know so much about him?'

But Agatha clammed up at once. She had a cousin married to a man stationed at Cleley, and word had come down from her that Bret had left the king's estate in Salcey Forest quite suddenly and under mysterious circumstances. There were rumours – and if they were true there was no need to worry that Bret would break Godiva's heart, or any other woman's, either. But there were other rumours, too, of quite a different sort. Agatha was far too confused to say anything about Bret to Godiva. It was best to play dumb, but keep a sharp eye on him. In time he would show his true colours. Men always do, so Bertha said.

Back in the saddle beside Bret, Godiva turned to him and asked him about his wager. Guardedly he admitted to something vague and innocent, and Godiva, satisfied, did not pursue the subject. They were silent for a while, and then she asked the question that had been on her mind since last night.

'Are you paid by my reeve?'

'Yes, of course, lady.'

'Then you are paid a pittance. And I suppose your father was not able to give you much when you left home?'

'Nothing. There were four other boys after me, and two girls. I went to my father's thegn with only the clothes I wore. He could not afford to arm me properly, and that's why he sent me on, into the king's service.'

'When you left Cleley, did you get a good parting gift?'

'A modest gift, lady. But I have to admit I like gambling a little too much. I left Cleley with a good bag of silver coins, but I went down to the gaming houses in Bristol and I lost most of it at once.'

'I like to bet too, but I hate to lose. If I lose I feel I must carry on gaming to get my money back. I've lost bagfuls of coins that way. Thank God, no one knows – only you now.'

Bret flashed her a wide smile and laughed conspiratorially as if they had shared many adventures and secrets already. Godiva felt at once that she had thrown herself into the embrace of youth, devilry and glamour. It was hard to resist taking his hand.

'We must talk again in Coventry,' she said, 'about how you could be advanced in our household. There are many ways in which a good man like you could do better than you are doing now.'

Bret expressed his thanks and then steered the conversation away from such personal matters as his poverty. He sang several songs and ran through some new riddles he had picked up from the men of Cleley, and then, as evening neared, he told her a terrifying ghost story. At the end of that second day of riding and talking, as their horses came to a halt at another farmhouse, she put her hand on his arm and whispered to him that he should consider whether he could become a *scopman* and entertain in the hall every night. Agatha, standing nearby to help her dismount, heard every word and scowled at Bret, who immediately adopted an air of embarrassment. Agatha continued glaring after him as Bret followed the other horsemen towards the back of the farm, and its barns and dossing stalls.

Two more days of fast riding, during which Godiva could do little more than exchange pleasantries with Bret, brought them to the eastern perimeter of the lands that made up Godiva's Coventry estate. This would be their last overnight stop before Coventry and she wanted to make the most of the chance to wash and tidy herself before being seen by the townspeople and meeting her household at Cheylesmore manor. Near the farmhouse there was a pool at which she often bathed, and since today had been another hot, humid day she thought she might swim there, even though the sun was declining behind banks of clouds. Agatha unpacked one of the travel bags and found clean clothes, soap and drying cloths, and then they headed down the path to the pool, leaving the captain with instructions that no one was to stray in that direction until they returned.

Their way led through trees and then on through tall grasses that edged the small streams that flowed slowly over flat land towards the river. They crossed over these at several points on stones that served as simple bridges, following a path that had been used since the earliest times to gain access to the crystal pool that gathered silently where a spring rose from the earth, feeding the river with fresh, clear water. There were no animals pastured here and so there were few flies, less mud and no dung. It was the only place on her estate where she felt a little of the happiness she had known on the banks of the Wye, when she had swum with Harry every sunny summer day, when he was little and all was well. She brushed away a tear and saw Agatha observing her. What should she do? Pretend she had a summer cold? Or confide in Agatha about Harry? The temptation was great, for the girl was canny and loyal, and she would hear gossip soon anyway, just as Bret had done in Winchester. Gossip flew like sickness, arriving for no apparent reason and with amazing speed, even in isolated places like Coventry. No. It would be best not to reveal anything now, for there was no telling what other troubles might lie ahead in Coventry.

'We mustn't stay too long,' she said. 'My nose and eyes are stinging.'

'But what about your hair?'

'Yes, I should wash it. It's full of dust and odours from that hostelry in Winchester. If I get a cold, so be it.'

At the spot where Godiva liked to bathe there were several big, smooth stones on the riverbank where one could stand comfortably while undressing and then jump into the waist-high water without stepping on sharp pebbles and slimy weeds. Agatha helped her undress and folded the dirty clothes away in a laundry bag she had brought with her. Then she unpinned and unplaited Godiva's masses of yellow hair, so thick with grease it uncoiled slowly like several snakes down her back.

'Swim first,' Godiva said, 'and wash afterwards. You too, Agatha, you smell bad now. Come and swim with me.'

Godiva plunged into the tepid water and swam quickly to a stone that rose like a platform in the middle of the pool. The sun was warm on her shoulders and the stone had retained the heat of the day. A moment later Agatha climbed up beside her. The two women, so different in rank, age and colouring, but both beautiful and naked, looked at each other and smiled.

'Thank you, mistress,' Agatha said shyly.

'For letting you swim? But you have every right, child, to be clean and comfortable. You work hard and you are sensible.' She noticed Agatha's budding breasts and determined little chin, growing more adult with each day. 'Your parents will want you to marry soon. When the time comes I'll give you some help with your dowry and trousseau.'

Agatha shook her head. 'Thank you, mistress, but I don't love anyone in Coventry. I did love Wulf, Odo's son, but he been sent away to help on his uncle's farm and I don't see him no more. The housecarls be nasty, and the other men be married already, or there be something the matter with them.'

'There's Bret,' Godiva said, and bit her tongue too late.

'Oh no, mistress! He be a wrong 'un all right.'

Godiva's wits came back to her and she sprang to her feet. 'I must swim across this pool twenty times, and then we'll wash,' she said, and threw herself into the shimmering, still water on the other side of the stone.

Swimming back and forth, mostly under the water, and aware only of Agatha's presence sometimes nearby, Godiva let her fears stream back behind her with her hair. Every so often soft weeds slithered through its strands, braiding her locks with green river ribbons, letting her fancy that she was a welcome guest at a feast in the underwater world and could stay there for hours. She wondered if this was how people felt when they prepared to drown. What a sweet way to leave this troubled world, with just one bubble of regret and then translucent peace. Why hang yourself like that poor tramp at Stivichall? Death should be a soft slipping away, not a violent plunge.

A shriek of anger cut across her reverie. Rising from the water, she could see Agatha standing on the stone where the clothes were, wrapped in a cloth and shaking her fist.

'You little bastard!' she was shouting. 'Pig's arse! Dirty son of a bitch! *Clawecunt!*'

'Agatha!'

'Mistress, there be a boy over there, in them trees on the other side of the river. He been watching us the whole time, I'll warrant. I've a good mind to chase after him and thrash him.'

'He'll be gone by now. Do you know him?'

'Of course I do. That be Tom, the tanner's boy, come here to fish, I suppose. I heard tell before that he peeps on women. His father already give him the birch for that, but it ain't stopped him. When he hears about him spying on you, mistress, he'll tan that boy's hide, good and proper. He won't sit down for a month of Sundays, mark my words!'

'Don't say anything yet. I'll see the boy and talk to him myself.' Godiva put her hand on Agatha's shoulder. 'When I get home there will be many problems to solve. I know I can depend on you to help me, and to be very careful with what you say to others. I want you to stay in the manor house as my permanent maid. Gwen is too busy these days to help me much, and your mother, well…'

'Oh, no one would want mother with them all day long. She'd have you in fits of tears, lady, by the end of a single day.'

'So, are we agreed?'

Agatha nodded vigorously and kissed Godiva's hand in thanks.

They returned to Coventry by a different route from the one on which they had ridden out, just over four weeks ago, entering through the main street and intending to pass by the town cross and the market. An outrider had gone ahead the previous night to tell everyone to turn out and greet the lady of their manor in the usual way, when she rode into town the next day.

Turn out they did, but they were not as she expected. How does hunger announce its presence? Godiva stared at them in disbelief, trying to decipher what she saw. Does it show first in slackened skin and lacklustre eyes, or in weak posture and unkempt hair? Or should she recognize it from the odour of neglect that hung in the air like a dark halo round their bowed heads? No: its clarion call was the unbearable silence of the children, clutching passively at their mothers' skirts, their eyes dry and their bellies swollen. She saw the shoemaker and realized he had lost two teeth in the last month. The innkeeper stood near him, and he looked angry. To the side stood the candlestick-maker's wife, the one who always had her new baby sucking at her breast. But there was no baby in her arms now. Suddenly Godiva felt violently ashamed. She and her retinue were parading before a famished town. But then, how much worse would it be for them to see the lady of their manor in disarray, too? She was the one whose money they were counting on to feed them, now that she was back. She had better look sharp about it.

At the town cross she ordered the captain to halt, and then she waited. Within moments the town crier arrived, out of breath, but eager for duty. In minutes the marketplace was filled with people, and her heart broke at the sight of them. Why had she not been told of their plight last night? The people at the farmstead must have known what was going on in Coventry. But farmers, she knew, have never cared much for townsfolk and never will. They lived in different worlds by different rules.

'Good people of this town of Coventry,' she began, and then choked and had to start again. 'Good people,' she carried on. 'I knew when I left that you were in danger of hunger, but I did not expect to see you struck down so quickly, so badly. You must tell me what happened. You first, Frith,' she said, pointing at the baker.

'There was want before you left, lady. Then the harvest died in the fields. And the stores of grain and flour went bad. Mould and rot. I've been making bread with old rye grain mixed with root peelings that women usually give to pigs. It's got no strength in it, and anyway there's little of that left, either.'

'And the cattle plague got worse,' shouted the tanner. 'We been sending the boys out to fish every day and trap birds, but they be town boys by now and don't catch too much.'

'Trade is dead,' the tinsmith added. 'People be afraid of

carrying the cattle plague back home with them, so they don't come to town no more. Anyway, most of the villages to the west of here have lost cows too and they don't have money to spend in Coventry no more. They're sending men to meet the Bristol merchants to buy grain, and that's costing them all they have.'

'I can help you with buying grain,' she started to say. But someone interrupted her. It was Father Godric's wife, Hilde, who had wormed her way through the crowd to face her husband.

'There be more than hunger in Coventry. There be bad spirits, too.' Someone shouted, 'Shut her up', but Hilde carried on. 'Folk be taking to the forest to make sacrifices. And others spread tales. They say the king hates Coventry for that we be bad people here – fornicators and adulterers and sodomites. The king will punish our sins, and the sins of the House of Lovric...'

At that someone clapped his hand over Hilde's mouth and pulled her back into the crowd, where she disappeared in a flurry of elbows and curses. Godric tried to apologize to Godiva, but she shook her head.

'I can only take one step at a time,' she shouted over the heads of the crowd. 'First I will give you what I have.'

The contents of her own purse, and the reserve of treasure with which she always travelled and which the captain of the guard protected, were now emptied out into the hands of the inn-keeper, because he, of all the tradesmen in the town, was the one most used to handling a lot of money. He counted it out slowly at the base of the cross before everyone, and then announced the total. Everyone who had a house was entitled to a share, and those with big families would receive an extra amount.

'Take this money and buy whatever grain you can get at once,' she said. 'Don't worry about getting a fair price. We'll settle scores in future with whoever overcharges us now. When I get to Cheylesmore manor, I will empty the barns all over my home farm for you and for whatever other villages are starving. By bedtime tonight everyone must have a full belly.'

A cheer went up, weak but hopeful. Godiva thought it the saddest sound she had ever heard, more like a moan than a shout, longing for life even when it was so cruel. Once again she felt hot with shame: just a few hours ago, beset by worries, she had dreamed of the stillness of a watery grave. She, who had never once seen her own flesh melt away, or felt hunger bite her guts, or seen a strong child's life dwindle to nothing at her breast for want of milk – she had idly dreamed of death. What a coward she had been.

In silence they rode on towards the manor, wondering what troubles might be waiting there. At first everything seemed unchanged. The manor's herds had not caught the cattle plague because they were kept apart from other livestock and their attendants had stayed on the manor to avoid contact with infected beasts. The milkmaids, being well fed, looked as they always did, plump and smooth-skinned. If there was a change it was subtle: their cheers, though warm and genuine, were slightly subdued, for everyone had family nearby and none of the girls could help them much. In the yard, the servants of the hall and the manor house were lined up to welcome the mistress, and they too appeared well. Godiva looked them over and felt relieved. She dismounted and went to shake everyone's hand, starting with Gwen. But Gwen wasn't at the head of the line, and suddenly she realized that Milly was absent, too. Instead Bertha had pride of place, and now she was standing in front of Godiva with her legs apart and arms folded, ready to give her a good dollop of bad news.

'There be sickness here, lady,' she said with grim satisfaction. 'Gwen got it bad, and Mistress Milly took to her bed yesterday.'

'What kind of sickness?'

'Fever and aches, coughing and sweating.'

'Nothing on the skin?'

'No. No rashes or pustules.'

'And the stomach?'

'No vomiting nor bleeding. Some headache, though. Gwen be complaining bad about her head.'

'Very well, this is not plague. They have a summer cold, that is all. How many here have it?'

'Just them two and a swineherd, but none else yet.'

Godiva turned to one of her men. 'This sickness could travel through the manor. I want you and one other man to go back to the town. Tell them we will bring the grain to them ourselves as soon as we can. No one must come to the manor from the town. If those hungry people catch this illness, they will die like flies. Go!'

She crossed the threshold into the manor house and instantly felt the joy she always felt at coming home, but now it was a joy tinged with concern. There would be so much to do, and do very quickly. To her surprise, Bret appeared at the door.

'Excuse me, lady,' he began diffidently, 'but I heard you say we will get the grain into town as soon as possible. Let me do that for you. The hall-men agree with me that we should get every cart and pack animal readied for haulage, and every hand, including all the women and children, over to the barns. If we don't act quickly you could break your promise that everyone will sleep tonight on a full stomach.'

'Thank you,' she said, deeply relieved to have this assistance just when it was needed. 'Reserve the contents of two barns for the manor's use. That should be enough to keep us going till we buy in more grain. And Bret, I am going to make you my foreman. Tell the reeve to come and see me about that. You are wasted in the forest.'

After Bret left, Godiva went at once to see Gwen and Milly in the sick-room. Gwen didn't seem to hear her come in. Milly raised her head, saw who it was and turned to face the wall.

'I'm sorry you are unwell, child,' Godiva said, taking Milly's hand and feeling how hot it was. Milly pulled her hand away as soon as she could. 'What is it, dear?' Godiva asked.

'You know quite well what is the matter, mother. My wedding is delayed and now I'm sick. The manor has been neglected because Gwen has been sick for nearly a week. Do you expect me to be glad, just because you're home? You should never have gone away in the first place.'

'You do not know the circumstances, Milly.'

'I doubt that you do either, mother. You wouldn't see a fly if it landed on your nose.'

The old impulse to slap Milly on the mouth came upon Godiva at once, and she got up to go.

'You are in good hands here with our nurse. So I will leave you now.'

'Good riddance,' said Milly into her pillow, too quietly for Godiva to hear. But Gwen did.

'You nasty little bitch,' she muttered, before yielding to such a noisy attack of coughing that Milly's retort could not be heard.

Godiva closed the door on them with relief. She was sorry they were sick, but it was just as well that they were in seclusion and out of her way. She would need all her presence of mind to get her people through the next ten days. If they survived that, they would live.

With this thought in mind she left the sick-room, picked her way through the herb garden and entered the yard. Suddenly she stopped, halted in her tracks by the scene of pulsing vitality that now confronted her. Bret had gathered in all hands from the manor grounds and already they were loading sacks of reserved grain and other dried supplies on to carts, donkeys, horses and the backs of some of the fittest young men. The campaign to feed the starving people of Coventry was under way. Thank God, she thought, for sending me Bret.

Ten

The next morning Godiva awoke to an unwonted silence outside her window. For a moment she thought she was still in the hostelry in Winchester, but her bed was empty and there was no sign of Lovric. She opened the window to breathe in the still, early morning air, and a puppy, frightened by the sudden movement above his head, yelped loudly. Then she realized what was wrong. The rooster was silent. He was missing from the dung hill on the north side of the palisade. He must be dead, she thought, for you could hear him crowing up to a mile away. And if the rooster was dead, what had happened to all the hens?

Cautious with drowsiness, she crept down the stairs and nudged Agatha to wake up and get breakfast started. Then she went out into the yard and looked about her. Something had changed while she was away. There was a slight air of abandonment about the manor. It was more than merely untidy after last night's activity; there was an underlying neglect. She almost tripped on a rake that had been dropped near a casually scooped pile of rubbish, and made a mental note to find out who had done that. Pulling her shawl tightly round her head to cover her unruly, undressed hair, she went in search of a servant. But there was no one to be seen. Without Gwen on the prowl, they felt safe to lie in later than usual. Only in the dairy would the maids be up, for the cows would bellow in pain if milking did not begin at the crack of dawn. Godiva sighed and began to walk to the milking sheds at the other end of the yard.

Working by the light of rush candles, eight dairy maids were busy on their stools, heads down and hands pulling away rhythmically beneath the healthy cows' bursting udders. It was a reassuring sight and Godiva lingered for a moment, watching them.

'I'm done with this one, lady,' said one of the girls, loosening the tether that bound the cow's knees and carefully removing her bucket before the cow could kick it over in annoyance. She patted the beast affectionately on her nose while saying some kind words in her ear. 'This here be Cressy,' the girl said, smiling proudly at Godiva. 'I brought her up from being a newly calved three-year-old what couldn't be doing with her calf, to her now being our best milker. I get such butter from her you can't believe.'

'Good, Ethel,' said Godiva, pulling back her shawl. 'But does anyone here know what happened to my rooster?'

The girls looked up from their milking and glanced at each other uncomfortably.

'Some say fox come in and kill some of the chickens,' Ethel said at last. 'Them that got away went up into the trees and won't come down for fear of God. The rooster, he just plain disappeared. Coward, I reckon.'

'Rooster pie, I reckon,' said a big girl, removing her pail and straightening her cramped back. Ethel frowned at her, but the girl went on. 'A man in the hall went out in the small hours last week, and heard some noise by the dung heap. Not a ruckus like hens flying from a fox, but a quiet noise, like men stealing around trying not to disturb the birds. There be one big squawk and in the morning rooster be gone, and a few hens, too. And all the eggs what got laid after pick-up time the day before, they be gone, too. We reckon they ended up as chicken soup and breakfast eggs in the town, lady. Sorry to say.'

'Thank you,' Godiva said, trying to hide her disappointment. 'Go back to your work now.'

As she closed the cowshed door she could hear a loud conversation breaking out behind her. It was punctuated only by the plaintive lowing of those cows whose milking was not yet finished, for there was none of the usual laughter one heard amongst the dairy girls once they had finished milking. They too are worried, Godiva realized. She thought of going back to tell them to have forbearance with the hungry people down the lane, but they must know that many of the barns had been emptied to feed the town. They would be too frightened for their own stomachs to feel much concern for others.

In the manor house, breakfast was on the table. Agatha had prepared wheat porridge, bacon, liver-sausage and fried bread, and a herb tea that might ward off the sickness that was going around. But no eggs. Godiva said nothing about that and started to eat quickly, vowing that she would not eat this well again until there was food for all. Then she began to run through all the things she had to do as quickly as possible. Suddenly she realized Agatha was very quiet and staying out of her way.

'Did you eat?'

'Yes, lady,' came a subdued voice from the back kitchen, where Agatha was scraping dishes into a pail. Godiva summoned her and Agatha, head bowed, reluctantly entered the room with her headdress pulled over half her face. Godiva immediately recalled Adel in Oxford and told Agatha to show her face. But Agatha stood stock still, holding on to a loose end of her headdress, and then she burst into tears.

'Who hit you?' Godiva asked, not waiting to see the damage. 'Well, it could only have been your mother. Last night, I suppose.

When you were down here and I was sleeping upstairs. Go and get her.'

But Agatha made no move.

'Very well,' Godiva sighed, getting up.

'Wait, lady,' Agatha burst out. 'It were my fault alone. Mother reprimanded me, and I gave her back-talk.'

Her eyes were dark with fear, for if Godiva told Bertha to leave the manor, the children in Bertha's cottage would starve like the children in town.

'My dear Agatha,' she said softly, 'I will speak to Bertha later. As for you, be careful how you address your mother. You have become her equal in the manor, and she won't like it.'

Agatha pulled herself together and went back to her chores.

Godiva dressed without her help and a few minutes later set off to talk to the master of the hall. She found Odo deep in conversation with Bret, both of them looking serious but relaxed, as though they had taken in hand all the most important matters that would prevent the crisis deepening.

'I sent for the reeve last night,' Odo said, 'but he sent back asking permission to stay out in Stivichall. There's been another suicide. Drovers came through again last week. He says no need for you to come down there this time, though, lady. It would be enough if you sent Father Godric to say a prayer when they bury him under the tree where he hanged himself.'

Godiva frowned. 'Shouldn't we give him a Christian burial, like the last one?'

'No, he had an idol on him. If he be buried under that tree, there'll be no more suicides there. Even folk who are looking to kill themselves don't want to go straight to hell's mouth with a pagan spirit for company.'

'Very well,' she said. 'I'll send Godric. Now, something else – I want someone to go from the hall to where the drovers' road enters my lands. Tell the farmers of Stoneleigh to block that road with trees and put a diseased cow's head on a post beside the barricade. There must be no more cattle movements over my lands or we'll never get rid of this plague. How is the culling going? Was there any trouble?'

'No trouble, but discontent. Anyways, we be almost done, lady,' said Odo. 'They killed on the last farm a week ago and we've heard of no new cases since.'

'Good.'

'Yes, but it were a sad, sad sight. I never seen hard farmers weep like children before. The piles of carcasses burned for hours and the stench lingered for days. You could see the smoke rising from all the villages, and it looked like the end of the world. Some be angry, saying they didn't agree with the cull.'

'Prayers. People need to be praying all the time until things get better, or else they will have the Devil for company soon. I'll go to the priory at once and arrange that. We'll send monks out to the villages.'

'Ha! They'll need spears in their backs. Them monks have closed the doors of the priory. There been no services, except for themselves, since just after you went to Winchester, lady.'

'I'll go and see Prior Edwin at once. Bret, come with me and get out the town crier to tell the people what we are doing to help them.'

She turned to go, but Odo seized her elbow.

'Wait, mistress. What about buying in grain? We should be doing that first, before anything else – before other lordships buy up what can be got.'

'You're right, Odo. I'll see to that now. You'll have to take the money with you under guard, for there'll be bandits in the forests by now. Where can we buy grain?'

'Grain merchants from Bristol have arrived already at Butt Field in Allesley, following the drovers' route. A party of us should go by barge along the Sherbourne and get what we can.

We could be back by nightfall and get food into town straight away. And replenish our own barns, too. I don't want men to grow nervous in the hall, thinking they may have to go hungry to feed the town.'

A little later, after counting out half the silver coins stored in her chest and giving them to Odo, Godiva set off with Bret on small ponies sometimes used by the manor for trotting back and forth to the market square. A breeze was blowing, lifting her lightly veiled loose hair. Bret could not help but glance at her and think how beautiful she was in the midst of all her troubles. Beautiful and good, too. He sighed heavily and rubbed the sweat from his brow.

'You have a kind heart, Bret. But don't worry, we will put things to rights soon. No one will starve in Coventry.'

He reached out and touched her hand. 'It is you who are kind, lady. And brave and beautiful.'

Godiva's eyes met his, and as there was no one to observe them she held his gaze and smiled back at him in a way that she had never done before. Bret's heart pounded with triumph and then with sharp desire. He took a deep breath and calmed himself.

At the town cross they parted, Bret heading to the town crier's house, and Godiva going to knock at the door of the priory, which was barred against the outside world as Odo had said it would be. To her surprise there was a prompt response, the bolts were withdrawn and Prior Edwin stood there in person to greet her.

'Thank God you are back,' he said at once, with more sincerity than she had ever before detected in his quivering voice.

'Come in at once,' he said, hurrying her inside. 'Look over there. It is what you always wanted.'

In the darkness of the priory it took Godiva a moment to

make out the softly gleaming ark that stood on a pedestal of granite not far from the door.

'That's a feretory. How did you get it?'

'I had it with me all along,' he confessed, 'but I didn't want the work of polishing it until it was ready for use. And now it is!'

'You mean you have the relic?'

'I do. It's in there already. Go and see!'

Godiva went up to the feretory and peered inside. Here indeed were the long bones with their silver fittings that had for years been kept in obscurity in the old church of St Michael's.

'I went and spoke firmly to the priests of St Michael's,' Edwin went on, 'and I told them exactly what you said. And they complied. It was like magic, dear sister.'

'Well, I am immensely pleased, dear prior,' Godiva replied. 'Nevertheless, there are more pressing matters to talk about. They say you have been barring people from services, ever since I went away.'

'But I explained to them,' he said sadly. 'I told them we had three or four cases of summer colds amongst the monks, and that if this got out amongst malnourished people they would succumb and die. Sometimes I believe the hardest problem God has put on Earth for us is to open the closed ears of those who will not listen.'

Godiva felt like agreeing, but she was still suspicious of Edwin, who had blossomed into a conscientious prior just when she was away and unable to nag him.

'Have you done anything for their hunger?' she asked.

'Of course, dearest lady. Every day we took half our bread and placed the loaves in covered dishes on a table near the door. Rain or shine they come at the hour when the loaves have cooled, and then take off like mice with pastry crumbs. Of course, it wasn't nearly enough, as I'm sure you could see when they came out to greet you...'

'I could not have asked more of you, Edwin,' she said. 'God seems to have moved your heart.'

'God moves in mysterious ways,' he agreed, and Godiva, sensing some irony on his part, raised her brows. But Edwin remained inscrutably virtuous.

'I am glad. I need to work closely with you over the next few weeks. There is enmity arising between people. Soon they will get out the dolls and the bodkins and start hexing each other...'

'And going to the forest to sacrifice.'

'Then we must bring prayer to everyone.'

He nodded agreement. 'Some of the brothers have spoken of this recently. About half of them are strong young men who can go about in all weathers. We will see about this at once.'

'Edwin, why are you so changed?'

'I honestly do not know,' he replied. 'Except that, perhaps, I wanted to please you.'

She smiled again and he tried not to flinch. What a fool she is, he thought, and how gullible. I put it right in her face – I am trying to please her. And she isn't even asking herself: *what for?*

Despite the midday hour, the market square was almost deserted when Godiva closed the priory door behind her. She looked back at St Mary's and felt again the queasiness that Edwin always caused her. But it was an unease she could not afford in the present circumstances, and anyway she couldn't justify it. He was doing everything she wanted and it was unfair to dislike him so much for petty matters such as his lisp, his pretentious turns of phrase and those pudgy fingers whose nails were always bitten down to the quick. Nevertheless the emptiness of the town square and the nearness of the prior's sickly presence made her long for her own house in its enclosed yard, filled with people she liked. She looked around her, hoping to see Bret, but he was nowhere in view. He must have left for Cheylesmore already.

Suddenly she longed to see his warm smile and be close to him again.

When Godiva returned to the manor house she noticed that the little pony Bret had ridden into town was still out of the stable. She summoned a stable boy and asked about Bret's whereabouts, but the boy only knew that huntsmen and foresters had come to the yard, looking for Godiva, and Bret had gone off with them into the woods. He couldn't have gone far, she thought, not on that pony and not without changing into a leather jacket for protection against brambles and low branches. Godiva pulled on her own leather jacket and then headed down the bridle path towards the forest.

He saw her coming from a grassy knoll on which he was sitting in the sunshine that had just broken through the clouds. He had sent the huntsmen away with thanks and the promise that he would tell Godiva the news himself: there were poachers at large in the forest, and some at least appeared to be towns-people, for their snares were often amateurish, maiming rather than killing, and leaving behind mangled animals with useless skins. After the huntsmen left, he took off his warm tunic and opened his shirt down to his waist. His pony was tied safely to a tree near a stream and was browsing tender leaves and sprigs. Bret smiled when he saw Godiva. Then he stepped into the pool of sunlight where she could see him, folded his arms and waited.

At the sight of him she reigned in the pony and sat stock still in the saddle. She felt as a deer must feel as she sees the hunter and her soft, beating heart is stopped by the arrow made especially for her breast. The breathlessness hurt her lungs. The stinging in her fingers and toes made them feel like the tips of frozen limbs thawing too quickly by a winter's fire. She looked away from him, wondering where she should go and what should she do. Then she called his name. He ran towards her and in moments she had swung down into his hands from the back of the pony. For the first time, they were utterly alone together.

'Bret?'

'Yes?'

As usual he held back from her, so that she thought it was she who pulled his face towards her, and she who pressed his soft lips to hers. But in moments she knew he would not stop what she had started. Everything he did felt new, and the years rolled away as her body seemed to melt and her muscles grew limp, so limp that soon she was falling on her back and her clothes were on the grass, and Bret seemed to be everywhere, kissing her from her ears to her toes, and all the places in between, places that she did not know men liked to kiss so much and for so very long. This must be wrong, she thought. Lovric has never done this, nor did my first husband. How does he know about this? This is the place I keep for myself, to comfort me and help me sleep when I am on my own. No man's tongue should find its way there, and yet there was no stopping its persistent, rippling touch. Without warning, the burning under her skin flowered suddenly into bright red, pulsing flame and she was lost to all thought. Only then, when he was sure that he had succeeded with her, did Bret do the usual, familiar thing that all men do, but coming after the misdeed that had gripped her whole being, it felt different, more complete than ever before and entirely unforgettable. He finished in mere moments and fell on to the grass beside her.

'Forgive me, mistress.'

'Mary and Jesus forgive us both,' she answered, but there was no sign of contrition on her face, merely a smile at the corners of her mouth, and fringed eyelids that remained closed.

She must have dozed for a few minutes, until she felt Bret

kissing her ear again and running a hand along her inner thigh, upwards from her knee. She had forgotten what it was like to lie with such a young man – how quickly they recover and start again. She had forgotten, too, what the second time was like: it was to be his time now, a matter of rhythm and continuation, until her resistance faded and for the second time he succeeded with her.

Neither slept after this. Bret wrapped her in his cloak and stroked her hair. He too looked contented now and she realized that she had never seen him look at ease until now. The angles of his face were softer and the green of his eyes so much darker that he could have faded into the forest background like a tree god.

'Can you come here with me again?' he asked.

'Would we be safe from prying eyes?'

'Yes. If we go there,' he pointed at a narrow path that led over the knoll. 'There is a bramble patch there that hides a pathway into a grove of oaks. It is beautiful in there, with cowslips and wild strawberries and dappled sunlight. I will take you there, for hours if you choose.'

She kissed him, and yet again her legs seemed to part according to their own volition. This time, though, because he was almost satiated, he pulled her up to ride above him and let her take as long as she wanted until, exhausted, she fell off him on to the grass and laughed.

'I feel eighteen again.'

'So will you come here to me again?'

'Yes. Again and again. So long as we can be secret and safe.'

'We can. I'll make sure of that.'

As he sat up, a hare that had been watching them stood up on its hind legs in the grass, blinked, leaped a few times and bounded off. It was soon followed by a deer and her fawn. For all

Bret's promise of secrecy, the forest seethed with life. Care would indeed be required, he reflected, for trouble not to land in his lap.

The barge came up the River Sherbourne from the landing station near Butt Field in Allesley and docked in Coventry at eight in the evening. Godiva and Agatha, Father Godric, Bret and others of the hall-men, the town crier and the town headman and the innkeeper, Prior Edwin and some of his monks, were all assembled on the muddy banks of the river, ready to assess the success of the meeting with the grain merchants of Bristol. Odo jumped ashore first, and from the unhappy look on his face it seemed that matters had not gone as he wished.

'We've got as much as we can load on this one barge,' he said, 'but we didn't get enough to load the mules. We've left them and some muleteers down in Butt Field as there's another delivery coming in four days' time. Early oats and new cheese next time from Wales. That there is wheat flour from Ireland,' he said, pointing at the bags that were being unloaded off the barge.

'How much money do you have left?' Godiva wanted to know.

'Over a half,' he said, handing several bags of silver to Godiva. 'The prices are not too bad. Lots of merchants coming up the Severn now, so there be competition between them. The problem is the supply. No one has the means to get heavy loads to places like Coventry. Reckon we'll have to make many trips to Butt Field until we've filled our barns up. We'll be more busy than poor, lady.'

Poor: the word clanged like a death-knell in Godiva's mind. She had never been poor in her life. Indeed for years she had actually been rich. Yet poor is what she would be before this famine was over. Poor for years perhaps. It was a strange, light feeling, as though she had divested herself of a heavy burden. Or perhaps it was adultery that made her feel like this: she had shed her virtue as well as her money and now she felt as light and insubstantial as a leaf. At the moment it made her feel powerful, as though immune to demands and fears. But how she would feel tomorrow, or next year, she had no idea. She shook her head to dismiss her futile thoughts.

'Let us go to the town cross,' she said, 'and begin the distribution.'

Torches flamed all round the market square, even though it was not yet fully dark, for the one thing everyone feared was that some deception would occur as the flour was being distributed. Fighting would then break out, which Godiva, in Lovric's absence, would not be able to suppress quickly. The few armed men at her disposal were all seated high up on war stallions to patrol the crowd that was forming rapidly in answer to the crier's announcement that the grain had arrived. Each horseman carried, as well as the usual arms, a whip with which to beat back rioters. As they walked their horses through the crowd, the hungry people looked up at them with a mixture of resentment and gratitude, for they too needed order now.

On Godiva's instructions, Prior Edwin opened the occasion with a prayer and a psalm sung by the monks, and then a short admonition that everyone should be mindful of his neighbour's want and of the merciful Lady Godiva's great love and care for them.

'And now,' said Godiva, brandishing a sharp knife, 'I will open the first sack. I will give every mother enough flour to make a small loaf for each child in the family and a big loaf for each adult. When I have finished with the mothers, I will feed those men who have no families. If you have no bags to carry flour you can use mine. This is intended to feed you until tomorrow night. By then we will have filled the town barns and made a reckoning of how much we have, how to dole it out and how long it will last.'

The women, knowing perfectly well the size of each other's families, quickly formed an orderly line that shuffled patiently forward as Godiva, helped by Agatha, dug ever deeper into the floury bags and shared out quantities of the light, life-giving substance into the hemp sacks that most people had brought with them. The single men, coming last, were less well provided for and needed to be given containers. These Godiva filled with their rations, plus a little extra flour, for it was amongst these that neglect and poverty seemed at their worst. By the time it was over she and Agatha were tired and sweating, dusted with flour and hungry.

'Tomorrow,' she said to the thinning crowd. 'We will meet here again tomorrow, before sunset.'

'God bless you, lady,' someone shouted.

'And God bless the good folk of the manor,' shouted someone else. 'Coventry ain't going to forget this night, not ever.'

'Wait! One thing more,' she said as they were about to depart. 'I'm opening my forests for hunting. But proper hunting, not careless trapping. I have reserved one stretch of the woods for my own needs and no one may enter there. Bret and the other huntsmen will show you where you can go. You will find wild pig, deer and rabbit, as well as mushrooms, berries, fiddleheads, and whatever else you want. Good eating to you all!'

Then Godiva and her people set out to return to the manor, leaving behind them a slowly dispersing crowd of thankful, relieved townspeople, all of whom would soon be at their hearths making unleavened bread as fast as they possibly could. By chance, it seemed, Godiva's horse fell into step alongside Bret's and she turned to ask his opinion of the evening's events.

'The food relief was quick and orderly,' he said, 'and they like the sound of your voice. If you were a man you would make a good commander. I would salute you and follow you into battle.'

Their eyes met for a moment. Luckily, Agatha and Father

Godric were preoccupied with an argument that had flared up between them, and everyone else was tired and looking at the road home. Still, thought Bret, I must be more careful. She might be in love with me, and that will make her careless. And I, God help me, must feel nothing whatsoever for her.

Eleven

The next few days passed in a delirium of activity as Godiva and the people of the manor continued their efforts to purchase more grain and distribute it fairly, to patrol the roads to ensure that infected cattle did not pass into the lordship, and to keep an eye on the forests so that the townspeople, now licensed to hunt at will, did not wreak havoc on the wild animals at their mercy.

But no matter how tired she was, Godiva would put on her sword belt and leave the manor every afternoon when the finger on the sundial touched five, and ride down the bridle path into that part of the forest from which everyone else was now prohibited, until she came to the knoll on which she had first seen Bret waiting alone for her. Here she would stop and tie her horse to a branch of a willow that stood on the banks of a stream, and then set out on foot along the slender deer track that led to the shaded oak glade where Bret sat, whittling a piece of wood and waiting for the sound of a twig snapping under her foot or a rabbit scurrying away from her soft tread. Every time she entered the clearing he would sweep her up and carry her to where his cloak lay spread out on a dry, grassy slope, strewn with flowers and scented so sweetly that it seemed they were in their own chamber, in a tower of their own castle, in a kingdom of which he was king and she was queen.

Bret, though, was worried. Whether because of exhaustion brought on by the current crisis, or the long summer of troubles that had preceded it, or whether Godiva had simply grown recklessly indifferent to her overbearing husband, she was too unconcerned about the secrecy of their meetings. She had taken only one step to preserve it, and that was to ban others from entering this part of the woods. But hunger bred lawlessness, and without guards at the trail heads, intruders were sure to show up soon. Then, too, she rode off every day in the wrong direction – if what she was doing, as she claimed, was going to bathe in that pool she liked so much. Her maid, Agatha, was a sharp-eyed little thing. She must have realized something was amiss by now. And Father Godric must be wondering why he could never find her at early evening prayers in the manor any more. She was lucky that the old housekeeper they called 'the corgi', and that bitchy daughter, Milly, had been confined for a while. But they'd be on their feet again soon and watching her. The odds were mounting against keeping their meetings secret, and Bret didn't like it.

One afternoon, while he was still in the early stages of making love with gentle kisses and light movements of his hands, he drew back sharply and turned his head to the side.

'There's someone nearby,' he whispered and, signalling her to stay still and quiet, he got to his feet and picked his way stealthily towards a broad oak, where he leaned against the trunk, listening carefully. A few seconds later he let out a loud whoop and went crashing through the undergrowth towards the far side of the glade. Godiva could hear shouts and curses, but could not distinguish any voices. In a few minutes he was back, his hose torn by the brambles and a nettle rash beginning to rise in scarlet blotches on his hands.

'It was that little bastard, Tom the tanner's son. Same one

as spied on you and your maid when you swam in the pool together.'

'How much could he see?'

'He didn't get close enough to see you. But he saw me all right. I slapped his head before he got away from me. Now he'll go back to town and tell everyone I was here, in the closed area of the woods.'

'Well, you have the right to be here. And in any case, he won't do that. His father would thrash him for disobeying the order to stay out of here.'

'But he could still put the word out – tell other children that he'd heard I was here on my own and up to no good. That kind of thing...' He took her hand and squeezed it apologetically.

'We could meet somewhere else,' she said.

'I don't know. The woods are full of people trapping and hunting now.'

'We could meet in the West Orchard, near the ruins of the old nunnery. People say they are haunted and no one goes there. Not even that wretched boy...'

He took her in his arms and almost relented in his resolve not to make love to her.

'No. I'll send you a message when I think I am under less suspicion,' he said. 'In a few days.'

He walked her to her horse, put the sword belt back around her waist and helped her to mount. For a moment she sat still in the saddle, unwilling to go, her beauty in sad tatters round her shoulders. Even before she uttered the words, he knew what she would say. She loved him. He felt like telling her, 'I know you do, because love is blind, and you are the blindest of all. Don't you know why you did not see Tom? Or hear him? Why not, Godiva?'

But that would be too cruel. It would also be self-defeating. Anyway, she probably wouldn't understand what he meant.

'And I love you,' he replied, not knowing or caring what he said.

Parting from Bret so unexpectedly had jolted her and left her distracted as she rode home along the bridle path. It fell to the pony, a small mare she had ridden for many years, to act as a lookout for any sign of trouble. To Godiva's surprise, only a few minutes down the trail the pony came to a standstill, pricked up her ears and refused to move another inch, not even swishing her tail against the flies. 'What is it, May?' Godiva asked, but got no response. She put her head down and placed her ear in line with the pony's and listened. In the intense silence that hung round the still animal's body she could detect soft sounds, at no great distance from where she and the horse now stood, sounds so low they could only have been made by some creature working away in great secrecy. 'Sh! Stay still,' she whispered in the pony's ear. Then she dismounted without so much as cracking a twig and, leaving May untethered, began to walk, half-stooping, in the direction of the sounds.

Moments later, as she crouched between thick ferns, she saw them. Two poachers had just killed a deer and were attempting to butcher it quietly on the spot. One was a thin boy of no more than fourteen; the other, a strong young man of about eighteen. She had never seen them before. They could only be drovers, she thought, entering the forest in defiance of the ban on cattle movements in the lordship. She wondered at their competence at butchering meat. She glanced round and noticed that the kill had happened at a place where there was no stream or other source of water to clean out the carcass. Nor did the bigger youth have a proper boning knife. Instead he was holding a small sword. As she watched, he plunged the sword into the animal's throat and ripped open the belly of the carcass from gullet to tail. Entrails and vital organs spilled out together on the bloody ground, followed by the bolus, the great green steaming ball of semi-digested grass from the second stomach. The youth jumped back in disgust and kicked the carcass.

'You, get over here,' he shouted at the smaller boy. 'Clean this shit and cut me some meat to cook.'

Godiva, angry at the ruin of good venison when people were starving, pulled out her sword and weighed the danger of attacking the youths. Just then, though, May wandered over towards her and gave a soft snort.

'Hey, a pony. With a nice saddle and all,' the older boy exclaimed. 'Go and grab her reins.'

'Leave her alone,' said the smaller boy. 'Someone will come looking for her.'

'I'll be on my way down London Road and selling this beast before they even know she's gone.'

'Uncle will flog you if he finds out. Send the bloody horse away and let's just smoke this venison.'

'Hmm,' the older boy rubbed his chin. 'Perhaps you're right. Well then, while we're at it, we could kill the pony, too. We could smoke all the meat at the same time and take it back to camp tomorrow. I'll warrant uncle don't know deer from horse in his mouth.' He wiped the deer's blood off his sword.

'You're not going to kill it now, with that sword? You're mad. You need a poleaxe. Send it away...'

'No, look...' The bigger boy made a slash at May, but succeeded only in grazing her neck. It was enough, though, for Godiva to rise out of the ferns in fury and charge him with her drawn sword.

'Fucking bitch, who you?' the older boy roared, waving his sword at her.

Godiva paused, realizing that a corpse would raise too many questions about her recent movements. 'I own that deer you just killed,' she shouted. 'You're trespassing. Go away.'

'Here, Alf,' he shouted at the smaller boy. 'Pick up a stick and help me beat the hell out of this bitch.'

He came at her now, confident that between the two of them they could have her down on the ground in no time. But May reared up against the smaller boy, teeth bared and hooves thrashing, until he retreated to the edge of the clearing, leaving the big one to face Godiva alone. By now, desperate to secure his catch and livid that a woman with a pony was holding him at bay, he was ready to kill her and hide her body under a mound of leaves. He slashed with his sword, and felt the surprising strength in her arm as she parried, to left, to right, then in a circle. Each handled the sword better than the other expected, and the fight seemed as though it would end by accident, when one tripped over a root and the other pounced in victory. But suddenly Godiva spotted a branch lying nearby and, swooping, seized it with her left arm. Moving so fast that the youth could do no more than parry in retreat, she got closer to him and started slashing at the side of his head with the branch. It confused him more than it hurt, but it gave her the chance to cut his arm with her sword. He shrieked at the sight of his blood and dropped his weapon.

'Spare me! I give up!' he said, beginning to sob. 'Keep the fucking deer.'

'No, you keep it,' Godiva said, picking up his sword. 'You've ruined the butchering. Take the carcass with you. Go on. Put it on your back and go, and don't ever come back to this lordship again.'

If the two youths thought it odd that they were being allowed to keep the meat, they did not show it. In moments they had vanished into the forest and Godiva was left alone to recover her breath.

'Come here, May,' she whispered, and threw her arms round

the pony's neck. 'We'll get you back to your stable now and put a big salve on your neck.'

The pony nibbled at her ear and for a moment Godiva could have sobbed with as much abandon as the youth she had seen off from the forest. But the moment passed and she straightened her clothes and hair, jumped into the saddle and set off once more for home.

In the kitchen of the manor house Bertha, Agatha and Milly had their heads down as they busied themselves with the rabbit pies they were making for dinner that night. Bertha had claimed the right to do the most skilled job – rolling out the pastry and cutting it into large, flat discs, some of which were fluted at the edges to fit snugly on top of the pie. With ostentatious caution, she lifted each one and then laid the pastry carefully over the pie trays so that no holes or gaps appeared from which the stew would leak and spoil the dish. Milly had taken the job of making the second batch of dough, because she liked to dig her fingers in and out of it, just as when she was six years old. Agatha had the job of filling the pie cases with the stewed meat, still hot from hours of slow simmering in spiced wine, and passing the pies to the slave who handled the manor house's kitchen oven. No one saw Godiva enter the room.

She stood for a moment, taking in the scene. So, she observed wearily, Milly was well again, and Agatha and her mother were on good enough terms, for the moment, to cooperate. Suddenly Milly raised her head from the kneading trough and saw Godiva.

'Mother!' she said in a raspy voice, still not fully cleared of her cold. 'Whatever happened to you? You're all mud and twigs.'

Agatha and Bertha, startled, looked up too, so quickly that Bertha dropped a pastry base onto the floor.

'Oh my!' she said. 'I never done that before. Mistress, what has happened?'

'Nothing. Just a fall. May got startled and I wasn't paying attention.'

'Yes, I'm sure,' said Milly. 'You look as though you've seen a ghost. Anyway, at least you're not as late as usual. I hear you go into the woods each afternoon for so long that everyone else has to have their evening meal an hour later than usual.'

'Never mind that,' Agatha said quickly. 'Pies can be eaten any time. You could have yours in half an hour, Mistress Milly, if you be truly hungry.'

'That's right,' Bertha said. 'Better for you to go off to bed early, young mistress. She only just come out of the sick-room,' she added, addressing Godiva. 'But Gwen still be there, though not with a cold any more. She has bad headaches and says her limbs are weak on one side. Could be "the corgi" had a small stroke. From all the worry, I'd say.'

Godiva sighed deeply. She would have to go to see her housekeeper as soon as possible. 'Are you sharing Gwen's work between you?' she asked, looking round at their hot, flushed faces.

'Yes, mistress,' Agatha smiled at Godiva. 'Mother knows Gwen's duties and she is teaching me well. And Mistress Milly is helping out, too. With kneading and such.'

'Only for tonight, though,' Milly snapped, 'and I certainly won't be going to bed early, Bertha. I feel quite well, thank you. And anyway,' she said, resuming her kneading and dropping her voice so that her mother could hardly hear her, 'I want to sit with father when he eats with us tonight.'

'What did you say?' Godiva shouted. 'Lovric will be home tonight? Why did none of you tell me straight away? Oh my God, he'll have Harry with him! Why else would he come rushing back at such short notice? That's more important than pies or housework or anything else.'

'Really, mother?' Milly asked blandly. 'That's good. I mean, it's good that father is more important than anything else, for there will be no more walks in the woods each afternoon for you, not with father back home and telling you what to do all the time.'

'Go and get some more flour,' said Bertha quickly, and Milly, sensing she had overstepped the mark, went out of the room.

'I need to be alone sometimes,' Godiva said as though talking to herself, while Agatha and Bertha concentrated on the pies. 'I have to have some interludes of peace during these worrying times.'

Still there was no reply from Agatha and Bertha.

'Have people complained of my short absences?'

'No,' said Bertha firmly. 'No one even noticed you were going out to walk until Milly asked Father Godric to pray for her and he refused, saying he had to be with you. Then someone told Milly that Godric went to sleep in one of the barns every afternoon, and from that she reasoned that you were away from the manor. But no one told her you were in the woods, not me and not Agatha. Didn't seem like it was Mistress Milly's business where you were. She be a one that likes to go off a-strolling herself. Sulking and that. She just made it up, I reckon, about you walking in the woods.'

Bertha's eyes met Agatha's, and for once mother and daughter were in perfect accord.

'Well,' Godiva said uncertainly. 'We had better prepare for Lovric and the housecarls.'

'Everything is in hand, mistress,' Bertha said. 'Not a real feast, what with me having such short notice, but there be food and ale in the hall already, and the big fire going, and the horse troughs filled with hay and water. We done all this in the last two hours, since the messenger arrived.' She paused and looked across at Agatha.

'True, mistress,' said Agatha. 'There be nothing for you to do but get yourself nice and tidy before master come home. I already put hot water in the small oak tub for you. It will be cool enough now. And I've put the flat-iron on a clean linen dress and laid it on your bed.' Godiva was silent. 'I could come with you now,' Agatha said. 'I'm nearly finished with these pies.'

'No,' Godiva said quickly. 'I'll bathe alone. Come up when I call you, to braid my hair and dress me.'

Bertha butted in. 'That's right. You've plenty work left on them pies, my girl.'

Agatha hurried to agree and the moment passed when it might have seemed too obvious that Godiva refused the usual help with her bath, because no woman who has lain with a man day after day would want another woman anywhere near her until she had bathed alone.

Lovric's horn sounded late in the evening, as twilight was verging on night. Recalling his rebukes the last time he arrived home to find her absent, Godiva went out into the yard with the best drinking horn full of mead. The hall servants and slaves, the stable boys and the manor's staff stood round in a semicircle, torchlight flickering on the faces of those who stood in the shadows, everyone breathless with the excitement that always fill-ed the air when the armed men returned home together.

But it was not to be like that this evening. Lovric trotted in with only the herald and one other man beside him, and wearing the ordinary thegn's clothing he had worn when he rode with Godiva through Wessex in secret. He was sweating and dusty, and looked like a man who had come home at top speed. Godiva stared past him as if she had not seen him, gazing at the entrance to the yard and willing Harry to appear. Lovric stopped his horse before her and shook his head.

'You didn't bring Harry home?'

'No. Put that drinking horn away. Send everyone back to their duties.'

He climbed down from his horse and handed the reins to a

stable boy without a word. Then he turned to face her, unsmiling and angry.

'We must talk at once, alone.'

'Won't you eat?' she asked. 'There is a good dinner waiting for you.'

'Must I tell you twice?' he fumed as he crossed the threshold.

Godiva hurriedly told Agatha to keep the oven on a low heat, and followed Lovric into their chamber. She poured him a goblet full of red wine, which he took in his hand, but otherwise ignored.

'The housecarls, where are they?' she asked.

'Please, Godiva. Just listen to me and ask your questions afterwards. Can you do that?'

She had never heard him address her so curtly. Suddenly she wondered if he knew about Bret. She looked down at his dagger, and then at his gleaming sword. No, it was impossible. And yet her heart was thundering.

'Yes,' she replied breathlessly, and took a long draught of her wine while he still clutched his goblet in both hands. 'Go on. I am listening.'

'Harry,' he began. 'Obviously you will want to know about Harry first.'

She slumped with relief that Bret was not the first word out of his mouth. Lovric noticed and stared at her, but with none of his usual interest. He seemed like a man who knew what he had to say and just wanted to get on with it. He coughed and started talking in a controlled but crackling voice, sounding as though he had suddenly aged several years. It frightened Godiva as much as his unexplained anger.

'The king still says that Harry has a vocation as a monk. I know this is not true. But just to be sure I sent messengers to Siward and the reply I got was unequivocal: when Harry was with him he showed no interest in Jesus Christ, the Virgin Mary or God the Father himself. He was instructed in the catechism, of course, and went to mass with the rest of the household, and as far as anyone knows he has had nothing to do with paganism. But as for having one splinter of holiness in him, let alone a vocation to lead the life of a monk, it is utter rubbish and a lie.'

'Did you tell the king that?'

'Yes, but he just made more excuses to refuse to let the boy go. I even raised the subject of Harry's relations with Edmund. I said that Siward and I both knew about this, and we countenanced their friendship as long as it remained restrained in public. Well, Edward knows that military commanders have always protected men like Harry and Edmund, and yet he pretended I was telling him about some unheard-of depravity. He ranted at me, accused me of degeneracy and then he said all our family was in danger of hellfire. Especially you.'

'Me? I don't understand this, Lovric. When he spoke with me in the cathedral he only talked of my sins in general ways. He talked passionately, and yet he was sympathetic, even encouraging.'

Lovric said nothing and put his goblet to his lips for the first time. Then he drained it empty in one long gulp and went to stare out of the window at the black and starless night sky.

'Well?' Godiva asked at last. 'What else was said? You are angry, Lovric, and you haven't told me why.'

Lovric now started pacing the room, occasionally glancing furiously at Godiva, who noticed that his hand was on the hilt of his sword and that he was squeezing it repeatedly.

'For God's sake, tell me what the matter is!' she snapped, her fear blotting out her understanding of Lovric.

Again he paced, and continued pacing while she stared at him as though he were a stranger she might recognize, if only she tried hard enough and kept her eyes fixed upon him.

'I have nothing to say,' he said at last, mumbling through

clenched jaws so that it was hard for her to understand him. 'But perhaps you do.'

Godiva did not hear his last words. She folded her arms and braced herself for what now seemed like an inevitable escalation of their quarrel.

'Well,' she said coldly, 'if you won't tell me why you are angry, at least tell me how your meeting with Edward ended. Was anything at all agreed about Harry?'

'No. Edward terminated the audience on just one word. "Filth!" Then he stalked out, leaving me standing there alone like a churl, to be shown the door by that Saxon traitor-priest of his.'

'Father Francis,' Godiva said.

'Yes. That's the one. You'd know, of course. You've been on close terms with these cross-wavers, haven't you, Godiva?'

'What do you mean? I told you everything about that meeting in the cathedral,' she said, beginning to grow angry herself. 'Everything! "Close terms" doesn't describe it at all, and you know that, Lovric.'

'Well, how do you explain this, then?' he asked, leaning forward into her face. 'You, Godiva, are to have special favours. It seems the king thinks you are not to blame for the sins of the Earls of Mercia. It is your own terrible sins that you must answer for.'

'Explain what you mean. I've asked you before – what sins?'

Lovric clenched his jaw angrily and Godiva felt her anxiety deepen to hopelessness. Whatever the king had said about her to Lovric would remain between the two of them.

'Why is there talk of sins and favours?' she said again, determined to wring some sense from him. 'You must tell me the truth, Lovric.'

'There is nothing to tell,' he replied bitterly. 'Nothing you don't already know. Congratulations. You seem to have gifts of diplomacy I knew nothing about.'

'What in God's name are you talking about, Lovric?'

'Edward called me back to another meeting with him, and told me he had taken stock of all the many ways in which my house has given offence to him as king and to God. As punishment, he said, he will demand payment of the army tax from all my lands.'

'*Heregeld?*'

'Yes.'

'But this is an outrage. When?'

'At once, in full.'

'But he can't! That tax is immense. It hasn't been imposed in Mercia for years. Besides, it was raised to pay mercenaries, for defence against the Vikings, so there's no need now ...'

'For God's sake, Godiva, do you need to tell me such things? Edward may not be in the right, but he is the king, and he can do whatever he wants. He can send in his soldiers and take the tax by force from the farmers on my lands. I can't stop him because my armed men are not deployed to defend my own estates, but to defend the country in dangerous areas. Most of them are out on the Welsh borders and in the Fens, and some are up with Siward. I did not think I would have to defend my lands against my own king. He has almost declared war on me.'

'I thought you were about to declare war on him.'

'Not yet. He's made the first move, much sooner than I expected. I've been caught off balance.'

'Then what will you do, Lovric?' she said, taking his hand as her anger at him subsided. He was afraid, she told herself – not angry with her about anything she had done.

'I will pay the tax myself, out of my treasure,' he said, pulling away from her and starting to pace about again. 'It is a huge amount, but I can manage it, at least this year. The alternative would be to let the king's troops take what they want by force, and they would not be gentle in going about it. I would lose all respect as the lord of the land and I could never count on my people's loyalty again. Wessex lords would start moving in, offering to help them, and it would not be long before the earldom of Mercia came to an end.'

There was silence as Godiva waited for Lovric to tell her more. But he seemed far away, as though thinking of something even more oppressive than the huge tax he had to pay.

'Lovric?' she asked at last. 'Is Edward going to tax my lands, too?'

'Oh, Godiva!' he sighed. 'He said he might exempt your lands, despite what he calls your terrible sins. But there is a catch. You, as the landlord, must go and plead with him in person for exemption from *heregeld*.'

'Is that all? Well then, I'll go. I'll go tomorrow.'

'What? No...'

'I will. We have all slaved here for a week to save Coventry from starvation – something you don't even know about yet. I'm not going to stand by and let king's men raid barns that I filled for my people at my own expense. As for paying the *heregeld* with my own money, I don't have enough left.'

'I'll pay the *heregeld* on your lands,' he said quietly.

'But this is unnecessary, Lovric, and too expensive. We'd have no reserves left to deal with any emergencies. No, there's no harm in my doing what he asks.'

'No harm? Do you think he'd give you something for nothing? I've just told you he thinks you are the most sinful of us all. If you go to see him he'll bargain with you, try to force you into something...'

'Oh. Lovric! That's not how he is. He may be oppressive about taxation, but he is sincere in his love of Christ. Where is Edward now?'

'He is at Cleley, in Northampton,' Lovric said, but now his

tone had hardened and his anger was returning. 'Take my advice on this and don't argue with me, Godiva. You are not going to Cleley. You've already had too much to do with the king, on your own, without me, saying things you should not have said. We must stand side by side in this matter and take the same approach in dealing with Edward. I forbid you to go to him. That's all I have to say.'

'How dare you, Lovric! This is my concern, and this is my solution for a problem caused by you. Your diplomacy has failed. Your scheming and manoeuvring have come to nothing. I must defend myself. Don't you dare cross me on this, or...'

'Or what?' he asked icily. 'Is it a divorce you have in mind, Godiva? That is what men and women want when they cannot agree. If that is what you want, it could be arranged, quite easily I believe.'

'Of course not,' she said. 'No. We shouldn't be quarrelling like this, Lovric. But you must try to see my point of view and not just bark orders at me as if I were one of your housecarls.'

'Very well,' he said wearily, like one who knew he had to go through the motions of cooperation, though his mind was already firmly made up. 'Go on, Godiva. Have your say.'

'No. Not with you in this mood. I know you won't pay attention when I start giving you the details. Actually, you never do. Go and talk to Odo when you are ready to listen to someone, and find out how bad things have been here. Then listen to him tell you how much we had to do to turn things round. As for me, just explain why you forbade me to go to Cleley. It is not far away. The king has said he might lift the taxes off my lands if I go. So why do you want to stop me?'

'I never thought of you as stupid before,' he muttered. 'But recently you don't seem to see what is important. It's as though you've become so busy with this little town of yours that you can't think clearly any more.'

'Stop it! You are patronizing and you are...' But she ran out of angry words. 'Just tell me why.'

'All right. Let me make it as plain as day. You know now that Edward has been trying to see you alone, without me, ever since he came here to the investiture, two years ago.'

'Yes, he told me so himself, in the cathedral. There was no harm in it. It was a matter of religious concern...'

'And he insisted I bring you to Winchester.'

'Yes, but when I saw him he only wanted to talk about religion. I keep saying that and you won't listen. What is wrong with talking about religion? Perhaps he is not as bad as you and Godwin say, perhaps he is sincere about loving my soul...'

'Don't be stupid, woman!'

'If you think I'm stupid there's no need to talk to me. Just impose your orders! But maybe it's you who are stupid, Lovric. Maybe if you understood Edward the way others do, you could work with him, instead of always being at odds with him. Many think he is a genuinely good man, deeply spiritual...'

'Who's been getting at you, Godiva? Who's been saying such things to you?'

'No one. It's merely a well-known fact that many speak well of the king.'

'"Many"?' he repeated sarcastically. 'And this vague entity, "many", carries more weight in your mind than my views and those of Godwin, both of us men who have spent much time with Edward and can judge his actions. I think, Godiva, that perhaps you have been too much in the company of one of the "many" who share their views with you, given your great beauty.'

Suddenly, quite unaware of any movement in her shoulder, she found her arm raised and her hand flying out to slap his face. He caught her wrist and pulled it down beside her waist.

'Never,' he said softly, 'never do that again.' And then he turned to leave the room.

'Wait,' she called after him. 'Tell me, where are our men? And how long are you staying in Coventry this time?'

'I'm not going to tell you anything, Godiva,' he said angrily. 'I don't trust you any more.'

'And I don't trust you,' she shouted at his back. 'You've always deceived me, and now you can't even be bothered to do that. It is you who has been thinking about a divorce, Lovric, and pretending to believe it was me. You say Edward plays games with people, but you do, too. Alfgar always said you were not to be trusted, and now I agree with him.'

She stopped as he turned to face her, his expression grim and cold.

'This is no game, Godiva. I hope you don't find that out to your cost.'

She listened to his footsteps as he descended the steep stairs, and heard him exchange a few words with Agatha. There was a brief commotion as Milly screamed, 'No!' It was followed by a silence in which she could hear only Milly's muffled sobs and the sound of Lovric's feet crossing the yard. A horse snorted and another neighed, and then he was gone. ·

Godiva lay back on her bed – their bed, though it hadn't been that very often in recent times. She sipped her wine, and then took more. To her surprise she was not crying and shaking. She felt slightly cold, and reached out for a fur cover to pull up over her legs. So, he was gone. What difference did that make? He was hardly ever there to help her anyway. And when he did turn up, it was only to interfere with her decisions, to criticize and belittle, and to make demands on her to satisfy his own needs. He had always asked for complete compliance from her, and when he didn't get it he stormed off like an angry child. Or a man who is tired of his wife, she thought bitterly. Isn't that what they all do at his age? Make excuses for their irritability and go raging off into the waiting arms of some young and calculating mistress? It was such a tawdry little story, too commonplace to be worth a second thought. Perhaps, indeed, they had never really loved each other deeply. Perhaps their affection over so many years was simply due to the absence of alternatives for her, in the remote manor houses where she had been compelled to rule servants and manage stores, while Lovric came and went at will. This summer was not yet over, and yet it had changed everything. It had started with their reunion, but it had led inexorably towards the ruin of their marriage. It was finished, she felt sure.

Twelve

Almost unrecognizable in the dull soldier's clothes of a minor thegn, Lovric entered Coventry unnoticed by the few townspeople who were still abroad on the darkened main street. He dismounted near the priory, tied his horse to the hitching post and told his attendant to wait outside for a few minutes. Then he banged on the door. Prior Edwin, who had already been told that a strange man who looked like Lovric was riding into the market area, came to the door at once to let him in.

'Will you pray in your chantry, sir?' Edwin grovelled.

'Not tonight,' Lovric replied. 'Lead me to the chapel of the Virgin, and leave me there to pray alone.'

The prior did as he was told, lit two tapers and left. As he shuffled off towards the back of the church he glanced back and thought he saw his lord's big shoulders shaking. My, my, he thought, the storm is already breaking. I'd better stay and hear what I can of the thunder.

In the little chapel Lovric gazed at the frescoes. Their bright colours, softened and fluid in the candle light, reminded him of Godiva's clothes strewn carelessly across their bed, and of her hands, like Mary's, offering love and tenderness. *Ave Maria* ... he prayed in a whisper, and carried on until he reached the point where he always forgot the prayer. 'Sorry, Mary. *That is how I am with prayers. I can't remember them. But still, I came to pay my respects and to ask for your help. For the love of God, protect my wife and for the sake of your son, Lord Jesus Christ, make my family whole again before the winter comes. I am being pushed into rebellion and I am not ready for it. Stay my hand for the sake of England. Make Godiva love me again. Let me love Godiva again.'*

The prior, eavesdropping with all his might, heard these last words clearly and pondered their implications as he crept away through an adjacent corridor. The earl and Godiva no longer loved each other. He rejoiced. Without her husband, Godiva would have half the standing she had before, or less. That would teach her a lesson. On the other hand, Lovric seemed full of regret. He would come looking for reconciliation one day. Then that haughty bitch would be bossing her prior around as much as ever before. *Ergo*, it followed that his own best interest lay in further discouraging the love between the earl and his wife. That shouldn't be hard, he thought, now that Godiva was eating out of his hand.

Whispering down the corridors of several Benedictine monasteries the rumours had filtered quickly into the heart of the priory of St Mary's, Coventry. The king, they said, was angry with the whole House of Lovric and intended to teach the earl a lesson in humility and obedience and God-fearing. He had taken counsel with Father Francis and with other knowledgeable men and recommendations had been made. Soon, praise the Lord, certain men of the sword would feel the whiplash of the men who prayed.

Thus, knowing that trouble was on its way, the prior spent an uneasy night following Lovric's visit. That visit, he thought, must surely be the warning bell he had expected to toll. His dilemma, and the cause for his insomnia, concerned his own role. Should he give Godiva false hope that she would not feel the king's anger herself? Or should he begin to drop sympathetic hints that soon she would pay a price for being Lovric's wife? She would like him the more if he took the first approach, but then later, perhaps, when she came to look back on her troubles, he might seem to have been a little too innocent for plausibility. He had to be careful there, especially if his efforts to blacken her character in the eyes of the king's senior clerics failed and she kept her grip on his priory. Yes, he mused, no one could count on church reform to sweep away the claims of the lay owners just yet. It would take time. It followed then that he should adopt the second approach – give her some idea of the trouble that might lie ahead of her, but offer himself as a source of advice and comfort, her rock in shifting sands and swirling tides. He could advise her, for example, to adopt an attitude of humility, for she was certainly going to need it. First of all, though, he had to learn exactly what Lovric had said to her before storming out of the manor and coming to the priory. What was that quarrel about? He could hardly wait to hear what Godiva would say, and got up to pray to pass away the time.

He was not long left in suspense. Only an hour after dawn the clapper of the door-knocker clanged against its iron cradle, and Edwin ran down the corridor to open the door with all speed.

'My beloved sister in Christ…' he started breathlessly.

'I need your advice,' Godiva said at once, and the prior smiled. This meeting was starting as he would wish.

'Advice about what, beloved?' he asked, as soon as he had settled her comfortably beside the fire in the small room by the refectory.

'About going to Cleley to see the king.'

Edwin affected concern while struggling with delight. She trusted him so much she was going to tell him everything, all at once, without any suggestive prying on his part.

'The king,' she went on, her eyes beginning to redden, 'is very angry at Lovric, and at all of us. You know about Harry, I think?'

'Yes, but not much,' he lied, and then took her hand gently and encouraged her to tell him the whole sad tale of a boy corrupted, and a father's indifference (in the eyes of the king), and the question of the poor youth's spiritual salvation and his future life on this Earth, where men like him are not treated kindly.

'Except by the Church, if they renounce sin,' Edwin managed to say before Godiva told the rest of her story.

He put his head back, closed his eyes and pressed his fingertips together like a church steeple, as though struggling to absorb too large an amount of information. In fact, though, he was trying to detect how much Godiva knew of her husband's military affairs. From what she said it seemed that the earl had not been very forthcoming at home. Or was Godiva keeping back something? No, he assured himself: she was not clever enough to know what to reveal and what to withhold. No wonder the earl told her so little. It was a pity. There would be fewer grounds to accuse her of treachery than Father Francis expected. He would send a word to Cleley and tell them to stick to accusations of another sort. God knows he'd given them enough information about the black arts for them to think of something else.

'What it boils down to is this,' Godiva said, 'I must plead with the king for mercy. If he takes pity on me, he will remove the charge of *heregeld* against my lands and my poor starving people. If my plea fails, king's men will raid the barns and take my remaining money. The people will run away. Some will sell their children to Bristol slave-dealers. I would hang myself.'

'Go to him in faith,' Edwin said at once. 'Trust in the king's goodness and mercy. Throw yourself at his feet and plead with him. Abandon your pride. This is what Christ demands of us. This is the way to life eternal.'

'I can't keep this visit to Cleley a secret,' she continued. 'But I don't know what to say to my people. I can't explain why the king believes we are a sinful family, deserving such a heavy punishment. I can't tell them about Harry.'

'But you will have to give them some reason why the king is angry with the House of Lovric. Say something about Alfgar...'

'No. One day he will be the earl. I shouldn't give people reason to hate him.'

Edwin, who hadn't anticipated this matter, felt stumped.

'I know,' he said, suddenly remembering his own earlier thoughts. 'Tell them that the king has learned there has been a rash of witchcraft in many parts of Mercia. Hence the punishment of *heregeld*. It's probably true, Godiva. People do make heathen prayers and sacrifices when hunger starts. And you have been quite tolerant in such matters, have you not?'

'Yes. I haven't investigated rumours. I suppose I could say that to them. Thank you, prior. Pray for me.'

She got up to go and Edwin walked with her to the side-door.

'One thing more,' she asked, 'did Lovric come here last night, as he left Coventry?'

'No. I heard the sound of his horse approaching from the manor, and I hoped he would come and pray with us. But no, I'm afraid he galloped off as though in a fury.'

Godiva said nothing and looked away. Then she crossed herself again and left.

It was mid-morning when she got back to the manor, where everyone had scattered to do their own work. She went to the hall and told Odo to assemble all the people at once. Then she sat down on the big chair that Lovric used when he presided over their feasts and looked round at the empty hall, its high, oak-beamed ceiling, its rush-strewn floor and its gigantic cindery fireplace. How often had they sat here together, and how clearly the songs they sang still echoed in her head, as empty now as the hall itself. Husband gone. Money nearly all gone. Sons gone. Daughter gone, too, in her own way. Future gone, or at least grown misty. Her beauty going rapidly, and after that her stamina, and then perhaps her life. If that was so, then all that mattered was today, and what she could make of it. But no surge of courage flooded her heart as she formed this resolve. Today was a necessity to wrestle with, leading to nothing except tonight and then another similar day, and yet another, stretching on to who knew what dreary lengths for the sake of mere survival and nothing more than that. The latch that connected her to the mundane and the routine had slipped when she had not seen it happen. She was like an unyoked ox, looking at boundless freedom and seeing for the first time that it was nothing but an infinity of grass, one blade just like another, a sea of green ending only where the sea of blue began and the horizon drew the line that showed where possibilities came to an end. Her mind wandered to the vagrants who had ended their lives on a branch above the pool at Stivichall. She had spoken some empty words then, about people laying down the burden of life. Only now did she know what that meant.

'Lady, a word with you!' Odo's mouth was close to her ear and he was whispering urgently. 'Before you address the manor's people, tell me what you are going to say to them.'

'Why? This is not your concern,' she said, trying to sound resolved.

'Yes, it is. There are rumours going round that the earl has left us. Tell me what you will say to the people.'

'I am leaving to go to Cleley to talk to the king. He is going to impose heavy taxes on us, the *heregeld*. This is punishment for the acts of witchcraft that have taken place in our forests. Sh!' She held up her hand to stop him interrupting. 'We all know these have taken place. I'm going to have to plead with him to spare us.'

'For God's sake, lady, don't tell them that. Don't even mention the *heregeld*. How do they know you'll succeed with the king? If one word about this threat reaches the townsfolk, many of them will leave at once, with whatever they have left, rather than risk being here when the king's men raid us. And if they leave you, you won't get them back.'

One or two people were already entering the hall.

'But what else can I tell them?' she whispered.

'A lie. The bigger, the better. Say Queen Edith wants your advice on developing a new manor she has acquired. Say anything, but not what you planned to say. And tell them Lovric will be home soon.'

Odo hurried away and began bustling around, checking to see who had turned up at the meeting and who was still missing. Moments later, when it seemed that everyone was there, he came back and told Godiva that Milly had returned to the sick-room and would not come out.

'She's not sick, though, not according to the nurse. But she's turned her face to the wall and won't eat.'

'Then she can go hungry,' Godiva said, and Odo smiled in relief. It seemed the mistress still had some common sense.

Godiva climbed up on Lovric's big chair and cleared her throat. Some called out a blessing on her name, and someone else blessed the house of Lovric. Then silence settled on the wary crowd.

'Good people,' she began. 'I must go away for a few days. I am going east, to Cleley in the Forest of Salcey, to talk with the king. And Queen Edith, too,' she added, unsure which explanation to offer. 'The hall will be run by Odo, as usual, with Bertha and Agatha running the manor until Gwen or Mildred is in better health. Lord Lovric will be back soon, perhaps before I return myself. I understand that our supplies are good, but you must all continue to enforce short rations and fair distribution in the town. The rules regarding hunting will remain the same and drovers are still barred from entering my lands. In addition, I want you all to be on guard for any signs of the spread of the summer cold, or malnourishment, or trouble of any sort in the outlying hamlets. Don't listen to rumours, and try to keep everyone calm. You have my word that I will not be gone long.'

She stepped down and only then did she realize that she had not offered them an explanation, and no one had shouted out to ask for one.

'Good,' Odo said. 'Least said, soonest mended.'

Odo found Bret as he was leading a horse across the yard to the stables.

'Mistress will ask you to ride with her to Cleley. Do you know the way?' Bret nodded. 'Good man. You'll be going with only four others, but all fully armed. Go and see her now and then get over to the armoury. I'll meet you there and get you the best weapons in the hall.'

As Bret entered the hall Godiva was deep in conversation with Agatha, giving her instructions and answering her questions. To his surprise, Agatha seemed to be having a disagreement with her mistress.

'I must go with you,' the girl pleaded. 'You'll need me to help you...'

'You'll slow me down,' Godiva replied. 'You don't gallop well enough yet, and your favourite horse has just taken a stone in her shoe. Anyway, Bertha will need you.'

'But, mistress, I do gallop well. You just ain't seen me ride because you was always ahead of me.'

'Nonsense. I've asked the captain and he says you must improve before we go on another long journey. Practise while I'm gone. Tell your mother I want you to take time away from your work, and get a good horse from the stables and someone to help you.'

'Yes, mistress,' Agatha said hopelessly, but just then she saw Bret and her little face turned dark as bad wine. 'He should stay here too,' she said heedlessly, and then she burst into tears and ran away.

'She guessed you're to come with me and she doesn't approve.'

'But Odo does,' Bret replied, glancing round to see if they were alone. 'Those days we spent apart were worth it, Godiva. If anyone suspected anything, they don't any more.'

He fell on one knee and kissed her hand, and though Godiva stood quite motionless and was at the other end of the hall from her, Agatha, lingering near the door, could have sworn that she was trembling. That bastard Bret, she thought. He's fooling everyone again. But not me. One day I'll make him pay for what he's doing to mistress, so help me holy Mary.

How different in every way was this expedition to Cleley from Godiva's journey with Lovric to Winchester. Then, while travelling south together, there had been intervals of leisure, while now there was only hard riding; then there had been singing and good humour, but now there was only the company of a small and worried band of men, all keeping some distance from their lady. They were dogged by low spirits and enervated by stilted, staccato conversation. Exhausting days were followed by dreary nights at farmhouses whose owners, paid for their hospitality, showed no pleasure in caring for the wife of the Earl of Mercia and her men. Nor did the land they traversed show them more kindness, or indeed show them anything at all, for this was the watershed of the middle of England, where rivers that could easily flow east actually drained to the west, and those that should have gone west followed some imperceptible rise in the contours of the land and meandered off to the east. In forests that were thick with undergrowth and bog, the tangle of twisting trails and bridle paths made it difficult for the horses to keep their pace, and the lead riders too were strained, being unsure in the absence of clear landmarks which route was the correct one at each fork in the trail, and gaining no compass from the sun that lay hidden in cloud beyond the dark-green canopy above their heads.

A few days into their short journey, as they approached Salcey Forest, the landscape changed. The swampy woods began to thin out and small villages appeared beside streams that cut into the lighter soils beneath the surface. In some places there had been forest clearance, and with the greater sunlight came an increase in flowering plants. Godiva had never before felt so thankful to see the earth once more alive with colour.

'Pottery,' Bret said to her, in one of their rare exchanges. 'Folk here use the clay soils to make fine vessels, but they live on drier land where they can keep garden lots by their houses. Most of the pots from hereabouts go to Cleley, to Egg Ring.'

'Egg Ring? We're not going there!' Godiva was dismayed, for Egg Ring had a lurid reputation.

'Yes.'

'I thought we were going to Grafton, to the king's manor.'

'No. The manor is small and only used occasionally by the queen when she visits. We'll be sent on to Egg Ring. That's where the king does his business. We should start running into his outlying guards soon.'

In the event they saw no guards for the rest of the day, and it was only as they approached the small farm where they were to spend the night that a messenger arrived bearing instructions for the remainder of their journey. The man, who was invisible inside his helmet, which he did not remove, rode up to Bret, ignored

Godiva and reeled off a list of directions about the route to be followed – to Egg Ring, as Bret had foretold. Godiva's men exchanged worried glances, then one of them spoke up.

'Bret, friend, what is the meaning of this? That man's tunic bears the cross of St George. English mercenaries up north wear this sign. Why are they down here in Mercia, with the king?'

'It's nothing new,' Bret said, trying to keep his voice steady. 'A core of Knights of St George joined King Edward in his first year in England. He keeps them in places like this, where few see them and no one will take offence that they are not men of the *fyrd*.'

'Places like this?' another asked. 'What does that mean, Bret? Does the king keep other secret places? And what for?'

'I don't think so,' Bret replied. 'Just Cleley and another place in Yorkshire, near the coast. He does this so as to receive missions from abroad in secrecy, and traitors are brought here for questioning. The Knights provide the guards at these camps.'

'I don't like the sound of this at all,' said Arne, who had spoken little since Odo instructed him to accompany Godiva. 'Why did our mistress have to come here? Why not somewhere more open?'

'It's not too far from Coventry,' Godiva said quickly, 'and the king happened to be here just when I needed to talk with him. That's all there is to it. Nothing to worry about, thank you, Arne.'

'Mistress, I must disagree. Odo confided the true reason for your visit to the king, and he swore us to secrecy so as not to frighten the people of Coventry. But I am frightened now, and so are the others.' He looked round at his companions, who frowned in assent. 'The king threatens you with *heregeld*, does he not? Those men in their red crosses have already burned villages in several parts of England, in the name of the king's law and God's word. They pretend to be well-born knights in holy orders, but they are ruffians. Just ordinary soldiers putting on airs. Many hold them to be as bad as Vikings, though they wear the cross. And those are the men he will send against Coventry, unless you can change his mind.'

'There is truth in what Arne says,' Bret intervened. 'The king does use them to carry out difficult tasks. His confessor, Father Francis, encourages that. But here, in Cleley, they are under strict control. The king has his own housecarls to keep them in check, and the priests question them closely. You have nothing to fear from them.'

But, Godiva thought, much more to fear from the king than she had thought possible before.

The group dispersed to their quarters, Godiva bedding down beside the farmer's kindly wife, while the men settled in the barn. The woman entertained her with stories of Cleley and its potters, and soon, bored but soothed, Godiva fell into a sleep in which exhaustion vanquished fear. Matters were otherwise in the barn, however, where the men peppered Bret with questions about Cleley, Egg Ring and the Knights of St George, until finally someone pointed out that whatever lay ahead of them, it was entirely beyond their control. All they could do was protect their mistress and pray to the Lord that she would find the right words with which to divert the royal wrath into some channel that did not lead to Coventry. They all said amen to that.

But the next morning their fear only deepened. They had just started to assemble for departure when the yard filled with a company of armed men, all wearing the tunics that displayed their membership of the military guild of St George. There were more than twenty of them and they completely surrounded the band from Coventry, who were quickly blindfolded and their horses tied to those of the knights. Godiva alone was left free to see.

'No man may look at the way into Egg Ring,' the captain of the knights said.

'And if he does,' another of them laughed, 'that's the last time he sees anything at all.'

He made a gesture that mimicked the way eyes are gouged out by executioners. Then he started imitating a newly blinded man, bewildered and crazed with pain, groping around for something to hold on to. Godiva turned away in disgust. Moments later the blindfolded group from Coventry was led out of the yard, while Godiva followed behind them, riding alongside the knights' silent captain.

At first she could see no reason why her men should be blindfolded. The road across Cleley lacked landmarks; no one unfamiliar with this parish could possibly find their way back to Egg Ring after just one visit. But then, as they rounded a corner, she realized why the blindfolds were a necessity. There ahead of them to the left, on a small hill, stood a gallows, and hanging from its cross-beam were the swaying bodies of four men. Who these might be she had no idea, but there was every chance that one of her men would know. As she neared the gallows she steeled herself for the sight of the dead men's faces and turned to look at them carefully. She still did not recognize them, but at this close range she learned something new. Each one had been badly beaten before he died, and one, presumably a spy, had two blackened holes where his eyes had been. Godiva crossed herself and looked straight ahead.

A few minutes later, however, a scene presented itself that was so astonishing that she realized that this, not the gallows, must be the deadly secret of Egg Ring. Spread out over a piece of cleared, sloping land lay a village of tents. It reached all the way from the lane on which they were riding up to the tree line, and with its leather and rope structures of different sizes and their peaks adorned with colourful pennants, it might almost have been a fair, but that the tents were laid out with military precision in orderly rows like the streets of a walled town. As they got nearer she could see groups of soldiers in the tunics of St George moving amidst the tents, while further along most of the inhabitants seemed to be monks. To one side stood a large enclosed field, and here several pairs of knights were jousting with each other, using wooden dummy weapons, but wearing full armour to get used to the weight. Two of these jousting pairs wore the robes of Benedictine monks, over which they had placed chain-mail armour and St George's tunics.

As they passed by the tent village, a square stone tower came into view, the first permanent structure they had seen in Egg Ring. At first Godiva took it to be a church tower, but then she realized that it had none of the features of a church – no bell tower and no pretty arched windows, for instance. Instead it had a heavily barred door on its front wall and at each side a flight of stone stairs going down to doors that opened to a windowless, underground cellar, or what English people had recently started calling – in the Norman fashion – a dungeon. Suddenly she understood the geography of the tent village. Men suspected of crimes against the king were taken to the dungeon first, where the priests would supervise their interrogation. Once proven guilty, they would be paraded past the tents and on to the gallows, where soldiers would execute them.

Leaving the tents, they entered a thicket of trees that had been left untouched since the days of Cleley's innocence. Moments later there arose before them the big grassy outline of Egg Ring, which Godiva recognized as one of the enclosures used by ancient, long-dead people, now regarded as the home of dangerous spirits. Was this where Edward held rustic court while visiting his forces at Cleley? It seemed incredible. Why should any king camp in such a place? And yet this was their destination.

The captain stopped the riders and signalled that their blindfolds be removed. Then, after a few moments of blinking and gazing around, the whole group followed him round the embankment of Egg Ring to where a steep-sided cutting offered access to its interior. Here a wooden gatehouse sheltered the watchmen, and the captain called out the password of the day, 'Chalice and Eagle'.

'Who do you bring?' the watchman shouted back.

'Godiva of Coventry,' the captain answered.

'Dismount and enter in the name of St George and King Edward.'

The horses were led away, the huge wicker gate that formed the barrier between the world and the interior creaked open, and Godiva glimpsed the inner passages of the king's secret place, the hidden fortress of Egg Ring. Despite the afternoon hour there seemed to be no light within, other than the flames of torches. She looked up and realized that the sky was shut out by a vast patchwork leather canopy that covered the entire enclosure. It was stamped with gilt and silver patterns, and inset with mirrors that sparkled like the stars in the night sky, and yet for all its richness this roof was suffocating and dispiriting. She felt as though she was about to be swallowed by a whale, and a wave of nausea swept through her.

'This way, lady,' said the captain, but he raised his sword and, with its flat side, barred Godiva's men from coming any further with her.

'You know we must stay with our lady,' Arne protested.

Bret stepped in front of him at once to protect him.

'He does not understand the rules of Egg Ring, sir,' he said to the captain, who had taken off his mailed glove and was about to hit Arne's mouth with it. 'I'll be in charge of these men, sir, if you agree,' he added.

The captain stared at him coldly, but nodded silent consent. Bret took hold of Godiva's hand and kissed it quickly, whispering, 'Courage' as he backed away from her.

She was taken down a narrow lane, lined with pavilions set

close to each other. As she walked she could sense the nearness
of other people, though the place was silent as well as dark. Now
it seemed more like a tomb than any living creature's belly, and
she clenched and unclenched her fists to make sure she was not
dreaming.

Suddenly the captain stopped and pulled back a thick curtain
behind which stood a door to a small wooden building. He
opened it and then pushed Godiva inside so roughly that she fell
to her feet. By the time she stood up he was gone and she was
locked in. Fear flooded her mind, carrying her reason away in
swirling confusion. He had pushed her like a prisoner. That
meant that she was certain to die. From here they would take her
to the dungeon she had seen, and then to the gallows. It was
inevitable. She felt tears come to her eyes, but sit there blocked.
If she couldn't cry she should pray. Suddenly she longed for an
image of Mary on which to gaze. She looked round and noticed
for the first time that the room, despite its small size, was a
chapel, for it had altars on three of the four walls. Behind each
altar was a fresco of a saint, his colourful figure dancing in the
faint light of the few candles that lit the chapel. Facing her was
an altar to St Michael the Archangel, with his wings and his
sword, ready to battle Satan's legions. On the left was St George,
his spear levelled at the throat of the dragon of evil. And to the
right stood St John the Evangelist, the everlasting virgin, with his
chalice and his eagle. There was no room for Mary here. This was
a chapel dedicated to celibate soldiers, such as the man she now
had to meet. Godiva put her head in her hands, longed for Mary,
longed for home and then composed herself for the arrival of the
king.

Thirteen

'Lady, do you weep?'

The king's voice was so soft that it seemed to drift in on the air. Godiva wiped her eyes and peered into the dark corners of the chapel. As at Winchester, so now Edward created an illusion that he did not walk through doors like other mortals, but emanated, ghostlike and irresistible, through some other medium.

'Beloved sister in Christ, are you weeping?' he repeated.

'No. I am angry. I was pushed to the floor by your guard, as though I have already been condemned.'

Edward raised his eyebrows at the defiance in her voice. 'And were you frightened? Or offended?'

'Surprised, and winded by the fall. I am well now, as you can see, sir.'

Edward smiled down at Godiva. The smile of a cat, she thought, who will play as long as he wants to with a trapped mouse. Defiance was not going to help her.

'May I speak, sir?'

Edward nodded politely.

'For over a week since I returned to Coventry from your city of Winchester, I did nothing but struggle to feed a town that starved during my absence. Then my husband returned from

Winchester with news that you will impose *heregeld* on my desperate people, for reasons that I do not know. He told me you said you might change your mind, should I come here to plead with you. So, here I am, great king, pleading. Whatever has angered you, punish me alone.'

'So noble, so good,' Edward muttered, shaking his head. 'And so much the worse that you have tied your fortunes, not just in this world, but also in the next, to the sins of the House of Lovric.'

'Tied myself? But Lovric said that if I pleaded with you ...'

'Said? Lied, you mean. Lied to you and misled you. Do you believe a word that man says, Godiva? He has deceived me so many times. And hasn't he deceived you?'

She looked away and made no answer.

'And where is he now, Godiva? You don't really know, do you? But I do. I have reports that he went towards Gloucester. But he won't stay there. Oh no. His designs lie further west. He has left you alone, to decide your fate with me.'

'He keeps secrets, of course. He has to. But he doesn't deceive me.'

She saw him smile and knew she had made a mistake to say anything about Lovric.

'But I know he has,' Edward persisted, shaking his head regretfully. 'He has misled you about his wars against me, about Harry's sins and about his women – his many women over so many years, while you were alone at home, working and raising children. Worse still,' he said, dropping his voice and sounding confidential, 'his lies have corrupted you. Your goodness is not what it seems. No, your pleading will carry no weight with me, not unless you first promise me that you will put Lovric aside. Only then can I come to terms with you. Leave him, Godiva. Annul your marriage. Save yourself and your town.'

'What? Divorce my husband? But the Church condemns divorce.'

'Not always. In this case an annulment could be arranged.'

'Why?'

'On grounds of incest. After all, he is related to you within the prohibited degrees of kinship – you are second or third cousins, so I am told. Furthermore, you are both in second marriages, and the Church is unsure that remarriage can ever be justified. So, it will not be difficult to invalidate your marriage. Afterwards you could put your personal estates under good management and retire to a royal nunnery. That would be safer than one of your own convents. Edith could arrange that for you.'

Godiva gasped. There it was – the thing that woman, that bishop's concubine, Estrith, had warned about, with her tale of the Kentish woman who annulled her marriage to her cousin. Estrith had told Lovric to prepare to defend their marriage. Godiva had scoffed, but now it seemed the warning had been timely. Her fear and confusion turned to suspicion. In the weak light she looked Edward up and down, trying to decipher him, feeling her anger mount.

'Harry, of course, would be bastardized . . .' Edward murmured.

'No! Leave my family alone! Whatever is between me and my husband is a matter for the two of us.'

'Ah, misplaced loyalty! Pearls before swine!' Edward said, reverting to his sorrowful stance. He sat down and signalled Godiva to take a seat, too. 'I have told you what I want. I thought I could persuade you, but you refuse me. Why, then, shouldn't I give the order to those men out there, who are ready to ride to Coventry at any moment and destroy it?'

'Please,' she whispered, fearful again as she remembered Edward's secret power – the tent village, its soldiers, dungeon and gallows. 'Please give me a moment to think about what you have said.'

She put her face in her hands and shut her eyes. Edward, she thought, was not putting as much pressure on her to annul her marriage as he could have done. Why didn't he play on her jealousy and say more about Lovric's mistresses? And suggest that there were bastard children here and there? Why didn't he try to bribe her by offering to release Harry into her care? No, he was after some other outcome to this meeting, but she had no idea what that might be. The best thing she could do now was to say little and keep listening to him.

'I have already said, sir – if I have done wrong, tell me what I have done, and then punish me alone.'

'So we agree on that at least. You deserve punishment. I'm glad that you concur, but oh, my dear! I do not want to inflict the appropriate penance on you. It is harsh indeed. So please, Godiva, reconsider. Leave Lovric. Get an annulment...'

'No. I can't. It would be utterly wrong. Whatever troubles we may have now, we have been truly married for many years. I will not lie and say it never happened.'

'But would you defy the authority of the Church? Do you think the prohibited degrees are of no account?'

'Yes. In England we have always married our cousins, and widows remarry too, and so do divorced people. These are old traditions. No one understands these new rules that are coming in from France and Italy.'

'Ignorance is no excuse. The authority of the Church must not be challenged. We are living in dangerous times, Godiva, surrounded by Satan's friends. Pagans abound to our north; heretics to the west; there is defiance of Rome in the east; and worst of all, Saracens, who follow the lies of a so-called prophet named Mohammed, are gaining power over our most sacred shrines in the Holy Land. Oh, Jerusalem!' he pressed his fists to his chest and began to pace the room. 'It breaks my heart to think of Jerusalem. My sister's husband, Count Drogo of the Vexin, died there before he could return from his pilgrimage. And so did Count Robert of Normandy. All I want is to make the pilgrimage to the Church of the Nativity before I die myself, and make it safe for my people to go there whenever they wish. One day,' he said, standing over her again, 'perhaps even in our lifetimes, Godiva, there will be a Holy War to make the East safe for good Christian pilgrims again.'

'But I too am a good Christian woman,' Godiva said. 'I too want to see the Church strong and able to fight evil and heresy.'

'Do you? Then will you join in the good fight to purify our land? We must do that first before we can undertake Holy War.'

'Yes, of course I will. But, sire, these rules on marriage that you talk of are new to us. You cannot expect couples to separate who promised themselves in good faith.'

'I understand,' Edward said, suddenly gentle again. 'The Church's knowledge of what God wants from us grows much faster than the flock's ability to comprehend. That is why obedience is required from the flock, while mildness is needed in the good shepherd. So, I will be mild with you, my sister in Christ. Let us put aside the question of your marriage, for the time being.'

'Then will you remove the demand for *heregeld* from Coventry?'

'Oh no. I cannot do that. You may keep your marriage, Godiva, but you must make some other atonement, some other sacrifice. My land cannot be pure when even my noble families are corrupt.'

'Corrupt? Do you mean the offence that Lovric has caused you?'

'No. You must atone for your own sins, Godiva. As I told you, you have been corrupted.'

'We are all sinners, but I go to confession, do good works and I pray. What more...?'

'Oh, much, much more, alas.'

He smiled sadly at her lovely face, with its big, lustrous grey eyes and perfect nose and mouth, lying there within his grasp like flowers waiting to be cut.

'Shall we start, for example – with witchcraft?'

'There have been some pagan acts,' she admitted at once. 'Out in the forests. It always happens when people feel threatened. Perhaps I was not strict enough, but the people were still going to church and praying to Mary for help.'

'Not *their* witchcraft,' he said quietly, as though ashamed for her. 'Yours.'

'Mine?'

'Yes. In the Vale of the White Horse. Edith found out about that. We were both shocked.'

'But that was nothing! People from all quarters go there to put a coin in the Horse's eye and ask for favours. It is a harmless comfort.'

'Harmless? The White Horse is an old goddess. If she is harmless now, it is only because her evil spirit is dormant. People like you will bring it back to life and then she will ride the night skies again, bringing wickedness to every place that comes under her eye.'

'My priest never said so.'

'These married priests are ignorant. You should have confessed to your prior, or to one of his wisest monks.'

She looked down at her hands and Edward, knowing full well why she never confessed to her treacherous prior, decided to move the interview on.

'I do not think you are an apostate, Godiva, though you need to be more observant. But these lapses from orthodoxy are less serious than the corruption of your soul. It is in this regard that we – your king, Queen Edith, Father Francis and several others – believe you stand in need of correction.'

'But my soul is not sick. I give thanks each day to God for all his gifts and I trust in his mercy, now and for ever. I am full of joy in my life and hope for my future salvation. How can I be said to be sick?'

Edward took hold of her hand. 'Your soul deludes you with vain pleasures – with what you would call happiness or joy. But behind these light and carefree breezes that blow through your life, your true life – your life eternal – is rotting like a sodden brown apple that has fallen to earth beneath the Tree of Life. Rotting from pride, for one thing, dear sister. *Superbia*. Haven't you seen depictions of this haughty sinner on her horse, her head adorned with jewels and held up high for all to see?'

'But, majesty, I work hard alongside the other women of my manor. And look at me now. I have on old riding clothes and I haven't bathed since I left home.'

'It isn't your working attire I have in mind. It was your appearance at Winchester that caused concern. Your feasting gown and veil did not cover your neck. Men could glimpse that place where the neck joins the shoulder, a place that many men long to kiss. That was evil. You brought lust to my table. Edith said that was why she spilled the wine; she was shocked to see such lewdness in her presence. And ostentation, too. Did you see my queen adorned with jewellery? No. But you looked like the starry sky at night, twinkling with self-regard in the eyes of all the assembly. It was disgusting, obscene...'

Godiva was on the point of defending herself, but stopped. She sensed that Edward was now about to get to the heart of the matter.

'The penance for *Superbia* is humiliation,' Edward said, growing calm once more. '*Superbia* loves to be looked at with admiration. Therefore she shall be exposed in all her vileness and looked at with disgust and ridicule.'

'What do you mean?' she asked, almost inaudibly.

'Your penance. I told you it would be harsh. I would not impose it if you honoured my request that you abandon Lovric.

But you have refused. So, this is your penance. You must mount a horse, like *Superbia*, and ride like her through some public place where everyone can see you clearly. In your case, naturally, you would ride from your manor house and up to the town cross on market day.'

'And wear sackcloth and ashes?'

'No, my dear,' the king said, taking her hand again and stroking it softly, 'you will wear nothing at all, and neither will the horse. You will ride bareback, and you will ride naked.'

Godiva sprang to her feet. 'That is impossible.'

'Then leave Lovric.'

'No.'

'Then let your people pay *heregeld*.'

'No!'

'Then you choose the naked ride.'

'No. It would be more than humiliating. It would be dishonouring. My family would be mortified and the people of my town lose all respect for me. It would be lewd beyond words.'

'Yes,' Edward said, 'as lewd as you really are, Godiva. You see, men do not lust after you merely because of your beauty. No, it is because they recognize you for what you are. A lustful woman, corrupt and dirty. You cause men to have evil thoughts and their bodies to grow inflamed and incontinent. You threaten their acceptability in the eyes of God. You are as the great whore of Babylon.'

'How dare you,' she spat her words at him and sprang to her feet. 'I'd rather you kill me than do this to me. You have me here in this bizarre prison...'

'Sanctum.'

'Whatever it is, I am your captive. Just kill me while you have me at your mercy. Let that be the atonement and leave my people in peace.'

'Killing you would not save your soul. The Church Militant

battles to augment the Kingdom of Christ with saved souls. I want your soul for God.'

'By making me look like a common whore?'

'During your exposure you will experience repentance of a more profound nature than you can imagine now, and then you will be saved. Believe me. This is for your own good, and the good of my kingdom, and the good of Mother Church. This is for Christendom.'

'I cannot do it. It is an appalling thing to ask of anyone, man or woman.'

'That is why this penance would be the most effective purge of your soul.'

'But it is not a Church penance,' Godiva said suddenly. 'I have heard of this before. It was done in some villages when I was a child, to prostitutes and notorious adulteresses. The Church banned the practice and imposed more decent penances.'

'Ah, but it is not the nature of the penance that signifies. You see, Godiva, it is the question of who administers the penance. If it is a crowd of villagers, no good is obtained. If it is the Church, or the king, souls are saved.'

'But this penance is so unjust,' she whispered, grasping yet another dimension of what Edward intended. 'If I were sent to a nunnery, whipped and made to live on bread and water for a year – that would be terrible, but at least it would be over when the fasting ended. But this other penance will never be over. Even men who never saw me ride – *especially* those who did not see me – will think of me forever in this way, for what men imagine is boundless and endless. No, I cannot do what you want. It is impossible.'

'Is that your final word?'

'Yes. I will do any ordinary penance, but not this dreadful thing you have in mind.'

'It must be the naked ride. Nothing else suits your offence.'

'But why?'

'Oh, my dear,' he sighed. 'Godiva, I did not want to confront you with this. But now, with this obstinacy of yours, I must. You see, I know. I'm afraid I must say the words. I know about your ... adultery. *Adultery!* The filthiness of it – and with a man of your own household, a man of no rank. A churl by birth, so I'm told.' His next words were almost inaudible as he choked with disgust. 'Whatever would Lovric think of you?'

Godiva struggled to get her breath as anger and regret almost overcame her.

'You're not going to deny it now, are you? I have good knowledge about your forest trysts.'

'You should have said this sooner.'

'But few women who claim to be good admit quickly to their adultery.'

'Most people succumb quickly to blackmail.'

'Godiva, I know you are angry. But now it is time to accept your fate. I suggest you pray. There are many chapels in Egg Ring. I will send nuns to attend you until you leave. They can conduct you to any chapel you want. The Virgin, I suppose. Or perhaps St Helena, the patron saint of adulterers. At any rate, you will be well cared for and allowed to rest before you begin your journey home tomorrow. Now, with regret, I must leave to see to other matters.'

Edward gathered his robes round him, gleaming and rustling with the gold threads woven into the dark-red silk of the fabric. He had almost reached the small door that led to some other secret room when Godiva sprang forward.

'Wait,' she shouted. 'One more question. What is the worst thing that Lovric has done to offend you? Tell me, because truly I do not know. He was not a man to talk in great depth about his concerns whilst at home.'

'So it is said. I'm not so sure. I think you know a great deal about my kingdom, Godiva.'

Terrified, she could think of nothing to say.

'Well, let me refresh your memory. Beyond plotting against me at the Welsh borders, and up in the north with Siward and over in the Fens – apart from all this, Lovric is guilty of one great, overwhelming offence. He does not share my vision for the future of England. He may not even know what it is. But I will tell you. I see our future as a matter for Christendom. He would make treaties with heathens to the north, and with heretics in Wales and Ireland, while I want to crusade against them and crush them. He wants to be merely English; I want to be a ruler in the Holy Roman Empire, reborn, purified and up in arms against the infidel. He cannot take part in the rule of England unless he shares my views.'

Edward stared into her face eagerly, expecting an excited response from her. But Godiva remained still, for one word had sprung to her mind and was burning there like a hot coal from the hearth: Normans. The kingdom of heaven was known to all Britons, but Christendom was a Norman vision. Edward's dream was for England to be ruled by crusading Norman knights. There would be no place in it for the Anglo-Saxon earls and their descendants.

'Believe in me, Godiva,' he went on. 'Trust me. If I inflict pain, it is only to create good. Become a part of my army in the fight against evil. Join in the Church Militant and look forward to rejoicing eternally in the Church Triumphant.' He could see she would say no more. 'Kiss me,' he said.

She began to kneel to kiss the huge ring on his finger.

'No,' he said. 'Kiss my lips as Mary Magdalene kissed Christ.'

She felt faint and reached out to steady herself against the wall, but Edward took hold of her arm, drawing her closer. Waves of fear and revulsion crashed against the walls that sustained her soul – duty, piety and the hope of redemption. She had not felt like this since childhood, when her grandmother's corpse was laid out and the children of the family were led around the bier to behold the once-loved face, now cold and contorted, and each one had to kiss those waxen lips or face a beating for violating the sacred custom. Like her eight-year-old self, she forced her face upward, closed her eyes and let his mouth meet hers. It was a moist but motionless kiss, in which the tip of his tongue barely entered her mouth and sat there lifelessly, like the head of a loath tortoise. When it was over, Godiva felt a revulsion that went so deep she thought it must be touching that place which Edward wanted to revile and expose to public gaze.

'You could almost be a saint,' he said, and then he released her head from the clasp of his hands and wafted out of the room into the darkness beyond.

As soon as he was gone, two beautiful young nuns came to escort Godiva through a labyrinth of small passages to a chamber that was sumptuously appointed for the use of a lady. The dim light of day faded into the true dark of night as the nuns fed her, bathed her, and prayed with her. Godiva could not remember a time when she had been better cared for.

She fell asleep easily at about dusk, but some time in the dead of night she sat up suddenly in bed. A horrifying clarity filled her mind, as though she had been awake for hours puzzling through recent events. The king, she felt certain, had tried to persuade Lovric to annul their marriage. Why else would Lovric have babbled on so senselessly about divorce during their quarrel? And when Lovric refused, Edward had cast doubts on Godiva's loyalty, saying – lying – that she had already agreed to an annulment, agreed in the aisles and shadows of Winchester cathedral, agreed when she realized how the sin of incestuous marriage had spawned a corrupt son. She could almost see Edward's face and hear the words he would have used as he made his case. He would have sounded regretful, even embarrassed; he would have lamented the great pity of it – that a noblewoman should so easily be persuaded to abandon her husband. But are not all women, especially beautiful women, weak and untrustworthy? What else should the earl expect? That Godiva would remain loyal?

So it must have gone. And when Lovric had quarrelled so fiercely with her, it was his own anguish that had angered him, not her defiance.

'Oh, my love,' she murmured to the empty room, 'you thought I was going to leave you. And I thought you had grown tired of me.'

In fact, Lovric had indeed left her. He had not said he would divorce her, but neither had he stayed at her side. He had galloped away, leaving her to deal with Edward on her own – as the king knowingly pointed out. Lovric had cracked. The great warrior lost his nerve. To Godiva that seemed even more tragic than her own abandonment, for what would Lovric be without his soldier's pride? Nothing. He would be nothing at all. She, abandoned and discarded, was still the woman she had always been. She sobbed with pity for her broken husband, until, rising like a monster from buried depths, her guilt joined forces with her sorrow and she vomited into a pot beside the bed. Oh God, how she regretted now that she had betrayed Lovric. Her husband's infidelities – if they had really occurred – were inconsequential compared to her adultery with a man of her own household, and a man known to the king. And how well known? That was another blow. If it was Bret himself who had told someone about their secret meetings, carelessly boasting as men do, it would be too painful to think about it. Thank God that at least she had not touched him until after leaving Winchester, and Lovric could not possibly know about it.

After a while, when she stopped crying, she started thinking about the atrociousness of the penance that Edward had demanded. It was to this that he wanted her agreement, far more than a divorce from Lovric. She wondered why the penance was so vicious. His humiliation of Gunnhildr was bland in comparison. Even his rejection of his wife's bed had at least a fig-leaf of pious chastity masking its cruel intent. And then it came to her: if Lovric would not divorce his beloved wife even when told she was disloyal, what wouldn't Godiva do rather than divorce her husband – also not wholly trustworthy, but also beloved? Anything. Edward must have guessed that she would do anything. Even this nightmarish ride. And so Unwed Ned, and Needy Eedy too, would be avenged. The galling vision of the love of the earl and his wife, a married love that the king and queen professed to despise and would never know, would be wiped out of men's minds and in its place there would be put a degrading image that would provoke obscene mirth.

Yes, perhaps. But Godiva was calming down now, and as she thought more coolly about the royal pair, it seemed that love was of no importance to either. Power, land, armies, keeping their crowns: that was all that mattered. Oh, and piety, of course. How could she forget that? That piety of theirs was the true bond between them – a glue as strong as the love for which most married people hoped. Edith was the perfect Christian wife, renouncing sexual pleasure, abandoning hope of children, submissive (as St Paul told all women they should be) to the will of her husband, as long as that will aspired to the eternal, fleshless life promised to those saved by Christ crucified. And yet Edith was not known for submissiveness. No, according to Lovric, she was regarded in court as a tough young woman, one who took difficulties and turned them into advantages. Godiva recalled the story of the newly married Edith greeting a priest in court with a kiss, and being upbraided by a bishop for unseemly contact with consecrated male flesh. Did Edith retire and sulk? No. That very night she circulated hawk-eyed amongst Edward's guests, on the lookout for similar lapses, no matter how small, and swooping down on some of the noblest women in England to excoriate them and preach chastity. Her reputation was then sealed as a master of the art of the feint, for Edith's blows entailed no risks to her, encased as she was in the armour of piety, but left her opponents off balance and vulnerable. Godiva could attest to that herself. But who was Edith's opponent now, and who her allies, as each childless year passed? Godiva ruminated: in the end she would turn against her husband, and seek alliances in her own family. Hadn't Lovric said there were rumours she was seeking lands for her brothers? Well then, the royal marriage was not as well glued as all that piety might suggest. Who then was Godiva's own chief enemy? Who was behind this horrible penance? Edward or Edith?

Dear God, how she missed Lovric! She realized now that it wasn't really true that they didn't talk much to each other. Undoubtedly he was reticent about his military affairs, but they had talked through very many problems over the years, and she had come to take that for granted. It was she herself, saying over and over, 'You never talk to me, Lovric', that had convinced her of his reluctance to communicate. If he were here now, what would he say? He would remind her, probably, of Godwin's warnings, remind her that the king was a ghoul of a man, quite capable of imposing the naked ride on a married woman of normal modesty. That was the sort of thing a man like Edward might want to do. And yet, that was not her personal view of Edward. It was not his manner. It seemed excessive, too openly sexual. She could think of nothing similar being done to any other of his victims. There was something more behind Edward's wish to force this particular penance upon her, but she could wring no more sense out of what she knew of the matter. The naked ride, in essence, remained an enigma.

A sleepless night lay ahead of her and she tried to make herself as comfortable as possible in the luxurious bed to weather the storms of worry and speculation that were sure to besiege her for hours. But as she nestled in the silky sheets she heard a slight sound coming from near the closed door. She got up and put her ear to it and listened carefully.

'Sh!' someone breathed. 'Don't be afraid. It's me, Bret. Please, let me in.' He must be insane, she thought, to come to her in this place. As quietly as she could, she untwisted the withy that tied the door knob to the post and slowly, trying to prevent it creaking, opened the door.

'What do you want?'

Bret was taken aback by her tone. 'To see you, to hold you...' he started, but with rather less of his usual confidence.

'Bret,' she began, about to rebuke him for risking her good name and his own life. But her confidence in him had gone, and she was unwilling to confide in him. Let him find out for himself that the king knew of their secret love. If love it was. 'Bret,' she resumed sternly. 'I cannot be alone with you again. Never. My husband is in danger and I am full of remorse that I betrayed him with you.'

'What danger?' he asked, as if he had every right to know.

'These are private matters, between husband and wife,' she said coldly.

He took hold of her arm and squeezed it a bit too tightly.

'I don't believe you. You still want me, I know you do.'

He crushed her in his arms and bit the side of her neck passionately. Then he kissed her as deeply and as long as he had ever done. But she stood in his embrace, so stiff and fearful that he knew at once the spell was broken and his hold on her was over.

He stepped away and pushed her to arm's length, thinking how much he would relish giving her something to really fear. Godiva stared at him and noticed his expression changing as he assessed her, the room and the situation. As clouds of murderous hatred gathered in his eyes, she put her fist to her mouth to stifle the scream that rose in her throat. Suddenly he lunged forward to pull off her nightgown.

'No,' she whispered fiercely, pushing him with both arms.

For answer Bret seized her arms, pushed her back towards the bed and pulled the nightgown up to her shoulders. He had one hand over her mouth while the other pulled at his own clothing. But Godiva wrenched herself out of his grasp and snatched a torch that was still burning in a wall bracket. Pushing the torch into his face, she hissed at him, 'You'll die for this. They'll cut off your balls and put out your eyes.'

He backed away, and shook his head as though he had just woken from a bad dream: her high rank and this royal fortress protected her from him. But had she been a woman of no importance, alone beneath a forest tree, he would have raped and sodomized her, bitten, beaten and finally strangled her. He dropped his bloodshot eyes, knowing they had given him away. She was right, it was over. He should go to his own bed. At the door he paused and looked back at her. The violence in his face had died away as quickly as it had arrived, and he looked once more like a handsome young man with whom any woman could easily fall in love. Godiva hesitated, and then she turned her back on him, whispering, 'Go in peace, Bret.'

In the morning light, outside the embankment of Egg Ring, the world was stirring. Godiva, dressed once more in riding clothes, found herself waiting in fine drizzle for her men to assemble. Their horses had already been brought from the stables, properly groomed and rested, and there was no reason for the men to be this late. Just as she was starting to lose her temper they all arrived at once, with the reason for their delay immediately visible. Bret was wearing a bandage round one side of his face and his jacket was torn.

'He came into our tent in bad shape,' Arne said. 'We patched him up and he'll be able to stay in his saddle. But not at a gallop, I reckon.'

'What happened?' Godiva asked with an affectation of mild concern.

Bret noticed she was taking care to conceal her anger, and wondered if this meant she might forgive him.

'It was my fault,' he said carefully. 'I was curious about Egg Ring. I'd gone prowling around and some of the guard caught me. They knocked me about, but they let me go. I'm sorry, lady. It was stupid of me.'

An icicle of new distrust pierced Godiva's heart and she stared at Bret with such displeasure that he turned away towards Arne and the other men.

At this moment the guards turned up, distracting everyone from Bret's misadventures. The blindfolds appeared again and everyone except Godiva prepared for the discomfort of several miles of sightless riding until they reached the farmstead where the hoods would be taken off. Indeed, if the men from Coventry wondered about anything during their dark journey, it was not about Bret, but Godiva. She said nothing for its entire duration. Nor did she grow more talkative during the rest of the journey, and they were left to their own speculations. What had happened at Egg Ring? What would she say to the people at home about the reason for her visit? She would have to say something, or tongues would wag. And yet she gave no sign. Nor did she send one of the men ahead at full gallop to announce her imminent arrival at Cheylesmore manor.

And so, because there was no forewarning, there was no one there to greet her and she entered the yard of her manor house like one who has been released from prison and wants only to lie down in private and hide her face away. This is wrong, Arne thought. People will draw conclusions and take fright. He looked at Bret, but Bret avoided his eyes. There is something wrong there too, Arne concluded. As soon as they had stabled the horses, he set off to find Odo and tell him: something is afoot. We must be on guard. Godiva's troubles are far from over.

Fourteen

$\mathcal{D}$espite the late hour Agatha prepared a bath for Godiva, and sat with her, gently soaping her tired back and limbs.

'Too much riding be bad for you, lady,' she said accusingly.

'Did you do as I told you?' Godiva asked wearily. 'How's your galloping coming along?'

'Good enough, they say, for you never to go off again on your own with no maid, like you just did. That weren't right for a lady...'

'There were young nuns at Egg Ring.'

'You went to Egg Ring?' Agatha repeated, looking horrified. 'You told us Grafton manor. People say such terrible things about Egg Ring. There be ghosts there, and a dark dungeon...'

'As I said, I was well tended by young nuns. Forget about my doings, Agatha; they are none of your business. Tell me about the estate, and the town. And your mother. How have you been getting on?'

'As well as always. At least she never thinks to raise her hand at me no more. Her tongue – well, that be a different matter.'

'I'll talk to her,' said Godiva.

'You did already,' Agatha replied. 'She can't change, mistress. She don't mean no harm, and anyway she ain't got no false front.

At least you can trust Bertha.' Godiva looked at her questioningly, but Agatha would say no more about the object of her distrust.

'The manor and the town,' she continued, 'not much change there, mistress. People be better fed, and no one else caught cold on the manor. But the outlook for the late crops ain't good. That mean the farmers won't replace the cattle they had to cull, because they'll need what money they got left to buy more grain. So milking will stay poor.'

'And Gwen and Milly?'

'One still a-bed, the other still a-sulking.'

'So, no changes then.' Godiva paused, embarrassed to have to ask her maid the next question. 'What news from the earl?'

'Nothing, mistress. But...' Agatha hesitated.

'Yes? Tell me.'

'There be rumours coming from the dairy that some of the housecarls have sent to say that they would be taking ship. They were in Bristol and to sail west.'

'Rumours!' Godiva said angrily. 'You mustn't listen to them, or repeat them. They mean nothing at all!' And yet they evidently meant a great deal to Godiva, who seemed to have plunged into sudden despair.

'Yes, mistress,' Agatha said, regretting the distress she had caused. And yet she had done the right thing. This was no empty rumour. Everyone in the manor and the town had heard it, and its meaning was clear: whatever was troubling the mistress, whatever had caused her to go to the legendary Egg Ring, and no matter how great the threat – she would be facing it alone. Or with a viper in her bosom.

Agatha blotted Godiva dry, rubbed lavender oil into her sore spots and dropped over her shoulders a soft new nightdress, the latest product of the sewing rooms. Usually she exclaimed with delight when something new came her way, but tonight she hardly noticed. Agatha pulled back her hair to braid it and keep

it tidy for the morning, and as she did this she caught a glimpse
of Godiva's neck in the light of a candle that had been placed on
a high shelf. There was a mark there that she had never seen
before and, taking it to be an insect bite, she asked if her mistress
would like some lavender oil on it. But Godiva recoiled as though
just stung, rubbed her neck and blushed bright red. And so did
Agatha, who now realized what she had found, for she had seen
many of these mouth-shaped marks before, on the necks of girls
whose mothers were less fierce than her own.

'It could be a heat spot,' she said as casually as she could
manage. 'This is the time of year for them. Better just leave it
alone and it will go by itself.'

Minutes later, as Godiva started to grow warm and sleepy in
her bed, Agatha sped across the yard in search of someone in
whom to confide.

Odo was in the stable when Agatha burst in.

'Take this horse out to pasture now,' Odo said to the boy who
stood nearby looking curiously at Agatha.

Once he was gone, she sat down in a crumpled heap in the
straw to tell Odo her worries.

'Mistress said nothing about *heregeld*,' she concluded, 'nor
anything at all about why she had to see the king. And she knows
nothing about Lovric and the housecarls going into western
waters. She was longing for tidings of him, but ashamed to ask
me. She looks very tired and weak, like she be sickening with
something. We should be helping her now. But what can we do?'

'Best we do nothing until we know more,' Odo replied. 'I
tackled Arne, but he had nothing to say. None of the men who
went with her to Egg Ring have any inkling of how things went
with the king.'

'I bet one of them does, though,' Agatha said.

'That's what Arne said, too. But I find it hard to believe anything bad of Bret.'

But no one else, thought Agatha, would put a love-bite on Godiva. She bit her lip, though. Many women lapse, she knew, and most are not discovered. Let Godiva be one. She was about to say something misleading about Bret to distract Odo, when the stable door flew open and in he limped.

Odo left without a word and Agatha, stepping back, took in the sight of Bret's damaged face, from which he had removed the bandage. It had swollen greatly on the left side and his ear was split.

'You'll get a cauliflower ear if you don't get that dressed right now,' she said.

'Would you do it for me? There's no one else to help me. Your mother won't do it and Gwen is sick. Would you do it, please, Miss Agatha?'

She had a strong urge to box his wounded ear, or put salt into a dressing and slap it on his cuts. But she knew she should not act out of turn, for whatever she thought of him, Bret must still be in Godiva's favour. And so, instead, Agatha decided that she would extract every bit of advantage that she could from attending to the odious man.

The stable was full of the tools of first aid, for this is where men turned up first when they had fallen or been lacerated by hanging branches. Agatha took some clean lint and wiped away the pus that oozed from beneath the badly knit new scab on his cheek. He winced, but held steady.

'You be brave. Some men scream when we clean out wounds.' He said nothing and she started to smear a salve on the wound. 'Bret?'

'Yes.'

'I know about the king's demand for *heregeld*. Everyone knows, and everyone be afraid. What happened at Egg Ring? Did mistress say the right words? Has she persuaded the king to leave us be?'

Bret ignored her.

'I won't carry on treating your face unless you tell me,' she said, putting one hand on a hip and wagging a finger in his face as Bertha would.

'Listen, girl,' he said, seizing her wrist roughly and twisting it, 'this is too serious for gossip.'

'Listen, boy, my mistress be too good for you. You left a red mark on her neck last time. I know it were you. If I tell people about that mark, everyone will believe you done it. We all seen how she looks at you.'

Bret got to his feet, glanced round to see if they were alone, and before Agatha could guess what he was going to do, he put his strong fingers round her slender neck and slowly, as he whispered in her ear, began to squeeze.

'If you threaten me again,' he breathed, 'I'll kill you. And make it look like a horse kicked your face in.' He released his grip on her neck, but kept a tight hold on her arm. Agatha, reeling and choking, tried to catch her breath. 'What do you want for your silence? Money? Answer me! What do you want?'

No one, not even Bertha, had ever terrified Agatha so much. 'Not money,' she managed to whisper.

'What then?'

'Knowledge. Mistress be looking terrible. I know something was agreed at Egg Ring. Must have been. Then why don't she say? Because it must be something bad.'

'Why must you know?' he asked, holding her at arm's length and looking at her searchingly.

'Because I be afraid of what might happen next. She might run away, like the earl, and leave us to be raided. Or she might kill herself, like them vagrants over in Stivichall. You could tell me, at least a little bit, about what is going to happen next. If you ever loved her even for a minute, tell me.'

Bret stepped back, still staring at her, and noticed her small fingers knitting together in ceaseless agitation. Suddenly he pictured them at night, unbraiding Godiva's hair and brushing it down like a white horse's fair mane. He breathed heavily, clenched his fists and forced himself to think of Godiva as a peaceful corpse who would never trouble any man again. After moments of holding this image in his mind, he calmed down enough to deal with Agatha.

'Finish with my face,' he said, 'and I'll tell you.'

Agatha bustled to give his wounds the best and gentlest dressing she could and then she waited.

'I can't explain my part in your mistress's life,' he began, 'and I don't expect anyone to forgive me. I loved her more than she will ever believe, and far more than I wanted to, but that's over now. And I'm trapped. I can't help her.'

'Well?'

'She is to undergo an ordeal.'

Agatha leaped as if burned. 'What will they do to her? And why?'

'A penance. You will find out when the time comes. She will need comforting afterwards. Be ready, and get others ready. Talk of her with nothing but appreciation in the next few days. Remember her kindness to you all. Spread a rumour that she has ended the threat of *heregeld*. This will probably turn out to be true.'

'But what has she done wrong? Why a penance?'

'Done? Nothing really. She is wife to a man the king calls an enemy. But no one believes Lovric is really an enemy. Godiva provoked envy, because she is far more beautiful than Queen Edith. But the king is not attracted to women, at least not in the usual way. Nor is she a witch, though she is ignorant of theology and tolerates minor sins. But everyone is like that.'

'Then what?'

'Perhaps you wouldn't understand, Agatha.'

'I understand more than you think. I knew what you were up to as soon as you showed your face here. And I knew you were pretending to love her, and that yet you really do love her too, both at the same time. If I had better words I could say this plainer. But I do understand, even what I can't say.'

'Yes? Well, try this. The king likes to dream up stories, but his tales are about real people. He draws them in and then watches them struggle as they try to get out of the net he has thrown round them. He can do this because he is a king...'

'And a child! That's not so hard to understand. We have a man like that here, in the hall, and I had an uncle who was a mischief-maker like that. No one believes a word they say, but everyone pretends to. King Edward never grew up. That's all there is to say about him.'

'But the king's jokes are far from idle. And you can never be sure who his victims are supposed to be.'

'Godiva and the earl, I reckon.'

'Yes, but others too. Me, for example. It's possible no one will ever know.'

'He is clever, then. Doing things in such a way that he can never be blamed for what happens at the end of his story.'

'You do understand. You are clever too, and very pretty.'

He stooped to kiss her hand and Agatha shuddered when his lips touched her skin. Poor Godiva, she thought, how she must miss her poisoned paradise.

'I want to make amends for frightening you,' Bret said, extending his hand. 'I don't think I'm going to need this, and it might help you to marry a good man. In return, you could pray for me sometimes.'

He pressed a small leather pouch into her hand and then, instead of heading back to the hall to sleep, he mounted his horse and rode out.

Agatha stared after him for a long time until she realized he had left the manor. Only then did she open the bag. It was full of silver coins, which she took to be his winnings from gaming. She picked up one of the enclosed glass lamps used in the stable and started to examine the coins, and then she realized they could not have been won at gambling, for they were newly minted. She raised the leather to the light and was just able to make out the crest stamped on the inside. It was a crown. The bag had come from the royal mint and, like the coins, it was utterly new. Bret must have received it at Egg Ring, as payment for something.

'Holy Mother Mary,' said Agatha, feeling like a criminal and falling to her knees in the straw. 'What in God's name should I do with this?'

Bret was approaching the bridge on London Road when he saw them. The moon had come out and, in its steely blue light, the white of their tunics had taken on a phosphorescent glare and the red of their crosses a colour that was dark as old blood. He saw at once that the riders' heads were so completely encased in helmets that no one could tell which men were those who were coming to Coventry from Cleley. His heart thundered as they got nearer. They had come upon him sooner than he expected and he felt unready. Their hidden faces unsettled him, too. He would be out of luck if one of them was the guard who beat him up a few days ago. Rapist, the man had spat at him, and then battered his head with the boss at the centre of his shield.

For a moment the urge to escape gripped him. But he could see no pathway leading away from the road and nowhere at all to hide. Now it was too late. One of the men had already spotted him and urged his horse forward. Seconds later he had the reins of Bret's horse in his grasp. The man pulled up his visor and Bret was relieved to see a young face that he did not recognize. But then the other man arrived and took over the situation.

'Bret,' he said, removing his helmet. 'Your orders were to stay in Coventry until you were told to leave.'

Bret trembled. 'My mission is already over, lord bishop. They told me in Egg Ring that the woman is going to agree to the king's demands.'

'It was not for you to decide when your mission was over. Why did you leave Coventry?'

He had taken off his mailed glove, but Bret, though he knew what would follow, could think of nothing to say to save himself.

'You were disobeying orders,' the man insisted. 'You were running away. Why?'

'I was in danger of discovery.'

'That would have been your fault.'

The expected slap on the mouth did not materialize. The senior officer turned to confer with his colleague for a moment and then told Bret to dismount. Both soldiers now dismounted too and drew their swords, the younger one standing behind Bret and the senior going ahead towards the riverbank. No one said anything. There would be no further questions, Bret knew. The senior man had the authority to decide what to do with him, and really there was little choice. They could not turn him loose, nor could they take him with them on their mission to Coventry. Suddenly Bret found he did not have full control of his legs. He looked up at the bright full moon and thought he saw in it the lovely face of the young girl who had lain with him, willingly he was sure, though she had put up a struggle and was too young to lie with any man. How sweet that was. But later she had called it rape. He closed his eyes and thought of Godiva. She too was sweet and, for a woman of her age, innocent. He wondered when she would find out the truth about him. He wondered whether she would survive the penance. He wondered if the man behind him was a skilled swordsman, or one who understood the garrotte. And then he slipped at the edge of the river and could not get up again. He flailed for a few minutes in the shallow water under the soldier's heavy heel, and then he lay still. The moon disappeared and the soldiers cursed as they stumbled back to their horses in the dark.

Prior Edwin was expecting them. He had sent all his monks to an early bed and given orders that no one but he should answer the door during the night. He himself had spent the entire day praying. Just a little before the midnight hour, they arrived, swathed in heavy cloaks to disguise their white tunics as they rode into Coventry, and with their visors pulled down over their faces. Their legs were wet, though there had been no rain all day, and they had a riderless horse following behind them.

'Put this one in your stables and hide him,' said the older of the two soldiers. 'In the morning get your butchers to slaughter him and burn the remains. If anyone asks, say he was found roaming and he was sick.' The man dismounted, while Edwin, rooted to the ground, stared at him. 'Get on with it,' said the officer.

'All my monks are asleep, as you ordered,' the prior protested.

'So what? You do it.'

'Me?' Edwin bridled. 'I am the prior here. You can't give me orders. I'll tell my bishop.'

The officer looked at him pityingly, and then took off his glove and put out his hand. Edwin stared in growing confusion at the huge ruby set in thick gold clasps that sat on the officer's ring finger, a ring that he now raised imperiously to the prior's floundering lips.

'I *am* your bishop,' the stranger said. 'Now stable that horse and get us some food.'

A few minutes later the prior returned with straw clinging to his robes and a long, bleeding scratch on his forehead.

'Everything is to your liking?' he asked, feigning confidence.

'Show us to your room, prior,' said the younger man. 'We have come to the conclusion that austerity is not equally distributed in this establishment of yours. It would be good for you to sample your own guest quarters. Now!' he barked, as Edwin remained immobile.

In despair, the prior picked up a candle and ushered them through the narrow corridor that led to his private quarters. As he walked he started coughing noisily, and the two visitors exchanged glances. Once the door to the prior's room was open, the bishop pushed Edwin aside and strode in. There, as he expected, a young boy was smoothing out the bed.

'Still nice and warm is it, son?' asked the bishop, glancing round the large room, noting its good oak furniture, its colourful tapestries and the large fire crackling in the hearth. 'And what is this?' he asked, picking up a flask of wine and sipping directly from its lip. 'Not English, is it? Burgundian perhaps. Expensive, certainly. There really is nothing that helps in the reform of the Church so much as inspecting the distant parishes in person.' Then he turned back to the boy and his tone changed. 'Out you go, you little whore.' The boy fled and the bishop turned on the prior. 'I will have more to say about the state of this priory, but not yet. First you must take your orders.'

'Yes, lord bishop,' Edwin mumbled.

'Get that woman, Godiva, in here as soon as possible. Offer her your help in preparing her and the town for the penance. You must agree a day with her as to when she will do it – in about two weeks' time. As soon as we know the day we will leave you and return to the king. Two men and guards of the king's household will return on the night before the penance is to be performed, and you will lodge them in your quarters. Now, repeat what I just said.'

Miserably, Edwin complied. Then, taking his candle, he found his way back to the draughty guest room and lay down to sleep. The boy tried to placate him, but Edwin pushed him away roughly.

'Pay attention, Cherub,' he grumbled. 'Those two are going to stay up there in my room as long as they are at the priory. You'll have to wait on them. But no special favours, mind, or I'll kick you down the stairs and back to Bristol market myself.'

Cherub, who was relieved that Edwin would not meddle with him tonight, went to the edge of the bed, where he pretended to cry at the rejection. But it was Edwin who was the truly unhappy one in that hard bed – deeply and wretchedly rueful, and unable to sleep most of the night for thinking what a fool he had been to bring the wrath of Mother Church upon his head. And all to bring Godiva down a peg or two. How he wished now that he had left well alone. How easy his life had been under her benign governance. What had he been thinking of on that fateful day when he gave Bret an audience? And then, a little later, when he gave Bret what he wanted – stories about witchcraft, stories about the earl's infidelities on his travels, stories about this and that; a bit of truth and a lot of plausible guesswork. He knew it was all destined for the ears of the king, and he didn't care. But now he did, now that his days at plush St Mary's were probably numbered.

Godiva came to the door of the priory next morning at a much earlier hour than Edwin expected, looking as if she should have stayed in bed, but couldn't get any rest. He pulled back the bar on the door and almost pulled her into his arms, weeping copiously as he did so.

'Oh, my beloved lady!' he cried. 'I know! I know! There will be some dreadful penance imposed on you. I have been told already. Messengers are here from the new bishop, telling me to assist you in all ways. But no one has told me what the penance is for, or what it will be.'

Godiva described the events at Egg Ring and then turned to the matter at hand. 'We must get on with the arrangements, Edwin. I must get this penance over with as quickly as possible, in case Lovric comes back and stops it, and lets Coventry go to hell. And for the health of my soul. The thought of it presses on me night and day like a boulder, so that I can hardly breathe at times.' She crossed herself. 'Can you suggest a date?'

He tried to remember his instructions. The bishop-knight had said the penance should take place two weeks after he left Coventry. If he could finalize the date with her now, the bishop and his attendant would leave today – and he could have his room and his bed and Cherub to himself again, at least for a little longer.

'It can't be in less than two weeks from tomorrow,' he said.

'What? I can't go on that long with this horror hanging over me.'

'I'm sorry, but for liturgical reasons it can't be any sooner. Saints' days, and so on. We can't have this shameful parade taking place while the monks are processing to and from the town cross and around the priory precincts. As for Lovric, he never returns quickly once he has ridden west.'

Gloom settled on Godiva and she said nothing for a while.

'Very well,' she said at last. 'In two weeks. I will pray constantly between now and then, and fast on bread and water.'

'Oh no,' Edwin said, alarmed. 'Only fast on the day before the penance. These rituals of humiliation are more of a shock than anyone realizes. You must be strong for this awful ride.'

'There is another matter. The king decrees that you must

address the townspeople from your pulpit on the Sunday before my penance. You should get a letter to that effect soon.'

Edwin bit his lip, remembering the sealed scroll that had been tossed at him last night before he went to sleep, and which he had not bothered to look at.

'You are to tell them the day and hour of my ride. And that I will be naked.'

'What? Good God! *Me*? I must say *that*?'

'Yes. And you must explain that this is my penance, which will be accepted by the king as a substitute for the taking of *heregeld*, which was going to be imposed on them because of the sins of all their lords, the members of the House of Lovric. Then they must be told the time of my ride. It will start when the priory's bell is tolled at the hour when the market commences. The bell ringer must keep tolling the bell until I arrive. I'm sure you'll get a letter setting out these details.'

'Oh great God!' Edwin exclaimed again, jumping up from his seat and pacing about. 'I can't believe that I have to play any part in this awful business. No one said anything...'

'Why should they?' Godiva asked sharply. 'Have you had something to do with my misfortunes, prior?'

'Of course not!' he spluttered. 'But there were rumours. I knew of the king's anger. I knew of many things. Harry, for example. Monks love to gossip between prayers. But believe me,' he said, placing his hand on the cross that dangled from his neck, 'I knew nothing about this damned penance the king has dreamed up.'

'What did you expect? Some other kind of pain perhaps?'

'I thought, perhaps...' He began to cough and then stumbled on, saying nothing very coherent until Godiva put up her hand.

'Stop it. I don't want to know what you thought a few weeks ago. That was a time when you hated me. Don't think I didn't know. I saw it, but I let it pass and hoped that you would find it in you to be my ally here in Coventry. I thought you had, in fact. But that was all pretence, wasn't it? Still, I don't really care, Edwin. You are the least of my disappointments. Whatever you did is by the way now. We are in this plight together and that is all we need to think about.'

He felt a strong desire to abase himself at her feet, so great was the rush of relief and self-disgust that swept through his veins at being forgiven. He fell to his knees and kissed her limp hand. She let him mumble his thanks repeatedly, while she grew ever more certain that he had played some part in her downfall.

'There is one more thing you must do for me. Write to my dear friend, the Abbess of Evesham, and explain my position. I intend to stay with her after the penance for several weeks, or perhaps longer. Now,' she announced, rising and moving towards the door. 'I will not see you again before the penance. Pray for me each night and day until then. No, don't get up and see me out. I know the way out of my own priory.'

The door, as it shut behind her, carried towards the prior a small rush of air on which there hung the summer scents of lavender, honey and thyme. Edwin slumped in a chair beside the fire, inhaled the fading sweetness of her presence and stared into the flames, letting his tears fall unchecked down his slackened cheeks and onto his soft, pink hands.

The manor was still quiet as Godiva stabled May, her small workaday pony, herself. As she gave her a quick brush and a pat on the forehead in thanks for the dawn ride, the other horses stirred and gave soft snorts of greeting to their favourite rider, the one who always seemed to know what they needed and what they liked most. She turned at the door to the stable and looked back into the dark, pungent interior at the animals she loved so much. One of these would have to bear her to her Calvary. It would have to be a big, strong horse that knew her well, and that would not get nervous when she failed to give clear signals, or if she trembled or cried. Then it came to her. She would ride naked on Starlight, her only white horse, and the one she had usually ridden through the forest to Bret. God, if he were watching, would know what that meant.

She crossed the yard and entered the kitchen of the manor house. Quietly, so as to let the household sleep on, she poured herself a small cupful of yesterday's souring milk and sat at a work table to sip it slowly. Overnight, she had made up her mind. The penance was going to be a kind of death. Nothing would ever be the same afterwards. Lovric would never reconcile with her, and neither would Milly. Any hopes of making St Mary's into a great cult centre for pilgrims would be dashed by the lewd image that her name would evoke. As for herself, she might stay on permanently at Evesham after the penance. She could put her estates under management, even perhaps give them all to St Mary's – though not with Edwin holding the priorship. She got up and poured a little more milk into the mug. She had many preparations to make and the acidic milk was beginning to invigorate her. Where should she start? Obviously, with putting her own house in order. The brass gong was on the table in front of her. She picked up the copper-headed maple mallet that had been under Gwen's control before her illness, and paused. When she struck the gong with it and called her people together, there would be no going back. The penance would begin now.

Odo, who had been called to the stables, had just arrived there when he heard the sound of the gong reverberate across the yard. He wondered if he should join in the meeting of the household that it announced. Strictly speaking he belonged in the hall and had no business in the manor house, but these were not ordinary times. He fondled the ear of the nervous horse that he had been asked to inspect and asked the groom his opinion.

'This be one of her ladyship's,' said the boy, 'I know him even though his breastplate been taken off, and all his tack. Look like someone was readying him for a poleaxe to the head.'

Odo examined the stallion carefully. 'He's been hurt,' he agreed. 'There's a gash at the neck. Some fool thought he could just slit his throat. He must have put up a fight and bolted. When did you find him?'

'Night watchman brought him in, in the small hours. Him not wanting to frighten the other horses, he put him in the guest stable, to let him calm down on his own. Terrible state he were in, shivering and rolling them eyes like he was going mad. Calmed down now, though. Look,' he said, putting a crab apple in the palm of his hand and extending it towards the horse's mouth. 'Eat up, Blackberry,' he said, and the horse made a quick, careful nip at the apple.

'Blackberry? Who used him?' Odo asked, though he already had a good idea.

'Bret, sir, and no one else.' The boy paused. 'Blackberry been gone since last night and no one seen Bret since then, neither. I asked around.'

'Right,' said Odo, digesting this news.

'Odo!' Agatha stood at the door, panting. 'Come at once! Come to the manor house. Mistress wants you at the meeting.'

As soon as they were beyond the stable boy's hearing, Odo stopped.

'Agatha,' he whispered. 'I'm thinking you know more than you let on about Bret. Tell me now.'

'I can't tell you that here, in the yard,' she protested. 'Just that he's no good.'

'And mistress loves him?'

Agatha said nothing and turned away.

'Well, Bret's gone,' Odo said.

'Run away from the manor?'

'Worse. His horse been found injured. Looks like someone wanted to destroy it. I reckon Bret be killed.'

Agatha felt the bag of coins that nestled against her skin catch fire. She clutched her throat and tried to move the bag away from her heart.

'Will you tell mistress?' Odo implored. 'Break the news to her?'

'No! Listen to me, Odo. Let mistress think Bret ran away because he loved her too much and was afraid of making trouble for her.'

'She'll find out...'

'Not if you get rid of that horse. Get someone to take him out to the marshes and turn him loose where there be wild ponies to lure him into the forest. If that be done tonight, mistress won't hear no stories about him. As for Bret's body – *if* there be a body and he didn't just get rid of his horse to fool us – it may be far from here. And what with the roads closed to most folk on account of the cattle plague, it could be a long time before we hear tell of him.'

'Are you sure?' Odo asked.

'Yes,' Agatha said. 'All this trouble be too much for any mortal soul, even mistress.'

Odo grunted assent, and together they crossed the yard to the meeting that was now assembling in the manor house. As she walked, Agatha made a quick, silent prayer: *Oh, Mother Mary, bless my lies. And make me good again when time be right.*

Fifteen

As the gong rang out, the manor's main room filled quickly with servants. Even Milly felt she should attend, and Gwen had come limping in from the sick-room. Godiva stood before them all, wearing a dull black dress that she only ever wore at funerals. With no jewellery and with her long, newly greying plait hanging down one shoulder, she resembled an ageing maiden. The effect was worse than funereal; she seemed to be dying on her feet before their eyes.

'My people,' she began. 'I have good news and bad. I know you have heard rumours that the king intended to raid our barns and our money-chests to wring *heregeld* from us. I went to see him at Egg Ring in the parish of Cleley and heard his accusations against the House of Lovric, and against me. He agreed to forego the *heregeld* if I underwent a penance. I have agreed to this.'

A great murmur of protest broke out. Over in the corner Milly, thinking of her marriage plans, felt her knees buckle as she leaned against the wall. Suddenly she pulled herself together and pushed her way angrily out of the room.

'Quiet!' Godiva commanded. 'There is no alternative. I have to comply. The penance will take place in two weeks, on market day. I will tell you what I must undergo on the night before the penance. Not now. In the meantime, I want to make arrangements for the continuation of the life of the manor when I am not here any more.'

'Not here? What do you mean?' someone shouted.

'After the penance I intend to go to the convent at Evesham to pray for my own soul's health.'

'But will you come back to us?'

'Yes,' Godiva said firmly. 'But now I must talk to you all in turn. I will start with Odo. The rest of you, get back to work. Life must go on. Foodstuffs must be preserved and stored. Cleaning. Cooking. Spinning and weaving. All the usual work. Off with you now.'

They scattered quickly and Godiva sat down with Odo. 'It is up to you to handle the men of the hall,' she began. 'On the Tuesday night, when I disclose what I have to do to the people of the manor, I want you to call the men of the hall together and inform them. I could not face them and tell them about it myself.'

Odo stared at her, unable to respond. Then he nodded silently.

'I also want you to be my voice in the hall. Tell them I am sure that Lovric will return. Also, tell them it is not his fault – this penance I must undergo. I must be sure they remain loyal. If we start to lose the few armed men we have, the manor will be vulnerable to robbers. Can I count on you?'

'Yes, mistress,' he mumbled, tongue-tied by his knowledge of Bret.

'And one thing more. Is it possible that your son...'

'Wulf?'

'Yes. Could you bring him back to the manor?'

'Oh, yes indeed. What Wulf want, mistress, more than anything on Earth except one thing, is to train in arms. He don't like farming and he be no good at it neither. If you could see fit...'

'Yes, he can come to the hall. But I won't be able to pay him the right wage for several months.'

'That don't matter, mistress,' Odo said, a smile creasing his wary face. 'But may I ask why?'

'Agatha should have a better life than growing old as a maiden servant. She loves Wulf.'

'And he love her,' said Odo, smiling broadly. 'I had to push the boy on to the cart to make him leave Cheylesmore.'

For the first time in many days, Godiva smiled too. 'Send Agatha to me now.'

Odo bowed his head and left. A few minutes later, Bertha announced herself.

'Agatha be down the dairy counting the cheeses,' she said. 'Can mistress talk to me next?'

'Why is Agatha counting cheeses? I gave no orders.'

'It were my idea, mistress. We be putting away a lot of cheese for the winter, but folk in the town have no milk at all now. The last milch cow down there was culled while you was in Cleley. We can afford to let them have half our cheese and butter, mistress. After all, we be getting by well on half of everything else and I don't hear none complaining of hunger.'

Godiva, who had never suspected any kindness in Bertha, looked at her curiously. 'Was this your idea?'

'Yes, mistress, I saw famine once before. My baby sister died and my father left home. I never forgot what hunger can do.' A shadow crossed her face and she continued in a half-whisper, her voice cracking with shame. 'Mother sold herself to passing drovers to get us food, and father wouldn't take her back after that. Hunger works evil more powerful than the Devil.'

'Let us not talk of the Devil now,' Godiva said, crossing herself.

'Yes, mistress. He be too close these days.'

'Bertha,' Godiva said, trying to sound brisk, 'you can be in charge of halving the dairy produce and getting it into town at the same times each week. We'll inform the town crier when you have decided these matters.'

'Anything else, mistress?'

'Yes. I will be getting rid of most of my clothes. The good ones...'

'No, lady,' Bertha wailed. 'All the work that went into them! And how beautiful they be, and you in them.' She started to cry.

'Hush. I won't ever go feasting again. Not even if Lovric comes back here to Coventry. I won't be able to.'

Bertha's brows shot up, but Godiva gazed out of the window and kept on talking about practical matters.

'I will offer them to Milly. If she refuses, I will offer them to the convent in Evesham.'

'Yes, ma'am,' Bertha muttered, hating the thought of those lovely gowns, which had been her babies, now going to other women.

'And I will choose from the simpler gowns, two each for you and Agatha. There, I have no more to say. Send Gwen to me now, and tell Agatha to be here soon.'

Soon after Bertha left, still wiping tears from her eyes, Gwen entered, leaning on a walking stick. She held her head on one side and there was a slight curl to her lip that was quite out of character. Godiva got up and embraced her, then sat down close to her to talk about their problems.

'I had a stroke,' Gwen admitted. 'But not a big one, and the nurse was very good, exercising me each day and giving me porridge and puddings until I could swallow again on my own.'

'Are you clean?' Godiva asked tactfully.

'I am now, thank God. But I have this ugly snarl on my face all the time, even when I am happy. I never look in a mirror no more. But then, no use complaining, I can use both hands to work again, though my right arm and leg are weak.'

'I don't want you to work any more. You have done enough for two lifetimes and you deserve to rest now. Gwen dear, after my penance I want you to come with me to the convent at

Evesham. I will need a personal attendant and Agatha is too young to go off to a nunnery. All that praying would make her melancholy and start thinking of taking vows.'

'But, mistress, how can I travel? I can't ride.' Gwen frowned with worry.

'I won't be riding there. Riding is another thing I am giving up. I'm going to go in the wagons...'

'The ones we use to carry the hay? But that's unseemly for a lady, for your dignity, mistress.'

'All the more suitable, then, for my future.'

'Oh, holy mother,' Gwen murmured, wanting to know more about the penance, but afraid to ask. Her face darkened and she began to wring her hands like a laundress, but Godiva did not recognize these signs that others knew to be the cue for leaving Gwen alone.

'It will be a slow but comfortable journey,' Godiva continued. 'You'll like Evesham. There are lovely gardens with birds and streams and small groves where nuns pray or read. I will try to learn to read while I am there...'

'Oh, mistress!' Gwen blurted out, her face twisting with the effort to suppress herself. 'The fucking nuns would hate me. Take someone else. Damn it to hell, Godiva, do as I say, you stupid fucking bitch.'

Godiva sat back in astonishment and stared at Gwen. The curling side of her lip had risen by a tiny fraction of an inch, but it was enough to evoke images of werewolves and other creatures of the night.

'You see!' said Gwen miserably. 'That was a perfect example for you. I was going to tell you, but it burst out of me because I was getting upset.'

'What?'

'Bad talk. Dirty words such as I never used in my whole life. The nurse said it might get better, but I don't see much improvement yet. If you took me to Evesham I would be agitated, and who knows what I'd say to all them lady-nuns they must have at a nice convent like that? They'd be saying I'm possessed by unclean spirits.'

'I wish someone had told me about this before now,' Godiva sighed. 'There is a monk at the priory who could help. Prior Edwin says he is an exorcist, but he is more than that. He is learned and wise about such things. I'll send someone to bring him here at once.'

'Can I be cured, then?' Gwen asked, her face alight with hope.

'I don't know. But at least there'll be no more talk of demons after you've been examined.'

'I'm still not sure of leaving here, though,' Gwen said, her anxiety returning.

'It will be better than staying here. Coventry might not be a restful place after I am gone. In Evesham I can make sure that you are untroubled, and that the sisters understand your condition. Trust in God's mercy, dear Gwen.'

'Very well, I suppose, perhaps, I agree,' said Gwen, surprised at how the conversation had ended.

Godiva walked her to the door and told one of the kitchen servants to lead her back to the sick-room to rest. She watched Gwen's laboured, listing walk and thought how cruel it was that one who had always been so tireless was now condemned to a lingering decline.

Just then she saw Agatha coming towards her, clutching her headdress round her face and studying the ground beneath her small feet. She had Odo with her and the two were talking as though exchanging secrets. Godiva smiled. Odo would be telling her of Wulf's imminent return, and Agatha would be recalling the promises Godiva had made about a dowry and trousseau. It helped to offset the pain of the forthcoming penance to think of all the good she was doing this day for the people who depended on her. She leaned against the door-post, watching, anticipating the conversation that would follow.

Odo patted Agatha on the shoulder, as though reassuring her about something, and then went off. As Agatha approached, Godiva smiled in welcome and ran her fingers along the smooth, jewelled rosary which these days hung about her neck both night and day, as much a part of her body as the thick, fading plait of fair hair in which the string of stones often lay tangled. Agatha's eyes followed her fingers and knew that Godiva was unwittingly counting each Hail Mary, her mind following the silent words of prayer as involuntarily as her lungs breathed in the moist air of Coventry. She is longing for salvation, thought Agatha bitterly. If she prays enough, perhaps He, the Lord or the king, will lift her penance. So she fingers that pretty thing of pearls and jet that she calls a rosary, but that I have other names for. Your halter, lady. Your chain. And even – though I hate to think of it this way and fear my guardian angel will take offence and desert me – your noose, mistress.

They entered the house together and Agatha closed the door behind her. With her back turned to Godiva she slowly let down her headdress. Then she raised her face and let Godiva look at her.

'Great God,' Godiva whispered. 'Not again! Bertha?'

She put her hand out to comfort her, but Agatha shied away, protecting her swelling eye and split lip as though expecting another blow.

'I hit her back this time,' Agatha muttered, 'and that were worse than her hitting me. She fell down and hurt her shoulder on a milking stool, and then I kicked her, too. I'm so sorry, mistress.' Suddenly Agatha's deadpan composure dissolved and she started to sob, shaking quietly with outrage. 'I do still love her, but she ain't got no right.'

'No. She has no right,' Godiva said, taking Agatha in her arms and dabbing her eyes with her own sleeve.

'She call me a whore,' Agatha whispered, 'and say she will tell Wulf's mother I ain't no maiden and he can't marry me, for I have another man's seed in my belly, and...'

'Sh! Drink this,' said Godiva, pouring her best red wine into a goblet and pressing it to Agatha's wounded lips. 'Now,' she said, 'tell me what is the matter.'

'I were in the dairy...'

'Agatha!' Godiva snapped, 'talk proper English. I know you can. I've heard Gwen teaching you.'

Her fear is overcoming her, thought Agatha resentfully, but nevertheless she made the effort to speak as Godiva wished, for at this moment she wanted nothing to do with anything that belonged to her mother, not even her broad Mercian dialect.

'I was in the dairy, just finished with wrapping the cheeses in straw and linen, and up comes mother behind me, creeping quietly like a cat, like she always does when she's snooping. So, she sees what I got on the table, and she pounces on me, and pulls my hair. Next thing she's hitting my face and head and calling me a whore, all because she saw the money I was looking at.'

'What money?'

'This, mistress,' Agatha said, reaching inside her clothing to produce a leather coin bag. She sighed sadly as she passed it to Godiva, who pulled out a coin, examined it and put it back.

'How many?'

'Twenty.'

'Pieces of silver. Newly minted. And in a bag stamped with the crest of the royal mint.'

'Yes, mistress. But I ain't no whore.'

'No. But explain yourself, Agatha.'

'It were Bret.'

Godiva squeezed her eyes tightly shut and clenched her fists.

'It was Bret,' Agatha began again. 'He loves you, you see, mistress, and he could not bear to see you so unhappy. He has run away...'

'Agatha, you don't have to lie to me. If Bret ran away, it was for his own good and no one else's.'

'Oh, mistress!' Agatha mumbled abjectly. 'But I'm still sure he loves you. He must!'

'Never mind that. He's gone, you say?'

'He didn't tell where. And no one seen him since yesterday.'

'And the money?'

'I don't truly understand, mistress. He was angry at me for something I said, and then he squeezed my throat and said he'd kill me. But straight away he was sorry for doing that and then he gave me the money and told me to use it as a dowry, so I could get married...'

Godiva held the little bag in her hand and felt its weight pressing into her palm. The distrust she had felt ever since Egg Ring had this at its foundation. This was the price of secrets given to the king. Then it was given away, as if it meant nothing, after all, to have these silver coins. He was a gambler, she remembered. Gamblers never did value money, even prize-money. Where was he now, though? Not at Cleley, where he still had enemies; not at his penniless parents' home. Where could he go without money? Nowhere. He was dead already, she was sure.

'Mistress! Lady!' Agatha was shouting at her and pulling her sleeve. 'Are you well? You been standing still as a post and just as deaf, for minutes now.'

'Yes,' Godiva whispered.

'He loved you, mistress. I know he did. He said so,' Agatha insisted so fiercely that Godiva almost believed her and for a moment felt tears behind her eyes.

'It doesn't matter,' she said.

'It does matter!' Agatha argued vehemently, entirely forgetting her station. 'It wasn't a good love for you, and he weren't a good man, but that don't mean his love was not a real love.'

'You are too young to know, girl. Hush now.'

'No. I know some things.' Agatha shouted. 'Even if he were a bad man and wicked in many ways, I still believe his love for you were no more false than many other loves, even the Holy Virgin's or the Lord's Himself. They let you down, too, just when you need them most. They let babies die, and bad people rule, and let all manner of suffering loose on the innocent, and yet them priests say their holy love be better than our poor love here on Earth. Well, I don't believe that, and I don't believe you should do no penance, neither. No one does. Whatever you done wrong, it were far, far less than all the good you done.'

'Agatha!' Godiva exclaimed. 'We have no right to question God's love. Evil is beyond our understanding...'

'Damn right it is. So for what do we take orders from priests, when no one understands anything? And who are they to make you do penance? Everyone in Cheylesmore manor and Coventry town know about prior and Cherub, and about Father Godric and the hermit nun, and about his whores, too. You should refuse to do this penance.'

'The king would send in his swordsmen to raid us.'

'Unjustly.'

'That never stopped any king before.'

'Then let us all suffer together. Mistress, why martyr yourself?'

'Because the people who work my lands, and make a living in my town, are all I have. If they are made to starve because of me and the earl, I would die of shame. It would be more dishonourable even than this penance I must do. One day, after it is over, we will live happily together again. I'm sure of that. That is why I must perform the penance.' She paused as Agatha's disapproval filled the silence between them. 'There's another reason, too,' Godiva continued. 'I feel that perhaps...' But she stopped, not wanting to put into words something she was not quite clear about herself – that by accepting the penance she would somehow be in a stronger position than were she to refuse. It made little sense, and it would make none to Agatha, and yet she was convinced that she was right.

Agatha scowled silently at Godiva, who turned away, ignoring her burning black eyes. At last Agatha dared to ask about what was uppermost in her mind.

'No. I will not reveal what I must do until the night before,' Godiva replied. 'I won't change my mind on that.'

Agatha folded her arms defiantly and took a deep breath before carrying on. 'Then I can't stay with you,' she said sternly. 'I can't serve you over these next days if I don't know what must come to pass. If you won't tell me, I'll beg your leave to let me go from the manor, mistress, and go and work somewhere else.'

'Agatha! What is this rebellion for?' Godiva asked, surprised and hurt.

Suddenly Agatha jammed her mouth shut, her lips disappearing into a hard line that perfectly replicated her mother's obdurate jaws. Godiva stared at her until she realized that Agatha would not say plainly what she meant: she could not serve a woman she no longer respected.

Godiva scrutinized her maid for several moments as the girl stared at her feet and clutched herself tightly with her crossed arms. She had grown since this summer began. She was still short and slight, but somehow she was more of a woman, and now she wanted to be her own woman. Regardless of the present turmoil on the manor, it was inevitable that she would have rebelled at her servitude in some way – though covertly, through episodes of clumsiness, forgetfulness and such like. It often happened with maids at her age.

'Then it would be best for you to go, child,' she said.

'No, mistress!' Agatha wailed, appalled at what she had just done.

'Go until the end of summer. Take the money with you, guard it well and tell no one else about it. Come and see me on the day before All Souls' Night. By then your Wulf will be back home and settled in. My penance will be over and I'll be back from Evesham, I trust. And Lovric might be back here, too, and perhaps the boys with him.'

'Oh, my lady!' Agatha's face puckered, then she curtsied like a little girl, turned and ran out of the house, almost knocking Bertha over as she went.

'Mistress, I so sorry,' Bertha said, and then she too started to cry.

'Stop it,' Godiva shouted. 'No work is getting done on the manor because everyone is in tears, or sick or angry. I have nothing to say to you, Bertha, except that you deserved a kicking from your daughter, and you must hurry and tell Wulf's mother that there is no truth in the lies you made up about Agatha. And,' she added, seeing Bertha's mouth opening, 'I know how that money came into Agatha's hands, and it is none of your business. Go and tell Gwen to get back to light work if she is able to. And tell Milly she must work too or she will not get fed. You must decide on their duties and do it without making everyone resent you. If you can do that, I will reward you. But if there is one more quarrel on this manor, you can join Agatha wherever she will be spending the rest of the summer.'

'What? Where is Agatha going?' Bertha interrupted.

'Find out for yourself and stop scowling at me like a bulldog. Now go and tell everyone what they are to do, and above all, tell them I wish to stay alone, in silence, in the upper part of my house. There must be no noise at all in the yard near the manor house. Do you understand? Now be gone.'

Only when she had been alone in the silence of the darkened room, stretched out and still in her soft feather bed for an hour or more, did Godiva start to feel her fatigue. It started somewhere near the pit of her stomach and filtered out from there through the conduits of bone and ligament, sinew and muscle, until finally it reached her heart, where it filled her arteries with something heavier than blood and water, some colder fluid that seemed more viscous and appeared to play a part in weighing her down, pinned to the bed, awake but not alert, silent but not at peace. It feels like oil, she thought – and then, bitterly, she imagined this pollutant in her veins as holy oil, clogging them with unearthly goodness, fit only for saints and useless to a worn and stretched mortal like herself. That is what rebellious little Agatha would have said, she thought, if only the girl had felt free to say such things.

Three days before the day of penance two elegant wagons drawn by massive, well-groomed carthorses, trundled as quietly as possible into the yard of Cheylesmore manor. Worried servants ran out of the stable to guide the drivers away from ruts and tussocks, and to warn them that silence was being maintained in the yard on the orders of the mistress.

'Yes, I know that,' came a crisp voice from inside the biggest wagon as, in a habit of the finest white wool, a middle-aged nun stepped out and gazed round the yard.

'Mercy! Charity!' she shouted, waving a small whip that hung from her wrist. 'We have arrived. Get out.'

Two more sisters in white now appeared, blinked in the bright daylight, and started ordering the grooms to unload the provisions and move them into storage.

'That is the mattress on which your mistress will sleep when we take her away with us to Evesham,' said the superior nun. 'So don't go tearing the cover. Get the wardrobe mistress over here at once to keep this bedding aired and clean.'

'Bertha,' a groom shouted, and Bertha appeared, red with fury at the noise in the yard.

'I am Sister Mary of the Assumption,' the nun announced with calm authority. 'I am deputizing for the Abbess of Evesham and I have come to prepare Godiva for her penance. Those two,' she said, nodding at Mercy and Charity, 'are novices. They take orders from me alone. And while I am here, so do you.' Bertha was too astounded to say anything and Sister Mary continued, 'We will have the manor house. I will sleep upstairs with Godiva, and those two will sleep downstairs. Whoever presently sleeps in the house must find other quarters. Is that clear?'

Bertha found her tongue. 'Can those two cook and clean?' she asked, looking the novices up and down with pure contempt.

'Of course. Godiva must be purified before her penance. Her food must be cooked our way and blessed by me. Look what I have brought for her,' she added, producing a small vial of liquid from the folds of her clothing. 'Holy water from the fountain of St Egwin in Evesham. I will give Godiva three drops of this in each meal she takes from now on.'

She smiled graciously at Bertha, as though expecting her admiration, and then turned on her heel and headed straight for the house. Bertha spat into the straw behind her and went to tell Agatha to find somewhere for them to sleep for the next few nights.

Inside the house, Sister Mary looked round curiously. So this is what an earl's manor house looked like? She herself was the daughter of a cobbler and had never seen anything more splendid than the convent at Evesham. That, she thought, was far superior to this manor, which was really only a very big farmhouse with glass windows.

'Godiva! Godiva! Where are you?' she shouted at the foot of the stairs.

'In my chamber,' replied Godiva in a tired voice.

'Well, come down at once. Slouching around in bed will make you frail. You know who I am, don't you?'

There followed a silence as Godiva composed herself to deal peaceably with this abrasive woman, sent to help her, ostensibly, from Evesham.

'Yes. I suppose you are someone the abbess sent from Evesham.'

'*Someone*? I am Sister Mary of the Assumption,' the nun declared. 'And while I am here you are under my rule as a penitent. You are now under the authority and protection of the Abbess of Evesham. Look,' she commanded, opening the door into the yard. Godiva stared out through strained eyes and saw two young novices standing guard on either side of her door, each holding a cross like a sentry holding up a sword.

'I didn't ask for this ... guardianship.'

'No? But you got it. Be grateful. Now go and wash and dress and put that disgraceful hair out of my sight. Then we can begin to pray.'

Since prayer was what Godiva wanted, it seemed futile to start arguing with Sister Mary about her domineering manner. Still, she wondered that her good friend, the Abbess of Evesham, had sent her this awful woman at such a trying time. She decided to let it pass and tidied herself up. A little later Sister Mary and Godiva, now dressed and with her head covered, entered Godiva's bedchamber. The nun took one look at Godiva's bed and refused to pray anywhere near it.

'I can only pray with any strength in pure surroundings,' she said, looking away disdainfully from the marital bed.

'There is a small chamber to the side,' Godiva said in quiet exasperation. 'My maid sometimes sleeps there.'

'A virgin?'

'Yes.'

'That will have to do. Let us begin.'

Sister Mary believed that comfort was necessary for sustained, concentrated prayer, and she quickly found four thick cushions on which they could kneel as they prayed. Godiva braced herself for tedium as the nun started to hurry through the paternoster and various psalms that seemed to have no connection with her coming penance and present state of sin.

After a while she stopped, and Godiva, assuming she would repeat herself as Father Godric always did, opened her eyes to see what was going on. To her surprise one of the young novices was standing at the open window, filling her lungs with deep breaths of fresh air. Suddenly she turned and started to sing a psalm in the sweetest, saddest voice Godiva had ever heard, a true perform-ing voice, naturally strong and trained to perfection.

'O Lord,' she sang in English, looking Godiva in the eye as she pressed her hands together, '*rebuke me not in thy anger, neither chasten me in thy hot displeasure.*' Godiva winced. This psalm was being sung for her, Godiva the penitent, and no one else on the manor.

> '*Have mercy upon me, O Lord; for I am weak; O Lord, heal me; for my bones are vexed.*
> *My soul is also sorely vexed — but thou, O Lord, how long?*
> *Return to me, O Lord, deliver my soul; oh, save me for thy mercies' sake.*
> *For in my death there is no memorial to thee; in the grave who shall give thee thanks?*'

Did they know she thought often of death, dreaming of the pool where drowning would be easy? How could they know that? The singer, who had paused, now resumed.

> '*I am weary with my groaning. All the night I make my bed to swim and I water my couch with my tears.*

*Mine eye is consumed because of grief; it groweth old because of
all mine enemies.'*

It was true. Her eyes did look old; her enemies were many;
and some who had not been enemies had wounded her even
more. Her husband. Her children. Now she began to sob quietly
as the singer, her voice growing stronger, continued:

*'Depart from me, all ye workers of iniquity: for the Lord hath
heard the voice of my weeping.
The Lord hath heard my supplication; the Lord will receive my
prayer.
Let all mine enemies be ashamed and sore vexed: let them go
away and be at once ashamed.'*

Perfect stillness now occupied the room as the singer folded
her arms across her chest and bent her head in thanks for her
gift of song.

Sister Mary opened her eyes and spoke softly for the first
time since coming to the manor.

'We are all sinners, Godiva. I was once a penitent like you.
Though,' she added quickly, 'my sin was not the same as yours.
Nevertheless, we all have to find the way forward from our sin,
and the only way open to us is true repentance. This means far
more than regret or even remorse. To purify your soul you must
cease to care about your own worth, not just in the eyes of others,
but – hardest of all – in your own eyes. That is what the penance
you will perform in the market square of Coventry will accom-
plish. It will debase you, and if you willingly receive that
degradation, you will be free to feel the love with which the Lord
fills the universe, even in the very air you breathe. Because, you
see, it is your own self that stands in the way of your own
healing.'

Godiva looked at her searchingly, surprised that the bossy nun was now speaking about such ethereal things. Her eyes were cold, grey and canny, her mouth thin and hard, and her nose dominant, but her brow swept upwards in a graceful curve to her hairline. It was a face that could have been fashioned by different workmen in the same mason's shed.

'Yes, it is hard to let go of one's own thoughts and feelings,' she replied. 'Mine have been almost drowning me recently. I even longed for death, or for a sleep that would be endless.'

'I know,' said the nun. 'That was why I came here. At the abbey we prepare people for death. Penance and death are alike, and you would be surprised which people go through the fire with grace, and which ones choke on their pride and stumble on like wounded dogs, without dignity, without understanding.'

Godiva sighed deeply.

'I know you must be afraid,' the nun continued. 'But we will be at your side from now until your ordeal is over.'

At that the other novice took up her position by the window to sing and started with a psalm so short that even Godiva knew it in its entirety:

'*O praise the Lord, all ye nations: praise him all ye people.*
For his merciful kindness is great towards us: and the truth of
the Lord endureth forever. Praise ye the Lord.'

As she repeated the psalm, the first singer joined in. On the third singing so did Sister Mary. On the fourth repetition the nuns signalled Godiva to join in. When they were sure she knew the tune, they began to sing in parts, with the first singer soaring into descant like a lark to the heavens. How like the Church, thought Godiva, to mingle the misery of penance with the sublime delight of music.

'This little psalm is what we will sing when we walk together into Coventry on market day,' said Sister Mary when they had finished with the sung devotions.

Godiva nodded. The penance was beginning to seem, if not less terrifying, then at least conceivable. It would have a form, and she would have companions.

'One thing more,' said the nun. 'This business of you riding the horse naked and, I understand, bareback – I do not like it at all and neither does the abbess. It seems extreme. It would have been better had you walked in bare feet and in sackcloth and ashes.' She had begun to assume her former administrative voice, the voice that crackled with authority. 'But there we are, king's orders. Ours not to question why, and so on. But what I want to know is this: *can* you do it? Have you ever ridden bareback?'

'Of course.'

'But naked, and without a saddle or even a saddle blanket beneath you?'

'It will hurt.'

'Ah,' sighed the nun, 'I was afraid you'd say that. I was afraid that was meant to be the main part of the penance. And it should not be. Public repentance should have been all.' She screwed up her mouth in distaste. 'Sometimes I think men should have no part in the spiritual discipline of women. There are some bishops…' She shook her head and then she stopped abruptly, pulled herself together and repeated her mantra, 'But there we are. Orders are orders. We must do as we are told, isn't that so, Godiva?'

'Indeed. That is the truth,' Godiva agreed, nodding her head vigorously.

Sister Mary gave her a sharp look. Godiva did not strike her as a naturally submissive woman. Agreeable, yes, but not biddable. But surely, with the horror of this penance facing her, she would not have the nerve to muster defiance of any sort, not even the weak defiance of sarcasm.

Sensing that the nun was scrutinizing her, Godiva turned her face away. She's hiding something, thought the nun, some secret rebellion. Most penitents do. Deep in their hearts they want to subvert their penance and neutralize it, giving it some secret meaning that lets them retain ownership of their own souls. So mistaken, so futile! One plays such games with God only at great peril.

Godiva turned back to smile at Sister Mary and saw at once the suspicion in her eyes.

'Good sister,' she said. 'Don't doubt my sincerity. I will prove it to you on the day of the ride.'

Flustered at having been so well understood, the nun said nothing. As well she should, thought Godiva. The matter of my penance is between me and the king, not between me and God. The king is playing a game that I don't yet understand. But I know one thing: for me to win, I must keep playing, too.

Sixteen

*O*n the night before the penance, the nun suggested that Godiva go to bed early, with the novices to sing her to sleep. She herself conducted the meeting of the people of the manor and disclosed what was about to take place.

No great reaction met her words. There was acceptance, repugnance and a few tears, but in general it seemed as if people had been preparing for the worst since the prior made his announcement in church on Sunday and snatches of rumour had percolated into the manor. She examined their faces and tried to read them, but the more she looked, the less she felt she understood. Were they docile out of love of the Lord and respect for the king and the bishops? Or were they perhaps full of loyalty to Godiva and the Earl of Mercia? (She crossed herself quickly, thanking God silently that he had not returned, stopped the penance and sent her packing.) More probably these people were simply oafishly, ignorantly obedient. Then again, they might be dissimulating – raging with hidden rebellion that found no open outlet. They worried her, but soon she would be gone and they would not be her responsibility. That was the good thing about orders. You knew what you had to do, and what you could forget about.

Everyone slept soundly in the manor house that night, as if nothing special were to take place the next day, and at dawn the two novices rose quietly and woke up Sister Mary and Godiva. As soon as they were finished dressing, the nun began the last set of prayers that would precede the penance. She had decided on the simple prayer to the mother of God, *Ave Maria*, and when she finished Charity and Mercy repeated the invocation, 'Pray for us sinners now and at the hour of our death', singing it together like two birds nesting on the same branch, until finally the nun raised her hand to signal them to stop.

'I hear it,' she said. 'The bell of the priory is tolling. It is time. Come, Godiva.'

They walked out into the deserted yard of the manor, the three sisters in white and holding up their silver crosses, and Godiva wearing only her cloak, and beneath it, against her skin, her glittering, priceless rosary. She breathed deeply and chanted the prayer to Mary over and over again without stopping, like a great sock crammed with words that she stuffed down her throat to plug it and choke her screams of anger, fear and refusal.

A groom appeared from the stable with the halter of the chosen horse in his hands. He removed the halter, and the horse, freed of his usual restraints, shook his head nervously for a few minutes, then settled down. The groom backed away, crossed himself, shook his own head disbelievingly like an angry horse and strode quickly out of the yard.

Godiva hung a bag round the horse's neck, and then took hold of him by his pale-yellow mane. She walked him slowly towards the stone mounting block that stood near the entrance to the stables, whispering softly in his ear, 'Starlight, my friend. Go slow. Go easy. Keep me from being hurt, dear friend.' The nuns watched her, and though they did not approve of horse-whispering – a prayer would have been far better – they left Godiva at this moment of crisis to make her own decisions.

At the mounting block she ascended the four steps and then placed herself astride the horse's bare white back, gripping his flanks with her knees and testing his sensitivity to being guided solely by careful tugs on his mane. She leaned forward and thanked the horse for his calm and for letting her guide him from a new direction, and then she called out to the nuns to let them know that she was ready to ride. At this, Sister Mary positioned herself to walk in front of Godiva, and started to ring a small, shrill silver handbell she had brought from Evesham, while Charity and Mercy placed themselves at either side of the horse and raised their silver crosses high. As they started to sing the chosen psalm, Godiva slipped off her cloak and let it fall onto the horse-block.

The shock of the cold morning air on her skin, and the strange sensation of the horse's hide between her bare thighs, heightened her alertness and helped her concentrate on the difficult matter of keeping a good posture while riding bareback. It was, therefore, like hearing something at a great distance that she first heard another horse's hooves galloping into the yard and slowing down to approach her. Like a dreamer awakening, she looked up and saw Agatha astride a horse she did not recognize, glaring at her defiantly as she swept up Godiva's cloak from the horse-block.

'I be coming too, mistress,' Agatha said. 'And when you done your penance, I'll wrap you in this. I'll warrant the king said nothing about you riding naked both ways.'

'No. It will tarnish your good name. You will be ridiculed. No one will let you forget it.'

'I doubt that, mistress. Whoever be telling your tale in times to come, it won't be no enemy, for you ain't got no enemies save the one that caused your clothes to fall off you today, and he don't tell no stories in our part of England. We'd best be off now, mistress, and do this deed. And take this to sit upon as you go.'

Godiva

Agatha passed Godiva a small pillow from a baby's cot. It was filled with dried linseed and covered in white lawn linen, and when she sat on it, it disappeared into the shape of her body.

'Thank God. Who thought of this?'

'Mother. She ain't so bad, after all, mistress. And she sent to say God bless.'

Sister Mary rang her little bell again and Agatha bit her lip until it turned dark red. Godiva looked up at the cloudy sky and sighed deeply.

'I am ready,' she said.

You could kill someone with such a thing, she thought as she pressed against the horse's flanks. Strange how quickly skin chafes when it is unclothed. Strange too the illusion that the horse was lurching, pitching like a boat in a storm, simply because there were no reins to control his head, just that mane of hair that kept tangling with her own, both coarse and a dreary pale colour.

Suddenly the horse almost stumbled in a pothole and Godiva, realizing she had no means to regain her balance, panicked. What if this happened in the market square? Imagine what such a fall would look like as she cartwheeled to the ground with her legs flying apart above her. From behind she could hear Agatha call out 'Steady now' and 'Whoa, Starlight' and the danger passed.

But now the little pillow that sat protectively between her legs was starting to give trouble. It was comfortable, but not stable. She had to reach down and pull it back into position every so often; to any lecherous eye that chanced to see this movement of her hand, she would seem to be doing something obscene. Her nipples were indecent too, for they had grown hard in the chilly drizzle that had started falling a few minutes ago. No one who saw her in her present state would merely remark on her nakedness. No, their thoughts would be on copulation. With her.

Great God in heaven, how disgusting this ride was! You could kill someone this way.

And no doubt it actually happened, from time to time throughout the land, that some man or woman was shamed to death. Tied half-naked to a cart-tail and whipped out of the village. Put on a ducking stool and choked on dirty pond water and their own vomit. Hoisted upside down by one leg. Left sitting in the stocks until the stench of their own excrement mingled with that of the offal and spoiled food thrown at them the day before and left to bake overnight on their livid faces. That was ha-ha time for all the little children. These village punishments were things she had always taken for granted, never realizing it was the shame that was the killer, not the pain.

'But then you never did notice much, did you, Godiva?' It was Lovric's voice, loud with exasperation. Next came Milly's, ringing with contempt and bitter with frustration. 'Blind! Deaf! Stupid!'

'And who are you to be so critical of me?' she retorted. 'You only complained when I did not notice *you* – husband and daughter, both with your mountain of needs. Go to hell, Lovric and Milly, and stop tormenting me.'

Agatha noticed that Godiva was mumbling to herself and sounding distressed. They were approaching the bend in the lane where it turned towards the market square. Suddenly Starlight lost his footing and Godiva flew off his back, landing in muddy grass at the verge of the lane. Agatha jumped off her horse, wiped the mud off Godiva quickly and told her to get back up at once.

'I can't,' Godiva said. 'There's no stirrup or mounting block.'

'Like this,' said Agatha, shutting her eyes and bending low so that Godiva could put one foot on her shoulder and lever herself back on to the horse.

'Go very, very slow now,' Agatha said. 'Don't worry about anything. The houses all have their shutters closed and there be no one around. The surface of the lane be good from here on. Starlight won't stumble again.'

Godiva slowed her horse down almost to a standstill and repositioned herself carefully for the walk up the main street. There, just ahead, was the house of the fletcher, whose arrows were not in much demand in Coventry, and who kept a vicious, mangy dog, as bad-tempered as its master. And next to him was where the tinsmith lived, and his young wife who kept a dangerous sow, greedy enough to bite the arm off a small child. Starlight ambled peacefully past these normally noisy households and came alongside the inn, on the opposite side of the street. The silence here was even more startling, for no one had ever seen the inn closed and barred before. Godiva could almost see the tavern girls, crowding round near the front door, offering help to arriving travellers and sizing up those who might want special services in the woods that came close to the garden at the back of the inn. They were silent now, those big, coarse girls, but she could smell the stink of old beer and lubricated flesh that clung to them like marsh gas, as though they were actually there on the street, arms folded, eyeballing her resentfully, the lady of their town whose beauty was enough, all on its own, to make them feel like the cheapest of whores. And where was their whore-master this morning? She had pretended to respect the innkeeper ever since he turned up, just when Coventry was getting going, with a good account of his tavern outside Gloucester, a sound business plan, accuracy in making small change, and local connections who vouchsafed for him. And yet as soon as she saw him, she had known him for what he was. He was a man who bought and sold anything he could, and anyone.

Her town was disgusting. The face of Tom, the tanner's son, flashed into her mind, leering as he pulled away frantically at his adolescent parts. Why was she going through this agony to save these people's skins? For a moment it seemed that the horse's lurching would make her throw up, as though she were seasick. She whispered to him to stop. God help me, she prayed. Keep my mind strong. Don't let me go mad today. Keep the Devil away. Agatha came alongside and asked if she could help. Godiva shook her head.

Just then, from the house of the candlestick-maker, a two-year-old-boy, naked and unsteady on his feet, came running out, shouting, 'Horsey, horsey' and making straight for Agatha's mount. His mother came after him at once, swooped down and carried him off, not once raising her eyes to behold the penitential procession that was passing her house. Godiva remembered giving the woman flour in the market square, and how grateful she had been, saying that now she could feed her son and save his life. She had felt so proud then, and everything had seemed worthwhile – all the effort, all the sacrifice, and the way they had all pulled together. She prayed for help to keep these good thoughts in her mind.

As they entered the silent market place the tolling of the priory bell seemed unnaturally loud. Godiva wondered where all the people had gone. Had they stayed away for her sake? She gazed at the edges of the square, looking for possible spectators, and it was then that she saw them – about a dozen men, fully armed and ringing the square, their heads down and their hands on the hilts of drawn swords, held vertically with their tips stuck into the earth. Edward had sent a guard. Judging by their white tunics with red crosses, they were from Egg Ring. They would not look at her and they would prevent anyone else from looking, and yet their presence, fully clad and with naked weapons, made her feel more exposed than ever.

They came to a halt. Sister Mary and the novices stepped back towards the town cross, while Godiva and Agatha guided their horses towards the priory's entrance. The nun, disconcerted by the unexpected presence of armed men, shook her handbell as vigorously as possible. The bell ringer inside the tower held his rope still and total silence fell upon the square.

'In the name of our Lord Jesus Christ,' the nun shouted in the voice of a far bigger woman. 'I call upon all who can hear me to bear silent witness that there will now take place the penance of the Lady Godiva for diverse sins known to her conscience, to the king, and to the Lord God Almighty. Amen.'

Charity and Mercy said amen too. Godiva crossed herself, and Agatha, who was wondering who might be inside the priory today, scowled at its tower, her gaze stripping it bare with cold, disenchanted eyes.

'I confess,' Godiva began quietly, then raised her voice, 'to all the crimes against God of which the king has justly accused me. I have been proud. I have consorted with demons. I have committed sins of the flesh. I offer my nakedness as the sacrifice for the redemption of my soul, and the redemption of my people from the payment of *heregeld*. And,' she added, 'to confirm that my repentance is true, I will do that which I have not been asked to do.'

She told Agatha to pass her the bag that hung round the horse's neck, and from this she pulled out a pair of shearing scissors. Then she gathered her hair together at one side of her neck and slowly, laboriously, hacked through the thick bunch of loose hair.

'This is for my vanity,' she said, and threw the great hank of long hair towards the door of the priory.

It fell on the slate paving stones that lined the small forecourt, the gold and grey threads of her head vivid against the cold blue slabs, and scattering in the light morning breeze like an unbound sheaf of wheat left in a field after harvest.

'And this too,' she said, taking off the rosary and throwing it on to the severed hair. 'May these jewels rest around the neck of the statue of the Virgin in this priory and bring blessings to those who pray to her.'

Behind her back Sister Mary watched Godiva's act of contrition with admiration, but also with dismay at St Mary's enrichment. Agatha, observing the nun's covetous eyes, decided that this was the time to cover Godiva. She flung the cloak in a broad circle and brought it down exactly where she wanted it, covering Godiva's shoulders and completely concealing her breasts, her back and most of her legs.

'There's even more, sirs,' Agatha said, addressing the tower of the priory in her best English. 'Whoever you are, and from wherever you are watching. Look what I have for you.'

From out of her clothing she pulled the pouch that Brett had given her and took out one of the silver coins.

'This is the Judas money paid to Beorhtric of Nottingham in Egg Ring. Here is one for the Holy Virgin, in thanks for my mistress's kindness to me.'

She threw the coin at the heap of hair and precious stones.

'And here is another for her protection of this town from famine. And a third for enriching this priory. And a fourth for burying our dead. And a fifth for feeding the lepers.'

'Stop it, Agatha,' Godiva said. 'You need this money.'

'Ite. Finit est,' said Sister Mary briskly. 'Let us go. It is over.'

'It is not,' said Agatha. 'Here's all the rest. Fifteen more pieces of silver as payment for prayers by the monks of this priory, every day for evermore, for the good health of the Lady Godiva, and long life to Lord Lovric.'

The coins flew through the air in a glittering arc and scattered all over the forecourt where, in a little while, the monks would be scrambling for them.

Godiva and the nuns now began to arrange themselves to leave the square in the same order as they entered, but Agatha remained where she was, her horse motionless beneath her. She stared up at the tower, at the place where the shutters of a window were slightly ajar, and listened. But there was no movement and no sound, just a deep sigh which she took to be the wind rising. Then, as she was about to go, she saw it: a slight movement of the shutter, and behind it the outline of a jewelled hand. Bastard, she said under her breath, and then she too decided the penance was over and it was time to go back to Cheylesmore manor.

It seemed like a long time until the little group, all now on foot and exhausted, reached the entrance to the manor's yard. The bell of the priory was tolling again in the background, signalling that people were to remain indoors until Godiva could reach home in privacy.

That was the plan. But there, standing in the middle of the manor's entrance, her hands on her hips and her head cocked to one side, stood Milly. Godiva and Agatha stopped as soon as they saw her, but Sister Mary, who had met and managed a lot of angry young women in her time, marched straight towards Milly, with Charity and Mercy following obediently behind.

'Out of the way, young lady. Orders are orders. Stay indoors until the bell stops. Go now.'

'Go to hell!' Milly snarled, not moving an inch other than to raise a malevolent eyebrow in her mother's direction.

Sister Mary backed down. 'Godiva,' she called out. 'You must see to your daughter.'

'Godiva,' repeated Milly, mimicking the nun's crisp tone. 'Do as you are told.'

Godiva sighed deeply and walked towards Milly.

'What is it, Milly?'

'You know perfectly well, mother.'

'I understand. This penance has mortified our whole family. That was the point. The king...'

'Oh, shut up, mother. I know all about that. I know you're going to say you made a great sacrifice for a good cause, and you're sorry if I'm embarrassed.'

'Yes, I was. But why are you enraged, and insolent? I did what I had to do. It should not concern you so much.'

'Mother! I can't marry Peter now – not until people have forgotten about what you did today.'

'They will get over it, in time...'

'Time? I don't have time! Look at me,' Milly shouted.

Godiva looked her up and down wearily, but saw nothing different about Milly and her angry face and clenched fists. Agatha, however, observing her carefully, noticed that her hair was shining and her skin glowing, her cheeks were full and her dark eyes rich with colour. If she wasn't twisted with anger, she would have looked beautiful for the first time in her life.

'She be expecting, mistress,' Agatha whispered.

'That's right,' Milly snapped. 'You could come with me, Agatha, when I go to the convent at Wilton – for the delivery of my bastard child.'

'No, thanks,' said Agatha swiftly.

'No, Milly,' Godiva said. 'Don't go away, child. Stay here and let me take care of you. This is not the end of the world. I'll talk to Peter Mallet's mother.'

'She won't talk to you. Not after the show you've made of yourself today. I saw Peter last night and he said his mother's maid was at St Mary's on Sunday and heard Prior Edwin talk about your penance. And do you know what Agnes Mallet called you when she heard what you were going to do? "A holy whore", that was one thing. "God's harlot" another. And then, what she said most often, "dirty Edward's fool". She says you were deceived into making a disgrace of yourself for Edward's pleasure, and that what you did was not a proper penance at all, but a bad joke, for which the king is famous. She laughed at you...'

'That's enough,' said Sister Mary, beginning to finger her whip. But Godiva, who had turned a deathly white, took hold of the nun's hand and forced it down.

'Let Milly finish what she has to say.'

'Agnes Mallet says Edward probably watched the whole thing from somewhere. If she could deduce that, why couldn't you? She says you are stupid and that no son of hers should have a stupid woman's grandchild.'

'Does Peter agree?'

'No. He still wants to marry me. But he can't have his portion to marry unless his mother agrees.' Milly sighed and hung her head. Suddenly she looked vulnerable and young.

'Oh, Milly, why didn't you tell me there was a baby on the way?' Godiva asked, struggling with tears.

Milly seemed about to say something, then gave up in despair.

'I'll send gold to Wilton,' Godiva said. 'And make sure you and the child are well cared for. I'll explain to the abbess that your marriage was unexpectedly postponed.'

Milly nodded and turned away.

'Goodbye, daughter,' Godiva said. 'I will pray each day for your safe delivery.'

There was no answer. Milly disappeared to the far side of the yard. Godiva stared after her, wondering once more why their paths had diverged so bitterly and inexplicably, so many years ago.

And yet, for all her regrets, there was no doubt that Milly's going would remove a small black thundercloud that had threatened everyone's peace for many weeks. Godiva stepped over her threshold into the dark of her own home and, standing still, let its familiarity and tranquillity envelop her and bind her wounds.

'Mistress,' Agatha said from behind her. 'A day in bed be a good idea now.'

'My idea precisely,' said Sister Mary. 'You can go now, Agatha.'

'No, she stays,' said Godiva. 'I am no longer a penitent. I am the lady of this manor, and I want Agatha at my side.'

The nun nodded curtly and went to another room to pray.

Lying in her bed, Godiva could hear in the distance the priory bell stop tolling. In the yard of the manor, people were stirring. A horse neighed as it came out of the stables and, for the first time in days, someone shouted as a cart trundled out of a shed towards the entrance. From further away the lowing of cows could be heard as they left the dairy and took the path to the pastures. Thank God for the routines of work, the backbone of life. She would get back to work soon, too. She would start with making an account of how much grain they had in store, and how much money she had left. Then she would find out if anyone was going hungry. Perhaps the famine was fading away as new crops came in. Perhaps the weather was improving; it was still rainy, but the air seemed cooler. Dry, fine weather might follow, with sunshine. Perhaps their luck would start to change. She felt much better than she had expected. She would cancel her plans to go to Evesham, for she no longer saw any need for special arrangements to recuperate from the penance. She would tell the nuns tomorrow that they could pack their wagons and leave. That was her last thought as she faded into the oblivion of a day and a night of healing sleep.

It was in the night, though, in the blackest hour just before dawn, that the fever struck. Godiva sat up and called out to Agatha that she felt dizzy and ill. Agatha felt her forehead and immediately pulled back the cover of the bed. Godiva's nightgown and the bed sheets were drenched in sweat, and there was vomit on the side of the bed. Agatha screamed and all three nuns ran to her aid.

'There's no connection,' Sister Mary said at once. 'The fever and the vomiting are separate things. When did she last eat?'

'She woke up and had some bread and milk just after sunset.'

'Well, it was probably bad and upset her stomach. She'll get over that quickly. The fever is what I need to treat.'

Agatha burst into tears.

'Now, now! Pull yourself together,' said Sister Mary. 'It is not uncommon for penitents to be sick for a few days after doing penance. It will do her no harm.'

Agatha looked dubious and said she was going to get the nurse.

'No,' said Godiva, shivering violently. 'Don't bring her here. She carries sickness on her skin and clothing. Just get clean clothes for me and boil some feverfew leaves.'

Agatha set about removing the soiled linen, while the two novices went to the kitchen to heat water.

'I had a dream,' Godiva said a few minutes later as she sipped the feverfew brew. 'I was on a white horse like Starlight, and I was pursued by a laughing demon that caught me and pulled me to the ground and started to eat me alive. I was bleeding and then I woke up in pain.'

'Oh, my God! What did he look like?' asked Sister Mary.

'Not "he". It was a woman, with blood on her lips and teeth,' said Godiva, shivering violently. 'She had horns on her head, but her face was pretty and she wore long earrings. I think I've seen her before.'

Abruptly Sister Mary's sensible demeanour dissolved in noisy panic.

'That was a vampire!' she shrieked. 'That vomit was not due to bad food. A vampire has been at your stomach.'

'No!' Agatha protested. 'That don't make no sense. Vampires drink blood, not vomit. Everyone knows that.'

'You know nothing, you ignorant little girl,' the nun shouted at Agatha. 'I know all about these matters. Female vampires are different from male. They are like famine ghouls: they eat anything. We must look for signs.'

She pushed Godiva back, and Godiva, too dizzy to stop her, let her look for what she expected to see.

'There!' the nun exclaimed at once. 'Two marks right there, one each at the inner side of both legs. These are the doors through which this vampire spirit comes and goes. Oh, Holy Mary, I must exorcise the demon!'

'But those marks be from riding bareback,' Agatha protested. 'See,' she said, holding up the baby's pillow that had been Godiva's seat during the ride. 'There is a little smudge of blood on one side, from the chafing.'

'Nonsense, girl. The Devil can go anywhere and do anything to trick you. It is he – in the form of a she-vampire – who marked that pillow with blood. It is a sign.'

'You're just making this all up!' Agatha shouted.

Infuriated, the nun lashed out at her with the little whip, and Agatha, her arm burning, leaped away.

Meanwhile Godiva lay still, as though all this talk of vampires and the Devil had nothing to do with her. Sister Mary stared at her intently and decided this was another sign that the evil spirit was taking over her body.

'I feel ill again,' Godiva whispered. 'I'm dizzy and frightened. There's something bad in this room.'

The nun took the novices aside and addressed them sombrely. 'The demon in her dream was real. She has taken up lodging in her stomach. Now she is entering her mind, and Godiva will grow confused and melancholy. I will give her something to calm her down, and I'll pray and sit with her through the time when demons are strongest, at the break of day. You two try to sleep. I'll call you later.'

Godiva had broken into a heavy sweat again, and Agatha wiped her brow with a cloth soaked in lavender water.

'Enough of that! The Devil likes lavender,' Sister Mary declared. 'And he likes unconsecrated virgins, too. Off with you now and leave Godiva in my hands.'

'But she's sick,' Agatha protested, 'and I am her maid. She's used to me.' She turned to Godiva. 'Do you want me to go, mistress?'

Godiva looked puzzled. 'What's the matter, Agatha? Why are you looking at me like that?'

'Doing what, mistress?'

'Glowering. Your eyes are big and dark as a wolf's.' She put her hand over her own eyes and muttered to herself, 'God help me, I am not myself.'

'You see?' said Sister Mary. 'You are exciting the demon in her. Leave at once.'

'No,' Agatha said, but the nun raised her whip again and Agatha backed away towards the head of the stairs.

Godiva's face was now wet with tears and her cheeks were livid with patches of bright red, as though part of her face was blushing and part was shameless. These were the blotches that many people said were the outer marks of guilt and unclean spirits.

'Oh, Holy Mary,' Agatha mumbled, 'save my mistress from whatever is making her sick, and from this nun, too.'

'Go,' said the nun, as Godiva began to toss and turn and scratch her itching face. 'Just go, girl.'

Agatha did not stay to see more, but stumbled down the stairs and ran out into the yard where she knocked on the stable door. A groom let her in and helped her bed down in the straw. He looked at Agatha's terrified face and glanced across at the manor house, where a candle's light could be seen flickering in an upstairs window.

'Everything all right up there?' he asked.

But Agatha had buried herself in a mound of straw and wasn't answering. He looked back at the window, but it was unlit now and the entire manor was in darkness again. The bats and hunting owls were swooping about above the yard, with its treasury of voles and mice, muttering their murderous intentions to the other spirits of the night. I'd best get in, he thought. It will be dawn soon and all manner of bad things will be flying off home and looking to take someone with them for company. He crossed himself and turned to settle back down to sleep. As he did so, a piercing scream came from the manor house, followed at once by a second and a third. Then a bat brushed past his head, and a bird sang the first note of day.

'God save us all,' said the man.

A few minutes later Agatha gave up trying to sleep and ran across the yard to the lodging hall.

'What a to-do! What's all this banging about?' Bertha grumbled. She got up, climbed over the sleeping Gwen and crossed the straw-strewn floor. 'It's you! I might have guessed.'

'Sh!' Agatha whispered, 'Let me in. I need help.'

'What is it?' Gwen called out from the bed in the corner of the room. 'Light a candle someone.'

Bertha fumbled with the candle, melting half of it in the cinders of the hearth fire before she got the wick to flame.

'Listen to me,' Agatha said when they could all see each other. 'Mistress be in danger. Them nuns say the Devil got into her and they be all set on exorcising him. That old one, Mary, she got a whip, and if the Devil don't run away quickly I swear she'll use it on mistress to beat him out of her. Then they'd cart her off to Evesham and she really would go mad, and we'd never see her here again.'

'Too fast,' Gwen said in her laboured speech. 'You said too much for me to understand. Why is there talk of evil spirits?'

Agatha recounted all that had occurred since Godiva first complained of sickness in the night.

'She ain't been violated by no she-vampire,' she snorted. 'She be in shock, from the shame of riding naked into town.'

'And from the chill of the drizzle on her skin,' Gwen added.

'And from them nuns praying non-stop for forgiveness,' Bertha pointed out. 'Prayer be like rich cake. A little be tasty and make you feel nice. Too much make you throw up.'

'I know what's wrong with her,' Agatha said, 'but I ain't going to tell them nuns. They'd twist what I said. Like old Sister Mary saying the Devil put blood on that pillow. That stain was plain proof mistress got chafed when she rode with no saddle. But no, it had to be the Devil. They ain't got no sense, thinking like that.'

'Well, what do you reckon then?' Bertha asked.

'Something is vexing her sorely, someone she saw in a dream, all done up like a vampire. Now, Miss Milly said that Peter Mallet's mother calls mistress bad names and laughs at her. I think Mistress Mallet be the vampire in the dream, for she be the one round here telling folk that mistress's ride was not a true penance, but a cruel joke played by King Edward.'

'If Godiva believes that, it would drive her mad,' Gwen nodded.

'Them nuns be driving her out of her mind,' Agatha said. 'But we can't stop them. They won't listen to any of us. What can we do?'

'I know what,' Gwen said. 'Send for Brother Michael – the exorcist at the priory. That Sister Mary would have to listen to him.'

'The one what came to see about you talking filthy?' Bertha asked.

'Yes. He said my stroke caused that bad talk, not the Devil.'

'Then come with me to the priory, Gwen,' Agatha said. 'We'll get this Brother Michael to help mistress before worse happens.'

'No,' Gwen said quickly, 'take your mother.'

'But she don't know him,' Agatha protested. 'And she be likely to speak her mind and offend someone.'

'True,' Bertha agreed. 'Anyways, why you be such a coward this morning, Gwen? After all mistress done for you?'

Gwen, looking ashamed, tried to make excuses, but Bertha would have none of it.

'Very well,' Gwen said. 'You ought to know. Coventry is rife with rumours. Ethel from the dairy told me last night. They are saying that a man, a stranger, was up in the tower, watching mistress ride naked. Some are saying what that Agnes Mallet says; that this was no penance, but a shameful spectacle contrived for some man's pleasure – some important priest, or bishop. Some even say, for the king himself. There's terrible anger in the town, and a lot of wild talk, and the monks are so fearful they won't open the priory door at all now.'

'They'll open to us, though, if we start shouting out what we want,' Agatha said.

'I'll come with you, Agatha,' Bertha said. 'And I'll stand at the priory door and start saying things that will make them do anything to shut my mouth. Come on, Gwen. Stop all this cowardice. Put on your clean clothes, and hurry up about it.'

They left the lodging hall and headed towards the back entrance of the manor's yard, the one that led into the fields where the housecarls' horses were pastured when Lovric was in residence. They kept their heads covered and bowed, and only for a moment did Agatha see anything that made her pause: three strange horses alone on the pasture. Altogether they were exposed to view for only a few moments, but long enough to catch the eye of Mercy, who was standing at the window to Godiva's chamber.

'The lady's servants are leaving the manor,' she said to Sister Mary. 'Agatha and two older women.'

'They are going for help,' said Sister Mary calmly. 'But they won't get it. The priory of St Mary, Coventry won't act against the abbey of St Mary, Evesham, not for mere serving women anyway.'

She adjusted her headdress and cast her mind back briefly to the days when she was a humble cobbler's daughter. She had learned since then how the world worked: it worked for the powerful and their supporters. It had once worked for that poor woman going out of her mind on her own bed, a woman who had been blessed with a great legacy – noble birth, great wealth, celebrated beauty and love as well – and who had squandered it all. She gazed with pity at the deeply sleeping Godiva. Ruined though she was, traces of her beauty survived. Why had she refused the king's demands – which must have been just – and earned herself a dreadful penance from which her good name, and perhaps her health, would never recover? Didn't she know that only great lords with armies could defy a king? A woman such as Godiva should have been compliant and ingratiating, dissimulating and canny. What was wrong with her that she placed the love of others – a town full of churls and an ageing husband – above her own self-interest?

Suddenly, as though answering her question, a long-unvisited piece of scripture came back to her, a relic of her days as a novice in Evesham when she had no status in the convent and sought only to find her spirit's way forward from the cold desert of her childhood. *Though I speak with the tongues of men and of angels, and have not love, I am become a sounding brass, or a tinkling cymbal ... Love is patient and is kind; love is not envious; love is not boastful and*

is not puffed up. Love bears all things, believes all things, hopes for all things, endures all things ... faith, hope and love, these three endure; but the greatest of these is love.

But she blotted out these futile sentiments by starting to pray. Patience and kindness were virtues she admired far less than discipline and order, and as for love, it had played no part at all in the great success that she had made of her life. It was an irrelevance. It was obvious – just look at her, Sister Mary, robed in authority, and then look at that other: Lady Godiva, cast up amidst the wreckage she had made of her own life. What folly. What waste. What a shame.

Seventeen

*H*ow Agatha missed her horse now. How she longed to gallop into Coventry in a cloud of fury as she came to the rescue of her maligned mistress. She felt like a vanquishing queen of the dark world, and she longed for burnished weapons with which to terrify all who stood in her way. But when people looked at her, all they would see would be Aggy, Bertha's girl, plodding up the dog-fouled main street of Coventry alongside her mother, who was supporting Gwen as she leaned on a walking stick on her lame right side.

The last time Agatha had seen this street was when Godiva rode in to do penance. Then it had been newly swept and the animals were tied up in their pens. It had been quiet, clean and respectful; today it was filthier than it had ever been, and hazardous, too. An underfed dog snarled at her from near the door of the first house. She hurled a stone and it ran inside, where a child immediately screamed and a man started shouting. Up the street, ahead of them, stood a white sow with her farrow suckling beneath its massive, garbage-filled belly. The strongest creature in town, the sow stood her ground as the three women approached, lowered its head and squinted ferociously. The women from the manor froze.

'Piggy! Come here!' shouted the tinsmith's wife, brandishing a bucket of slop as she ran into the street. The sow glimpsed the bucket and trotted off towards the pig-pen at the back of the house. The nervous women resumed their trudging progress up the incline, which – though slight – was making Gwen gasp and complain.

'Wait,' shouted the tinsmith's wife behind them. She was not much older than Agatha and caught up with them quickly.

'I must warn you,' she panted. 'The street is dirty because things in town are bad. People say we got no future here and it be better to think of going back where we come from. Be careful up by the town cross, in case some insult you. What you want in town, anyway?'

'Mistress be sick and we be going to the priory for help,' Bertha said, scowling at the young woman.

'Mistress Godiva, sick? What kind of sickness?'

'None of your business,' Agatha snapped.

'Well, you be going the wrong way, looking for help at the priory. Prior be gone, and Cherub, and some others, too.' She crossed her arms in satisfaction as she saw the confounded look on their faces.

'Gone where?' Agatha asked, less haughty now.

'No one rightly know. But they rode off yesterday afternoon, right after Godiva's penance. There were two important men with them, and a group of soldiers guarding them all. One of the men was very tall and thin, and the other was very strong and had on a great big ring. They all wore helmets with visors and no one here knows who they be.'

'We'd best continue,' Agatha said to Gwen and Bertha, 'and find out what we can at the priory.'

But they had only reached the door to the house of Frith the baker when they were stopped again. Frith came out to meet them, and so did the tanner and his wife and their boy Tom.

Then came the cobbler, the wood-turner and the candlestick-maker and his wife. They gathered round the three women, enclosing them in a ring of surly, jostling faces.

'How is our lady?' Frith began. Agatha quailed, for it seemed he was sneering. But she could not be sure. 'I hear say she be a-bed,' he went on, insinuating that he had heard much more than just that. 'In bed, and tired, like.'

Agatha didn't answer him. Frith had been at the fore when Godiva gave out the flour rations that saved people's lives. If he now openly despised her, what would others think? She shivered with fear, and her mother, noticing, folded her arms high across her bosom as though expecting more trouble.

'Does Godiva know what has happened in the priory?' asked the cobbler.

Suddenly they were all talking at once, bombarding Agatha with questions. She was unprepared for this interrogation and folded her arms like her mother and stared back at them with narrowed, hard eyes.

'And when will she lift the barriers at the roads and let the drovers back through? I get no skins to tan these days. The culling be done. She should get out of bed and open the roads.'

'And we're hungry again,' the candlestick-maker's wife said. 'I lost one baby and now my other little one be ailing. When is Godiva going to be mistress here again?'

'When she's well, of course,' Agatha said, finding her tongue. 'Now tell us about the priory. We know nothing at the manor, except that nuns came to us from Evesham...'

'To cure the lady of devils!' said the wood-turner's wife. 'For she be a witch, and that's why she done so bad a penance. That's what some folk say.'

'That's what them nuns say,' Agatha shot back. 'But I didn't expect treachery like that out of your mouth, missus.'

'That ain't no treachery, for many of us be thinking that.

Watch your mouth,' said a hefty girl who helped out at the inn. She had brought some friends up from the inn with her and now they closed in on Agatha, breathing foully into her face and muttering soft curses.

'Come on, Aggy,' Bertha said, putting herself between Agatha and the gang of girls. 'No use talking to this lot.'

'Wait,' shouted the cobbler. 'There's more. Some are saying that the tall, thin man, what stayed in the priory the night before the penance, got into the tower and could watch Mistress Godiva come into the square. And they say the other man had a big ring on his finger and bossed all the monks around like he were a bishop...'

'That's enough,' said Agatha. 'These stories are of no use. I don't know what be true.'

'But listen to this, then,' the tanner butted in. 'They've found the body of that huntsman from the manor. The one they say the lady liked.'

'Where?'

'In a stream, on the road to London. And it weren't no accident. He been pushed into the gravel so hard you wouldn't know his face. Them that found him knew him only by his clothes. And one thing more, beside his body they found something you would not expect on a huntsman – a silver cross with a garnet in the middle. Valuable. Looks like the killer were a man in orders, and he lost his cross when he struggled to keep the fellow down.'

'And then, too,' Tom butted in, 'there be the matter of Bret's horse.'

'What do you know about that?' Agatha asked fearfully. 'You been peeping again, Tom?'

'In a manner of speaking,' said the boy cockily, risking his father's hand. 'One evening Bret disappeared, and that same night

I saw two men ride into the priory yard with Bret's horse tied to the saddle of one of them. I reckon...'

'*We* reckon,' said his father.

'We reckon the men who came to the priory killed Bret, and one came back later with a third one, him what was fixing to watch Godiva, and these men be high-ups in the Church.'

'And there's something else,' said the cobbler. 'There be some new monks running the priory now. The Prior and Cherub and a few others be taken away. Looks like they'll be before a church court to answer some questions.'

'Now listen here, you good women of the manor.' It was Frith the baker, more worked up than ever. 'What we here in town all be asking is this – why was Godiva never sent to no church court? How come she be sentenced to a cruel penance, just like that? It don't seem right. Rich or poor, all should be punished according to law. Even the prior going to get law. But it look to us like she were punished according to whim, by some bishop, or even by that unmanly king that we never see but everyone say can't lie with no woman, but only look at her instead.'

'And we don't like it,' said the town crier, who had just joined the growing crowd. 'None of us ain't going to pay no tithes to them there monks, priors, abbots and whatnots, till we be sure they got nothing to do with setting a trap for the lady of our manor.'

'And,' added Frith, 'some be saying worse. Like, they would burn the priory down and take whatever they have in there. And give Godiva back her rosary. And you, missy,' he said to Agatha, 'they want to give you back that bag of coins you said was Bret's Judas money.'

'No! Stop all this talk!' Gwen interrupted, jabbing with her stick at those who had moved too close to Agatha. 'You people want to burn down the priory while your lady is still sick in bed? How would that help her? Have you lost your reason?'

'Not as much as you have, crone,' the innkeeper sneered. 'Folks here have lost hope. Lost their faith in Godiva and the earl. They see themselves going back to poverty in some small hamlet in Arden Forest. What reason do they have to expect a turn for the better? Even if Godiva gets her strength back quickly, what can she do? She's impoverished and so are we; her priory will probably be put under another monk's rule; and we here are ripe for plundering by bandits, for we have no protection. The earl and his soldiers have gone away and may never come back.'

'Exactly!' exclaimed the candlestick-maker. 'Why should he? His wars be always in the west and his family here be ruined. They say Alfgar be practically an outlaw, and Harry a...' he avoided the word, 'and his wife is being called "the holy harlot" and such like. That whole family be ruined. The king don't like them, that's why.'

'Godiva should never have gone naked through town,' shouted one of the tavern girls. 'It were too rude, and she a lady.'

Another girl pushed forward, shaking her fist furiously. 'She should have defied the king!' she screamed. 'Told him to fuck off and stuff his penance up his bald arse. She be a coward and she shamed herself.'

'Yes,' shouted several new men's voices, drunk despite the early hour. 'Fuck off, king! Fuck yourself, Neddy!' Then others took up the refrain. 'Fuck off, priests! Fuck off, monks! Fuck off, Lovric! Shame! Shame! Shame!'

Then someone pointed at Agatha. 'Away with you, you manor rat,' he shouted. 'Out!'

It was the old community war chant against the Vikings and they all took it up now with abandon, heedless of the fact that no one had seen a Viking for decades.

'Out! Out! Out!'

A boy kicked Agatha on her ankle and a tavern girl spat on her as she fell to the ground. Agatha scrambled to her feet and pushed the girl so violently that she fell back amongst her friends, winded and surprised at the counter-attack.

'I won't listen to you no more,' Agatha screamed, pressing her hands to her ears. 'Cowards you be, and traitors. Mistress stood up for you at the worst of times, but you can't stand by her for a short while until she gets better. Plague on you all! I hope you starve to death. You didn't deserve no help. Mistress should have taken her money and gone away and let the king's men take all you have for *heregeld*. You ain't worth a farthing, none of you. You men be no stronger than lambs' cocks, and you women be...'

'Enough of that,' said the tinsmith, stern and conciliatory at the same time. 'You be a young woman now, Agatha, not a girl, and you must see more than one side of things. Coventry be likely to die. If that happens everyone here will suffer. But you manor folk will never suffer as long as you live. If Godiva goes away, she will take you with her. Even if she dies she will make provision for you in her will and you will go to serve with other noble families. But we are not servants, miss. We are mere *tenants*. She don't owe us more than fairness in setting the rent we pay on her property. If the property decays, we must move on. We be free men and women, and we be on our own. That's all there is to it. You can't blame folk for worrying about that.'

Agatha looked him up and down, then nodded imperceptibly.

The tinsmith took her arm and turned to face the crowd. 'She don't mean no harm,' he said. 'She be upset, like we all be upset. Reckon we should go with her to the priory. When she talks to them monks we could add our voices. We ain't never been heard up there, by the town cross. Who says we follow Agatha to the priory?'

There was a roar of approval, and Agatha, horrified, now realized that as quickly as a leaf turns over in the wind, she had become their heroine. She bit her lip remorsefully, recalling her mother's admonition: beware the wish that comes true. Her eyes met those of Bertha, who shrugged slightly: things were out of their hands now.

The crowd surged forward up the hill, and once more the chant of 'Out, Out, Out' rang forth, menacing, primitive and mean. Agatha, who walked so quickly she left them all behind, stopped to catch her breath and look back. There, following behind her, came her mother and Gwen, surrounded by the town crier and the innkeeper, the tanner and his wife and their son Tom, the cobbler, the crier, the wood-turner, the tavern girls and a gang of drunks, the tinsmith and Mrs Smith, Frith the baker, and the candlestick-maker and his desperate wife. And from the doors of the houses people were pouring out to join this kernel of protestors, all of them now converging on the priory, ready to call for justice from the lords of the Church. Agatha felt a rivulet of cold sweat trickle down her back. For such things they torture you, to find out the names of your fellow ringleaders. Then they would make charges of witchcraft or heresy, which she would never understand well enough to deny, for the talk would all be in Latin, and then they would burn her alive or flay her, or whatever they do to rebels.

A rebel – Godiva had accused her of being one when she objected to the penance. Her mistress, who was so often accused of ignoring things, had found in Agatha's soul something she herself knew nothing about: mutiny. And it had come to pass, for here she was, the obvious ringleader in a peasants' revolt.

'Quiet, all of you!' she shouted as the crowd milled about her. 'I promised my mother she could have the first rant against the priory. Who wants to speak after her?'

Most of the hands in the crowd shot up at once. Agatha felt at a loss.

'Mother first, and then we'll just have to see,' she said.

'First of all,' Bertha shouted at the priory gate, 'we are not satisfied with paying tithes and having monks lock us out of their services. Second of all, we are not satisfied with seeing all manner of bad living amidst the priests of this parish and none held to count...'

She was wagging her finger as fiercely as ever, but affecting a manner of proper speaking that leached all the usual acid out of her words.

'Pipe down, Bertha,' someone shouted. 'Call a spade a spade or shut up. Them priests be arse-boys, all of them, and get no punishment. But our lady be made to shame herself. We want vengeance.'

'Vengeance!' the cry went up, raggedy at first, but soon in unison like a big wave crashing, drawing breath, then crashing back again. 'Vengeance! Vengeance!'

Agatha panicked, seeing the crowd lathering itself up for a riot. The priory would never open its doors now.

But just then, incredibly, a door swung slowly open. A monk stood before them, holding up a cross.

'Peace be upon you, brothers and sisters in Christ,' he said softly.

'And upon you,' they answered automatically with one voice as though in church.

Gwen nudged Agatha. 'That's the exorcist, Brother Michael.'

Anxiously, Agatha looked round at the faces in the crowd. But none of them seemed to know who Brother Michael was and what he did.

'Your complaints are well known,' he said disarmingly. 'But this is not the place or the manner for discussion of these grievances. One matter, however, can be redressed at once. The girl Agatha, who is she?'

Agatha, terrified, stepped forward.

'This money is tainted,' he said, holding up Bret's coin bag. 'It cannot be donated to a consecrated house. The prior did wrong in taking it. Keep it, or give it to the poor.'

Agatha reluctantly took back Bret's bag of money. A murmur of approval passed through the crowd.

'Now, what else can I do to help you?' the monk asked them.

Someone shouted out 'arse-boys', but the tinsmith took the wind out of his mouth with an elbow jab to his stomach.

'Agatha has a request,' he said, pushing her back to the front of the crowd.

'But I need to speak to you in private,' Agatha whispered.

The monk signalled the crowd to be silent and asked them to wait patiently while he conferred with her inside the priory. Murmuring and intrigued, the crowd settled down to gossip quietly and wait to see what would happen next.

As soon as the door was shut behind her, Agatha started explaining her mission frantically. But at the first mention of nuns from Evesham, the monk, sighing, stopped her.

'When Prior Edwin was taken away to the bishop's court, some of us made a search of his papers. They were full of un-opened letters. One was from the Abbess of Evesham, stating that she was in ill health and sending her deputy, Sister Ethelfled, to care for Godiva during the penance. It seems that someone substituted herself while the abbess was unable to intervene. I have a pretty good idea who this might be. Stout? Carries a little whip? I will send monks with you to the manor at once.'

'Please, will you come too? There be talk of demons.'

'Yes. I'd better come too and bring our herbalist.'

'Now?'

'Yes.'

He disappeared into the interior, leaving Agatha astonished at the new benevolence and potency of the priory. This Benedictine reform that she had heard the earl and Godiva talk about was surely a blessed thing if it took away the prior and produced good deeds like this morning's surprise at St Mary's.

She looked round and for the first time absorbed the grace of the lines of the priory's pillars and windows, the peace of the shadowy interior and the familiar sacred scent of incense. This is what Godiva had loved so dearly in her priory. This is what she had sought when she wandered off on that fateful day into Winchester cathedral. This – Agatha sought a word, and virtue came to her mind – this gracious virtue was still there in this and any other church, a possibility shimmering behind the veil that men smeared with their greedy hands. Her eyes wandered towards the painting of the Virgin that Godiva had spent hours contemplating. Agatha had never prayed in church beside her mistress and now she imagined what it had been like to be Godiva, a mere few weeks ago when all was well and she came here often. Perhaps that good life could return. Perhaps she should pray for it, though no one had properly taught her how.

She pretended she was Godiva and went to kneel before the painting. But no words came to her untutored mind other than the opening lines of *Ave Maria*. The rest she had forgotten over the last few weeks for lack of use. A pang of familiar bitterness passed through her. She felt deprived, as though a secret healing existed, but it was only made available to some, and not to poor young women like herself. She emptied her mind of words and let her eyes dwell on the painting. It didn't look like a real woman, she thought. The image was stiff and the proportions wrong, but the colours glowed and the face suggested the infinite love of a mother for her infant. If God is love, as the priests preach, then we only ever know Him through our mothers. But not mine, Agatha thought, suddenly tearful. Then it occurred to her: my real mother is Godiva. And she is mother to this priory and to the manor and to the town. And she who had been forbearing, generous, forgiving and caring had been wronged so deeply it had pierced her heart and sickened her to the point of death.

'Oh God!' she shouted out aloud at the Christ child in His

mother's arms, 'I don't know how to pray. I only know that you should do something. Help us now, or go away forever and let me forget about you.'

For the rest of her life Agatha was to believe that miracles can happen, for what took place next was what she least expected. A noise caused her to turn, thinking that Brother Michael had come back. But there was neither monk, nor herbalist, nor exorcist behind her. Instead, there emerged from the shadows the huge figure of a warrior, looming and threatening, and coming straight at her.

'Oh, great God help me,' she whispered.

'Get up, Agatha, and come with me,' said the warrior. 'You have much to tell me, I believe, about my wife.'

Half an hour later Agatha reappeared before the waiting crowd. With her was Brother Michael and Brother David, the herbalist. Clever Agatha, Gwen thought. Good girl. But Agatha had a strange, tight look on her face – not at all like one who knew she had been clever. Something is up, thought Gwen. Dear Mary, let it not be more trouble.

The crowd dispersed in a mood of satisfaction as the monks and the manor women walked silently out of town and towards Cheylesmore. Already one or two residents were out before their doors sweeping up their patch of the lane, and every so often someone called out, 'God bless' and 'Praise be'.

Once they rounded the bend in the lane, Brother Michael stopped and embraced Gwen, saluting her improved health.

'I never thought I'd see you walk to town again,' he said.

'Nor I. As for mistress, I know she thought I'd just go down-hill and end up demented.'

'Has she had madness on her mind, then?' asked the herbalist.

'Now you mention it, I think she has.'

'And she was yearning for a deep, long sleep, almost like

death,' Agatha added. 'She frightened me when we went swimming a little while ago. She stayed under the water too long and said it was beautiful down there amongst the weeds. Even then I thought she wasn't quite right, but I thought she was coming down with a cold, no more than that.'

They talked on, about all the events of that summer, and soon the gate to the manor yard appeared before them.

'Godiva was exhausted and in low spirits, even before the penance,' said Brother Michael. 'Afterwards she went into shock.'

'Don't you believe in Satan then?' asked Bertha.

'Yes, but he is no more busy interfering with mortals than is the Lord. His visits are very rare.'

Charity and Mercy spotted Agatha and the others as soon as they entered the yard.

'You were right as always, Sister Mary,' said Charity. 'They did go for help to the priory.'

'But, alas, they got it,' said Mercy blandly.

'What?' the nun gasped. 'Hurry, make this chamber tidy and see that Godiva looks tidy, too. Pull the covers right up to her chin. Take out the chamber pot and rinse it. Get to it!'

The novices flew around the upper part of the manor house, putting everything in order. The nun, meanwhile, quickly hid her book of spells against the Devil, which, though widely used, was not approved by her abbess. She hid her little whip as well.

Moments later a loud banging on the manor-house door announced the presence of Sister Mary's rivals for authority. She let them wait a while before she slowly descended the stairs with maximum gravitas and dignity.

For several moments everyone sized each other up. Sister Mary noticed that the two brothers from the priory were ordinary monks and that she therefore had superior standing in holy orders. However, she was not in her own precinct, and they were men. She had better be careful. Agatha noticed that Sister Mary had replaced her whip with a cross.

Sister Mary, hoping to take charge of the situation, spoke first. 'You three,' she said to Agatha, Bertha and Gwen, 'get out. Now.'

Bertha opened her mouth, but Agatha nudged her into silence.

Alone with the monks, the nun now called on the novices to stand at either side of her. 'Well,' she began, 'what is the meaning of this intrusion? No authority has informed me of the need for a visitation from the priory.'

'If exorcism has taken place here, you have acted beyond your station, sister. There is an allegation against you, and we have come to investigate.'

'Nonsense,' the nun said confidently. 'I am perfectly capable of dealing with evil spirits. That is my role in Evesham. Is it not, my daughters?'

'She casts out spirits, sir,' said Charity.

'They go howling away, so it is said,' added Mercy.

'But you are not the exorcist at Evesham,' Brother Michael persisted. 'His name is Peter of Little Stow. I know him. We studied and trained together in Exeter. Where did you train?'

A lie quickly sprang to her lips, but Sister Mary did not want to give the novices evidence to use against her in future. 'That is none of your business,' she replied angrily. 'It is not right that you come here and challenge me, after all the good work I have done for the poor soul who lies up there, ravaged by the forces of darkness.'

'Whatever you have done, your abbess did not authorize it. There is a letter from her in the priory. It states that Sister Ethelfled was on her way here from Evesham. Now show us to the sick-bed.'

No one moved. Then Brother Michael pushed the nun and the novices aside and took the stairs two at a time.

Inside the darkened room he could barely make out the figure of a woman, lying under layers of bedding despite the mild summer weather. She was motionless and so pale against the white linen sheets that she seemed drained of blood. The herbalist felt her pulse and temperature. The exorcist opened the shutters, one after the other, and then started to open the windows to let in air.

'What do you think you are doing?' Sister Mary fumed. 'This woman has been in a high fever all night. She must be kept warm.'

'What did you give her?' asked the herbalist, holding Godiva's wrist and then letting it drop lifelessly onto the sheets.

'Feverfew tea, of course. What else?'

'Yes, what else? She has been unconscious for hours.'

'Well, of course, I had to sedate her in the night. She was calling on Beelzebub and the Green Man, and Freya, too.'

'You overdosed her on Set-wall. Valerian. You might have killed her.'

'And you are lying when you say she called out the names of devils,' said the exorcist. 'Those who are genuinely possessed are strong and hearty. She would have thrown your tea in your face and ripped up your book of spells.'

'What book?' asked the nun defiantly.

'That little, well-thumbed thing, on the table over there. I've seen it many times before now.'

Sister Mary stared in horror at the table. Someone had removed the cloth that she had flung over the book in haste when the monks arrived. She turned to accuse the novices, but the two girls stood mutely staring at their feet.

'That has nothing to do with me,' the nun protested.

'Rubbish, no one in this room can read apart from you, me and Brother Michael. You can't read yet, can you, girls?' he asked the novices. They shook their heads.

'I've heard enough,' Brother Michael said, pulling back the bedclothes.

In the strong daylight the exorcist could see that Godiva was unkempt. No one had seen to her hair or washed her skin for a while, and the smell of old sweat was growing offensive. He pulled back an eyelid and saw that the inner lid was pale and yellowish, suggesting some reaction by her liver. Her pulse was steady, but weak, and her temperature seemed low. Other than that there was nothing remarkable about her condition. No marks of the Devil, no bestial growling in her throat, nothing at all, just weakness and drowsiness from an excess of the roots of the pink and white flowers that had driven her into unconsciousness.

'I should examine her body for signs,' he said, and started to turn her over.

'No!' shrieked the nun. 'That is indecent! I forbid it.'

She lunged forward and tried to place Godiva as she had been, lying on her back, but as she pushed and strained, Godiva woke up, screamed at the sight of the nun's face and fell onto her side with the loose nightgown falling off her shoulder. Everyone in the room saw clearly the long, red marks that ran from her neck to somewhere beneath the gown.

'My God, you'll pay for this,' said the exorcist.

'I can explain,' the nun protested.

'Yes, to your own abbess. Did you arrive by wagon? Then go back as you came. Now!'

'Wait,' the nun said, and then she began to cry. 'I was only doing my best for her. I thought what I did would cure her. And I was so frightened myself. These devils hate the ones who struggle with them. I thought I would be possessed, too ...'

'Enough,' said the exorcist. 'Say all these things to your abbess. She will no doubt offer you a suitable penance and a cure for your soul. Go now.'

Sister Mary and the novices vanished down the stairs, and

soon the sound of wagon wheels could be heard, creaking too rapidly for safety as the nuns' driver urged the carthorses to make the fastest getaway possible from Coventry.

'My good lady,' said Brother Michael, taking hold of Godiva's hand, 'I am sad that we should meet again like this. But you will recover quickly now.'

The herbalist approached the bed and put a small silver spoon to her lips. For several minutes, as the tincture worked its way into her head, Godiva lay back with her eyes shut as the dizzy reeling that had sickened her slowly calmed down, grew faint and passed away altogether. After a while, when her head was clearer, she asked the monks why the Abbess of Evesham, who had once been her good friend, would have sent Sister Mary to her.

'She didn't,' the exorcist said. 'That nun tricked her way in here while the abbess was unwell. Sister Mary is notorious for imposing her will on weaker nuns. She has exceeded her authority for years, most recently by attempting to heal those whose minds are confused – something for which she is untrained. She probably came here, knowing how the penance would lower your spirits, and hoping to prove her merit as a healer so as better to defend herself in the bishop's court. But now she has gone. So have some others, Godiva. You'll find the priory much changed. Prior Edwin, a boy known as Cherub and several members of the choir have been taken to say what they can in their defence. Your confessor, though – a certain Father Godric – was deemed to be merely disorderly and was released to the care and admonitions of his wife.'

'I should have dealt with them all myself,' Godiva said, 'but there were so many pressing matters, and they are cunning men.' She thought for a moment. 'Poor Cherub! What will happen to the boy now?'

'Who can tell? As you know, lady, he suffers from fits. It

would be a great kindness were you to let him come back to the priory. He has no enemies at St Mary's and nowhere else to go.'

Godiva nodded.

'She seems strong enough,' the herbalist said to the exorcist.

'Then let me break the news,' Brother Michael said to Godiva. He opened the palm of her hand and enclosed in it the huge, familiar gold ring that Godiva had seen on Lovric's hand for years. The gold warmed her fingers quickly. Then, reluctantly, unwilling to face the message it conveyed, she held it up to the light and confirmed its ownership.

'Tell me at once, does this mean he is dead?'

'No. The earl is at the priory. He asks when he may visit you here.'

For several minutes Godiva said nothing. The herbalist offered her some more of the tincture, but she refused. Her mind was clear enough: it was her heart that lay in two halves, one full of love, the other of anger. No medicine would bring them together. At last she took the exorcist's hand.

'Tell Lovric I need more rest. He could see me here tomorrow evening. Until then, if he will, let him look into the affairs of my priory.'

As soon as the monks had gone, she eased herself out of bed, stretched her stiffened limbs and gingerly fingered the weals on her back. Contemptuously, she reflected that worse scratches were to be had from brambles on forest paths; a few drops of lavender oil would soon erase the irritating reminder of that hideous nun and her little instrument of spite and fear. Her muscles were still weak, it was true, and she felt tired and unable to stand as straight as she used to. But that would pass. As for her mind, the chaotic visions of the night after the penance seemed to have acted like a yellow bristle broom, sweeping the debris of the penance and the clutter of the summer's miseries from all its corners, leaving it clear, untroubled and ready for whatever would happen next. Even ready, she thought, to face Lovric tomorrow.

A few minutes later Agatha knocked excitedly at Godiva's chamber door.

'Them nuns from hell be gone already,' she said gleefully. 'I've warm water here to wash you clean, mistress. Gwen be making you a good breakfast. I'm going to put clean linen on your bed, with lavender flowers under the sheets, and you will have a day and night of perfect rest before the earl come here. You going to be well again, mistress, and beautiful too. The good old days have come back to us here in Coventry, praise Mary and all the saints.'

Agatha rushed downstairs to help Gwen. But Godiva did not hurry to wash. She lingered by her chamber window and watched as the monks departed, and in the ensuing interval of silence, as the smell of frying bacon and sausages came up the stairs, she became acutely aware that the aching in her limbs was beginning to ease and fade away like mist steaming out of the wet earth when sunshine falls on sodden fields. Despite this, she sighed deeply. Old times, she knew, would not be coming back. Some things had changed forever, and tomorrow, when she saw Lovric again, she would find out what could continue and what had gone forever.

Eighteen

The Earl of Mercia would come in secret at dusk, riding an ordinary horse from the priory's stables and wearing a monk's robe over his cloak, its hood pulled over his forehead. His messenger said he wanted Godiva to send the servants out of the manor house, the yard and the stables. And he wanted a good dinner ready for him when he arrived. He is hopeful, she thought, but uncertain. He wants no premature shouts of welcome. 'Yes,' she said to the messenger. 'Tell the earl that I await him at the appointed time.'

That afternoon Gwen went into a frenzy of cooking, scouring the pantry for any delicacies that had survived the recent frugality. Agatha left her to it, and turned her attention to Godiva's torn and faded beauty. She too was over-anxious to do the things that she had always done, to make the past come back to life at once. She offered to prepare a bath with soured milk in the water, and produced tinted cornflower for dusting Godiva's skin after the bath. She found the oil used on the hooves of newborn foals and suggested a manicure. Then she got hold of some camomile and talked of washing her hair. But Godiva would have none of this and lay down alone on her bed until it was nearly time for Lovric's arrival. Bored and unsettled, Agatha went off to find her mother. Bertha was in the store room, brushing everything she could get her hands on and scowling ferociously.

'Them nuns,' she said resentfully, 'poking about, looking for the Devil and bringing moths in here with them.'

'Hush, mother. No more about them.' Agatha, discomfited by the too-recent memory of the nuns, wriggled around on her seat and stared at the lengths of fabric her mother had laid out on the table. Suddenly her eyes alighted on a long head-wrap she had not seen before. 'What's this?'

'It be old. Mistress say she wore it when she first met the earl.'

Agatha shook it out and whistled with admiration. The length of shimmering mauve silk was finely embroidered at its loose end so that a cascade of seed pearls would seem to fall down the neck of the wearer onto her breast. How beautiful Godiva must have looked in this.

'When she gets up I'll show it to her,' she said, wrapping up the silk carefully into a neat little scroll. 'Perhaps she'll remember, then, how she ought to look to meet the earl.'

But Godiva showed no interest in the pearl-strewn veil. Nor did she want her hair braided in the style Agatha had invented for her short hair, nor her face blotted with the tinted cornflour, nor her dry lips dabbed with reddened wax. Gwen's delicacies were set aside in favour of a light stew with rye bread.

'I appreciate your efforts,' Godiva said, reading the surly contours of Agatha's face. 'But I want my husband to see me as I am now, not as a shadow of what I looked like before our troubles.'

Agatha's lip curled slightly. Mistress had taken to calling her horrible penance, her shame and her delirium '*our* troubles'. She seemed to want to remind everyone of the link between the famine, the threat of *heregeld* and her penance. But in the town the talk was only of the king's dirty mind and how the lady had been fooled by the great and ghastly *scopman* of England. No one could get over it.

'Very well,' Agatha said sullenly. She still loved Godiva, but she was bursting to tell her to stand up for her good name. 'How shall we do your hair then? We can't just leave it dangling down like rats' tails. It look truly bad, mistress, like you be not right up here,' she said, patting the side of her head.

'Agatha, how dare you!' Godiva snapped.

Agatha bowed her head in confusion, realizing she had gone too far.

'Just make some small braids at the sides to keep it tidy, and then go away and leave me in peace.'

Silently and deftly, her little fingers flying like a weaver's shuttle, Agatha made several minute plaits that she finished off with bits of gold wire.

'Sorry,' she mumbled and ran out of the room.

Godiva watched her go, and felt her weariness return. It was immense, like a sea in which she bobbed about aimlessly, the lapping of its waves giving incessant voice to one idea: dear God, I am sick and tired of other people's thoughts. My own are enough trouble for me. God help me tonight if Lovric tests my patience, for I truly have none left.

The knock, when it came, was as it always was. Loud, insistent, but not too long. It was the knock of a man who expected to be let into his own home. Agatha answered the door, assured the earl that no one but Godiva was in the house and ran off to the lodging hall.

Lovric, thinking how pretty the girl had become, watched her cross the yard and saw Odo's boy, Wulf, run up to her, take her arm and say something. Wulf had grown at least four inches in the year since he'd last seen him. Nothing stays the same, Lovric reflected, and braced himself for the sight of Godiva.

'In here,' she called from the back of the house.

He crossed the floor of the main room and stepped down into the kitchen. She was standing facing the hearth, stirring a small cauldron that contained the stew they would eat for supper. It would be a simple meal, served by a woman who seemed frailer and thinner than she had ever been before.

'Eva?' he said warily.

She turned slowly and let him take his time absorbing what he saw. A spasm of pain crumpled his brow. She was almost as dismayed at the sight of him. He looked ten years older than when he had ridden away.

'Did you know?' she asked.

'About the penance? No. Only that you had agreed to an act of contrition of some sort.'

'Where were you when you heard? Who told you?'

'In Bristol, about to take ship to Anglesey.'

'And go to war against Edward?'

'Yes. Eva, ever since I left you I have been making preparations to wage war against him. The only thing that delayed me was bad weather on the Irish Sea and the failure of some of the Welsh and Irish to rendezvous with me in time. That, and Godwin's sudden loss of nerve. As things turned out, I never did go to war. On the day you left Egg Ring messengers reached me from Edward. He praised you and said he had forgiven all our sins. And Alfgar and Harry, too. I had no idea what he was up to. And no idea what he had told you to do. I only learned about this ... so-called penance ... in the priory, last night. I came here from Bristol as fast as I could, but I was too late to stop it.'

'I see,' she said, suddenly having nothing more to say. He too found he couldn't carry on. After several moments she turned back to stirring the stew.

'What shall we do, Eva?' he asked eventually.

She put down the ladle, folded her arms and turned to look at him.

'The last time I saw you, you accused me of wanting a divorce and then you stormed off. The thought had never even crossed my mind until you mentioned it. I was angry at you, but I never wanted a divorce, Lovric.'

'I know,' he said softly. 'I was wrong, and I'm sorry.'

'It was Edward, wasn't it? He misled you – told you in Winchester that I had agreed to annul our marriage, agreed when I met him in the cathedral?'

'You guessed?'

'Yes. But not until I was in Egg Ring, listening to him give me reasons why our marriage should be annulled. That's when I realized he must have said the same things to you, in Winchester. In fact, though, I had agreed to nothing at Winchester. It was later, at Egg Ring, that he said he would lift the threat to Coventry, and spare me the penance, if I agreed to divorce you. But by then you had already left me in a fury – and yet I refused to divorce you.'

Lovric, remorse and anger clashing, looked away. 'Eva,' he said carefully at last, 'don't take what I am going to say now as an excuse for my actions. I said I was in the wrong, and I don't mean to excuse myself...'

'Then what?'

'I was afraid you were leaving me, and that made me act rashly. But there was something else, too. Something that made me so angry I couldn't talk clearly with you. I couldn't believe you didn't realize what that was, while we were quarrelling. It seemed as though you wanted me to put it into words, so we could argue about it and toss it around like any other matter about which we disagree. But it was too painful.'

She ransacked her memory, but nothing came to mind.

'I thought it might be obvious. It was to me, after Edward said it.'

'But what?'

'Godiva, you're not going to deny it, are you? I've forgiven you already, so let us not go through lies and inventions now.'

She folded her arms again, and was about to tell him to stop speaking in riddles, when she stopped. Her eyes met his, and she understood his meaning as plainly as if it had slammed into her face.

'Oh Eva,' he muttered. 'That man, Bret.'

Eyes shut, reeling, she leaned back against the wall. Minutes seemed to pass and neither spoke. Then she began to collect herself, retracing the events of the last month and looking amongst them for something she knew to be there, some key, lying amongst the chaos of conflicting stories and disparate memories. She went back to the point where Lovric had arrived in Coventry, blazing with anger, and her fear that he knew about Bret. She remembered in precise detail how his dagger looked, and the hilt of his sword in his hand, her own panic, and then her reassuring certainty that he could not possibly know anything about her infidelity. And then, as her memory grew ever sharper, she saw it: the little key to the big lie. Of course he did not know.

'But, Lovric,' she said slowly, 'how could Edward have told you about Bret in Winchester? It is impossible. Nothing had happened between me and that man. Later – yes, I must admit it, but not then. Not in Winchester.'

'I'm not lying to you, Godiva. That is what Edward said – you lay with that huntsman.'

'Yes, Edward told you about it – told you *before* it happened.'

Now it was Lovric who closed his eyes in shock. He said nothing for several moments, unwilling to admit the king's victory in his game with them.

'That man,' he said at last, 'that man was sent to seduce you. It was planned by Edward. My God, Bret didn't even love you.'

'No. He deceived me. And Edward deceived you.' She paused, and for the first time in all their years together Lovric saw Godiva's face in its bare, essential structure, unadorned by smiles or any other expression of concern for him. 'I can explain how Bret deceived me. I was tired and lonely, and he was young and handsome. If you had stayed at my side when I asked you to, I would not have gone with him. But as for you, how can you explain how the king deceived you? Why did you so quickly think badly of me? For years I put my jealous feelings aside and kept faith with you. But you...'

'It's true. I believed Edward instantly. I remembered how you and Bret looked when you left Winchester, seated beside each other. You seemed made for each other, happy together, good for each other. And I knew that was not true of you and me. I felt old, and I felt tarnished by all the compromises I've made and my half-truths. I could easily imagine you wanting another man instead of me.'

'But why didn't you act on your misgivings? It would have been so easy. One promise from you, one token of concern, and Bret would never...'

'Stop it, Eva,' he shouted. 'I don't ever want to hear that man's name again. It's worse still when you say it was my fault.'

'That's not what I meant...'

'Anyway, the bastard is dead. I didn't kill him, but somebody did,' Lovric gloated shamelessly.

Godiva blanched. 'I'm not surprised,' she murmured.

Lovric paused, feeling less triumphal and a bit ashamed that he had broken the news so roughly. 'Some scouts who were coming back to meet me found him near the London Road. He was face down in a stream. They believe he was murdered by king's men from Cleley.'

'I'm not surprised,' she said again. 'He made enemies wherever he went.'

Lovric hung his head for a while. Then he remembered something else that had long been on his mind, a detail from the time of their angry parting. 'I went to the priory and prayed for you before I left Coventry. I prayed that we would love each other again one day. Didn't the prior tell you? He was listening behind a pillar.'

'No. But I'm not surprised at him, either. He would have liked us to separate. With me away in some distant convent, he could have done as he pleased.'

Once more it seemed as though they had no more questions for each other. Godiva stirred the cooking pot haphazardly, and Lovric stared round the kitchen as though making an inventory for his quartermaster. Then suddenly, despite his better judgement, he reached out for reassurance.

'You didn't really love that man, did you, Godiva? Not even for one second, not even when...?'

The impatience that Godiva had feared would ruin their meeting sprang to life.

'Stop it, Lovric,' she snapped. 'You've no right. Not unless you tell me all about Estrith first.'

For a man who wanted to win back his wife, Lovric was making a dog's dinner of the conversation. He looked towards the cauldron and thought of saying something nice about the stew. But that would be ridiculous at such a serious moment. He thought next of saying something flattering about Godiva's appearance. But she knew how she looked and she would laugh bitterly and get angry. He could think of nothing at all to say. In desperation, he got to his feet and threw off his cloak.

'Come here,' he said, his voice rough with tension.

'No.'

'For God's sake, woman,' he shouted as he sprang across the

few feet of floor that separated them and pushed her arms behind her back. 'I love you,' he said. 'I never stopped loving you.'

He forced a kiss on her mouth and she felt repelled. His beard was stale and rough. His lips lacked the soft youthfulness of the last man who had kissed her. But yet his lips clung to hers, and the longing in his mouth was greater than anything she had felt for years. Her heart echoed its answer: I almost died for lack of love. I want to be loved again. A warmth came into her kiss, a mere spark, but enough for him to know he could come home again. He picked her up in his arms, feeling her to be light and fragile as the leaves that were just beginning to fall, and carried her up the stairs, which creaked as they had done each time he mounted them, and then he laid her on the bed, pushed back her short hair and bathed her in his tears.

Some time later, Lovric, contentedly chewing a hunk of fresh bread, took her hand. 'I've got news, Godiva.'

'Harry?'

'Yes, and Alfgar, too. Harry has been released from the cathedral.'

'Thank God almighty.'

'He is on his way north.'

'*North*? To Siward? Not to us?'

'To Edmund. Both boys volunteered to serve with Siward's Scottish frontier soldiers, on condition they could serve together. I consented to this, but I said I wanted Harry home for Christmas. And Alfgar will be back as well.'

'And you? Will you be here too, my love? Say yes, if only for a few weeks...'

'I'll be here too. But for more than a few weeks...'

'What?'

'Yes. At Christmas time I am going to invest Alfgar as Earl of Mercia. I've seen with my own eyes how well he is doing. Even some of the Irish leaders seem to like him now, and as for the Welsh, they are talking of inter-marriage even before he has children. The king has agreed. Alfgar's days of disgrace are over. And my days of peace and comfort will begin.'

'But why?' Her joy gave way to alarm. 'Aren't you well?'

'To all appearances. But when I was about to take ship and start waging war against Edward, I realized I no longer had the heart for it. Something had gone from me – that urge to fight enemies that I've had all my life. I could feel the absence of the fire in my belly. I thought I was sick and saw my physician, but he could find nothing wrong. He advised me, though, not to start a campaign in that state. "What state?" I asked him. "Broken, sir," he said.'

'Broken?'

'My fighting days are over, Godiva. I think they ended when I ran away after quarrelling with you, ran away from all my own mistakes. If I had gone to war as I intended – if I had not learned of your troubles and come rushing back here – I would have died in battle. Edward's soldiers would have killed me. He has forces at Cleley that can quickly go anywhere in the land and crush any army I could raise.'

'I know. I'm glad you didn't start an uprising. For a short while I thought it was the way forward, but I came to see it would be hopeless. What will happen now?'

'England will be safe from invasion while Edward lives, though not afterwards. Our family is safe for the duration, too. That was your achievement.'

'Not much of an achievement. Peace only for our short time.'

'It's the best we can get, and not to be despised. Men have always gone to war hoping to gain wealth and power for generations to come. Every bloodied sword is held up as a peacemaker. But how often does war produce lasting peace and prosperity? Defeated enemies don't vanish from the Earth. They come back, reincarnated in their children and grandchildren. At least we have now, Eva, and it's your doing. Your actions tilted the king's power in our favour. You held your nerve like a warrior going into single combat, and you won. I am immensely proud of you.'

'Tell that to Coventry. The people there think I'm dishonoured. They're still muttering about revenge.'

'I'll show them, then. On Sunday we'll walk together to St Mary's. Wear your Sunday best and let everyone see that you are my wife and my queen.'

She would look beautiful again? A bubble of laughter rose in her throat.

'What are you laughing at?' Lovric asked, quickly on his dignity.

'Myself. *Superbia*. How quickly she came back.'

'A good thing too,' said Lovric. 'I have no patience with sulkers.' That brought Milly to mind and he asked where she was.

'She was always a grievance of a girl,' he said after Godiva finished explaining. 'I was wrong to keep her waiting so long for her wedding feast, but she'd have got into trouble anyway. She's hot-tempered and sharp-tongued. A stay in a convent might do her good.'

Godiva pressed her hands together and sighed. 'There's something I never understood. Why does Milly hate me so much? Was I too harsh? Unfair?'

Lovric just grunted. 'She's still young. The baby will change her.'

Godiva disagreed: childbirth could make Milly much worse. Silently she vowed that as soon as the most important matters were settled in Coventry she would get a monk to write a letter to Milly at Wilton. Then she winced – it was always like that for Milly. She never came first.

*

As it happened, Lovric and Godiva had to wait until they could parade to church together, for the following Sunday a messenger arrived from the priory, saying that one of Lovric's spies had arrived in the night, bearing news. As was customary, he was disguised as a monk and was waiting in a secret cell of the priory. Lovric, unwilling to take himself away from his big breakfast, demanded to know the nature of the news. The messenger glanced round nervously and then announced: 'Queen Edith is imprisoned. Her brothers have gone into exile. Godwin is rampaging in the south.' The man smiled with satisfaction, knowing that Lovric would now abandon his bacon chops and fly like a bolt of lightning to the priory.

'Come with me, Godiva,' Lovric said. 'Whatever has happened to Edith, it took place around the time when I received Edward's message of forgiveness. This has something to do with your penance.'

'That bad joke...'

'Whatever it really was, it appears to have been put to great use.'

How beautiful the priory looked, thought Godiva, as she entered the familiar door and accustomed her eyes again to the shadows of the cloisters, and how peaceful and safe it felt to be here with Lovric and without Prior Edwin. Just then, around the corner came Cherub, his golden ringlets bobbing and a broom in his hand.

'My lady,' he gasped. 'Sorry to be cleaning now. No one said you would be coming here...'

'Are you well, Cherub?'

'Better every day,' he replied and ran off, as light and awkward as a storm-damaged angel, his splendid new feathers just growing in.

The door to the secret cell where Lovric saw his spies was already open, casting a bright pool of candlelight into the cloister. Godiva followed Lovric inside, looked round for the thin, sly man she expected to see, and then stopped in confusion as a tall, beautiful woman rose to greet them.

'Greetings, Godiva. At last we meet properly,' said Estrith Gudmanson.

Seeing her clearly for the first time, Godiva realized she had no cause for jealousy. Estrith was beautiful, but she was also remote, as though something had happened that had closed her heart against others. If ever Lovric had loved her it was long ago, before that happened.

Estrith poured them all some wine, and then, after a quick exchange of information with Lovric about several unrelated matters, she turned to Godiva.

'The real reason I am here is to bring you information, Godiva. You need to know about what happened to you – that horrible penance – and why it happened. It was Robert de Champart's idea that I come: he and the other prelates want to make their peace with you. They would apologize, but of course they are not able to.' She paused and sipped her wine carefully. 'Edward set traps for you, Godiva, many traps. But, you see, the traps he set for you were really meant to catch another.'

Godiva's hand suddenly trembled and she put down her wine. 'I thought all along that something else was on Edward's mind – that he wanted something else. The penance was part of some game I couldn't fathom.'

'Yes. There was a game going on at court – a game of pious posturing in which everyone competed in holiness, self-denial and militant Christian fervour. Edith played this game to the hilt.'

'I remember that very well.'

'And as I told Lovric in Winchester, the bishops were at it, too. They were on a ferocious campaign to force people like you to renounce their marriages.'

'Edward tried to persuade me, at Egg Ring. But I told him it was nonsense: every noblewoman in England is married to her first or second cousin.'

'Then think what riches would fall into the hands of the king and the Church if even a quarter of these land-owning ladies annulled their marriages and entered convents. The amount that came Robert de Champart's way when that woman from Kent agreed to leave her husband – it was staggering. I still haven't finished counting it all. Well, Edith was the bishops' greatest ally in the annulment campaign, and she astonished Edward with her mastery of the prohibited degrees and the various schemes for reckoning kinship. Now – listen carefully, Godiva – when you went to Egg Ring, Edith was staying nearby at Grafton manor. The night after you went back to Coventry she hosted a small, celebratory feast at Grafton for the king and several bishops. I accompanied Robert, and I was the only other woman there. At the dinner Edith could talk of little else but the debauchery of your sons and the wrongfulness of your marriage. After your penance – whose details she withheld – she said you would suffer extreme shame and be in low spirits. At this point Robert sat up and paid attention. He asked what care would be given to the health of your soul during this difficult time. Edith said Edward had already thought about this. Edward looked at her, said nothing and let her carry on. "Yes," said Edith, "the Abbess of Barking has been instructed to send a group of high-born nuns to take care of Godiva." Robert looked round the room, smiled at everyone and predicted that these lady-nuns would whisk you off into luxurious seclusion at Barking Abbey and pamper you in every way until you lost all remaining interest in your manor, your town, your priory and your husband – all of which were hard work and disappointment. Everyone laughed at that.'

'But, Estrith – no nuns came from Barking. A monstrous woman came here from Evesham, but she had nothing to do with the king.'

'Exactly. Nothing happened. After Robert made his comment, the king grew quiet and thoughtful. Then he stood up, raised his glass and declared a toast. "To the lady of Coventry, Godiva."

'What?'

'Those very words. A nervous silence fell on everyone as Edward raised his glass and slowly sipped his wine. "This woman's sweet and humble acceptance of my penance affects me deeply," he said, and then he sat down. Edith went white and the entire roomful of bishops and clerics remained speechless. The king was going into one of his about-faces, when no one could guess what he would say next. Everyone waited. Edward then addressed Edith, praising you, extolling your piety, your courage and, in great detail, your ravishing beauty, and the beauty of your soul. And then he talked about your goodness to the people of Coventry, and how they could not possibly have a better lord than Godiva. He even said it was regrettable that you did not have royal blood, for then you could have married into the ruling line of England when you were young and fertile. "She is the same age as I am," he said, staring at Edith's bosom – which, as you know, Godiva, is as flat as a Shrove Tuesday pancake – "and if only had fate permitted it, she would have borne me sons such as a king could be proud of." Well, at this point Edith realized that Edward had been leading her on for weeks, until she had made it obvious to everyone how much she hoped to see you off to a convent and pass your estates to her favourite brothers. That night, at Grafton, she was lured into showing her hand. Edward, meanwhile, had concealed his. She felt like a fool, and with that reference to you as an ideal royal bride she felt mortally insulted. She jumped up from the table, stormed around the room ranting and railing, until finally Edward, wearied, told the servants to bring him the chess board. He pointed at her queen and said, 'Checkmate.' Edith went mad then. She screamed that they had both – king and queen – intended your penance as a hoax, and that while she wanted your lands (yes, that was true, she admitted recklessly), he, the king, had wanted the penance so as to obtain the only gratification of which he is capable: sinning with his eyes.'

'Good God. She said that in public?'

'It gets worse. Edward didn't answer her. He merely shook his head sorrowfully and looked at Father Francis as though to say: see what I have to put up with? The unspeakable coarseness of this Godwin girl. The silence grew until Edith could bear it no more. "*Scopman!*" she screamed at him. "Watchman! Masturbator!" But she had gone too far now. There was muttering amongst the bishops and much throat-clearing, and then Robert got up and he and I took her by the hand and led her away, cursing and sobbing. She spent the night under lock and key, and the next day Edward expelled her from court. She is imprisoned now in Winchester.'

Godiva let out a deep sigh, as though she had been holding some part of her breath ever since she saw the king in Winchester cathedral. 'Now I understand my penance,' she breathed.

'Yes, it was the bait that lured Edith on until she thought she had won. When she realized she had been deceived, her piety dissolved right under the noses of the bishops. She is destroyed, perhaps forever.'

'But I still do not understand the king,' Godiva said. 'His piety seemed so deep and sincere that I had come to believe in it. I can't believe that everything he said about sin and repentance was no more than a posture to disguise his intentions.'

'Sincerity?' Lovric exclaimed. 'No one will ever know this king's mind. Nor whether he means to hand his crown to one of his Norman kin, or keep them living in false hope of gaining

England. For the moment, though, it is clear that I and my house are no longer the chosen enemy. It is Godwin and his children who occupy that position now. I am glad.'

The next morning Godiva called Agatha to her chamber.

'I understand Bret's money was returned to you?' she asked. Agatha nodded. 'And Lovric says you and Wulf went to the forest last night.' Agatha blushed and nodded. 'Do you want to marry?'

'Yes, but Wulf have no money, and we ain't got nowhere to live.'

'A churl's farm on the London Road is falling into my hands because there are no heirs. Bret's money should just about cover the cost of the freehold. What do you say?'

Agatha was stunned. 'Go away from here, mistress? Have I offended too much?'

'No, but this summer you grew out of being a serving girl. It is time for you to have your own house and man and, God willing, your own children.'

'Thank you, mistress, for thinking of me. You are right, it is time. I ain't no virgin no more, and Bertha going knock the living daylights out of me if I end up like Miss Milly.' Despite the unintended insult, Godiva smiled. 'But I'm going to sore miss the manor and all the folks here,' Agatha continued. 'It be lonely, out in your own house and garden.'

'And there's something else to consider. There is a stream running along this farm's border. It is where Bret was found dead.'

'Who told you, mistress?' Agatha gasped.

'The earl. His scouts said they thought the king sent knights from Cleley to kill Bret. And he guessed that the king had sent him here to me in the first place. He was able to piece together the rest of it.'

Agatha examined Godiva's face, with its softening lines and

reviving beauty. There was no expression there: one might have thought that Bret had never existed. Nor was there any trace of shame: the earl and his wife had made their peace with past disloyalty.

After she had dried her eyes and wiped her nose, Agatha left to continue her chores. Godiva sat by the table for a few minutes, wondering who she would train to replace her. She was so deep in thought that she did not hear the sounds of shouting and running feet until Bertha flung the door open and cried out, 'Help, lady! Come quick.'

Godiva ran to her front door, and immediately collided with Tom the tanner's son, who threw his arms round her, wailing, 'Sanctuary, sanctuary.' Behind him followed a gang of townspeople, all shaking their fists and sticks, and cursing. They stopped in confusion when they saw Godiva before them, pointing her sword.

'Sorry, we be trespassing,' said the innkeeper, inching away.

'We had to catch the little bastard before he get out of town,' said the tinsmith. 'Even his father don't want him no more. Ask him, mistress.'

Godiva pulled Tom out from behind her skirts and looked at him. He had a fresh bruise coming up on one eye, and the other was already closed from a punch he must have received last night. He could not stand up straight.

'What have you done, Tom?' she asked. 'Tell your story quickly.'

'Everyone in town say it be me that spied on you, and carried stories about you to Cherub, who told the prior, and that's why the king made you do the penance. They want revenge on me, but it's not true...'

'But you did spy. So what is not true?'

'That I would go and meet Cherub. All I did was follow him, to see what he was doing in the forest.'

'I think you'd better come inside,' Godiva said, pushing Tom into the house and closing the door on him before she addressed the crowd. 'Good people,' she said. 'I do not want revenge for what I was forced to do. The king has made his peace with me and all members of our family. As for Tom, he does peep and he is a nuisance. But he has done me no damage at all. Nor was Cherub involved in slandering me. The matter only concerned the prior, who has been sent away, and Beorhtric of Nottingham – Bret – who is dead. Go home now and let me talk to the boy.'

She turned away from them and went inside. Behind her she heard a cheer go up, praising her name. Inside, the twelve-year-old boy was huddled amongst last night's cinders in the hearth, shivering like a dog expecting the next kick.

'Why did they turn on you, Tom? Even your own father?'

'I know why, but I couldn't tell them or it'd only be the worse for me.'

'You can tell me, though.'

He looked at her searchingly with eyes that had long grown used to reading people's faces and postures.

'Yes, all right. But it be a bad story, mistress. I did follow Cherub. And I seen him meet a man sometimes, over by where the woods come close to the back of the inn. It were the innkeeper, mistress. He would hurt Cherub and bugger him and make him cry. Then he would give him money.'

'Why would Cherub consent?'

'To save up money and run away from the prior. Everyone knows Cherub were a slave bought in Bristol and he don't have nowhere to go. He don't even have a name, though I hear he be Irish and called Malachy. Prior treat him cruel. Stands to reason Cherub be wanting money to go away.'

'Does someone else know about this?'

'Yes, and that's my touble. Innkeeper seen me last time he

had hold of Cherub. It were pure bad luck for me. I were up a tree and a woodpecker started banging right near me. Innkeeper look up and what did he see beside the woodpecker but my face, watching him finish with Cherub. After that he told my father that I'd spy on you and pass on stories for the prior. So I got a first beating for that. Then, when folks started talking of revenge, innkeeper tell them I was the one they should punish, because they could never give the king the whipping he deserved. I got kicked round the market square for that. They were going to put me in the stocks, too, but I slipped away and ran here.'

'You'd better stay exactly where you are,' Godiva said. 'I'm going to talk to the earl about this.'

A little later Gwen came in and examined Tom's bruises and cuts. While she washed them carefully with warm water and smeared green balm on the worst sore spots, Agatha made him some broth. Neither talked to Tom, who avoided their rebuking eyes and stared fearfully into the flames of the fire.

At last Godiva returned, accompanied by Odo. They stared at Tom, folded their arms and then broke the news.

'Well, young man,' said Godiva, 'this is what the earl says. You are to leave this town at once – but as a soldier, attached to Lord Alfgar. Earl Lovric says he never has enough good spies and you obviously have the makings of a fine one. But you must be obedient, brave and hard-working.'

'And no more spying on people when they are private,' said Odo. 'Any more of that and you'll be back in Coventry. In the stocks. I'll put you there myself.'

Hope sprang up in Tom's eyes. 'No, sir. That be boring anyway. It always be the same old thing. Shirt up, trousers down, bang-bang like a woodpecker, then finish in a big sweat and go home.'

'Off with you!' Godiva shouted.

Odo bundled the boy out and ordered him straight to the hall to find out what he should do next. Then he turned to thank Godiva.

'So, Wulf and Agatha be all set up. And now Tom, too. I see you be back to work, mistress. Putting this place in order. Thank God for that, lady, and for this cruel summer be coming to an end, too.'

'Amen to that.'

The summer straggled on, however, as though reluctant to loosen its grip on the victims of its bad humour. The late crops were a disappointment and the weeks of hunger had left many susceptible to coughs and wheezes, irascibility and pessimism. Nevertheless everyone was glad of the dreary calm that now prevailed. Some, too, appreciated the changes that were stirring in the priory. Sundays were becoming more of an occasion for those who toiled during the week. A new prior arrived from Evesham who encouraged the parishioners of St Michael's to walk from the old parish church and through the priory precincts to see the newly displayed feretory, within which St Augustine's arm rested in proper dignity at last. And in the priory, for the first time, the humble and the failed were made welcome and regaled with pageantry and beauty in such abundance that they glimpsed for a moment a world in which the spirit soared and the heart was unchained.

Godiva followed these developments with interest, but to Lovric's eyes she did not seem to gain the satisfaction that he would have expected from the improvements in the priory. It was as though the events of the summer had left some part of her so damaged it was beyond being healed by her daily life. He probed, but to no avail. And then, since Godiva would not tell him what was oppressing her, he made a decision and took matters into his own hands.

*

Four months after the penance, on a brilliant autumnal day, a wagon drew up in the yard of the manor. Godiva, who was in the manor house showing Ethel, her new maid, how to help Bertha with the clothes in storage, paid no attention to its arrival until Lovric came in and called to her from the foot of the stairs.

As she descended the staircase, looking carefully at her feet, she heard a small cry like the mewing of a cat and looked across towards the door. A beautifully dressed young woman stood at the threshold with her back to the sunshine so that it was hard to make out who she was. Then the baby in her arms cried again, and she stepped forward.

'Mother?'

Godiva halted and swayed for a moment and then, taking Lovric's hand, she descended the rest of the treacherous stairs, crossed the floor of the room to the door and put out her hands to take the baby.

'Her name is Godiva, mother. And here is Peter Mallet, my husband.'

Godiva heard, but had eyes only for the new face that bore her name. After she had held her for a while, Lovric took the baby in his scarred arms and kissed her downy forehead. He was about to say 'as lovely as her grandmother' when he stopped.

'She's as beautiful as her mother,' he said, and congratulated himself when Milly's face lit up with a smile as broad as Godiva's.

Turning, Godiva caught sight of them all in the big mirror and realized for the first time just how much she had aged during that summer, the summer in which Milly had come into her prime. It is autumn, she thought. The time of the falling of leaves. She passed the baby back into its mother's arms and felt a contentment that surpassed anything she had known before. That grudging, painful summer, the summer of her naked ride, had yielded its fruit and come to its end.

Postscript

Godiva in history, legend and fiction

A few years after the events referred to in this novel, Lovric died, peacefully it seems, at his estate in Bromley, in present-day Staffordshire. Godiva did not remarry. She survived the Norman Conquest and kept possession of most of her lands, perhaps because her sons did not oppose William of Normandy in 1066 on the battlefield at Hastings, or perhaps because she remained in favour with King Edward's advisers until his death in that same year. It is uncertain whether she died in 1067 or in 1085, but in any case it is said that she was buried alongside Lovric in adjacent chapels in her beloved St Mary's. Eventually a great Norman cathedral was built on the site of Godiva's old priory, and around it the city of Coventry thrived and continued to grow. This cathedral was intact until 1940, when aerial bombardment reduced it entirely to rubble. Recently, however, shards of medieval glasswork that seem to depict a fair-haired, beautiful woman have been found on the site. Some believe these are the remains of a medieval stained-glass window, installed in honour of Godiva.

The descendants of Lovric and Godiva were not exterminated after 1066 as were those of Earl Godwin of Wessex, but they suffered the fate of most of the Anglo-Saxon aristocracy: they gradually fade out of the historical record. (There is a hint that Alfgar, son of Lovric, continued to ally with the Welsh after his father's death, for his daughter Edith married Gruffydd ap Llywelyn, King of Gwynedd.) On the whole then, the House of Lovric, which was itself the last hurrah of the royal clan of the old tribal kingdom of the Hwicce, has left few marks on the pages of history. Nearly all that remains to recall its once-powerful grip on the English midlands is the story of Godgifu – the startling and mysterious legend of 'Lady Godiva'. The opacity of the story provokes curiosity: who was Godiva, and did she really ride naked through Coventry?

It is surprising, given her gender and the fact that she lived about a thousand years ago, how much is known about her. In her time she was referred to simply as *Godgifu* (see the note on pronunciation, p. vii), not as 'Lady Godiva' and certainly not as 'Countess Godiva' (a Norman-era embellishment). As depicted in this novel, *Godgifu* acquired considerable landed wealth through inheritance from her parents. She had connections with Nottingham and may have lived there as a child. She was widowed young (having borne at least one child), and made a long-lasting second marriage with *Leofric* (known as Lovric in this novel), Earl of Mercia, during which at least one other child was born. At some point the family lived in Hereford, but later, probably under political pressure, they settled in Coventry where Godiva became an 'improving land-owner', deeply involved in promoting the growth of the town as a market and as a centre of worship. She was probably born around the turn of the first millennium and was therefore in her forties at about the time when the naked ride is thought to have occurred. The date of her death is also uncertain, but she is known to have survived the Norman Conquest, and may have lived on until the 1080s. She is mentioned in The Anglo-Saxon Chronicle and in Domesday, as well as in the St Alban's manuscript in which the legend of the ride first appeared.

A great deal is also known about Godiva's milieu. The most important circumstance affecting her life was her husband's political eminence. Lovric was one of the three earls who kept King Edward the Confessor on his shaky throne. The other great factor shaping Godiva's story was her position as founder of St Mary's, a new Benedictine abbey in Coventry. Her husband's political career, and her own status as the founder-patron of an abbey, would have drawn Godiva close to the vortex of eleventh-century rivalries, plots and conflicts.

What kind of society existed in Britain, during the last years of Anglo-Saxon England? A contemporary time-traveller would find it both a strangely familiar and deeply alien society. Divorce, for instance, was available to women as well as men, and women with property were able to retain their possessions after divorce or widowhood. Remarriage must have produced families with stepchildren just as it does today. Continuity can also be found in the practice whereby children of well-off families were raised away from the family hearth: in the eleventh century this meant sending the child not to a boarding school, but to be 'fostered' in another household of equal or better status than the parents'. But the result was not dissimilar. For more than a thousand years upper-class English children have been sent away to broaden their social connections, and to dilute their attachment to close family and neighbourhood ties.

These similarities render the differences all the more startling. Slavery was an accepted institution of Anglo-Saxon England, with Domesday recording slaves in every region of England (the percentage rising from east to west). Criminal law enshrined inequality, for those without property were subject to severe corporal punishment, while those with property could settle any offence – even murder – by paying a fine. What is more, the fines payable to victims varied according to the property-level of the victim: it was much costlier to offend a noble than a common peasant.

The built environment of the Anglo-Saxons would have looked more backward to modern eyes than the towns and villages of the later Middle Ages. Walled towns were fewer, cathedrals were squatter and castles less imposing. Nevertheless standards of living and population levels rose gradually throughout the Anglo-Saxon period, with all branches of technology improving, and textile production (mainly women's work) achieving memorable levels of skill, beauty and international value.

The intellectual life of the age was dominated by piety. The Benedictine monastic reform was gathering momentum, promising to bring knowledge of the scriptures to every village and to sweep away such practices as clerical marriage, toleration of divorce and lay ownership of churches. At the same time, the aristocracy was beginning to take a greater interest in the expansion of Christian power in the Holy Land; it was during this period that attitudes and ideals emerged that led to the appearance of the crusader knights a few decades later.

But above all, perhaps, the eleventh century was an age of great insecurity for the political elite of the British Isles. Beginning in the ninth century, Vikings had raided and colonized all parts of Britain; the terror they instilled remained fresh in people's minds in the eleventh century. Actual raiding had ceased by Godiva's time, but the threat from the North Sea had merely taken on a new form – the dynastic designs of the Norse/Danes on the throne of England. This threat loomed ever larger as the Duchy of Normandy (Norse-man-land) began to emerge as a strong military force across the English Channel.

The coronation of Edward 'the Confessor' as King of England in 1043 crystallized this threat, for the new king was Norman on his mother's side and by upbringing. On his accession he brought with him to England a circle of Norman supporters who were soon followed by others, all hoping for lands and favours. The Anglo-Saxon leadership pinned its hopes for survival on the birth of an heir to Edward by an English wife, an heir that they could control and bring up as English. But Edward refused to cooperate. Though he married Edith, daughter of the most powerful of the earls (Godwin of Wessex), he refused to have sexual intercourse with her. Neither would he divorce her and remarry, nor take mistresses and produce bastard sons. This situation persisted until his death in 1066 when, as feared, a Norman army attacked at Hastings, and Anglo-Saxon England came to an end.

Godiva's story, as I have envisaged it, is tied to the country's deep malaise – its political paralysis and the sexual obsessions of its king. I have based my characterization of Edward as a clever, cruel joker and fantasist on Frank Barlow's authoritative biography, *Edward the Confessor* (see Further Reading on p. 343), though I have elaborated on some of the conclusions that may be drawn from this study. Apart from the king, most of the major characters in this novel are known to history. These are: Godiva herself, her husband Lovric, his son Alfgar, Earl Godwin of Wessex, and his daughter Queen Edith. Other important historical characters also flit in and out of the story: Queen Emma, Siward of Northumbria, Lady Macbeth and Gruffydd ap Llywelyn, all of whom were at large in the first half of the eleventh century.

The incidents in this novel are largely fictitious, but some important events, such as Queen Edith's fall from grace in 1046 and the alliance between the Mercian leaders and the Welsh, have a historical basis. My depiction of the Church's attempts to disrupt marriages where the partners were within the 'prohibited degrees' of kinship is likewise historically based.

So much, then, for Godiva herself, in history and in this novel – but what about the legend? Does the old tale contain any truth? The answer to this question cannot be a simple one, for the life of the legend has had an intriguing history of its own. In the words of the literary historian Daniel Donoghue (*Lady Godiva: A Literary History of the Legend*, Blackwell, 2003, pp. 26–7), 'For more than a century after Godiva's death, no written source makes even the faintest allusion to her legendary ride or to anything now commonly associated with it, such as nakedness, the horse, or taxation … Nothing would lead anyone to anticipate the sensational story that abruptly appears a century later, when chroniclers in the Benedictine abbey of St Albans insert a fully developed narrative into their Latin histories. The story comes under the entry for 1057, the year of Leofric's death. After praising the couple's piety and their generosity to religious institutions, one account continues:

> Yet this pious countess, wishing to free Coventry from an oppressive and shameful servitude, often begged her husband, the count, under the guidance of the Holy Trinity and the Mother of God, to deliver the town from this servitude … She persevered in her request and relentlessly exasperated her husband with it, until she finally forced an answer from him:
>
> 'Mount your horse naked,' he said, 'and ride through the town's marketplace from one end to the other when all the people are gathered, and when you return you will get what you demand …'
>
> Then the Countess Godiva, dear to God, mounted her horse naked on the day agreed upon and, by loosening the braids of hair on her head veiled her whole body except her brilliantly white legs. And when she had finished her journey unseen by anyone, she returned rejoicing to her husband, who considered it miraculous. And Count Leofric, releasing the city of Coventry from its servitude, confirmed its charter with the stamp of his own seal.
>
> (quoted by D. Donoghue
> from Matthew Paris's *Chronica Majora*, c. 1250)

The 'abruptness' of the appearance of the legend in writing, and the subsequent addition of further details, such as the nature of Coventry's 'servitude' and the role of Peeping Tom, have caused many commentators (including the above-quoted scholar) to reject the possibility that there is even a kernel of literal truth to the legend. On this point I would only say that the exclusion from the written record of a story about important figures from a conquered native aristocracy is not at all surprising. It is not evidence, *per se*, that the story was fabricated. Nor is it surprising that when the story emerged in ink after some time on the tongues of monks, it had acquired such a sickly hue of conjoined piety and lubricity that incredulity would be the most likely response of modern critics.

A couple of other points can also be made in defence of the actuality of the naked ride. One concerns the nature of the ride itself, which reeks of the Middle Ages. Shameful ritual punishments that somehow fitted the crime were characteristic of the period. Several are described in the texts of the laws of medieval Wales, and one of these was even 'international', having a close parallel in Swedish law of the same period (see Nerys Patterson [now Jones], 'Honour and Shame in Medieval Welsh Society: The role of burlesque in the Welsh laws', *Studia Celtica*, 1981–2). Such punishments, like more recent tarring-and-feathering, were often inflicted outside the arena of formal institutions and therefore few detailed accounts of their enactment survive. But where they exist they can be just as shocking as the Godiva legend. The *popolo* of Viterbo, for example, when they rioted in 1387 seized the city prefect and dragged him to the town square, 'where they ritually humiliated him, pressing his mouth up the anus of his prized steed and that night sent him naked out of the city in a casket' (Sam Cohn, 'Popular Revolt and the rise of early modern states', *The Historian*, Spring 2006).

Another matter on which there has been hyper-scepticism is the nature of the 'servitude' of the people of Coventry, from which, so says the legend, they were released by Godiva's penance. There can be little doubt that 'servitude' refers to taxation, just as later versions of the legend maintain, for the essence of free status in the Middle Ages was freedom from the many kinds of taxation imposed on communities and individuals. The taxes in question, however, could not have been imposed on Godiva by her husband, for she was the title-holder to her considerable estates. But there was one tax to which all land-owners were liable, namely the war tax, *heregeld*, used by the Danish kings to support their mercenary armies. Barlow comments that, 'Ethelred had instituted this tax in 1012 and Edward abolished it thirty-nine years later. It is uncertain, however, whether its collection was suspended for long. Geld was certainly unpopular. Not only was it associated with Viking raids and foreign rule, it was also "a tax which had to be paid before all other taxes and it oppressed the English people in many ways".' (Frank Barlow, *Edward the Confessor*, Yale University Press, 1970, p. 155). While Godiva would never have owed taxes to her husband, as a noble land-owner she would have had to pay the king if he demanded *heregeld*. His demands for this payment were, it seems, subject to his own private agreements with individuals, some of whom escaped liability when they made special arrangements with him (ibid., p. 156). This is the situation which, in this novel, I have taken to lie behind Godiva's vulnerability to Edward's demands.

It is futile, however, to press on with arguments about whether Godiva's ride 'really' happened. In my view, far more important than the literal truth of the legend is the fact that the historical Godiva lived at a moment in time when the history of women was about to take a sharp turn for the worse. Up until the age of the Norman Conquest women throughout Britain, whether in England, Wales or Ireland, could inherit and bequeath substantial property, including land. Women could also instigate divorce (where there were grounds that were legally acceptable), and retain access to their children and to their share of the marital property. Widows and divorced women could also remarry. During marriage, women were protected by law against violence and neglect and were not, in general, prohibited from practising specific crafts or skills, or from riding, bearing arms or travelling. The basic social model for the pre-Conquest adult woman was that of partner in a marital relationship: sometimes a lesser partner, often equal and occasionally superior.

Over the centuries following the Norman Conquest, under the influence of Church lawyers, all these advantages that women in Britain had hitherto possessed withered away and passed into history, leaving women of all social ranks subject to vastly increased male authority in the family, dispossessed of property in everything but name, and in general degraded to a state of inferiority – disarmed in an age of 'chivalry', unemployed in an age of guilds, and uneducated in an age of growing literacy. Men and women were set on routes of social change that split the age-old customs of partnership and introduced the enmity of the genders. The overwhelming responsibility for this unhappy change is borne by the Catholic Church, which obtained jurisdiction in all matters to do with the family and pushed forward an agenda for the dispossession of women – especially powerful, land-owning women – which found keen support in ruling military circles in Norman England.

The question for modern readers of the St Albans legend, cited above, is whether its writer was consciously reflecting on the changes that the Conquest had brought about. Donoghue writes that 'the story ... emerged sometime before 1220 as a fiction posing as a historical fact' (op. cit., p. 45). Something about the story resonated with matters that were affecting St Albans in the years leading up to 1220. What this might be is not hard to guess: in 1215 Magna Carta was ratified, forming the basis of a new agreement between King Stephen, the Pope and the English barons. One of the bitter disputes between the barons, the princes of the Church and the king concerned his unbridled raising of taxes through *scutage*, a tax imposed as a substitute for direct military service. In essence, *scutage* was similar to the *heregeld* of Godiva's era. Both taxes were resented as 'servitude' by English land-owners. In reworking Godiva's story the monks of St Albans found the ingredients for framing an allegory of their oppression under King Stephen: the tax was unjust, it was imposed by someone who, though claiming the right to impose it, actually exceeded his authority (Godiva's husband, symbolizing the king). Lovric became the villain, forcing Godiva into a sexually humiliating display, and Godiva herself, being female, served as a symbol of the subject community, constrained but morally powerful. Perhaps it was Godiva's pre-Norman, Anglo-Saxon female identity, and the monks' awareness of the extent to which post-Conquest English women were losing power, that made her an ideal icon for a story about oppression and about the dishonour imposed on women in a subject society – an allegory, really, not of the Norman Conquest *per se*, but of any conquest, at any time.

With this interpretation in mind, it seems less surprising to discover that the chroniclers of British legendary history thought that Godiva was a kinswoman of that other sexy icon of English popular resistance – Robin of Loxley, or Robin Hood. She was also said to be related to another, less famous guerrilla of the Fens, Hereward the Wake. In different ways, these three figures of medieval legend defied authority and evaded conquest. All three paid a huge price for resistance – exile in a wilderness of forests or fens, and the social exile incurred by degradation – but notwithstanding hardship and injustice, legend has it that all three survived, eluding their enemies to the end and evading any definitive understanding of who they really were and exactly what they did.

February 8th, 2007
Caernarfon, Gwynedd

Further Reading

Anglo-Saxon studies at university level are enjoying a surge in popularity – in part, it is said, because of the immense popularity of Seamus Heaney's translation into modern English of the Anglo-Saxon horror classic, *Beowulf*. Many current course syllabi and reading lists are now available online. Another resource for those who want to know more about this period is the historical re-enactment society, *Regia Anglorum*, and its wonderful website (www.regia.org).

For a sense of the personality of Edward the Confessor, this novel drew extensively on the work of Frank Barlow (including, *inter alia*, *Edward the Confessor*, Yale University Press, 1970). A readable outline of the history of the whole Anglo-Saxon period is to be found in the work of H. R. Loyn and is still to be recommended (*Anglo-Saxon England and the Norman Conquest*, Longmans, 2nd revised edn, 1991). James Campbell, et al. (eds, *The Anglo-Saxons*, Penguin, 1982) discuss and illustrate the culture as well as the history of the Anglo-Saxons. For an exhaustive, fully illustrated account of Anglo-Saxon clothing, Gale Owen-Crocker's *Dress in Anglo-Saxon England* (revised edn, Boydell and Brewer, 2004) is unsurpassable. Godiva's Coventry receives detailed attention in G. Demidowicz, *Coventry's First Cathedral* (Paul Watkins, 1994) and in the first chapter of Richard Goddard, *Lordship and Medieval Urbanisation: Coventry, 1043–1355* (Boydell and Brewer, 2004). Though not bearing directly on Godiva's story, the following accounts of the lives of royal women of the period are enjoyable and illuminating: Harriet O'Brien, *Queen Emma and the Vikings* (Bloomsbury, 2005); Pauline Stafford, *Queen Emma* and Queen Edith: Queenship and Women's Power in Eleventh-Century England (Blackwell, 1997).

Relatively few novelists have ventured into the Anglo-Saxon world, in part because the Arthurian mystique casts a long shadow over adjacent centuries, dinting their glamour and their interest. An exception is Bernard Cornwell, with his stories of Viking England, and recently of King Alfred.

The field of Anglo-Saxon studies, including the archaeology of the period, and the related fields of Irish and Welsh medieval studies are unfolding rapidly. New findings and new perspectives are likely to reward those who pursue their interest in this, one of the most formative phases of British history.